RECIPES FOR LOVE AND MURDER

RECIPES FOR LOVE AND MURDER

A TANNIE MARIA MYSTERY

SALLY ANDREW

HARPER
AVENUE

Recipes for Love and Murder

Published by Harper Avenue, an imprint of HarperCollins Publishers Ltd

First Canadian edition

Originally published in the United Kingdom by Canongate Books Ltd. in 2015.

HarperCollins books may be purchased for educational, business, or sales promotional use through our Special Markets Department.

HarperCollins Publishers Ltd
2 Bloor Street East, 20th Floor
Toronto, Ontario, Canada
M4W 1A8

www.harpercollins.ca

Designed by Suet Yee Chong

Library and Archives Canada Cataloguing in Publication information is available upon request.

ISBN 978-1-44344-302-9

Printed and bound in the United States
RRD 9 8 7 6 5 4 3 2 1

This book is dedicated to my amazing parents,
Bosky and Paul Andrew.

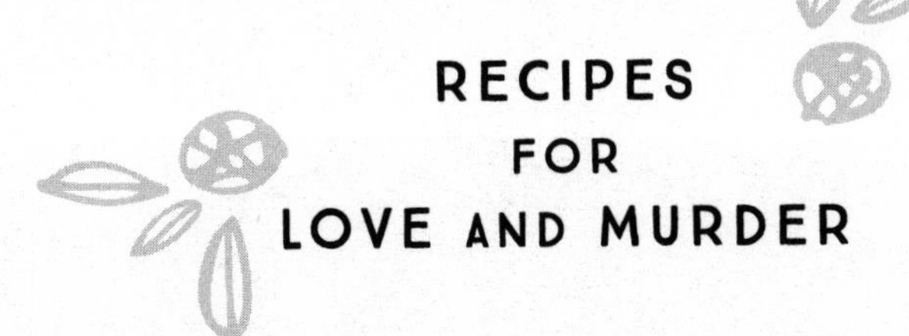

RECIPES FOR LOVE AND MURDER

ONE

Isn't life funny? You know, how one thing leads to another in a way you just don't expect.

That Sunday morning, I was in my kitchen stirring my apricot jam in the cast-iron pot. It was another dry summer's day in the Klein Karoo, and I was glad for the breeze coming in the window.

"You smell lovely," I told the appelkooskonfyt.

When I call it apricot "jam" it sounds like something in a jar from the Spar supermarket, but when it's konfyt, you know it's made in a kitchen. My mother was Afrikaans and my father was English and the languages are mixed up inside me. I taste in Afrikaans and argue in English, but if I swear I go back to Afrikaans again.

The appelkooskonfyt was just coming right, getting thick and clear, when I heard the car. I added some apricot kernels and a stick of cinnamon to the jam; I did not know that the car was bringing the first ingredient in a recipe for love and murder.

But maybe life is like a river that can't be stopped, always winding toward or away from death and love. Back and forth. Still, even though life moves like that river, lots of people go their whole lives without swimming. I thought I was one of those people.

The Karoo is one of the quietest places in South Africa, so you can hear an engine a long way off. I turned off the gas flame and put the lid on the pot. I still had time to wash my hands, take off my blue apron, check my hair in the mirror, and put on the kettle.

Then I heard a screech of brakes and a *bump* and I guessed it was Hattie. She's a terrible driver. I peeked out and saw her white Toyota Etios snuggled up to a eucalyptus tree in my driveway. I was glad to see she had missed my old Nissan bakkie. I took out the melktert from the fridge. Harriet Christie is my friend and the editor of the *Klein Karoo Gazette* where I write my recipe page. I am not a journalist; I am just a tannie who likes to cook a lot and write a little. My father was a journalist and my ma a great cook. They did not have a lot in common, so in a funny way I like to think I bring them together with my recipe page.

Hattie was in her fancy church clothes, a pinkish skirt and jacket. Her high heels wobbled a bit on the peach pits in my walkway, but when she stayed on the paving stones she was okay. I still feel a bit ashamed when I see people coming straight from church, because I haven't been since my husband, Fanie, died. All those years sitting nice and pretty next to him on those wooden pews and listening to the preacher going on and on, and then driving home and Fanie still dondering me, kind of put me off church. Being beaten like that put me off believing in anything much. God, faith, love went out the window in my years with Fanie.

I've left the windows open since then, but they haven't come back in.

So there was Hattie, at my door. She didn't have to knock because it's always open. I love the fresh air, the smell of the veld with its wild bushes and dry earth, and the little sounds my chickens make when they scratch in the compost heap.

"Come in, come in, my skat," I said to her.

A lot of the Afrikaans ladies stopped being my friends when I left the Dutch Reformed Church, but Hattie is English and goes to St. Luke's. There are more than forty churches in Ladismith. At St. Luke's, coloureds and whites sit side by side quite happily. Hattie and I are both fifty-something but otherwise we are different in many ways. Hattie is long and thin with a neat blond hairstyle and a pish-posh English way about her. I'm short and soft (a bit too soft in the wrong places) with short brown curls and untidy Afrikaans. She has eyes that are blue like a swimming pool, and mine are pond green. Her favorite shoes are polished, with heels, but I prefer my veldskoene. Hattie doesn't bother much with food (though she does like my milk tart), while for me cooking and eating are two of the best reasons to be alive. My mother gave me a love of cooking, but it was only when I discovered what bad company my husband was that I realized what good company food can be. Some might think food is too important to me, but let them think that. Without food, I would be very lonely. In fact, without food, I would be dead. Hattie is good company too, and we are always happy to see each other. You know how it is—some people you can just be yourself with.

"Good morning, Tannie Maria," she said.

I liked the way she sometimes called me Tannie, Auntie (even though she says it in her English way, as if it rhymes with "nanny," when in fact it rhymes with "honey"). She leaned down to kiss my cheek, but she missed and kissed the dry Karoo air instead.

"Coffee?" I said. Then I looked at the clock. The English don't like coffee after eleven o'clock. "Tea?"

"That would be super," said Hattie, clapping her hands in that Mary Poppins way of hers.

But she wasn't looking so super herself. Her frown was wrinkled, like the leaves on a gwarrie tree.

"Are you okay, skat?" I said, as I prepared the tea tray. "You look worried."

"I do love your house," she said, patting my wooden kitchen table. "All the Oregon wood and the thick mud walls. It's so . . . authentic."

When Fanie died, I sold the house we had in town and got this one out here in the veld.

"It's a nice old farmhouse," I said. "What's the matter, Hats?"

She sucked in her cheeks, like the words were falling back down her throat too fast.

"Let's sit on the stoep," I said, carrying the tray to the table and chairs outside.

From my stoep you can see the garden with its lawn and vegetables and all the different trees. And then on the other side of my low wooden fence is the long dirt road leading up to my house, and the dry veld with its bushes and old gwarrie trees. The nearest house is a few kilometers away, hidden behind a koppie, but the trees make good neighbors.

Hattie smoothed her skirt under her as she sat down. I tried to catch her eye, but her gaze jumped all over the garden, like she was watching a bird flying about. One of my rust-brown hens came out from where she was resting under a geranium bush and helped herself to the buffet on the compost heap. But this wasn't the bird Hattie was watching. Hers flew from the lemon tree to the vegetable patch, then hopped from the lizard-tail bush to the honeybells and back again. I heard birds calling all around us, but could see nothing where she was looking.

"Can you see something there in the veld plants?" I asked.

"Heavens above, it's warm," she said.

She took an envelope from her pocket and fanned her face with it.

"Let me give you some milk tart."

I cut slices and put them on our plates.

"It's just got to rain soon," she said.

Now she was following the invisible bird as if it was jumping all over the table. I pushed the plate toward her.

"It's your favorite," I said.

I could tell Hattie had more to say than the weather report. Her face was red, as if there was a hot thing in her mouth, but the corners of her lips were tight where she was holding it in.

Hattie was not one to be shy to speak, so I did not try and rush her. I poured our tea and looked out at the dry veld. It had been a long time since the rain. Across the veld were those low hills of the Klein Karoo, rolling up and dipping down like waves. On and on, like a still and stony sea. I picked up my melktert and bit off a mouthful. It was very good, the vanilla, milk, and cinnamon working together to make that perfect comforting taste. The texture was just right too—the tart smooth and light, and the crust thin and crumbly.

Hattie looked into her cup, as if her imaginary bird had jumped in there. I could see a real bird in the shadows of a gwarrie tree, too far away to see what kind. I love those old trees. Some of them are thousands of years old. They are all knobbly and twisted like elbows and knees, and their leaves are dark green and wrinkled.

Hattie sat up straight and had a sip of her tea. She sighed. This is what stoeps are for. Drinking tea, and sighing, and looking out at the veld. But Hattie was still looking inside her cup.

"Delicious," I said, eating the last melktert crumbs on my plate.

My bird flew closer and landed in a sweet-thorn tree. It was a shrike. Hunting.

Hattie did not touch her milk tart, and I couldn't sit still any longer.

"What *is* it, Hattie, my skat?"

She swallowed some air and put the envelope on the table.

"Oh, gosh, Maria," she said. "It's not good news."

I felt the tea and melktert do a small twist inside my belly.

TWO

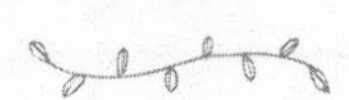

Now I'm not one to rush into bad news, so I helped myself to more tea and milk tart. Hattie was still drinking her first cup of tea, looking miserable. The envelope just sat there, full of its bad news.

"It's from the head office," she said, running her hand over a bump in her throat.

Maybe the air she had swallowed had gotten stuck there.

Hattie didn't often hear from the head office. But when she did it was to tell her what to do. The community gazettes are watchamacallit, syndicated. Each gazette is independent, and has to raise most of its own funds through advertising, but they must still follow the head office rules.

The shrike dived from the branch of the sweet-thorn tree down onto the ground.

"Maria, they say we absolutely must have an advice column," she said.

I frowned at her. What was all the fuss about?

"Like an agony aunt column," she said. "Advice about love and such. They say it increases sales."

"Ja. It might," I said.

I was still waiting for the bad news.

"We just don't have the space. Or the funds to print the four extra pages that we'll need to add one column." She held her hands like a book. I knew how it worked. Four pages were printed back to back on one big sheet. "I've tried to rework the layout. I've tried to see what we can leave out. But there's nothing. Just nothing."

I shifted in my chair. The shrike flew back up to a branch with something it had caught.

"I phoned them on Friday," said Hattie, "to tell them, 'Sorry we just can't do it, not right now,' I said." Her throat became all squeezed like a plastic straw. "They said we can cut out the recipe column."

Her voice sounded far away. I was watching the shrike; it had a lizard in its beak. It stabbed its meat onto a big white thorn.

"Tannie Maria."

Was the lizard still alive? I wondered.

"I argued, told them how much the readers adored your column. But they said the advice column was nonnegotiable."

Was the butcher bird going to leave the meat out to dry, and make biltong?

"Tannie Maria."

I looked at her. Her face looked so tight and miserable—as if her life was going to pot, instead of mine. That recipe column *was* my life. Not just the money. Yes, I needed that too; the pension I got after my husband's death was small. But the column was how I shared what was most important to me: my cooking.

My throat felt dry. I drank some tea.

"But I've been thinking," Hattie said. "*You* could write the advice column. Give advice about love and such."

I snorted. It was not a pretty sound.

"I know nothing about love," I said.

Just then one of my chickens, the hen with the dark feathers around her neck, walked across the lawn, pecking at the ground, and I did feel a kind of love for her. I loved the taste of my melktert and the smell of rusks baking and the sound of the rain when it came after the long wait. And love was an ingredient in everything I cooked. But advice columns were not about melktert or chicken love.

"Not that kind of love, anyway," I said. "And I'm not one to give advice. You should ask someone like Tannie Gouws who works at CBL Hardware. She always has advice for everyone."

"One of the marvelous things about you, Maria, is that you never give unsolicited advice. But you *are* a superb listener. You're the one we come to when there's anything important to discuss. Remember how you helped Jessie when she couldn't decide whether to go and work in Cape Town?"

"I remember giving her koeksisters . . ."

"You listened to her and gave her excellent advice. Thanks to you, she is still here with us."

I shook my head and said, "I still think it was the koeksisters."

"I had another idea," Hattie said. "Why don't you write a cookbook? *Tannie Maria's Recipes.* Maybe I can help you find a publisher."

I heard a whirring sound and I looked up to see the shrike flying away. Leaving the lizard on the thorn.

A book wasn't a bad idea, really, but the words that came from my mouth were, "It's lonely to write a book."

She reached out to take my hand. But my hand just lay there.

"Oh, Tannie Maria," she said. "I'm so sorry."

Hattie was a good friend. I didn't want to make her suffer. I gave her hand a squeeze.

"Eat some milk tart, Hats," I said. "It's a good one."

She picked up her fork and I helped myself to another slice. I didn't want to suffer either. I had no reason to feel lonely. I was sitting on my stoep with a lovely view of the veld, a good friend, and some first-class milk tart.

"How about," I said, "I read people's letters and give them a recipe that will help them?"

Hattie finished her mouthful before she spoke.

"You'd need to give them some advice."

"Food advice," I said.

"They'll be writing in with their problems."

"Different recipes for different problems."

Hattie stabbed the air with her fork, and said, "Food as medicine for the body and heart."

"Ja, exactly."

"You'll have to give some advice, but a recipe could be part of it."

" 'Tannie Maria's Love Advice and Recipe Column.' "

Hattie smiled and her face was her own again.

"Goodness gracious, Tannie Maria. I don't see why not."

Then she used the fork to polish off her melktert.

THREE

So it was on the stoep with Hattie that we decided on *Tannie Maria's Love Advice and Recipe Column.* The column was very popular. A lot of people from all over the Klein Karoo wrote to me. The letters I wrote back gave me the recipes for this book: recipes for love and murder. So here I am, writing a recipe book after all. Not the kind I thought I'd write, but anyway.

One thing led to another in ways I did not expect. But let me not tell the story all upside down, I just want to give you a taste . . .

The main recipe in this book is the recipe for murder. The love recipe is more complicated, but in a funny way it came out of this murder recipe:

RECIPE FOR MURDER

1 stocky man who abuses his wife
1 small tender wife
1 medium-size tough woman in love with the wife
1 double-barreled shotgun
1 small Karoo town marinated in secrets
3 bottles of Klipdrift brandy
3 little ducks

1 bottle of pomegranate juice
1 handful of chili peppers
1 mild gardener
1 fire poker
1 red-hot New Yorker
7 Seventh-day Adventists (prepared for the End of the World)
1 hard-boiled investigative journalist
1 soft amateur detective
2 cool policemen
1 lamb
1 handful of red herrings and suspects mixed together
Pinch of greed

Throw all the ingredients into a big pot and simmer slowly, stirring with a wooden spoon for a few years. Add the ducks, chilis, and brandy toward the end and turn up the heat.

FOUR

Just one week after I sat on the stoep with Harriet, the letters started coming in. I remember Hattie holding them up like a card trick as she stood in the doorway of the office of the *Klein Karoo Gazette*. She must have heard me arriving in my bakkie and was waiting for me as I walked down the pathway.

"Yoo-hoo, Tannie Maria! Your first letters!" she called.

She was wearing a butter yellow dress and her hair was golden in the sunlight. It was hot, so I walked slowly down the path of flat stones, between the pots of aloes and other succulents. The small office is tucked away behind the Ladismith Art Gallery & Nursery in Eland Street.

"The vetplantjies are flowering," I said.

The little fat plants had pink flowers that gleamed silver where they caught the light.

"They arrived yesterday. There are three of them," she said, handing me the letters.

The *Gazette* office has fresh white walls, Oregon floorboards, and a high ceiling. On the outer wall is one of those big round air vents with beautiful patterns that they call "Ladismith Eyes." The office used to be a bedroom in what was one of the original old Ladismith houses. There's room for only three wooden desks, a sink, and a little fridge, but this is enough for Jessie, Hattie, and me. There are other freelance journalists from small towns all over the Klein Karoo, but they send their work to Hattie by email.

On the ceiling a big fan was going around and around, but I don't know if it helped make the room any cooler.

"Jislaaik," I said. "You could make rusks without an oven on a day like this."

I put a tin of freshly baked beskuit on my desk. Jessie looked up from her computer and grinned at me and the rusk tin.

"Tannie M," she said.

Jessie Mostert was the young *Gazette* journalist. She was a coloured girl who got a scholarship to study at Grahamstown and then came back to work in her hometown. Her mother was a nurse at the Ladismith hospital.

Jessie wore pale jeans, a belt with lots of pouches on it, and a black vest. She had thick dark hair tied in a ponytail, and tattoos of geckos on her brown upper arms. Next to the computer on her desk were her scooter helmet and denim jacket. Jessie loved her little red scooter.

Hattie put the letters on my desk, next to the beskuit and the kettle. I worked only part-time and was happy to share my desk with the full-time tea stuff. I put on the kettle, and got some cups from the small sink.

Hattie sat down at her desk and paged through her notes.

"Jess," she said. "I need you to cover the NGK church fete on Saturday."

"Ag, no, Hattie. Another fete. I'm an *investigative* journalist, you know."

"Ah, yes, the girl with the gecko tattoo."

"That's not funny," Jessie said, smiling.

I looked at the three letters sitting on my desk like unopened presents. I left them there while I made coffee for us all.

"I want you to take some photos of the new work done by the patchwork group—they will have their own stall at the fete," said Hattie.

"Oh, not the lappiesgroep again. I did a whole feature on them and the Afrikaanse Taal-en Kultuurvereniging last month."

"Don't worry, Jessie darling, I'm sure something interesting will come up," said Hattie, scribbling on a pad. I didn't think she'd seen Jessie rolling her eyes, but then she said, "Or else you can always find work on a more exciting paper. In Cape Town maybe."

"Ag, no, Hattie, you know I love it here. I just need—"

"Jessie, I'm truly delighted you decided to stay here. But you are a very bright girl, and sometimes I think this town and paper are too small for you."

"I love this town," said Jessie. "My family and friends are here. I just think there are big stories, even in a small town."

I put a cup of coffee on each of their desks, and offered the tin of rusks. Hattie never has one before lunch, but Jessie's eyes sparkled at the sight of the golden crunchy beskuit and she forgot about her argument.

"Take two," I said.

When she reached into the tin, it looked like the gecko tattoos were climbing up her arm. I smiled at her. I like a girl with a good appetite.

"Lekker," she said, and her hip burst into song.

Girl on fire! it sang.

"Sorry," she said, opening one of her pouches. "That's my phone."

The song got louder as she walked toward the doorway and answered it.

"Hello . . . Reghardt?"

She went out into the garden and her voice became quiet and I couldn't hear her or her fire song anymore. I sat down at my desk, and dipped my beskuit into my coffee. It had sunflower seeds in it, which gave it that roasted nutty flavor. I looked again at the envelopes.

The top letter was pink and addressed to Tannie Maria. The *i*'s were dotted with little round circles. I took a sip of my coffee, then I opened the letter. By the time I'd finished reading, I was so shocked I stopped eating.

This is what it said:

Dear Tannie Maria,

It feels like my life is over and I am not even thirteen. If I don't kill myself, my mother will. But she doesn't know yet. I have had sex three times, but I only swallowed once. Am I pregnant? I haven't had my period for ages.

He is fifteen. His skin is black and smooth and his smile is white, and he said he loved me. We used to meet under the kareeboom and then go to the shed and play ice cream. He said I taste like the sweet mangoes that grow on the streets where he comes from. He tastes like chocolate and nuts and ice cream. These are things I used to love to eat. I tried to stop the visits to the shed, but then I saw him there in the shade of the tree, and got hungry for him.

I fanned myself with her pink envelope and carried on reading.

When I told him I might be pregnant, he said we mustn't meet again. I go past the tree after school but he's never there.

I have been so worried that I can't eat. My mother says I am wasting away. I know I'm going to hell, which is why I haven't killed myself.

Can you help me?

Desperate

I put down the letter and shook my head. Magtig! What a tragedy . . .

A young girl who can't eat.

We had to get her interested in food again. I needed a recipe with chocolate and nuts. And ice cream. With something healthy in it.

I would of course tell her that you can't get pregnant from oral sex. And in case she really was not able to talk to her mother, I would give her the number for the family-planning clinic in

Ladismith. But if I could just come up with an irresistible recipe for her, it might save everyone a lot of trouble.

Bananas, I thought. They are very healthy, and would help her get strong again. How about frozen bananas, dipped in melted dark chocolate and rolled in nuts. I wrote out a recipe for her with dark chocolate and toasted hazelnuts. That should help her get over him. And in case the boyfriend read the paper, I put in a recipe for mango sorbet too. Mangoes were in season, and the good ones tasted like honey and sunshine.

FIVE

Sjoe, but it was hot and those cold recipes looked good. There were still two unopened letters on my table. The letters did not call as loudly as the frozen bananas.

"I'm going to work from home," I told Hattie. "I need to test some recipes."

"Mmm-hmm," she said.

She had a pencil in her mouth and was frowning as she worked.

"Hattie, what time is Saturday's fete?" asked Jessie.

Jessie was at her desk, taking a little notebook out of one of her pouches.

"Fiddlesticks," said Hattie, pressing buttons on her computer. "Hmm? Two P.M."

I stood up, the letters in my hand.

"It's important the recipes are good," I said. "Irresistible."

Hattie looked up from her work.

"Maria, darling. Go."

My little bakkie was parked a few trees away from the office, beside Jessie's red scooter. We tried to stay a bit of a distance from Hattie's Toyota Etios; I already had one ding she had made on the door of my car. My Nissan 1400 bakkie was pale blue—like the Karoo sky early in the morning. With a canopy that was white like those small puffy clouds. Though the canopy was usually dustier than the clouds are. I'd left all the windows open, and it was in the shade of a jacaranda tree, but it was still baking hot in there. It really was a day for ice cream.

I popped in at the Spar to pick up the ingredients. It was a quiet time of day so I was lucky to get out of there with chatting to only three people. Not that I mind chatting. It's just that those sweet cool dishes were calling to me quite loudly, so I couldn't listen properly.

I could smell the ripe mangoes as I drove past the farmlands, through the open veld and between the low brown hills. I turned into the dirt road that goes toward my house, drove past the eucalyptus trees, and parked in my driveway, next to the lavender. Two brown chickens were lying in the shade of the geranium bush; they didn't get up to say hello.

I went into the kitchen and plonked my grocery bag on the big wooden table, then peeled six bananas right away and put them in a Tupperware container in the freezer. Then I chopped four mangoes and put them in the freezer too. I stood over the sink to eat the flesh off the mango skins and suck their sticky pits clean. It was a messy business.

Then I crushed the hazelnuts with my wooden pestle and mortar and lightly toasted them in a pan. I tasted them while they were warm. I broke the chocolate up and put it in a double boiler. I would do the melting when the bananas were frozen. I tasted the dark chocolate. I ate some together with the nuts just to check the combination. Then I prepared some more nuts and chocolate to make up for all the testing. It would take a couple of hours for the bananas and mangoes to freeze. How was I going to wait that long? My letters. I had brought back my two letters from work.

I decided to take them outside so I could focus without distractions. I sat on the shady stoep and opened one. It was from a little girl who liked a boy and didn't know how to make friends with him. I gave her a nice easy fridge fudge recipe. Little boys never say no to fudge.

The next letter I opened said:

> *Oh hell, I'm such a total idiot. Please tear up that last letter. If my husband ever sees or hears about it . . . I'm a fool. Please don't publish it. Destroy it. I beg you.*

What last letter? What was she afraid of? I looked at the postmark on the envelope. Ladismith. The date was two days ago. I phoned the *Gazette*, and got Jessie.

"Hey, Tannie M," she said.

"Did I leave a letter on my desk?" I asked.

"Hang on, I'll check."

I looked at the kitchen clock while Jessie was gone. Not even an hour had passed since I'd put the bananas in the freezer.

"No, nothing. But mail did arrive after you left. And there's a letter for you."

"White envelope," I said. "Postmark Ladismith, sent two or three days ago?"

"Mmm . . . ," she said. "Yup."

"I'm making some choc-nut frozen bananas," I said. "If you want to pop over sometime . . ."

"Why don't I shoot across in my lunch break? I'll bring your letter."

"Just right," I said.

I didn't have a good feeling about the husband in the woman's letter. It gave me an uncomfortable worry in my belly. I decided to put something sweet in my stomach instead. The banana wasn't frozen yet, but it tasted good with the nuts and chocolate. I needed to test the recipe properly—with frozen banana and melted chocolate—so I stopped at just one banana.

To get myself out of the kitchen I put on my veldskoene, old clothes, and straw hat and went into the vegetable garden. I had two pairs of veldskoene: one light khaki, which was smarter, and the other dark brown, which was better for gardening. It was like a roasting oven outside but there was a part of the garden that was in the shade of the lemon tree, and I kneeled down there and started pulling out weeds.

There were some snails on my lettuce and I chucked them onto the compost heap where the chickens would find them.

I was lucky I had good borehole water to feed my garden from below. It had been too long without rain. The Karoo sun tries to suck all the moisture out of the plants and people. But we knyp it in, holding on. The little vygies and other succulents do the best job of holding on to it. I put olive oil on my skin at night so I don't turn into dried biltong. But I don't use it when I go outside or else the sun would fry me into a Tannie Maria vetkoek.

After a while the sun was too much. I stood up and brushed the soil off my knees and washed my hands under the garden tap. I took my hat off and splashed my face with cool water and wiped it with my handkerchief. Then I went inside and put the chocolate in the double boiler to melt and took the mangoes out of the freezer. They were frozen, but not rock hard, which is just perfect. I whizzed them in the blender, then put this nice sorbet in the Tupperware and popped it back in the freezer.

I heard Jessie's scooter coming so I took the bananas out of the freezer and the melted chocolate off the stove. I used my little braai tongs to dip the frozen bananas into the bowl of dark chocolate and then roll them in the plate of toasted nuts.

Jessie grinned as she came in the kitchen.

"Wow, Tannie M, something smells lekker. Jislaaik, what is that?"

She put her helmet and denim jacket on a kitchen chair and looked at the chocolate-nut bananas that I was putting on wax paper. When I had done five bananas, I popped them in the freezer.

"First, our starters," I said, and dished us out two bowls of mango sorbet.

"Ooh, this is awesome, Tannie. What's in it?"

"Mangoes."

"Ja, but what else?"

"Just mangoes."

"No. Really?"

"Ja. The Zill ones are the best, but they aren't in season yet. These Tommy Atkins are very nice too. Oh, and a bit of lime juice on top, to give it that tang."

"Wow. Amazing."

I put our empty bowls in the sink, and got us two plates for the main course. Jessie adjusted her belt.

"What *is* all that stuff on your belt, Jessie?" I asked as I dished the bananas onto our plates.

"Mmm," she said, patting the different pouches that hung across her hips. "Camera, phone, notebooks, knife, flashlight, pepper spray. That kind of stuff." She was looking now at the chocolate banana. "That looks, um, delicious."

"They do look a bit funny like that," I said. "Not quite right."

"Do we eat them with our fingers?"

"I'm not sure," I said. "I've never done this before. Here's a knife and fork . . . Wait a minute. Cream. That's what they need." I put a big dollop of whipped cream on our plates. "There, that looks better."

We started with a knife and fork but ended up using our fingers because they were too delicious to waste time fiddling.

One of the best things about Jessie is that she appreciates food. She has a sensible body with padding in the right places.

We didn't talk as we ate, but Jessie closed her eyes and moaned a bit.

"Jislaaik," she said, when she had finished, "that is the best banana I've had in my whole damn life."

I smiled and dished up her dessert. Another frozen choc-nut banana and cream. I gave myself one too, to keep her company. I wished that I could send Jessie's sensibleness to the girl I was sending this recipe to.

Jessie cleaned the last smudges of chocolate off her plate. Then she sighed and stroked one of the geckos tattooed on her arm. She sometimes does that when she is happy.

"I'd better get back," she said, standing up and opening a pouch on her belt. "Here's your letter."

It felt hot in my hands.

SIX

When Jessie left I did not even clean up; I went outside and sat on the metal chair in the shade of the lemon tree and opened the envelope. The handwriting was the same as the other letter.

Dear Tannie Maria,

I've always enjoyed your recipes. I read them every week.

I am ashamed to be writing to you now for advice. I've made my bed and I should lie in it, but then after what's just happened . . .

I promised to love and obey this man. My husband. The love has dried up, but I do my best. He does his bit too; he pays for our son who has cerebral palsy and is in a special needs home.

The beatings only happen when he is drunk or jealous. If I don't fight back it's not too bad. He says he is sorry afterward, which in an odd way I believe, and that he won't do it again, which I don't. Sometimes something snaps. It might be to do with his own father and with his time in the army. He has nightmares about the army. Not that I'm making excuses for him—I'm just saying he's not a monster.

My mouth was dry and I stood up, leaving the half-read letter on the chair. I went inside and poured myself a glass of water from the fridge. My hands were shaking a bit. My chest hurt as I swallowed. It happens when I drink cold water too fast. I went back to the letter in the garden and carried on reading.

The beatings are about once a month. The sex once a week. So I have twenty-five days a month when he doesn't bother me much. I have a lot of happy hours with my woman friend, who comes to visit when he is out. I work only two mornings a week, so am at home a lot. She and I have a kind of love for each other, though I prefer to keep it platonic.

She gave me the ducks. Three white ornamental ducks. We fixed up the pond for them to swim in.

Those ducks were the first things I've ever loved in a totally pure way. Without guilt or pain. Pure bright joy. I could just watch them for hours. Swimming. Waddling. Rooting in the grass. Lying with their beaks tucked into their feathers

He shot them.

All three of them.

With his fucking shotgun.

They were sleeping.

I wanted to kill him. I grabbed a kitchen knife and ran at him. He held my arms until I'd cried myself into exhaustion.

My husband had drunk a bottle of Klipdrift brandy. He was jealous of my friend and of the ducks. But the final straw was the curry I made. He said the lamb was tough and the curry too spicy. He said I didn't care about him. He was right on both counts.

Could you please give me a recipe for a good mutton curry? And any other advice?

Yours sincerely,

Bereft woman

I sat there for a long time with the letter on my lap, looking at my veldskoene, remembering things I didn't want to remember. The sun slowly chased me out of the shadow and I felt its warmth on my legs and shoulders. But I was shivering and felt cold. Then suddenly I was hot, the sun burning my skin. A wind rustled the leaves in the tree and I stood up and went inside.

There were unhappy feelings in my tummy. I ate the last frozen banana, and it pushed aside those feelings. I couldn't feel much other than chocolate bananas in my stomach anymore. But my mind, my mind was still going where I didn't want it to go. My hands were shaking again.

I made myself a big mug of coffee with lots of sugar and took it outside to the stoep table, with the woman's letter and my pen and paper. I thought the sweet coffee would pull me right. But even after that whole mug of coffee I still felt down. I was full of a sadness that I couldn't shake off. All those years that I had spent with a man who was much the same as her husband. Not exactly the same. He had not shot my ducks. I did not have ducks. Or a good friend to give me white ducks. And my beatings were more like once a week, and the forced sex once a month. If I was lucky. But still the story felt the same. Even the Klipdrift brandy was the same. I didn't ever run at him with a knife. And I didn't leave him. I had been scared of dying. And scared of living too.

When Fanie got a heart attack and died, something broke free in me. But while he was alive, I just could not escape. Even the priest at our church said it was my duty to stay by my husband, so I stayed and stayed.

I hoped this woman would not do the same. I picked up my pen. We would of course not print what she wrote, but we could publish a recipe and a letter from me. I spent a long time working out what to say, writing and crossing out. It took me two hours and a bowl of mango sorbet. In the end I said:

I lived for too many years with a man who beat me. Bruises and bones can heal. But the heart, the heart can be damaged forever. Love is a precious thing. If you are with a man who abuses you, you should leave him. I know there are many reasons why it is hard. But you can find a way

You can do better than I did. You can save your heart.

Then I wrote out my best recipe for a slow-cooked lamb curry. (My mind jumped to a duck muscatel dish, but of course I didn't write it.) You will find the mutton curry recipe at the end of the book, with all the other recipes. It is a very tender and delicious curry with excellent side dishes.

SEVEN

A couple of weeks later I was walking in my veldskoene down the path to the office, in the morning heat. I could hear voices as I got close to the door.

"That's super-duper," said Hattie, "I knew you could write a great fete article."

"Ag, Hattie, please. Now, the story I wanted to discuss with you. Local farming practices and how overgrazing and pesticides are totally mucking up the ecosystems . . ."

"Maria," Hattie said, clapping her hands together as she saw me, "just look at that pile of letters on your desk. Isn't it marvelous?"

I stood under the ceiling fan and felt the air dry the sweat on my face and neck. My brown cotton dress felt rumpled and sticky though it was perfect when I put it on this morning. Hattie was sitting at her desk and she brushed a speck of dirt off her smooth apricot cotton trousers. I don't know how she always managed to look so smart. Jessie grinned as she handed me a glass of cold water. Her smile was bright in her round brown face.

"Dankie, skat," I said and gave her a Tupperware container. "Bobotie for you."

"Ooh, lekker," Jessie said, and put it in the small fridge.

She stood for a moment with the fridge door open, and lifted her thick ponytail up, away from her black vest. She let the air cool her face and the back of her neck.

Girl on fire, sang Jessie's cell phone. She took it out of its pouch and pressed a button that turned the song off.

"Just a reminder," she said.

"Goodness, Jess. We don't need reminders that it's hot," said Hattie.

"No," said Jessie, smiling. "It's reminding me to check on a certain website that should be ready by now . . ."

She went and clicked some buttons on her computer. I sat down at my desk with my glass of cool water. It had been two weeks since we'd started the column and the letters were flowing in. A lot of people were hungry for my recipes and advice. It was quite a responsibility, but I was enjoying it. When I gave someone a recipe, I usually cooked it for myself too. When I wasn't writing, I was cooking. More than I could eat myself. Sometimes I froze the extra food; often I brought it to Jessie.

I put down my glass and picked up the thick handful of letters on my desk.

"Jinne," I said. "How am I going to choose?"

I laid them out like a solitaire game on my desk. There was only space to print one or two letters per week, and I felt bad for the people I couldn't answer. Some of them gave addresses, and I sent them replies. But most of them didn't.

"Maria, darling, we've been working on your problem," said Hattie. She looked at Jessie, who was in front of her computer. Jessie nodded and gave Hattie a thumbs-up sign. "And we are delighted to tell you we've got a website up now. I got sponsorship from Klein Karoo Real Estate Agents. We can post loads of your letters up on the website. And people can email their letters to you."

"Come have a look," said Jessie.

"Oh," I said. "Thanks, skat." I didn't want to sound ungrateful. "The thing is, I am sure most of the people who write to me don't have web thingies. They are just . . . ordinary people."

"You'd be surprised, y'know," said Jessie. "Many people have the Internet in their homes. And lots of the little towns have Internet cafés these days."

I went to look at the website on her screen. It was called the *Klein Karoo Gazette*, just like the newspaper. Jessie clicked on something and a page came up that said: Tannie Maria's Love Advice and Recipe Column. There was a drawing of a nice tannie who didn't look like me, holding a lovely cake in the shape of a heart.

"It does look nice," I said. "I know I'm behind the times and all . . . with this website stuff."

"Oh, do tell her, Jessie, what you organized."

"I spoke to the manager of the Parmalat cheese shop," said Jessie. "They have bought some ad space next to your column, and . . . you know how they have that notice board up in their shop with announcements and stuff? Well, they've agreed to put up a second board, just for Tannie Maria's letters and recipes."

"Ag, moederliefie," I said, smiling at them both. "That is so sweet."

"And now," said Hattie, "we can pay you a bit more for your work. What with all the extra letters you'll be posting."

"Most people keep their letters anonymous," I said, "so I can't mail the replies to them."

"No, darling, I mean posting on the website, and the notice board."

"About Parmalat," said Jessie. "They ask if you could put dairy products in your recipes. Cream and cheese and that."

"All of them?" I asked.

"Um, no, but in a lot of the ones that go up on the board."

"That's okay," I said, "I like cheese."

I was going to make some coffee before starting work, but the handwriting on one of the envelopes stopped me. I pushed the other letters aside and sat down and opened it.

It was from the woman with the dead ducks.

It said:

A note for Tannie Maria (not for publication)

The mutton curry was superb. It seemed to pacify my husband a little. I kept some for my friend, who loved it.

I am making a plan that will allow me to leave. I will just have to tread water till I get it right.

Thank you.

Sometimes I wished the letters to me weren't anonymous. That I could write back. I suppose there was the danger that the woman's husband could get his hands on my letter. I wrote back to the duck lady inside my own head: *You can do it! I'll send you every recipe I know to help you.*

I have a drawer in my office where I keep my thank-you letters. But I didn't put her letter there. I felt worried about her; she hadn't escaped yet. I was going to take her letter home and put it in a special place.

I made us all coffee and then read through the other letters. Hattie and Jessie were arguing about an article, but I tuned their voices out while I worked on my laptop. I like writing by hand but it's easier to fix mistakes on a computer.

By lunchtime I had a headache but a good feeling in my heart. There were only two letters left to answer. To all the other people—teenagers and grannies, men and women, writing in with their problems and their dreams—I had given some small advice and a good recipe. The best recipe, the one that kept reminding me it was lunchtime, was the potato salad with mint and cream. I needed to go home at once and test that one out. I also wanted to take the duck lady's letter home. I couldn't reach her, but I could look after that letter as if it were a piece of her.

"I'm going home," I told Hattie.

My house was cooler than the office. And I had some ice-cold homemade lemonade.

"Goodness gracious," said Hattie, glancing at her watch. "It's one o'clock already."

"I've done most of the letters, and will bring them tomorrow," I said. "I just need to work out which are for the paper and which are for the cheeseweb."

Hattie laughed. She had a tinkling sort of laugh. Cool, like water.

"You know what I mean," I said. "I'm too hot and hungry to talk right."

Before I got in my little blue bakkie, I opened the doors on both sides and chased the heat waves out. Still, the seat burned my skin wherever my dress wasn't covering me. I left the windows open when I drove and the air dried out my lungs.

The hills were lying low, as if they could escape the heat. Towerkop rock, on top of the Swartberge, wasn't shy of the sun, sticking its bald, split head high up into the sky. The sides of the mountain looked fuzzy and wobbly.

When I got to my house, before I even poured myself that lemonade, I took the letter to the kitchen shelf. To the big recipe book my mother had given me. I opened the pages of *Kook en Geniet*. I folded the duck lady's letter between the pages, and closed the book around her words. As if it was holding her, sending her everything she needed.

I spent the afternoon with my potato salad, preparing it and eating it at my stoep table, and then I sat beside the leftovers with my last two letters and my pen and paper.

One letter was from a young girl with no friends and a school cooking project. The other from an old man living alone on a farm, with too much ground meat in his freezer. I could feel the unhappiness of the writers, and I sat with it for a while, trying to work out what I could give them. They were asking me for recipes, but it was obvious that they were lonely and wanted love. I did not have a recipe for love.

But if I could give them really good recipes, easy ones they could make themselves, they could invite someone to eat with them. I knew the recipe for a perfect macaroni and cheese that I could give to the girl. And for the old man, the best spaghetti Bolognese. And even if they ended up eating them on their own . . .

"If you are honest with yourself," I said to the potato salad, "is the feeling of love really any better than the satisfaction you get from a good meal?"

Food is good company, but it doesn't answer back, not in words anyway. Maybe that is one of the reasons it is good company. But it did communicate with me somehow, because next thing I knew I was polishing off the leftovers of that cream and mint potato salad.

My mouth was full of delicious flavors and my tummy full, and I answered my own question: "I think not."

EIGHT

The next morning my phone rang. It was Hattie.

"Have you heard?" she said. "Nelson Mandela died last night."

When I put the phone down, I made myself a cup of coffee and took two rusks and sat out on the stoep. But before I could bring the coffee to my lips, the tears started leaking out of me.

Mandela was ninety-five and had been sick for a while, but it still came as a shock. I looked out at the brown veld and the wrinkled gwarrie trees and the distant mountains. My tears made it seem like rain was falling, but the sky was wide and empty. I knew that people all over the land were crying with me for Tata Mandela.

Then my belly started shaking and tears from deep inside me came up and I realized I was crying for my own father too. My pa who had left me too soon.

I looked out at the veld and let my heart be filled with my sadness and my pride for my father and for Mandela.

Sometimes I thought that my father left my mother because of Mandela. But of course I couldn't blame Mandela, who had, after all, sat for over twenty years in prison on Robben Island, a long way from the Klein Karoo. I knew my father did love my mother—with her brown eyes and soft hands, and her delicious food—but I also knew that the Klein Karoo, even with its big veld and open skies, was too small for him. And my mother's mind too narrow.

To my pa, Mandela was a freedom fighter and a great leader; to my ma he was a terrorist and a kaffir (though she did not use the *k* word in front of my father). They did not often argue in front of me, but this was a disagreement that I heard more than once.

My father was the African correspondent for a newspaper in England, the *Guardian*, and he would travel a lot. Over the years, he came home less and less, and then he stopped coming back altogether. He would send money and postcards. The cards made my mother angry. Eventually the postcards stopped, although the money carried on every month. When I missed him I would read the old postcards that I had rescued from the trash can (and sometimes had to stick together where my mother had torn them). I kept them in a book my father used to read to me when I was little—Rudyard Kipling's *Just So Stories*. And I waited to grow up, because when I was eighteen I would go and find him, and visit some of the wonderful places on the postcards and in the *Just So Stories*. But that's not how it turned out.

When I was eighteen my mother got a long-distance phone call, saying my father had died in an accident. She seemed just as upset that it was a black man who gave her the news as by the fact that my pa had died.

The money from my father stopped, but the *Guardian* continued with a small pension for my mother. I got a job at the AgriMark—the farmers' co-op—to help cover the bills. I lived with my ma right through my twenties.

In 1990, the apartheid government finally lifted the state of emergency. Political organizations—including the African National Congress—were unbanned, and all political detainees and prisoners were released. Mandela was free at last. But the country was full of fighting and blood.

Mandela led the reconciliation talks and somehow took us down a path to peace. In 1994 all South Africans were allowed to vote in the first nonracial democratic election. The ANC came into power and Mandela was our president.

My mother, along with lots of other whites, was terrified. She bought boxes of canned food and put bolts on all the doors and windows. I did not know what to think about the politics, but I felt more and more trapped in the house. It was then that Fanie started courting me. I was thirty-three. When he asked me to marry him, I was just glad to get out of my mother's home.

Fanie had done his compulsory two years of service in the apartheid army and was angry with the Afrikaner National Party government for getting "all buddy-buddy" with the ANC. This same Afrikaner National Party had trained him to kill these "ANC terrorists," and had now let "the enemy" take over our government. Mandela eventually charmed my mother, but Fanie never relaxed with him, or with the black government.

"I like the way he dances," my mother said of Mandela. Of Fanie she said, "He has a good job at the bank, and the Van Hartens are a respectable family. His father was an NGK priest, you know."

It was only when she had relaxed the bolts and started shopping normally (though she still kept two big sacks of flour in the pantry) that she told me the truth about my father: He had been an underground member of the African National Congress. Even though the organization was unbanned and my father already dead by the time she told me, she whispered the news to me, and told me to keep it secret.

She would not tell me more about what he did or about what kind of accident had killed him, or why we didn't have a funeral for him.

I hoped Mandela would cure her of some of her anger toward my father and the blacks who stole Pa from her, but she held on to a lonely kind of bitterness until she died.

Because Mandela was a good man, and was ANC, like my father, I started listening to him as if he might have the same sort of advice as my pa would have given me. Before that I had not paid much attention to politics; it all happened far away from me. After all, as we saw on TV, most of the unrest was trouble with the blacks, and in the Klein Karoo there were mainly coloured townships. After listening to Mandela, I didn't vote ANC (in fact I didn't vote at all), but I joined the NGK women's group that raised funds for coloured schools and AIDS orphans. I did a lot of baking for those church fetes.

And when I was married to Fanie and he started to beat me, I took courage from Mandela. Mandela stood up for women's rights and criticized violence against women. Sometimes after listening to him, I felt I must just walk away from Fanie. But my fear was stronger. So was the voice of my husband, mother, and church: Staan by jou man. Stand by your man.

Still, even though I stayed with Fanie, Mandela's wise words helped with the loneliness and the pain, and made me think maybe, just maybe, it wasn't all my fault.

When I had finished my coffee and brushed the rusk crumbs off my lap, I found myself crying a bit more. And the tears for my father and for Mandela, the father of our nation, were all mixed up on my cheeks.

NINE

Over the next week, South Africa mourned Mandela's death and celebrated his life. People from all over the world came to pay their respects. At the memorial service in Johannesburg, the heavens opened up and it rained and rained. We listened to parts of the service on the radio in the *Gazette* office. The office was hot and dry and we sat still, listening as the fan turned slowly around and around. The president of Tanzania reminded us that in Africa, rain is the biggest blessing. Rain will fall when a chief arrives. The skies were celebrating as the chief, Mandela, went to heaven.

"His grandmother was San, you know," said Jessie. "The Bushmen know how to make rain."

During Barack Obama's speech Jessie started crying and even Hattie was dabbing at the corner of her eyes with a handkerchief. I had already done my crying. I was surprised to see how moved Jessie was. She was too young to know Mandela. But he was the kind of man whose story and whose dreams reached across the ages. And like Mandela and Obama, Jessie was passionate about justice.

We all liked the lines that Obama quoted—the ones that kept Mandela going when he was in prison for all those years—about being the captain of your own soul.

The day of Mandela's funeral was an unofficial public holiday.

I was surprised that even Ladismith took the day off to honor Nelson Rolihlahla Mandela. Twenty years ago the whites, and even many of the coloureds, would have seen him as a terrorist, like my mother did. But Mandela in his life and in his death managed to win their hearts. He reminded us all of the goodness in ourselves and each other.

I met up with Jessie and Hattie at the Ladismith Hotel, and the bar was full of people watching the funeral service on the big-screen television. The hotel served coffee and beskuit at no charge, and had brought in a whole lot of white plastic chairs alongside the usual wooden ones. The curtains were closed so we could see the TV nicely.

The bank manager, in a suit, was sitting alongside the old coloured man who begs outside the Spar. And the young black policemen were drinking coffee with the old white women who work in the furniture store. Everyone was sitting together as if they were old friends, in a way you don't usually see in Ladismith.

When they carried Mandela's coffin off, I had to work at not crying. Jessie, Hattie, and I sat there, with our heads held up high. I hoped that Mandela's spirit would live on in us somehow.

TEN

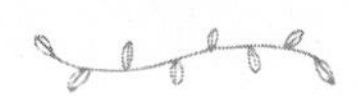

The next day we were at the *Gazette* office, and everything was back to normal. Though I did have a feeling that from now on everyone in South Africa would treat each other with respect and kindness. I was wrong about that . . .

I was leafing through a new batch of letters. The fan on the ceiling was going around and around. It was like an oven with a Thermafan. Jessie, Hattie, and I were all being evenly baked as we sat at our desks.

Jessie had on her usual black vest, her fingers moving so fast across her keyboard I don't know how her thoughts were keeping up with them. The geckos on her arms swayed a little as they followed her typing fingers. Hattie was at her computer, wearing a peach linen short-sleeved shirt and matching skirt. Linen, and still it wasn't creased.

"There are five emails for you, Maria," said Hattie. "Isn't that marvelous?"

Jessie's phone sang, *My black president.* It was the song Brenda Fassie had written in honor of Mandela. But I did not look up; the letter on my table was pulling all my attention. I ran my fingertips over the writing on the envelope. I could learn a lot about someone before I even opened their letter. This writer used capital letters and pushed too hard with the pen, as if their message was very important. The address was written in the Afrikaans way, with the number after the street name, Elandstraat, 7. The words of the letter were pressed onto a lined page with a black ballpoint pen:

TANNIE MARIA. I'M SCARED MY FRIEND'S HUSBAND IS GOING TO KILL HER. HE BROKE HER ARM. HE THINKS SHE'S LEAVING HIM AND HE SAID HE'LL KILL HER. SHE DOESN'T WANT TO CALL THE POLICE. SHE SAYS I MUSTN'T GO TO HER HOUSE. IF I KILL HIM IN SELF-DEFENSE OF HER, FOR HOW LONG WILL I GO TO JAIL?

I put my head in my hands.

"Hey, Tannie, what's up?" asked Jessie.

I gave her the letter. She read it in three seconds.

"Gosh, you look peaked, Maria," said Hattie. "Can I make you a spot of tea?" I nodded. "What's the letter say?"

"It's another bastard dondering his wife," Jessie said, handing the letter to Hattie. "Threatened to kill her. Jislaaik. I wish there was a giant insecticide for these guys. DDT that we could spray from an airplane."

"There was that other lady of yours," said Hattie, looking at the letter, "with the husband who was also a rotter."

"Yes," I said. "The lady with the ducks. Without the ducks."

"The bastard shot them, didn't he?" said Jessie.

"I got another letter from her recently," I said, "telling me she was making a plan to leave. I think the woman who wrote this letter is duck lady's friend. The one who gave her the ducks."

"Is there no return address?" said Hattie.

I shook my head.

"Nearly all my letters are anonymous," I said. "But it's got a Ladismith stamp."

"It might be someone else," said Jessie. "One out of four women in South Africa is beaten by her husband or boyfriend."

"I don't think she's one of those. I've just got a feeling that it's my duck lady. She spoke about her friend who loved her. I told her to leave her husband. And now he might kill her."

"Fiddlesticks," said Hattie, putting a cup of tea on my desk. "There's no need for that sort of nonsense. Let's get a response to this woman right away. I'm sure you can help her. We can put your answer on the website now, and the Parmalat board, and we can get your letter into tomorrow's *Gazette*."

"Eish. We'd better act fast," said Jessie. "I've got the number here for People Opposing Women Abuse." She was looking at her BlackBerry phone. "This is serious. At least three women are killed by their partners every day in South Africa. Okay, let's give her the numbers for the battered women's shelter, Life Line, and legal aid."

While Jessie wrote the phone numbers down on a bit of paper, I had a sip of my tea, and tried not to think of all the women in South Africa who were beaten, raped, and killed, nor of my years with Fanie, but only of this woman and her friend, asking for my help. What did they need right now?

"I can tell you this for sure," said Jessie, handing me the phone numbers, "self-defense won't work as a legal argument, if she's killing to protect her friend. The woman who's being beaten can get a protection order and a warrant for the man's arrest. If he breaks the protection order, the police will arrest him. The wife must organize this. A friend can help, but can't do it for her."

I spent an hour making phone calls and another half hour writing the letter telling her what I'd learned. Jessie was right. There was not much the friend could do. The woman had to act for herself. She must ask for the domestic violence clerk at the Ladismith Magistrates' Court, and get a protection order. Her friend could give her all the information and the phone numbers. There was counseling and legal aid, and a shelter in George where she could stay.

If duck lady was reading the paper—or the Web or the Parmalat board—she would get this story herself. I don't know why I hadn't sent these numbers in my first letter to her. That was really stupid of me. I should have asked Jessie earlier. I wish I'd known about those phone numbers when I was with Fanie.

I wanted to give the woman who had written to me some comfort food, recipes for chicken pies and chocolate cake. Things you could rely on when everything else is deurmekaar. But I knew that she would probably not be in the mood for baking, even if she had a Thermafan oven. And I had no way of taking the food to her myself.

Then I remembered that Tannie Kuruman made the best chicken pies. Soft and juicy inside, with flaky pastry crusts. I phoned her and got her recipe and put it at the end of my letter, saying that the pies were for sale at the Route 62 Café.

Jessie put the letter on the website, and I went and pinned a copy on the Parmalat notice board. On the way back I stopped at Tannie Kuruman's café and bought two warm chicken pies.

I sat in the shade of a big umbrella, watching the mountains, the Swartberge, with the Towerkop peak, there above the town. The heat made them look farther away than they really were. The shadows on their flanks were purple and green, like bruises.

The pies were delicious. The first one I ate for duck lady. The second for her friend. In case they didn't get a chance to buy their own.

ELEVEN

The next two days I went to the *Gazette,* and replied to my other letters and emails. For lunch on both days I went to the Route 62 Café and ate two chicken pies. I sat on the bench in the umbrella shade and looked up at the mountain. Tannie Kuruman came and sat down beside me.

Tannie Kuruman smells of the kitchen. It's a nice smell. She's a coloured lady in her sixties, and even shorter and rounder than me. She wears a doek over her head, a little cloth to tidy her hair away. Her skin's a bit browner than mine, and her hair frizzier. But coloureds and whites do not look so different from each other out here in the country.

"It's so dark up there," I said, when I had finished chewing, "in those mountain gorges."

"Ja," she said, "it's where the tall trees grow. When it rains there are lovely waterfalls over the rocks."

That night I struggled to sleep. I was worried about those two women. I knew too well what could happen to them, and I tried not to remember what had happened to me. But sometimes these flashes just come to me as if it all happened only yesterday instead of years ago. I calmed myself down by reciting my mother's muesli buttermilk rusk recipe. Butter, flour, sunflower seeds, dried apples . . .

I had run out of beskuit at home and at the office. And rusks should dry out overnight. So I got up and made a big batch and put them into two baking trays in the oven. I let the warm, sweet smell fill my lungs, and somehow it helped fight away the memories, and the worry. Maybe duck lady's husband was not as bad as my husband. And even my husband didn't kill me . . .

When the dough was baked and had cooled a little, I cut it into rusk-size pieces and put them into the warming drawer. I ate two of the biggest pieces while they were still soft, with a cup of tea. They were like buttery cake. I went back to bed and kept my mind on the sweet bread that was becoming rusks, all safe and warm and dry, and I finally managed to fall asleep.

I woke early, just before the birds, and sat on the stoep in my nightie and looked on the dark shapes of the veld and the hills and drank coffee and ate two of the golden-brown beskuit. I put on my veldskoene, walked around to the side of the house, and opened up the chicken hok. I checked that all five hens were in there, and listened to their sleepy chicken noises. I always close the hokkie door at night, because you never know when a jackal or rooikat is in the area. I threw some crushed mielies on the lawn and called *kik kik kik* and they woke up fast.

The flashbacks were gone with the morning light, but the worries were still there, and my mind wouldn't settle. So I made my farm bread with oats, sunflower seeds, and molasses.

I put the dough into a cast-iron pot and took it outside on my stoep where the sun was now shining.

I phoned the *Gazette* but there was no reply. When the dough had risen, I divided it into two bread pans and put them in the oven. While they baked I got dressed, but stayed barefoot. Then I brushed the loaves with butter and wrapped each one in its own cloth.

I ate the soft warm bread, with butter and apricot jam on one slice and cheese on the other. I am not sure how settled my mind was, but the food settled very nicely in my belly.

While I cleaned up I listened to a cicada's buzzing song. I

wondered if he was screaming for rain—the days were just getting hotter. But I suppose he was shouting for a mate. Cicadas aren't shy about calling and calling. After years of living underground, he comes out for just a short while and makes his mad music. But it seems he only plays one note, which goes on and on. I suppose his life in the sunshine is too short to be fussy. Maybe what sounds like a desperate racket to me is beautiful music to a lady cicada.

I filled a tin with muesli buttermilk beskuit for the *Gazette.* I didn't want to go in to the office; I couldn't say why. But I brushed my hair and put on lipstick and my khaki veldskoene and headed for the car.

Lying near the front tire of the car was a small feathered thing. It was a dead bird. A dove. I wondered if I had hit it, but it didn't look run over. It was all in one piece, just soft and dead. I put the rusks down on the passenger seat, and picked up the bird. It was so light in my hands, but it gave me a heavy feeling in my heart. I laid it under a bread-flower bush on the edge of my driveway. The bush had little red flowers.

My sky blue bakkie was not too hot, thanks to the morning shade of the eucalyptus trees. I wound down my windows as I drove and the warm wind unbrushed my hair and dried my lipstick.

At the *Gazette,* I pulled in some distance behind Hattie's Etios, which was parked very askew. As I walked up the path to the office, I could hear Hattie talking loudly.

"Golly, Jess," she was saying. "I wouldn't have thought you an ambulance chaser."

Jessie's voice: "Aw, Hattie . . ."

"And privacy for the poor chap? The bereaved?"

"I used a telephoto lens, he didn't even see me."

"Were you invited there? Or did you really just follow the ambulance?"

"C'mon . . . Its siren was on, it was right in front of me. I'm an investigative journalist."

"Pish-posh."

The door was open and they were at Jessie's desk. Hattie was frowning but she tried to rearrange her face when she saw me.

"Maria . . . ," she said.

"Hello, Tannie." Jessie grinned.

Hattie was too polite to carry on skelling out Jessie in front of me. But Jessie wasn't going to let it go.

"Just have a look at the photos," she said to us both.

I looked at the pictures on her computer.

The first photograph was from a bit of a distance: a farm, an ambulance, and paramedics.

She clicked slowly through a few pictures:

Men in white. A stretcher, a woman's body, her arm in a plaster cast. Pretty nose and mouth, brown hair loose across her shoulder. Pale skin, eyes closed. Maybe in her forties. A man in his fifties, standing, hands hanging useless at his sides, the ambulance driving off. His hair wiry with scraggly sideburns, his mouth a little open. His face full and empty at the same time.

A photo of the same man, squatting on the ground, in front of a pond surrounded by reeds, his face buried in his hands.

"Is she dead?" I asked, although my bones already knew the answer.

Jessie nodded.

"I spoke to my ma, at the hospital," she said. "Her name is Martine van Schalkwyk. The husband is Dirk."

"Can you do a close-up on that picture?" I said. "No, not his face, the pond."

At the edge of the water, caught in the base of the reeds, were a few feathers. Small and white.

I felt strange and had to sit down. I managed to get to my desk chair.

"Maria, you're pale as a ghost," said Hattie.

Jessie put the kettle on while Hattie fanned me with a piece of paper.

They pulled up their chairs and sat down on either side of me. Jessie handed me a cup of coffee and I took a big sip. It was sweet and strong.

"The ducks," I said. "It was the lady with the ducks."

"Oh, heavens, yes, the one who wrote to you," said Hattie.

"The bastard," said Jessie. "He killed her."

"Oh, if only . . . ," I said, but the list of the things I wished was too long to say.

"Have some beskuit," Hattie said, opening my tin and offering a rusk to me.

"Let me investigate," said Jessie, standing up. "Please, Hattie."

Hattie sighed.

"Talk to the police and the hospital," she said. "But you leave that husband alone."

Jessie opened her mouth as if she was going to speak but then closed it again. She grabbed her notebook, helmet, and jacket and headed off.

Hattie shook her head.

"That girl."

"I think she'll go far," I said.

"Maybe too far," said Hattie.

TWELVE

We heard the buzz of Jessie's scooter fading away and then the rattling of a big car arriving, its brakes screeching as it stopped, a door slamming, boots stomping up the pathway.

Hattie peeked outside. Her eyebrows shot up and she scooted backward, her hand on the door, like she might close it.

"Haai!" a woman shouted. "Ek soek, Tannie Maria!"

She was looking for me. Her voice was rough but had some sweet flavor, like a Christmas cake with pits in it.

"I'm afraid she's not currently available," said Hattie.

"Where is she? Who're you?"

"Would you like me to take a message?"

Hattie was blocking the door but the woman pushed past her.

"Blikemmer," she swore. Tin bucket. "I must see her."

She was wearing men's coveralls and no makeup. Her hair was short but deurmekaar, like she'd been running her hands through it. But you could still see she was a good-looking woman in her thirties, her eyes brown with dark eyelashes.

"And you?" she said when she saw me.

She looked like she was going to klap one of us. Who was she going to smack first? She wasn't as tall as Hattie, but she looked strong enough to take us both on.

I was going to tell this rude woman that I was the cleaning lady and she was messing up the floor with her dirty shoes.

But then I saw, stuck to the mud on one of her big leather boots, a little white feather.

"I am Tannie Maria," I said. "Sit. Sit. I'll make us coffee."

She sat on the edge of Jessie's chair and frowned at me, as if she didn't like the way I was putting sugar in her coffee. But I carried on anyway, and added milk too.

Then there was a sound like someone had stood on a puppy, and I got a fright. The woman's face crumpled and the sound was her crying. Then she was tjanking, howling like a dog that's been left alone. I put her coffee along with the tin of beskuit on the table next to her, and pulled my chair closer to hers.

"Heavens above," said Hattie and closed the door.

But she needn't have worried because the woman got much quieter. Tears ran down her face, right into her mouth; you could see the lines because her cheeks were a bit dusty. She was tjanking softly now, and I could make out some words:

"Tienie. My Tienie," she said. "I love her."

The tears kept streaming down. Ag, I felt sorry for her.

Then there was a loud knocking, and Hattie went to open the door.

"Police!" barked a man's voice. "I am Detective Lieutenant Kannemeyer. We are looking for Anna Pretorius. Her bakkie is outside."

Hattie said nothing and for the second time someone pushed past her. The policeman was big and tall with short hair and a thick handlebar mustache. It had a nice shape, like he took care of it. His mustache was a chestnut color and his hair was a darker brown with silver streaks above his ears.

The woman jumped up from her chair, knocking the tin and spilling the rusks onto the floor.

"Anna Pretorius," said the man, "you must come with me for fingerprinting."

Anna wiped her face with the back of her hand and then, with that same hand full of dust and tears, she made a fist and punched the policeman in his jaw. He jerked back and touched his fingers to his face. His eyes were a storm-cloud blue. He reached out his long arm. The long arm of the law, they say, but I'd never seen it in person before, you know, reaching out like that. But she ducked under his long arm and darted for the door. He seemed to move more slowly than she did, but somehow he caught her. She was jumping, and beating out with her fists, her face as red as a beet. But he just wrapped his arms around her, like a giant bear, and pinned her to him until she went still. There was sunlight shining on his arms and you could see that chestnut-colored hair again.

"Konstabel Piet Witbooi," he said.

A little guy with the high cheekbones of a Bushman popped up beside the detective. His hair was like peppercorns and his skin was wrinkled and yellow-brown, like a sultana raisin. His hands moved quickly and quietly as he slipped handcuffs around Anna's wrists. I thought she was still going to kick and bite, but when I saw her face I realized the fire had gone out of her. The tears were slipping down her cheeks again.

"Why do you need fingerprints?" I said to the policemen.

They did not reply, but I knew the answer. Anna was a suspect in the murder of her friend.

"You've got to help me," Anna said, looking at me with her wet brown eyes.

I knew that I would try. But I also knew that I would never be able to help her with her biggest trouble. That huge eina loss of the one she loved.

And then, it was funny, and I know it was a selfish thing to do, but I felt jealous of her, standing there looking so miserable, with the big policeman holding her. I envied her love. That deep love I had never had.

Konstabel Witbooi and Detective Kannemeyer and Anna left Hattie and me standing there, looking down at the muesli buttermilk rusk crumbs, trampled all over the floor.

I shook my head. What a sad story.

THIRTEEN

"You blerrie dyke bitch," said the pink-faced man in khaki shorts.

Now that wasn't how I expected to be greeted when I went into the Ladismith police station. I was there to tell the detective about the *Gazette* letters I'd gotten from the dead woman and her friend. I hadn't gotten a chance to talk to him earlier.

The rude man was swearing at Anna: "Blerrie bitch."

Anna stood in front of a long wooden counter next to Konstabel Piet Witbooi. He turned and greeted me with a nod. Anna's handcuffs were off and there was ink all over her fingers. The room was big, with pale yellow walls and small metal-framed windows, and an old humming air-conditioning unit. There was a corridor leading off this room, with doors to smaller offices. On the other side of the counter sat a young black policewoman at a wooden desk, busy with some paperwork.

Anna glared at the rude man, her eyes bright and her nose twitching. "She hated you, you ugly warthog," she said. "Vlakvark."

He did look a bit like a warthog: stocky, his eyes small and his hair wiry. A big nose. And brown and gray scraggly whiskers on his jaws. Where had I seen him before?

"You blerrie fat rat," he said.

She was baring her teeth at him now, but not in a smiling

way. She didn't look like a rat, more like a rock rabbit, a dassie. With her soft fur and dark eyes. I wondered if the dassie was going to sink her teeth into the warthog.

"She was mine," he said.

Now I recognized him: Dirk van Schalkwyk—from Jessie's photographs.

The policewoman said something, but I could not hear, because at that moment the air-con unit made a loud rattling sound.

"She hated you," Anna hissed.

"I'll blerrie kill you, you fat kakkerlak," he shouted.

That was just silly. She looked nothing like a cockroach.

"Hey!" said Detective Kannemeyer, coming out of the office at the back. He stared down at us all. He really was a tall guy. "Stop that."

"Go ahead, warthog," said Anna, standing up straight, pushing her shoulders back. "Kill me, you murderer."

"You're not gonna get away with it," said Dirk, pulling a gun out from under his shirt.

I thought she would kick him or throw herself on the floor but she just lifted her chin a little higher. Maybe she was happy at the thought of joining her Tienie.

Piet moved so quickly I hardly saw him. He knocked Dirk's arm up into the air as a shot rang out. *Boom!* Bits of plaster and dust fell down from the ceiling.

Detective Kannemeyer clamped Dirk's wrist in his big hand, and took the gun from him.

"Enough," said the detective.

Kannemeyer twisted Dirk's arm behind his back, and Dirk made a snorting noise. They both had ceiling dust on their hair.

"You fat rat," Dirk mumbled as he was pushed past Anna, out of the room.

I shook my head. Such rudeness. So unnecessary.

Anna really was not at all fat. She had some padding, like any woman who ate three meals a day. But to call her fat was just wrong.

Now the police station was full of people who'd popped in to see what the shouting and shooting were about.

"Hello, Tannie Elna," I said to the woman who worked in the shoe shop next door.

She was small and thin, hopping up and down like a meerkat to get a good view.

"What's going on?" she said.

"Would you say she is fat?"

I pointed to Anna, who was being led away by a policewoman. Elna put her head to one side and scrunched up her mouth, then shook her head.

"No," she said, "not really . . ."

"Was someone shot?" asked a man from the Spar, the manager.

He had one of those silly little mustaches, like a little boy who's drunk chocolate milk. The hair on his head was combed sideways, to hide the bald spots.

"Dirk van Schalkwyk was here," said Elna.

The Spar manager's nostril curled up.

I don't know how Elna knew about Dirk; I hadn't told her. But that's what it's like in a small town. Sometimes news travels faster than the things that are actually happening. I was once told of an old lady's death before she died. But she did die, the next day, so she managed to catch up with the news.

"I hear Martine van Schalkwyk was killed," said Tannie de Jager from the library.

"Who is she?" said a lady wearing a pink floral dress.

"She's married to Dirk, who works at the AgriMark," said Elna. "She does the books at the Spar."

Then they were all talking at once, saying and asking I don't know what. I was looking around for somewhere quiet to sit when the detective came back in again and said very loudly: "Show's over. Go away."

The people went quiet and looked at him and each other.

"Voetsek!" he shouted, making a shooing movement with his hands, and they scuttled out like chickens.

But I stayed, standing to one side. Kannemeyer ran his hand through his short hair.

"Can I help you?" he said.

"You look like you could use a nice cup of coffee," I said, looking up at him.

He smiled. It was a nice smile. Slow and warm, and it went right to his eyes. His mustache curved up at the corners. His teeth were white and strong.

"Ja," he said. "You were at the *Karoo Gazette*."

"I need to talk to you," I said. "About Martine van Schalkwyk."

He sighed and took a pen out of his pocket.

FOURTEEN

The next morning I stood on my stoep and watched the early light make long shadows of the hills and the thorn trees. The sun was warm on my face and I had a good feeling but I wasn't sure why. It was probably because of the lamb. I was going to make slow-roasted lamb, with potatoes, pumpkins, and green beans. And a buttermilk chocolate cake.

Detective Kannemeyer hadn't listened to my whole story at the police station, but got my address and said he'd come around to my house the next day to take a statement. I could see he had a lot on his hands, so I didn't argue. He said he would call first.

On the way home from the police station, I'd stopped at the butcher because they had a special on leg of lamb. There is no better-tasting meat than Karoo lamb. You can taste the Karoo veld, and sunshine and the sweet wild herbs the lambs eat.

I was in the mood for my nice cream dress, the one with the little blue flowers. I took off my veldskoene and found my blue shoes with the low heels. I put on my apron and started with the lamb.

Once the lamb was in the oven, I went outside to pick rosemary for the potatoes. The red geraniums were flowering, and I cut some to put in a vase on the kitchen table.

When I was in the garden, the phone rang. My shoes interfered a bit with my walking, and on account of this and the distance between the geranium bush and the phone, my heart was beating fast when I picked up.

"Hello."

"Tannie Maria?"

"Hats," I said.

"You all right, darling? You sound a tad breathless."

I put the rosemary and the geraniums on the phone table and sat down on the chair.

"What did Jessie find out?" I asked.

"Can you come in to the office? To discuss the murder case."

"The case," I said, because it felt good to say.

"Well, it's not as if it's a big murder mystery. We know jolly well who did it. But we don't want the rotter to get away with it, do we?"

"I can't come yet," I said. "Detective Henk Kannemeyer is coming here today."

"The big chap," she said, "with the strong arms."

"To take my statement. And read the letters."

"Jessie went to interview him, but he wouldn't tell her anything. Maybe you'll have better luck."

"I'll do my best. What did Jessie find out at the hospital?"

"Nurse Mostert, Jessie's mother, heard that it may've been an overdose. Sleeping pills."

"Suicide?" I leaned forward in my chair.

"Maybe. They still have to do the autopsy."

"Look, I mustn't stay on the phone. You know, in case Kannemeyer calls."

"You sound like you're waiting for a date."

"Don't be silly, Hattie. I must go."

I rubbed the geranium leaf between my finger and thumb and breathed it in.

Suicide. Selfmoord as they say in Afrikaans: self-murder. Sjoe. In some ways it felt worse than murder. If a man treats a woman so badly that she ends her own life, it's like he has killed her twice: her heart and then her body.

When I was with Fanie, I thought of killing myself. I even got as far as buying sleeping pills.

There was a pressure on my chest like a bag of potatoes. I just let myself sit there, next to the phone. Then I was suddenly crying. For Martine, for Anna, for myself. I hadn't cried for years and there I was, crying for the second time in just a few weeks. Maybe it was not a bad thing. When I was finished, my heart felt a bit lighter.

I hadn't killed myself. I was here now, alive. I had chickens that gave me beautiful eggs, a stoep with the best view, and some real friends.

I took another sniff of the geranium and got up.

I peeled the potatoes and sprinkled rosemary, salt, and olive oil over them, put them in the oven, and turned up the heat. Then I took the letters from Martine and Anna outside to the stoep table, along with some coffee and beskuit, and read through what the women had written, and my responses to them.

"No," I said to the last beskuit. "This woman didn't kill herself. She had plans to escape."

I went inside and chopped up half a pumpkin, and sprinkled it with sugar, cinnamon, and blobs of butter.

"I wonder if I left the phone off the hook," I said to the pumpkin as I put it in the oven.

I checked the phone. It was okay. I nipped the ends off the green beans and prepared the batter for the chocolate cake. I was greasing the cake tin, my fingers covered with butter, when the phone rang.

FIFTEEN

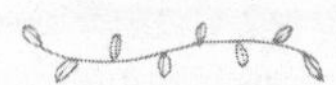

"Mevrou van Harten? It's Detective Lieutenant Henk Kannemeyer. Can I come around now?"

I looked at the clock on the wall. It was noon.

"Could you make it at one o'clock, Detective?"

He cleared his throat. Everyone in Ladismith knows business is not done between one and two. All the shops close so that people can go home for lunch. Except for the Spar. And the police station.

"I can give you a bite to eat," I said. "That is, unless . . ."

Maybe he was expected at home.

"It's okay," he said. "I've got sandwiches."

"No, no, I've made roast lamb."

"Roast lamb?"

"With potatoes and pumpkin. Soetpampoen."

"Oh. Well then . . ."

I wondered who made him his sandwiches.

I put the cake in the oven and took the foil off the lamb. Then I prepared the chocolate icing. I added the rum and buttermilk and tasted the dark mixture on the tip of my little finger.

"Mmmm," I said. I added a pinch of salt and then tasted again. "Perfect."

I cleaned the kitchen and laid the outside table. The big jug of lemonade with ice and fresh mint stood next to a tray with the letters from Martine, and her friend Anna. My replies were there too.

The heat had melted the dark blue out of the sky, leaving it that pale Karoo blue. But the trees and tin afdak kept the stoep cool.

I took off my apron, tidied my hair, and put on fresh lipstick. I heard a car heading my way and I smoothed my dress and went outside. A bokmakierie was calling to its mate in the thorn tree. I saw his police van pulling up in my driveway. Those birds make such a beautiful trilling sound, it goes right through your heart. I walked up the pathway to wave at him. Just so he knew he was in the right place.

I watched him get out. Long trousers and his khaki cotton shirt a bit open at his neck and chest. He touched the tip of his mustache and dipped his head as he greeted me.

"Just listen to those bokmakieries," I said.

"Ja. Lovely."

We walked to the stoep together. He sat down, fitting his long legs under the table.

"Smells good," he said.

"Lemonade?" I poured some into a tall glass for him. He smelled good too. Like sandalwood and honey. "Here are the letters I told you about. I'll just be in the kitchen."

He started reading as I went to look after the roast and the chocolate cake. The cake needed to cool before I could ice it.

When I came out with the roast lamb and vegetables, Kannemeyer was holding the letters in his hand, and looking out across the veld at our red mountain, the Rooiberg. I could still hear the bokmakieries calling, but they sounded farther away now, maybe in the big gwarrie tree.

He jumped up to help me put the roasting tray on the table.

"Shall I carve that for you?" he said.

I handed him the knife.

"I'll get the handwriting checked," he said, slicing the lamb, "but I think you're right—these were written by Mevrou van Schalkwyk and Mejuffrou Pretorius." He shook his head. "Those white ducks . . ."

"You read my letters too?" I said, spooning potatoes and pampoen onto his plate.

"Ja. I read them all."

"So you can see why I feel involved. Responsible, even," I said, dishing out the green beans.

He frowned.

"If I hadn't told her to leave, he wouldn't have killed her," I said.

"You can't blame yourself, Mrs. van Harten."

"If I had told her about people, organizations, that could help her, keep her safe," I said, putting some of the best lamb slices on his plate, "she could be alive today. Like me. About to eat a nice lunch."

The thought that she would never eat lunch again made me very sad.

"Tannie Maria," he said, "we don't even know it was the husband. It might have been suicide. Maybe it was Anna. We don't know yet. You can't blame yourself."

"It wasn't suicide. And you don't really think Anna—"

But I didn't want to ruin the meal with an argument.

"Let's eat," I said. "Help yourself to gravy."

The food was perfect. The lamb was dark and crispy on the outside and tender on the inside; the potatoes, golden brown; the pumpkin sticky and sweet. Kannemeyer closed his eyes when he ate his first mouthful. We did not talk while we ate. I could hear the bokmakieries again, out in the veld.

When he'd finished eating, he said, "I haven't had such a lekker roast since— For a long time."

A little bit of gravy was on the tip of his chestnut mustache. He smiled. That lovely white smile again. But his eyes looked sad. He wiped his mouth with his napkin. It was time to set things straight, while the food was still warm in his belly.

"Detective Kannemeyer," I said, "you know it was her husband who killed her."

"Maybe. Maybe not. You need evidence to convict someone."

"You've read the letters," I said. "I was there when this . . . man tried to kill Anna in the police station."

"Ja, Anna must press charges against him. But that is a separate matter."

"Have you got evidence that someone else could have killed Martine?"

"We are waiting on . . . reports."

"What reports?"

I was wondering about Anna's fingerprints and the autopsy.

"Ma'am," he said, "Mrs. van Harten. We are handling it, you don't need to worry."

"But, Detective, we do worry. The man can't just get away with it. We could help you investigate the case."

"We?" he said, glancing at the watch on his thick wrist.

"Well, us, at the *Klein Karoo Gazette*," I said. "We've got an investigative reporter, we know people in the town. We could find evidence—"

"Mrs. van Harten," he said, standing up, "I appreciate the information you have given me, but this is a murder investigation for the police to handle."

"There's cake," I said. "Buttermilk chocolate cake. With rum in the icing."

"Sorry. I have to go."

The bokmakieries had gone quiet now; from far away on Route 62 came the sound of a truck driving up toward Oudtshoorn.

SIXTEEN

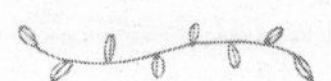

Now of course I was cross with Kannemeyer after that. He was stubborn. Rude, in fact. How could he leave without cake? But I was more cross with myself. I should've brought it out sooner.

I went into the kitchen and began icing the cake. If he had only seen it. Or smelled it.

"I messed up," I said to the cake. "If he had a taste of you. He would have agreed to anything I asked." I licked a bit of rum-and-chocolate icing off my finger. "Anything."

I called the *Gazette*. Jessie answered.

"Kannemeyer's come and gone," I said. "Can you two come here for a meeting? I've got a chocolate cake asking to be eaten."

"Yes," said Jessie. "Tell the cake yes."

The three of us sat on my stoep in the hot afternoon. Jessie's eyes were wide because she had been driven here by Hattie. Little yellow birds were eating insects on the lawn, while the chickens lay in the shade of the geranium bush.

"You look nice, Tannie M," Jessie said, looking at my cream dress with the blue flowers, and my blue heels.

"Yes, you should have told us we were dressing up for tea," said Hattie.

"Ag, Hats, you always look smart," I said.

She was wearing a fitted shirt and long white cotton skirt. Jessie was in her sleeveless black vest and shorts. I poured our coffee and tea. Jessie's eyes opened even wider when I cut her a slice of cake, then they rolled toward the top of her head as she took a big bite. For the second bite, her eyes were closed.

"Darling, just a sliver for me, please," said Hattie. She patted her neat blond hair. "So! How was the meeting with the big detective?"

"He read the letters and agrees they fit. He'll get the handwriting tested."

I handed her a thin piece of cake, and cut myself a nice piece.

Jessie's phone sang, *Light my fire.*

"Sorry," she said. She took it from her pouch and glanced at it and smiled. "It's just a message. Go on, Tannie M."

"But I messed up with him," I said. "I didn't give him cake in time, and he wouldn't tell me anything. And he doesn't want our help. He wants us to stay out of it."

Jessie said something but her mouth was full of cake, so I couldn't understand it.

"What she is attempting to say," translated Hattie, who had not yet touched her cake, "is that Kannemeyer wouldn't speak to her, but Reghardt did."

"Who's Reghardt?" I asked.

"Reghardt Snyman is an old school friend of Jessie's who happens to be a policeman. And who happens to be sweet on her."

Jessie wrinkled her nose at Hattie.

"What?" said Hattie. "I've seen how he looks at you."

Jessie stroked a gecko tattoo on her arm. The cake was making her happy. And maybe the mention of Reghardt too.

"Kannemeyer did say that maybe it wasn't Dirk who killed his wife," I said. "He thinks it might've been suicide, and it seems like they suspect Anna too."

"This cake is totally awesome, Tannie," Jessie mumbled between crumbs. "Is there brandy in the icing?"

"Rum," I said.

"Did Hattie tell you about the sleeping pills?"

"Ja," I said. "But Martine wrote to me that she was planning to leave. I don't think she was suicidal." I picked up the letter and read: " 'I am making a plan that will allow me to leave. I will just have to tread water till I get it right.' "

"Maybe she meant leave this mortal coil," said Hattie as she nibbled on her cake.

"My ma was on shift at the hospital when they brought the body in and she saw that there was a wound on Martine's head," said Jessie. "Then the LCRC came and took the body to Oudtshoorn; they will do the autopsy there."

"The LCRC?" I said.

"Sorry, the Local Crime Registration Center. They do the forensic testing for this region. Though some things they send off to the forensic lab in Cape Town. And Reghardt told me—off the record, of course—that the LCRC was given a fire poker for fingerprinting."

"A poker?" I said. "Did her husband klap her with it?"

"Well, if she was hit on the head, then I suppose we can rule out suicide," said Hattie.

"She could've drugged herself and, like, fallen and hurt her head," said Jessie. "Or he could have hit her with the poker and it was just the last straw and she killed herself."

"I don't believe it," I said, passing the letters to Jessie. "Look at these again."

"Didn't you give these to the detective?" asked Hattie.

"No. I let him read them, but when he didn't want to stay for cake, I was a bit upset and told him they were *Gazette* property and I would make copies and drop off the originals tomorrow."

"He could've just taken them, you know," said Jessie. "Being a murder case and all."

"He's a real gentleman, that detective," said Hattie.

"Elna le Grange said Martine was a bookkeeper at the Spar," I said.

"Ja, that's true," said Jessie. "My cousin Boetie works there.

He says she went in twice a week. A nice lady, he said. Quiet."

She quickly read through the letters I had given her.

"Dirk was a pig," she said. "But Anna might have been moerse angry when Martine told her not to come around anymore."

She read out loud from Anna's letter: " 'She says I mustn't go to her house.' "

"Oh, golly," said Hattie. "Maybe that's why they wanted her fingerprints. To see if they matched the ones on the poker. But Dirk is the abusive one, not Anna. He got wind of her plan to leave, and killed her."

Jessie's cake was finished. She got out her pen and paper, and started making notes.

"I know it seems obvious to us that the husband did it," she said, "but we need to find a way of proving it. It's also possible, objectively speaking, that someone else did it." She took a sip of her coffee. When she was writing, Jessie spoke in a different way. Less like a small-town coloured girl and more like an SABC-TV presenter. "We need to establish cause of death. Identify suspects and possible motives. We also need to find evidence to convict the guilty party."

"You're right," I said, cutting another slice of cake for Jessie. "I suppose Anna's letter shows she might kill for love. Then Martine told her not to come around. That might've upset Anna a lot. Maybe Martine was planning on leaving not just her husband, but also Anna."

"Love does funny things to people," said Hattie, looking at the first letter. "Martine said she wants the relationship platonic from her side. Perhaps Anna wanted more."

I gave Hattie some more tea.

"And," said Jessie, "Martine's son is in George. Maybe she was planning on leaving Ladismith altogether to be nearer him."

We were all quiet for a while, drinking and eating and feeling rather pleased with ourselves as investigators. On the grass, termites were gathering grass and sticks, just like we were gathering clues.

I was also feeling pleased with the chocolate cake. It was perfect. Moist, dense, rich, and satisfying. You can hold the idea of the best chocolate cake in your mind like a memory from childhood; but when you eat a real cake it's often a bit of a disappointment. Not this one.

I heard the bokmakierie calling in the veld. I felt bad. Anna had asked for my help, and here we were talking against her when maybe all she was guilty of was love.

"I think I should go and take Anna some cake," I said, "and see what she has to say."

"Good idea," said Hattie, "she trusts you."

"I could also take a slice to Kannemeyer," I said, "along with the letters."

SEVENTEEN

"You're here bright and early this morning, Tannie Maria," said Hattie as I walked into the office. "Bee in your bonnet?"

The heat had not yet settled on the day, and the ceiling fan was off.

"I can't ignore all the other people who write letters just because some are in trouble or dead."

I put Martine and Anna's letters and a Tupperware container with two big pieces of chocolate cake onto my desk, and picked up a pile of envelopes and some pages of email printouts. I heard Jessie's scooter arriving and I turned on the kettle. Then I sorted through my post. It was important to start the day with the right letter.

"Haai, Hattie and Tannie M," said Jessie. "What's up?"

She was eyeing my Tupperware container. You couldn't see through it, but Jessie had a sixth sense when it came to cake.

"Sorry, my skat, it's for Anna and Kannemeyer. Could you make copies of these on your scanner thingy?" I handed her the letters. "So I can give the originals to the detective." I rattled the rusk tin to distract her from the cake, but it only had crumbs in it. "Coffee?"

Once we all had our coffee and tea and no rusks, I chose a plain brown envelope with a thumbprint of black grease next to the Riversdale postmark. Riversdale is a big town, about a hundred miles away. Well, not really big, just not as small as Ladismith.

The letter was from a guy in trouble, who signed his name as Karel. He had a lot to learn, but he seemed willing, and I did my best to help.

Dear Tannie Maria,

I am writing to you for love advice. Don't bother with the recipes. I can't even boil an egg.

I met this girl at a Brandy Festival and I like her a lot. She has eyes that sparkle, and an amazing smile. Her name is Lucia. We sat together at a wooden table and I hardly said a word but I offered her my slap chips and she ate some.

When she smiled at me, I felt like a bunch of birds was trying to fly out of my chest.

I wanted to say something but I couldn't.

I am a mechanic, and my fingernails are always a bit black, no matter how much I scrub them. Lucia is clean and smells so good. She is small and neat, like a Mini. I am more like a truck.

I feel like such an idiot. I want to see her again, but I don't know how to talk to her.

And what if I ask her out and she says no? Or what if she comes but I say nothing the whole time?

Karel

I got out my pen and paper and wrote:

Dear Karel,

What if she says yes? Ask her out by text message. Take her to a movie.

There is no need to feel like an idiot. You might think boiling an egg is simple, but it is really quite a tricky thing to do. The perfect egg is one that's been boiled for exactly three minutes. The problem is that if you put the egg straight into boiling water, the shell cracks. But if you put it into cold water, it's hard to know when to start timing. There are three different ways to deal with this. I like the first way best.

Heat the egg before you add it to the boiling water. Do this by putting the egg into a small bowl which is about one quarter full of cold water, then slowly add hot water from the kettle. Use a spoon to lower this warm egg into the boiling water.

or

Add a teaspoon of vinegar to the boiling water—this makes the egg think twice about cracking.

or

Put the egg in cold water and stand and wait till it boils.

Have a spoon and egg cup ready and eat right away, because the egg carries on cooking inside its shell. Serve with toast, butter, salt, and pepper.

I was sure a lot of people would be glad to see my response. How to boil an egg is a question that many are too embarrassed to ask. Karel was brave to bring it out in the open like that. I had high hopes for him.

I had just started to study another small blue envelope when the phone rang. Hattie answered.

"The detective," she whispered. She winked as she handed me the phone. "For you."

"Maria speaking," I said.

"Anna Pretorius has been arrested," the detective said. "She won't call a lawyer. She wants you."

"Arrested?"

"Can you come down to the station?" he said.

"For hitting you in the jaw?"

"For murder, Mrs. van Harten."

"Did she kill that man who tried to shoot her?"

I know I was being dense, we'd discussed it ourselves, just yesterday. But I didn't want to believe it.

"For the murder of Martine van Schalkwyk."

This was really bad news.

But on the plus side, I could deliver both slices of cake at once.

EIGHTEEN

I pulled into the shade of a rubber tree in the police station parking lot. On the passenger seat beside me were the letters for Kannemeyer, and a Tupperware container holding two slices of chocolate cake.

Piet popped his head out of the station door, then came across the dusty tarmac to meet me. Oh dear, I thought, what about a slice for Konstabel Piet?

Piet smiled at me as I got out, his yellow-brown face became even more wrinkled, and his almond eyes narrower. He led me to the station, through the busy reception area and along a passageway to Kannemeyer's office, moving silently in his leather sandals. Kannemeyer was on the phone and I sat down to wait for him. Piet left, which took pressure off the cake situation.

The detective nodded at me, but carried on with his call. He looked big, even when he was sitting down. His desk was solid teak and had a polished reddish glow that went well with his chestnut mustache.

"Mmm . . . uh-huh . . . ," he was saying, leaning back in his leather chair.

Outside his office window were thorn trees, and the shadows of the branches fell on the white walls and on his shirt and chest.

My chair was also wood and leather. It was the comfortable

office of a man who spent a lot of time there. I wondered about his home life.

There was a fan on his desk, and I leaned toward it to feel the breeze on my face. My dress was sticking to me from the heat. Between the files and papers on his desk, I saw a photograph in a silver frame. It was Kannemeyer, younger, with his arm around a woman. She was pretty and her face was turned up to him like a flower to the sun. And he was shining love down on her.

"Okay. Ja . . . Ja nee. 'Bye," he said.

He put down the phone and cleared his throat.

"Mrs. van Harten," he said.

"I brought you some cake," I said. "And a slice for Anna."

I pushed the Tupperware across the table and opened it so he could see the two big pieces wrapped in wax paper. He did that slow smile of his that showed off his white teeth and lifted his chestnut mustache at the corners.

"Thank you," he said.

"So, what's happening with Anna?"

"There is quite a case against her." He ran his fingers across his mustache. "Her prints were on a fire poker that was used to hit Martine van Schalkwyk. Fresh tire tracks from her bakkie were in the dirt driveway."

"What does she say?" I said.

"She won't talk to us. She won't call a lawyer."

"Anna wouldn't kill her friend. She had no reason to."

"Could be a crime of passion. Photographs were smashed. Including Martine and Dirk's wedding photo," Kannemeyer said, glancing at his own photograph. "Van Schalkwyk says the woman was in love with his wife. Your letters support that. Did you bring them?"

I put my letters on his desk, but I didn't want them used like that. He was laying out the evidence against Anna. Neatly, like he was laying a table. I didn't want to eat at that table.

"The letters show that Martine's husband was threatening to

kill her," I said. "He broke her arm. It's him you must arrest."

"There's no evidence that he did kill her."

"Were his fingerprints on the poker?"

"No."

"Isn't that a bit funny?" I said. "Wouldn't he use the fire poker in his own house?"

I took his piece of cake from the Tupperware and put it on the table. The corner of the wax paper fell open, showing a small, dark corner of glistening icing. He looked at the chocolate cake and then at me, as if he had just seen me properly for the first time.

"Ja, we found it strange," he said. "Only Anna's prints were on the handle."

"Sounds like someone used it and then wiped their prints."

Kannemeyer moved in his chair and looked out of the window. There were a few big clouds in the sky. Fat with rain that would probably never fall.

"It wasn't the poker alone that killed her," he said at last. "She had taken—or been given—a strong sedative. Then she was hit on the head with the poker. Afterward she was suffocated. Probably with a pillow. There were bits of the cushion fiber in her mouth."

"What?" I said.

"I'm sorry," he said.

Suicide was like killing her twice. Heart and body. But this way she was murdered three times over. I could not believe Anna would do that.

"It doesn't sound like a crime of passion to me," I said. "It must have been planned."

"You know, Tannie Maria," he said, "I've been thinking the same thing myself."

"So why arrest Anna?"

"We need to go on the evidence we've got. She's arrested, not convicted. She can apply for bail. I'm hoping you can talk some sense into her. You are the only one she's asked for. Convince her to get legal help. And to press charges against Van Schalkwyk."

"What does Dirk van Schalkwyk say? Did you question him?"

"Of course we've questioned him. What he said is police business. I am only sharing Anna's story with you because she needs your help."

"Let me see her then. Can you organize us some coffee, please?" I said, picking up the Tupperware from his desk and closing it. "To go with her cake."

"I'll take you to her."

Kannemeyer led me down a darkened corridor to a back room with a small window and an enamel-topped table and two plastic chairs. The walls were yellow-white and cracked, like a smoker's teeth.

A policewoman led Anna in. Anna wore jeans and a khaki shirt that hadn't been ironed. Her short dark hair needed a brush. She scowled at Kannemeyer and the policewoman.

I opened the Tupperware and put it on the table. We sat down and Anna tried to smile at me but her mouth was too tight.

The policewoman scooted forward to see the cake. I bet she had never seen such a nice chocolate cake, but she wasn't getting any. Even if Anna offered to share it with me, I'd say no. I could see she needed every crumb of it herself. At the approach of the policewoman, Anna held her mouth even more closed. Her lips almost disappeared. I would have to get her to relax if she was going to talk or eat.

"Konstabel Witbooi will bring coffee," said Kannemeyer, at the doorway.

"Can we be alone?" I said to the policewoman. "Please."

The woman glanced behind her as if I might be talking to someone else.

"I am here for your safety," she said.

I looked up at Kannemeyer. He moved his chin to tell her she could go. The door clicked locked behind them.

"How are you doing?" I said.

Anna looked at me with those big brown eyes.

"Oh, Tannie," she said.

She lifted her fingers to her forehead and let her head fall into her hands.

Piet came in with coffee.

"Dankie, Konstabel Piet."

When he'd gone Anna sat up and looked at me again. I was adding milk and sugar to our cups.

"Bloody hell," she said, kicking the table leg with her boot. "I messed up."

The coffee wobbled and the cake did a little dance. The icing was melting. I passed her coffee to her and tried to take a sip of mine, but it was still too hot. Anna rubbed her hands on her thighs.

"She's dead. Dead. And it's all my fault," she said.

Was she giving me her confession now?

"Oh, Anna," I said, then I kept quiet.

If she was going to talk, I'd listen.

"I got there too late," she said.

She ran a hand through her hair, messing it up even more.

"I knew the bastard would kill her. I could've stopped it. But she'd told me not to come around and I didn't. I was stupid, I should never have listened to her. On Tuesday I was feeding my ducks when I felt like I was punched in my stomach. I rushed to her house." Her gaze shifted to the wall. "But it was too late . . ."

She was not looking at the cracking paint, but at another picture inside her mind.

"Have some cake," I said.

But she didn't. She had a sip of coffee.

"The poker," I said. "It had your fingerprints on it."

"When I found Tienie dead, I was so upset and angry," she said. "I was angry with him. With Tienie. With myself. And that blerrie wedding photograph. It sat there, staring at me, lying to me, like it did every time I came to visit. I know it was stupid, but I was just so blerrie freaked out, I picked up that poker and klapped that wedding photograph across the room."

I took a sip of my coffee.

"Did you hit Martine?" I asked.

Her eyes went wide.

"Tannie Maria, I loved her."

I kept looking at her.

"No," she said. "I would never hurt her. Never. But Dirk . . ." She took a big sip of coffee. "He's going to pay for this."

I peeled the wax paper off the cake and pushed it closer to her, and she started in on it. Now I knew she was going to be okay. She nodded at me, her mouth full, and gave me a thumbs-up.

"Have you pressed charges for what he did at the police station?" I said when she was finished.

She licked the icing off her fingers and shook her head.

"This is between me and him."

"Anna, you must get legal help. I brought those phone numbers from my letter. Call legal aid. Apply for bail." I took the paper from my pocket. "Here."

She laughed, but it was not a happy laugh.

"Tannie Maria," she said, "do you think I care if I go to prison?" She took the piece of paper but she didn't look at it. "Do you think I care if I die? Have you ever loved someone? I mean, really loved someone?"

I found myself wishing I had brought an extra piece of cake for myself. That was a big slice she ate all on her own.

"No," I said, into my coffee cup.

Henk Kannemeyer came to the door to fetch me and my empty Tupperware. He had chocolate icing on his bottom lip.

"Will she apply for bail?" he said as we walked along the corridor.

"I gave her some legal aid phone numbers," I said. "I don't think she did it."

"That cake," he said. "Very good."

As we came to his office, I saw that he'd shared his piece with Piet. Piet was studying every crumb on his plate for clues to how such a perfect chocolate cake was made. The phone rang on the desk, and Kannemeyer stopped to answer it. He lifted his hand, asking me to wait one minute. But I hurried past. I wanted to get home as soon as I could. There was still half a cake in my kitchen.

NINETEEN

When I woke up the next morning, I had a bit of indigestion so I chewed an antacid.

On the kitchen table was one last slice of buttermilk chocolate cake. The rest I had eaten the night before while I was not thinking about what Anna had said about love. I made some coffee and went and sat on the stoep to watch the day arrive. It happens all of a sudden in the Karoo. One minute the light is soft and full of the night's shadows, and then the sun is blasting everything awake. The Rooiberg changes from red to orange to ochre yellow before you can finish a cup of coffee.

The birds and insects were calling and flying about: the bulbuls eating the purple berries on the gwarrie trees in the veld, the bokmakieries hopping in the branches of the sweet-thorn trees.

All five of my chickens came to say hello, their wattles and combs wobbling and their rust-brown feathers trembling as they ran toward me. I reached into the bucket of crushed mielies that I kept on the stoep and threw them a handful.

I drank my coffee and searched the sky for rain clouds, but there were none. I was wearing my thin blue cotton dress, and had bare feet, but I was already hot.

I packed a fresh tin of muesli rusks for the *Gazette* office. I looked at the cake on the table. It was the last slice of what may have been the best chocolate cake I had ever made. It was quite a responsibility.

I could not eat it myself. Not just because of the indigestion. (That would pass. It always did.) It needed to be put to good use.

"I am wondering how you could help with the case," I said to the cake. "The other slices did a good job at the police station yesterday. Poor Anna, I hope she gets out soon. I am sure prison food is terrible." I sat down at the table. "But someone is going to have to eat it."

My stomach was feeling a bit better after the antacid so I got up to boil myself an egg. Just one. I sat and ate it at the kitchen table with bread and appelkooskonfyt.

"I think it is that husband Dirk who should be eating jail food," I said to my egg as I knocked the top off with a teaspoon. "I think we should go and have a chat with him."

When I had finished, I said to the slice of cake in front of me, "But I need to be prepared. You can't just walk up to a murderer unprepared."

I tidied my breakfast away and made two big roast lamb sandwiches with farm bread. One for Dirk and one for me. With mustard and gherkins and lettuce. I cut them each in half and put them in a Tupperware container. The cake slice glistened under its chocolate-rum icing. I wrapped it up in wax paper and popped it into the Tupperware too.

The Tupperware and the tin of rusks came with me to the *Gazette*. I parked in the shade of the jacaranda. The phone was ringing as I stepped into the office and Hattie waved hello to me as she answered. There was no sign of Jessie.

"Harriet Christie," Hattie said. "Yes, Mr. Marius . . . Certainly, Mr. Mar—"

On my desk was a thick cream envelope with my name and address written in beautiful handwriting. The postmark was Barrydale.

"We are doing our best, Mr. Marius," said Hattie.

Mr. Marius was a *Gazette* sponsor. Real estate. Hattie pulled a face at me, pointing her finger at her tongue to show he made her feel sick. I was glad I didn't have her job. I tuned out her voice as I sat down and read my letter:

> *Tannie Maria, I like your style. You are one plucky lady.*
>
> *I am an interior decorator who left Cape Town to retire—sort of—in one of these quaint little Karoo towns. Mostly it's divine, but some days the small minds of these folk just make me want me to tear my hair out by the roots and scream for mercy. But let me not digress. It is my boyfriend's birthday later this month, and I thought I would make him a special meal. I have bought a set of pale turquoise ceramic crockery for the occasion, handmade plates that are just exquisite. He is a growing lad and he loves his meat and carbs, but I think the occasion and the plates call for something more than pap en wors. Any ideas? Something with the right flavors and colors to go on these plates. Something special and feisty—like my boyfriend. Something with balls.*
>
> *Marco*

I closed my eyes, and I could imagine those lovely turquoise blue plates. What I saw on them was frikkadelle, tamatiesmoor, and yellow mieliepap. Ja, those spicy meatballs, together with that chunky tomato sauce, and polenta, would be very nice on that blue plate. And maybe a side plate with big chunks of bright roasted vegetables, like beets and butternut squash and yellow pepper. And feta. Oh, it looked beautiful . . .

"Hey, Tannie M." Jessie's voice dissolved the picture. "Who you dreaming of?"

"Jessie," I said. "You gave me a fright. I was thinking of meatballs."

"How did it go at the jail yesterday?" Hattie asked as she put down the phone.

"Did they enjoy your cake?" said Jessie.

"Oh, yes," I said, getting up and filling the kettle. "Coffee and tea?"

"Ja," said Jessie.

"Please," said Hattie.

"I don't suppose there's any more of that cake?" said Jessie, eyeing the Tupperware on my desk.

"There's one piece left," I said. "But I've got plans for it. I brought you some muesli buttermilk beskuit."

I told them about my meetings with Kannemeyer and Anna.

"Does sound like someone wiped off their prints before Anna picked up the poker," said Jessie, taking her coffee and a rusk.

"And it simply doesn't make sense for Dirk to wipe his own poker, you'd expect to find his prints on it," said Hattie, accepting her tea and ignoring the beskuit.

"Ja, but he is a bloody idiot," said Jessie, "so he might do such a thing."

"I think we must talk to him," I said.

"But would he talk to us?" said Hattie. "I gather he's not a friendly chap."

"I have a piece of that chocolate cake," I said, "and a lamb sandwich. With mustard and gherkins. That could make him talk."

"I don't think we should be giving that bastard cake and lamb," Jessie said. "He deserves a sharp kick in the balls."

"The man has a gun, you know," said Hattie. "But I agree he's more likely to talk to a tannie with food than a pair of *Gazette* investigators."

"Okay," said Jessie. "You can try going in with the food and I'll wait outside. If you shout, I'll come running with that kick. And pepper spray."

I could've used Jessie in my days with my husband. I gave her another beskuit.

"Dirk's staying at the Dwarsrivier Bed and Breakfast," said Jessie. "I saw his car outside and I spoke to Tannie Sarie, who cleans at the B and B. He's booked in for a couple of days."

"Why'd he move out?" I asked.

"It's a crime scene. The forensic team from Oudtshoorn was here—the LCRC. They've put that yellow tape all over the place."

"Goodness, Jess. How do you know all this?" asked Hattie. "Are you seeing Reghardt then? Does he tell you these things?"

"Not exactly," said Jessie, twirling her ponytail around her finger. "We have seen a bit of each other, though, and I did overhear him talking on the phone, and then I just happened to drive by the Van Schalkwyk farm. Came straight back when I saw the LCRC vehicles."

Hattie shook her head.

"I think we should visit the crime scene ourselves," Jessie said. "Soon. Before Dirk goes home. The LCRC will be finished there today and the police guard will be removed."

"Oh, golly, Jess, I don't want you getting into trouble," said Hattie.

"Anna's the one in trouble, for a murder she didn't do. We've got to try and help her."

"We can't go breaking the law," said Hattie.

"Maybe *you* can't," said Jessie. "You're the boss. But I'm an investigative journalist; I'm expected to break the law."

"Maybe we can stretch the crime-scene tape a little," I said, "without breaking it."

Harriet sighed, and said, "Girls, girls, please don't do anything stupid."

Jessie winked at me. We both looked at Hattie with wide, innocent eyes. Jessie had her last sip of coffee. Her hand touched the pepper spray on her belt.

"Let's go," she said. "I bet Dirk's hungry."

TWENTY

The Dwarsrivier Bed and Breakfast was only two blocks away, but the summer sun can fry you on the pavement, so we went in my bakkie. There were a lot of cars outside the B and B; I had to park a little way down the road. We walked slowly toward the building in the skinny shade of some thorn trees. It was one of those low, square houses they built in the seventies, painted a pale brown without much character. Nothing like the original Victorian Ladismith houses. But it had a nice lawn in front of it with edges of pink flowers and a bench in the shade of a Karoo willow tree.

"That's Dirk's Toyota," said Jessie, pointing out a white bakkie.

There was also a Hilux van outside the guesthouse, and a family was unloading backpacks from it.

"They don't look like hikers," I said.

They were well dressed, not the type to get their boots muddy. On the side of their van was a picture and some writing.

"Seventh-day Adventists," said Jessie. "I did an article . . ." She was looking up the road. "Isn't that Anna?"

Yes, it was her, jumping out of her farm bakkie. Now she was striding toward the B and B. She was farther away than us, but moving fast, her head down and her eyebrows coming together in a frown.

"She must have gotten out on bail," I said.

"She's also coming to see Dirk," said Jessie.

"I bet she's not bringing cake," I said.

"Anna," I called and waved. She didn't look up. We moved faster. "Anna!"

She saw us, but didn't look happy about it. Jessie ran ahead and stood at the gate entrance, blocking her way. But Anna didn't slow down; she was going to crash right into Jessie.

"Anna. Wait!"

I wasn't running, because I don't believe in running, but I was walking very fast and my breathing interfered with my shouting. Anna stopped and glared at me. She was wearing those farm boots and jeans and a man's white shirt.

I wiped sweat off my forehead and waited for my voice to catch up with me before I said, "What are you doing?"

"Tannie Maria," she said. "Stay out of the way."

She pushed Jessie aside as if Jessie were as light as a meringue and barreled up the concrete path to the front door. A man with a big beard jumped out of her way and into a flower bed. Before she stepped inside she rested her hand on a bulge at the back of her shirt. It was a gun, tucked into her jeans.

Jessie pulled out her pepper spray.

"That's no match for a gun," I said.

"I know," she said, "but Dirk's got a gun too, and she might need help."

"Jessie, no," I said but she scooted up the path and into the building.

I plodded after her, armed with only my Tupperware. I crossed a dark carpet with a mottled pattern to get to the reception area where there were some beige couches and a young redhead behind a desk. There was no sign of Anna or Jessie.

"Call the police. Now," I said. "And an ambulance."

The girl just looked at me with her mouth hanging open. I grabbed the phone off her desk and dialed.

"Ma . . . ," called the girl.

She wrapped her finger around a strand of her hair, and twisted it around and around. The policeman who answered the phone tried to ask me twenty questions but I got him to put me through to Detective Lieutenant Kannemeyer.

"Anna's just arrived at the Dwarsrivier B and B where Dirk is staying," I told the detective. "She's got a gun."

"I'm on my way," he said.

"We may need an ambulance too," I said, just before he hung up.

"What room is Dirk van Schalkwyk in?" I asked the girl.

"*Maaaaaa* . . . ," she called, her eyes wide.

I heard noises and saw an open door leading to a courtyard. A woman in a floral dress with a scarf covering her curlers came waddling out of a little office.

"Jaaa . . . ," she said to her daughter.

But I was already on my way outside. A row of guest rooms opened on to an area with a pool, a table and chairs with a big umbrella, and some deck chairs. Kids and teenagers were swimming, and lying around the pool. Jessie was trying to get them to move into the reception area but they were ignoring her.

"Emergency evacuation," said Jessie. "Move it!"

A girl on a deck chair rolled from her back onto her side.

"I was here first," she said.

A little boy ran and jumped into the pool, splashing us all. It was a rude thing to do but I welcomed the cold drops on my face and arms.

Anna was moving along, checking on each of the rooms. Her gun was held behind her back. These were badly behaved youngsters, I thought, but they didn't deserve to get caught in a gunfight. I slipped off my shoes, stood on the first step of the pool, and opened up my Tupperware. I unwrapped the cake, and held it out in front of me. I had their attention.

"Cake," I said. "If you hurry inside now, you will each get a piece. Stay inside till I call you."

The kids were up and in that room like spring hares. I could hear the redhead and her ma shouting at them as they dripped water across the carpets. I felt bad lying to them about food. But I had a plan, so I wouldn't really be lying.

"Clear out," said Jessie, waving her pepper spray at a couple peering out from one of the rooms. They looked at Jessie and Anna then scuttled away.

There were just two more unopened doors.

"Don't do it, Anna," I called. "Come sit and talk and with me. I've got a lamb sandwich and cake." I clutched my Tupperware to my heart. "Please."

But she was as focused as a lioness stalking her dinner. Jessie was following her, getting closer.

"Fok off," Anna said.

She turned the handle on the second-to-last door, and opened it a crack. I closed my Tupperware and took a few steps back. Things were looking bad. Jessie gripped Anna's shoulder and Anna struck out at Jessie, sending her flying backward. Jessie lost her balance and toppled into the pool, splashing us with some more cool water.

Anna pushed the door open with her foot, holding her gun out in front of her. The room was empty.

Then I heard a toilet flushing, and the sound got louder as the bathroom door opened. It was not Dirk who stepped out, but a woman in a long dress.

"Voetsek," said Anna, chasing her from the room.

The woman shrieked and ran into the main house.

There was still the sound of gurgling and splashing . . .

Oh my God, Jessie! She can't swim, I remembered.

I jumped into the pool and managed to get a grip on her chin and hold it out of the water. She sucked in air. I held her head up and dragged her to the shallow end, where she sat on the step, coughing.

Anna was rattling the door of the last guest room. It was locked. The curtains on the windows were closed. She stepped back a couple of paces from the door, the gun at her side. I thought

I saw the curtains twitch slightly, but I had water in my eyes and couldn't be sure.

Anna ran and kicked her big boot smack into the door. I heard a crunch as the lock splintered; it fell open and she flew in.

Then the shooting began. It was loud. So loud.

Then it was quiet. Very quiet.

The silence was broken by sirens. Getting closer. They were here at last. But it was all over now. Dirk came staggering out of the room, his face and sideburns all bloody, his arms bleeding. There was blood on his hands, dripping off his fingertips. I watched him stumbling toward the pool. He couldn't see.

I should've called out, to stop him. But I didn't.

He fell in. I could've jumped in to try and rescue him. But I didn't.

Jessie and I rushed to the room. Anna was sprawled across the floor. Her jeans were darker than they should be and her white shirt was blotched a bright tomato red.

"No," I said. "Anna . . ."

I tried to go to her, but big hands were pulling me back, out of the way. Men in uniforms were everywhere. Then I was sitting. On a chair, outside, I think. *Anna.* I wondered if she was where she wanted to be now. Together with her love. United with Martine.

People, people were swarming all over.

But I felt so alone.

TWENTY-ONE

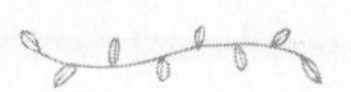

"Are they all gone, Tannie? My ma said it was firecrackers but Pa said it was shooting."

I am not sure how long I had been sitting there in my own world before this little voice pulled me back. My blue dress had dried, sticking to my skin.

"And then I saw the people with the blood," he said, "so Pa must have been right. Firecrackers can't do that to you, can they, Tannie? Ma says they are dangerous. There were policemen here, Tannie, there are still some."

He was looking up at me with big eyes, his hands held together in front of him. A skinny boy in swimming shorts and hungry ribs. There was a policeman putting yellow tape around the room. POLICE was written in blue capitals across the tape. Another policeman was taking photographs.

"Are they dead, Tannie? Are they?"

"I don't know," I said.

"Me and my sister went inside, like you said. We were hiding behind the couch."

I realized I was clutching the Tupperware to my chest. I relaxed my grip and put it on my lap. His gaze followed the food.

"I was scared, Tannie. We were all scared. But it's over now, isn't it?"

"Yes," I said, "it's over now."

The adults and some of the children were going back into their rooms, but a few of the children stayed in the safety of the main house, peering out from the doorway. They were frightened and needed something for the shock.

"Cake," I said, standing up, pulling at my dress to get it straight.

The little boy raced ahead of me into the house, saying, "It's the tannie with the cake. It's all over now, she says. She's going to give us cake."

I sat on a beige couch and the kids shuffled closer to me, to my Tupperware. The couches were pretend leather; they felt plastic and sticky. There was a policewoman in the office talking to the ma in her curlers.

"Children," I said, "I promised you all cake. And you will get it."

"We were scared, Tannie," said a little girl. "It was loud. And there was blood. We saw it."

"Like tomato sauce," said an older boy. "All over. A big mess."

He pointed to where the young redhead was busy cleaning the mottled carpet.

"I was trying to get you safe quickly," I said, "so I didn't explain very well. I have only one piece of cake here."

The children's faces dropped like the sinking dough of a cake when you open the oven too soon.

A small girl started crying, "I'm huuuunnnnngry."

"But it is a big piece, and you will each get a taste of it," I said as I opened the Tupperware. "And then I am going to go home and bake you a cake, and bring you back a big piece each."

That seemed to cheer them up a bit. The little girl stopped crying and reached out both her arms toward me and my food.

"Okay, you can have the sandwiches too," I said, though I was feeling quite hungry myself. "Now, we need a knife . . ."

A pale lady came rushing forward, but instead of giving me a knife she said, "Wait. What are you feeding them?"

So I told her. And I explained that I'd bake another cake for them and that I needed a knife, but she just stood there. Maybe she wanted the cake herself, but I thought that was greedy of her, because the children obviously needed it more. Then Jessie came and gave me the Swiss Army knife off her belt, opening a blade for me. That girl really knew how to make herself useful.

"I gave my statement to the police," said Jessie. "They wanted to take yours too, but you weren't in the mood for talking earlier. I told Kannemeyer you would go down to the station later."

"Kannemeyer was here?" I said, as I cut the cake into nice little pieces.

Jessie nodded, and said, "You don't remember?"

"The cake," the lady asked. "It's made with butter and eggs?"

"Oh, yes," I said, "my own chickens' best eggs. And buttermilk."

Maybe she wanted the recipe. But before I could tell her, she pulled the little girl and the skinny boy away from me, and lifted up a hand to say stop.

"Sorry, we don't eat meat or dairy," she said.

My mouth and the little girl's mouth fell open at the same time. She threw back her head and wept. The boy's lower lip was wobbling. I felt like crying myself. It had been a very strange day.

The carpet under my feet started shaking and it looked like the walls were swaying. Is this what an earthquake felt like?

"Tannie Maria," Jessie said, "are you okay?"

Jessie took the Tupperware from me because my hands were not holding it properly. Then she sat down on the couch, as if there was no earthquake at all. Mothers were trying to pull their wailing children away, but the children were digging in their heels.

"It's not so bad," said Jessie, patting my shoulder. "I spoke to my ma at the hospital. They're still alive. Flesh wounds and blood loss, but no major organs hit. A bone in Anna's leg was fractured by a bullet. Both her legs are hurt but she'll be okay. That pig Dirk will be all right too, though his arms are pretty damaged. It's amazing they didn't kill each other."

The mothers called in the fathers and they carried all the children away. It was just Jessie and the Tupperware and me left on the couch.

"You in shock, Tannie?" said Jessie. The room was not exactly swaying anymore, but it wasn't quite still either.

"I'm sure we need this more than Dirk or those kids," said Jessie, looking down at the food on her lap.

She raised her eyebrows at me then passed me a sandwich and helped herself to one. The sandwiches still looked fresh, even after such a hard day.

"Mmmm mmmm mm," she said, as she closed her eyes and sank her teeth into the bread.

I felt better already. The food was firm in my hands. The ground was solid under my feet. Ooh, ja. Gherkin and mustard and lamb.

"These people are Seventh-day Adventists," Jessie said after she'd swallowed. "They believe it's the end of the world. Again. They've had a few false alarms over the years, but this time they think it's for real. They've flocked here from all over because the Klein Swartberge are supposed to be a good place to ascend. There's some spot at Dwarsrivier where the rocks look like Jesus."

The end of the world. It felt like that, just now, when the woman refused my food and the ground started shaking. I suppose if I couldn't eat meat or dairy it might seem like the end of the world.

"Have some cake," Jessie said when we had polished off the sandwiches. "I was thinking . . . With Dirk and Anna in the hospital, it's a good time to visit the scene of the crime."

The sugar and rum had settled my nerves nicely and the chocolate was clearing my mind.

"What are you up to tonight?" she asked.

"I guess I'm going on a little outing with you," I said, and she winked at me.

TWENTY-TWO

On the way home, I stopped at the police station and gave my statement to the young paperwork woman. She seemed bored by what I told her. Maybe she had heard it all before. There was no sign of Reghardt or Piet or Kannemeyer. She told me Kannemeyer was at the hospital. She was a slow writer and the air conditioner hummed and rattled. It seemed to take her forever just to get my name and address, so I made the story I told her very simple.

"We will contact you if we have any questions," she said once I had signed the statement.

I was tired when I got to my house late that afternoon. I sat on my stoep with some beskuit and a cup of tea. I looked up at the sky and yawned. But I was not going to lie down.

"I don't believe in sleeping in the day," I said to my tea. "It's confusing. When I wake up I don't know whether to have breakfast, lunch, or supper." I dipped my muesli beskuit into the tea. "I suppose I could just eat beskuit. Any time of day."

I looked up at the clouds that were gathering in the north. They looked nice and fat and I hoped it would rain. A cool breeze was blowing and the leaves on my lemon tree were stirring.

Here in the Klein Karoo, the sky is so big. Usually it is blue and empty, but now it was putting on a fancy show. I sat watching the movement of the clouds. I wasn't thinking on purpose, but after a while ideas started gathering at the back of my head. Thought clouds. In the sky clouds I could see shapes. A duck. A woman. Martine, dissolving. Anna and Dirk puffing up, dark and fat. A long poker, like a cut across the sky.

It didn't make sense that Anna would wipe the poker clean before using it on Martine. But if the poker was wiped, then the murderer wasn't wearing gloves. There might be other prints. Did the murderer wipe those too?

I rested my eyes and allowed my mind to think.

When I opened my eyes again my tea was cold and the clouds had come closer; they were big and inky blue. The plants and trees were all looking up, hoping for rain. But not expecting anything. Karoo plants are very patient. They wait for months and months without a taste of water. But they don't get bitter, or shrivel up and die. They just hold on to the little moisture they've got and keep on waiting.

I don't think I could manage that myself.

TWENTY-THREE

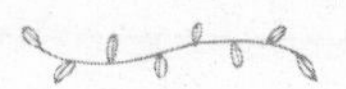

I fried bacon and made toast with my farm bread, then prepared bacon-and-marmalade sandwiches. I put them in a Tupperware for Jessie and me to eat later that night. Then I made an extra one, which I ate on the stoep, watching the fat underbellies of the clouds turn pink then blood red. Then they were gray, and growing closer, bigger, darker. I knew I should be pleased, because they held rain somewhere in there, but they looked so black and heavy, and in their shapes I saw the faces of men with bad thoughts inside puffy foreheads and dark beards. My husband, Fanie, was dead and gone, but sometimes it felt like he was with me again, like a bad taste in my mouth. Suddenly I could see the expression on his face just before he would hit me. My forehead was sweating and my heart beating fast. It was like I was having a bad dream, but I was wide awake.

I was pleased to hear the sound of Jessie's scooter heading my way. I rinsed my mouth, washed my face, and put on my khaki veldskoene.

Jessie came into the kitchen carrying two helmets and a small backpack. She was wearing jeans and black boots and her jacket, as well as the usual pouches and stuff around her belt.

"Are you sure there's no one at Dirk's house?" I said.

"We'll soon find out."

"But the police are finished with the crime scene?"

"Yes, they've taken photographs, dusted for prints and all that. They're just leaving the crime-scene tape up awhile. In case, you know."

"Are you sure? We don't want to mess up their investigation."

"We won't mess up anything," said Jessie. "We'll only try and help. The more brains on this the better."

"I wonder if I should change," I said, looking at her black clothes and at my dress.

"Ja, better you wear trousers. And dark clothes. We should go on my scooter," she said, "then we can hide it in the bushes."

"Me on the scooter? I can't even ride a bicycle."

"I'll be driving. You just sit there."

"Isn't it dangerous?"

"You'll be fine. You got a jacket for the wind?"

So there I was, sitting on the red scooter behind Jessie. I'd changed into my brown veldskoene, navy blue pants, and a dark green raincoat. And I was wearing a helmet and Jessie's backpack. The clouds were hanging above our heads; they were now so dark and heavy that the sky was struggling to hold them up.

"Hold tight," she said. "But relax. If the bike leans when we turn a corner, go with it."

I took a deep breath as she started the bike and we zoomed off.

I could feel the road under us. *Bump bump bump.* Like my heart beating. When we turned a corner, I thought the bike was going to fall over. But we were fine. The wind was rushing across my cheeks. I could feel the hum of the bike in my whole body. It did feel dangerous, but not a bad kind of danger. With Fanie, I was always so careful, trying to keep out of danger, I ended up scared of my own shadow.

We went up a slope toward Towerkop, and I could see the lights of the little town of Ladismith, and up there on the Elandsberg, Oom Stan se Liggie. Oom Stanley de Wet set up that little light high on the mountain about fifty years ago. A bicycle light and a dynamo, charged by a waterfall. If there's no water falling, there's no light, and we know that our water's running low. Three hundred times and more he climbed that mountain in his veldskoene to check on his light. Oom Stan died a couple of years ago, but his liggie is still there, shining into the darkness.

I took some courage from that little light. Then there was a flash of lightning that showed us the Langeberge, the mountains in the distance to the south.

A rabbit darted into the road, and Jessie wiggled, but we didn't fall. She slowed down but the rabbit kept running back and forth across the road.

She stopped the bike and turned off the engine. But the rabbit still jumped back into the road instead of heading off.

"Ag, stupid thing," she said.

"It's not stupid," I said. "Just scared."

"Scared of its own shadow," she said.

Because of the lights of the bike, when the rabbit ran toward the side of the road, its own giant shadow leaped out at it, frightening it back into the road. It was scared to stay in the road, because we were there, but it was just as scared to leave.

"Turn off your lights," I said.

In the darkness the rabbit shot off into the bushes.

A yellow moon with fat cheeks pushed through a gap in the clouds and lit up the road for us, so we kept the lights off as we traveled up the dirt road toward the mountain.

Jessie stopped at a gate with a sign: Van Schalkwyk. Soetwater.

"Let's walk from here. Was that okay, Tannie M?" Jessie asked, as I climbed off the scooter.

I pulled off my helmet, and smiled.

"Ooh, ja, that was fun!"

She took her backpack from me and then pushed the bike behind some spekboom trees that grew thick at the side of the road. We went through the gate and walked along the dirt driveway that led down to the farm.

Below us was a dark farmhouse with the stoep light on, and at the bottom of the farm was a small cottage, its windows yellow with candlelight.

"A farmworker and his wife live down there," she said.

We walked toward the main house in the valley. The moon was behind the clouds again, but bits of light leaked through and lit up the stony road. Among the dark shapes of some aloes ahead of us, I saw a pair of glinting eyes.

"Haai!" I said.

"It's just a jackal," said Jessie.

As we got closer, the jackal trotted away, its bushy tail trailing behind. We stopped in the black shadow of a giant eucalyptus tree behind the house.

"Sh-sh-sh," said Jessie.

I held my breath. What was that sound? Footsteps. Heading this way.

My shoe got caught on a root, and I stumbled, cracking a twig.

The footsteps paused.

"Hey!" a man called.

His steps were getting closer. I hugged the trunk of the tree. It was big and wrinkled. Lightning flashed. There was a rustling in the bushes and the jackal darted across the veld.

"Hah!" said the man's voice. He stood on the other side of the tree, and we heard the sound of a match striking and the inhalation of a cigarette. Jessie and I looked at each other, our eyes wide.

Thunder rumbled. The man strolled off. We heard him cough and spit as he walked around the house, then his footsteps getting farther away.

When all was quiet, we peeked out. We could see the red glowing speck of a cigarette heading toward the distant cottage. By the soft light of his front doorway we saw the shape of his body, his stooped shoulders.

"Sjoe," said Jessie, "let's hope he stays there."

She opened her backpack and took out a pair of surgical gloves for each of us.

"Now," she said, "to get inside."

We kept away from the stoep light, and tried the doors and windows at the back of the house.

"Nope," said Jessie, testing the back door. A strip of that yellow-and-blue tape was stuck across it. She took out a card and tried to slide it down the side of the door, like they do in the movies. "No good. It's bolted on the inside."

"Here," I said, "this sash window isn't locked."

Jessie helped me slide it open. Then she sat on the sill, took off her black boots, and passed them to me before she climbed through.

"Better not to leave prints," she said.

I took off my veldskoene and put both pairs of shoes next to a big flowerpot. Jessie opened the back door. She lifted up the crime-scene tape for me and I ducked under. We stood there in our socks, looking at each other. In the darkness I could see the white of Jessie's teeth as she smiled.

"We did it, Tannie M," she said. "We're in."

A jackal called. A crazy, wild sound. In the dark shadows, I smiled back at Jessie; I was not afraid.

TWENTY-FOUR

"Careful," Jessie said. "Looks like broken glass. Let's close up, then we can turn on our flashlights."

"I didn't bring a flashlight," I said.

Jessie closed the curtains while I did the shutters. Now it was really dark.

"Here," she said, turning on a flashlight, and handing me another. "It's a headlamp. Fit the strap over like this. And press this button, to make the light dimmer or brighter."

She helped me fit it on and I looked around the big room. It was an old farmhouse, bigger than mine, but a similar style. Like in my house, the wall had been removed between the sitting room and kitchen. There was a wooden table and a small pantry in the kitchen part, and a fireplace against the wall in the sitting room.

"Ouch," said Jessie.

I thought she'd cut herself, but it was what she'd seen on the floor that hurt. It was a photograph of Martine, all young and glowing in her wedding dress, and Dirk, not quite as young as she was, but looking like not such a bad guy after all. There were spears of glass around them, as they smiled up at us.

"That's the photograph Anna told me about," I said.

I shone onto another picture among the broken glass: two men in uniform.

"It's Dirk," I said. Young and without sideburns. "And his father, maybe."

They were wearing the old South African army uniform. Dirk was grinning but the older guy had thin straight lips.

"His pa looks like a mean bastard," said Jessie.

My husband did his two years in that army. They didn't train them to be good men.

"Look," said Jessie, shining onto a dark brown smudge on the couch. "Blood."

I nodded, trying not to feel the sadness, trying to think like an investigator. The couch was not far from the fireplace.

"Yes," I said. I shone on the floor next to the couch. In the pool of light was a tiny dark circle. "And a drop of blood there too."

I stepped around the glass and went across to the kitchen and opened the fridge. Clean shelves. Lettuce. Ladismith cheese. Sauces. It was not very exciting, but it made me feel hungry. It was too soon for our sandwiches, though. We needed to do some work first.

"You carry on here; I'll check out the rest of the house," said Jessie.

I closed the fridge. Next to the stove was a spice rack, labeled in alphabetical order. The pantry had shelves of cans and jars and packets, also very tidy and labeled. Not alphabetically, but by group. Vegetables, Meat, Baking, Recipes. There was a small row of recipe books on a shelf, organized according to size. I saw she had a copy of *Cook and Enjoy*. I had the Afrikaans version, *Kook en Geniet*.

I looked around the pantry and kitchen. There was fine black dust on one side of the sink and on the edges of the wooden kitchen table. The kind of dust the police used for fingerprinting. I took the headlamp from my head and shone it from this angle and that, then leaned down closely to examine the dust.

"Nothing much in the bedrooms and bathroom," said Jessie, coming into the living room. "But Martine's got a study full of papers. She's totally organized. Bills, letters, documents, all neatly filed. I bet she was a good bookkeeper."

"Look at the table here, Jess. It's been wiped. Just this part, where the two chairs have been pulled back."

"Ja?"

"Only half the table. Wouldn't you wipe the whole table, if you were wiping it?"

"No. I'd just wipe off the messy bit. You think it got messy in here?"

"Uh-uh," I said, shaking my head. "The murderer wiped their prints off the poker. Which means they weren't wearing gloves and might have left prints in other places. Martine wasn't the kind of woman who would wipe only half the table. Look, there are still some little crumbs and dust in the middle there. She wouldn't have left it like that. Look at her spice rack."

"Whoa. Ja. Like her filing system. But maybe she was in a hurry. Or she's got a maid who's a bit slack." She shone across the black dust on the table. "The police were looking for prints here."

"But they wouldn't find any because it was wiped. I think the murderer sat down at the table with her," I said, touching the back of a chair.

"And they drank tea together?"

"No, the teapot is up on the shelf. High and dry. But there are two glasses washed up at the sink."

"So it might be someone she knew." Jessie glanced at her watch. "Let me get back to those papers."

While she was in the study, I opened all the kitchen drawers. I put the headlamp back on my head again because it freed up both my hands. Everything was very netjies in the drawers. Cutlery, dishcloths, all neatly stored. Plastic shopping bags folded in little triangles like samosas.

I poked through the trash can. There was a Spar packet crumpled up in there. Why wasn't it folded? Her arm, I remembered. She had a broken arm. Could you fold a packet properly with one hand? I tried it. It wasn't easy but I could do it. Even with a glove on.

I went back to the fridge and looked at the expiration date on the package of lettuce. It was for today, Friday. Spar likes to keep their lettuce fresh, so this one was bought within the last few days.

"How did you get here?" I asked the lettuce. "And when?" I turned the package over in my hands. "Sunday and Monday, the Spar has no fresh lettuce. So you must have been bought on Tuesday or Wednesday. Did Martine buy you on Tuesday? The day she died. Her arm was broken, so I don't think she could drive. Did Dirk drive her or did he maybe shop himself?" I put the lettuce back on the shelf. "I don't know what it is about men and salad, but I've never heard of a man buying lettuce for himself. Did someone else shop for Martine?"

I closed the door of the fridge. I was sorry for the lettuce; it was looking wilted, and it's a sad thing to see good food going bad. But I had to move on.

At the sink was a dishcloth that I studied in the lamplight. It was white with blue checks. There was a faint reddish mark on one corner. I shone all around the sink. I spotted a small red drop of liquid, beside the tap. I dipped the tip of my gloved little finger into the liquid and then touched it to my tongue and closed my eyes.

I knew that sweet metallic taste.

"Psssst! Jessie!"

TWENTY-FIVE

"You may be right, Tannie M," said Jessie. "I can taste the iron."

"I know I'm right," I said. "I grew up with a pomegranate tree in our garden."

"So they were eating pomegranates," she said.

"Or drinking pomegranate juice," I said, pointing to the glasses.

We heard a light drumming on the tin roof of the stoep.

"Rain!" said Jessie.

We went to the back door and turned off our headlamps and watched the rain fall in the darkness. Soft, cool rain. Jessie and I grinned at each other. At last. The ground sighed with relief as it fell. I took in a deep breath.

"Ooh, that smell," I said.

The first rain on the warm dry earth. Nothing like it. Then after the smell of the earth came the smell of the plants. It was as if each plant gave something of itself to say thank you for the rain. All the smells mixed together to make a delicious air soup for us to breathe in.

"Let's have a sandwich to celebrate," I said.

She handed me the Tupperware from her pack and I gave us each a bacon-and-marmalade toast sandwich.

"The lights are off in the cottage," said Jessie. "We should have a talk with that guy sometime. Wow. Lekker sandwich, Tannie."

"I could make him some vetkoek," I said.

"With curry, maybe," said Jessie.

"Did you see any grocery slips, in Martine's papers?"

"Ja," she said.

"I am looking for one with Tuesday's date. I think someone shopped for her, and it could have been the murderer."

I explained about the lettuce date, and the package, and Martine's broken arm.

"Let's go have a look," said Jessie.

We brushed the crumbs off our surgical gloves and went into the study.

"Look how organized this all is," said Jessie. "Personal letters, bank statements, bills, papers about her son in that home. Grocery slips." She shone her headlamp onto the papers as she sorted through them. "Here it is . . . Her most recent shop at the Spar was on Friday the fifth. I've looked in her purse, but there are no slips there."

"Looks like she didn't shop for herself on Tuesday then . . ."

"Maybe Dirk, Anna, or someone else . . . You might be right, Tannie, it could've been the murderer. I wonder if the police have taken samples of that pomegranate juice. Did you find the bottle the juice was in?"

"No," I said.

I touched a file marked "Letters, Personal."

"Has she got any of our *Gazette* letters?" I asked.

"Nothing here," said Jessie. "But I wonder if she'd hide them somewhere. Away from her husband."

"So who are the letters from?"

"A couple from a boring brother in Durbanville. But most of them from an interesting cousin. Old letters from her at a Texas address. Then the last few years she writes from New York."

"Ja?"

Jessie took out a smart cream envelope and a cheap brown one.

"The cousin is Candy Webster; her apartment overlooks Central Park. Sounds like she's in the fashion business, travels all over, sends postcards to Martine from cool places. They seem quite close. Lots of hugs and kisses. The brother, David Brown, has written a letter whining about 'Father,' and his lack of appreciation for everything David does." Jessie lifted a file marked "Jamie." "These are the reports from the doctors and social workers in George about her son with cerebral palsy."

The rain started hammering down, then there was a flash of lightning and a thunderclap. Really close and loud. I pulled the curtains back and peeked out the window.

"Jessie, look!"

Through the branches of the gum tree we saw the shape of a big car on the top of the hill, creeping down the drive.

"Oh, shit," Jessie said, jumping up. "Flashlights off!"

"I think it's turning around."

We peered out the window, watching the car do a three-point turn. But instead of driving away, the car stopped and its lights went off. The rain went quiet for a moment, like it was holding its breath. Then there was a very big flash of lightning. In that moment we saw a white car, big, like a bakkie or a 4x4, and in front of it, walking toward us, was a man.

He had a rain hood over his head, a flashlight in one hand. And a gun in the other.

Rain hammered down on the roof, and the next crash of thunder sounded like the sky itself was shooting down at us.

TWENTY-SIX

Hemel en aarde," I said.

"Bliksem!" said Jessie.

But neither heaven nor earth nor lightning stopped the man walking toward us, his flashlight heading for the front of the house.

Jessie pulled out her pepper spray and went into the living room, toward the front door.

"He's got a gun," I said.

"We can't just run," she said.

I took in a deep breath. I didn't want to be a rabbit in his lights, but I wasn't ready to fight him.

"We need to know who it is," she said.

"Let's hide," I said. The rain was quiet again and we could hear noises on the stoep. "In the pantry."

We slid into the pantry in our socks. With our flashlights off, it was really dark. There was a big key on the outside of the pantry door. I managed to pull it out, but my hands couldn't get it into the keyhole on the inside.

We heard the front door open and I stepped back, bumping into Jessie. But we didn't make a sound. A line of light cut the living room in two. The key was cold and still in my hand.

The beam swung slowly across the kitchen, the light sliding

through the gap in our door and onto a can of baked beans on the shelf. I held my breath. We heard a rustling, like footsteps on plastic bags. The sound headed away from us. We peeked out. His flashlight was in the study. He was going to wish he had a headlamp if he was looking through papers. But I wasn't going to lend him mine.

"Shall we call the police?" I whispered to Jessie.

"They'll want to know what we're doing here. Maybe it's Dirk."

"Did look like his car. But I can't believe it, he's in the hospital."

"There might be bandages under that raincoat. Those bloody loonies don't know when to lie down. Could it even be Anna?"

"She walks a bit like a man," I said.

I managed to get the key into the door, but it seemed silly to lock ourselves into the pantry.

"Let's sneak out and get the car registration," said Jessie.

We tiptoed to the front door, but as Jessie opened it, we saw the small glow of a moving cigarette. A shadow was coming out of the night, approaching the stoep.

We slipped back into the pantry. We left its door a little open, which gave us a view of a dark patch of the living room wall. We stood very still and listened. The guy outside coughed and spat before stepping onto the stoep. He knocked on the front door.

"Meneer?" he called.

It was the man we had heard earlier that night.

"Meneer. It's me. Lawrence."

His voice got louder; he must have opened the front door wide.

"Sorry, Meneer, jammer, but the police asked me to watch out here. People mustn't come in the house, they said."

I could hear the soft rain again, falling on the tin roof.

"Jammer, Meneer."

His voice got louder still, as if he'd stepped inside.

"I didn't mean to get you in trouble, Meneer. That day."

Lawrence coughed.

"Meneer?"

Footsteps rustled out of the study; we saw a flash of bright light across our strip of view.

"Meneer? . . . Hey, the light."

Was he shining his flashlight in Lawrence's face?

Boom. Boom. Gunshots.

The sound of something falling.

"Jesus," said Jessie, under her breath.

I pulled the pantry door closed.

My hands were shaking but they somehow managed to lock the door. I saw a dim light in Jessie's hand as she pressed buttons on her phone. Her fingers were shaking and it looked like she wasn't getting the numbers right.

The footsteps came right up to the pantry and turned the doorknob. When it didn't open, a fist thumped the door. Luckily it was one of those old solid doors. Teak, I hoped. We moved away, pressing ourselves against the far shelves.

Ka-ting! A shot.

A metallic ringing sound in my ears.

He tried the door again, but it didn't give. The sound of my drumming heart filled the whole pantry.

I heard a kind of wailing. At first I thought it was Jessie's phone ringing, then I realized it was a police siren. How could they have come so fast? Jess hadn't even made the call.

There were two more gunshots: so loud and close I felt sure they must have hit us. I checked my stomach and chest, but found no holes. The footsteps rustled away. The siren was still going, but I wasn't sure if it was getting any closer.

Something soft settled on my skin. Maybe goose bumps. I reached out for Jessie and for her hand. Even through my gloves, I could feel there was something sticky all over her fingers.

"Oh, no," I whispered. "Jessie?"

Her fingers moved weakly.

"Are you okay, Jessie?"

"I'm not sure," she said. "I feel a bit weird and there's stuff leaking on my arm. Has he gone?"

"Listen."

The siren noise stopped and we heard what sounded like a 4x4 revving and racing away.

"How does the switch work on this headlamp again?" I said. "Wait, here it is."

I managed to turn it on and shone it on us both. We were covered in white powder, and Jessie had sticky orange stuff all over her arm and hand.

"Apricot jam," I said, putting my fingers to my mouth. "And cake flour."

The shot jam can and the exploded bag of flour were on the shelf above us. Flour was all over the cans and the recipe books. Jessie licked some jam off her fingers, and the sugar did its job. She took off a glove and managed to make that phone call.

"Reghardt," she said. "It's me."

"Are they close by?" I said when she hung up. "The siren's stopped."

"No," she said. "There was no siren. It was a ring tone I played on my phone."

We unlocked the pantry door and looked out. A black man lay still on the floor, a red hole in his forehead and a dark stain spreading across his chest.

"Lawrence?" said Jessie.

He wore a faded blue shirt that was frayed at the sleeves and collar. On his khaki pants you could see dark lines where raindrops had fallen. Jessie kneeled beside him.

His eyes were open, like he was staring at the ceiling. I wanted to close them for him, but instead I turned on the light. As if that could make things normal again.

His right arm lay above his head, his left by his side. Resting in his left palm was a half-smoked cigarette. He had pinched the tip of it closed so he could smoke the rest of it another time.

Jessie checked his pulse. She looked up at me and shook her head. There would be no other time for Lawrence. She got up, opened the back door, and stood staring out into the darkness. A cold breeze moved through the house, in the front door and out the back.

I had seen two dead bodies before this one. In coffins. My mother's and my husband's. At the sight of each of them, strong feelings had swum up from deep inside me and taken the air from my mouth.

But I did not know this man, Lawrence, at all, so I was surprised to find such feelings coming up in me again.

He was not in a coffin. His blood was still fresh. Just now he'd been walking in the rain, smoking, talking. He was alive. Then someone shot that out of him. *Boom. Boom.* Stole it from him forever. Murder is the worst kind of stealing.

Martine's life had been stolen. And now Lawrence's.

"Tannie Maria!" said Jessie. "Our shoes. They're gone."

TWENTY-SEVEN

The thunderstorm had moved on to the south, but it was still raining softly as we sat waiting on the stoep. There were flashes of lightning over the Langeberge as the police sirens got closer.

"What're we going to tell them?" I asked Jessie. "We shouldn't be here."

"Jislaaik. There are two murders now. I think we should come clean."

"Too late," I said, looking down at our messy clothes. "Where are those napkins?"

We were dusting the flour off our pants when the police arrived, their headlights shining straight on us. When they turned them off, I could see the men by the stoep light. Piet and Kannemeyer got out of the van, and a young man stepped from a car. The man was tall and thin. Next to Piet he looked very long, but he was not as tall as Kannemeyer.

My feet wanted to run to Kannemeyer, which is strange because as I've said, I don't believe in running, and anyway I was wearing socks.

When the men got closer, Jessie looked like she wanted to run too, but we both stayed standing on the stoep. Piet was leading the way with a flashlight, pointing here and there to the ground. He wore his khaki shorts and leather sandals.

"It's all messed up with the rain," said the young man.

He had a pale face and his soft dark hair fell across his forehead like a teenager's.

Piet shone the flashlight down low, and spoke quietly, "Look, these come from there." He pointed toward the cottage. "And these are different. Look there. The heel."

"Ja," said Kannemeyer, "it's wider."

Piet showed them where to walk so they did not interfere with the tracks.

"What are you doing here?" said Henk Kannemeyer, frowning, as he stepped onto the stoep. "Are you all right?"

He was wearing jeans and a long-sleeved white cotton shirt. The top few buttons of his shirt were open and the hair on his chest was that chestnut color.

"The man is dead," I said, pointing toward the front door.

Kannemeyer went in and bent over the body. The young man stood close to Jessie. Next to her he looked very tall.

"Jessie," he said.

His eyes were dark and soft, like the center of a black-eyed Susan. He had thick eyelashes and eyebrows.

"Reghardt," she said, looking up at him.

"Are you hurt?" he said, touching her arm gently.

"It's just jam."

Piet and Reghardt went to the doorway as Kannemeyer put his fingers to the man's neck. The three of them just stood there awhile, looking down at the dead man as the rain fell softly on the tin roof.

"Warrant Officer Snyman," Kannemeyer said to Reghardt. "Make the calls. But wait a few minutes before phoning EMS. They can't help him now, and I want a good look around before they come trampling all over the place."

"Emergency medical services," Jessie whispered to me.

Reghardt walked to the edge of the stoep and spoke quietly into his cell phone. Kannemeyer signaled to Piet, who stepped inside—his eyes, nose, and hands doing tiny movements as if he could sense things that we could not. Piet was tasting and testing the air, like a wild animal arriving in a new place.

Kannemeyer came out and stared at me. He looked like he wanted to shout, but instead he spoke very quietly, which somehow made it worse.

"You could have been killed," he said.

His mustache looked a bit rough. He had probably been fast asleep twenty minutes before. There were raindrops on his shoulders.

"What happened?" he said.

"Um, we came to see . . . ," I said, losing my sentence as I looked up at Kannemeyer. He was so much bigger than me. "We . . ."

"Who did this?"

"Ah . . . ," I said. Somehow the words were getting stuck under my tongue. "Um . . ."

"We came to investigate a story," said Jessie. "A big white car arrived. Around ten past eleven. It was dark, but it looked like some kind of four-by-four, probably a bakkie. A man got out with a flashlight and a gun. We saw his silhouette in the lightning. Medium height and build. Wearing a raincoat with a hood. We hid in the pantry, and he came into the house. We didn't see him. He made an odd sound as he walked, kind of a rustling, and he went into the study."

Piet and Reghardt also came to listen to Jessie, the reporter. Piet's eyes moved over her too, looking for clues.

"After a short while, Lawrence, that man there, came up to the house. I think he's the worker who lives in the cottage down there. We were in the pantry, so we couldn't see. But we heard him at the door calling to the man. He called him Meneer. He said the police had asked him to watch the house."

Reghardt nodded. Maybe he knew about Lawrence, or maybe he was just encouraging Jessie. Piet was studying the stoep now, his eyes moving about like dragonflies. Shooting from there to here, then hovering in one place.

"I should arrest you both for trespassing," Kannemeyer said, glaring at Jessie and me.

Jessie continued as if he hadn't spoken. "He also said that he was sorry, that he didn't mean to get Meneer in trouble."

"So he knew the murderer?" asked Kannemeyer.

I shook my head, and Jessie explained.

"Maybe not. He might have thought he knew him. But the man was out of his sight while he spoke. He might have seen his car, or been expecting someone. Lawrence couldn't see him when he was calling to him. He probably thought it was Meneer Dirk. Then we heard footsteps, and saw the flashlight, and Lawrence said, 'Hey, the light.' I think the murderer shone a bright flashlight in Lawrence's eyes." Jessie looked at me, and I nodded. "Then we heard a shot. Two shots. We locked the door of the pantry and the murderer realized we were there and when he couldn't open the door, he shot at it. I played a ring tone on my phone that sounds like a police siren." Reghardt smiled at Jessie's cleverness, but Kannemeyer did not look impressed. "He shot twice more, the bullets came right through the door, and then he drove off. We came out and we found Lawrence."

Kannemeyer's lips were pinched tightly together under his mustache. Piet walked around Jessie and me so he could see us from all sides.

"You should not have been here," Kannemeyer said, running his hand over his short thick hair. "You could both be dead."

I looked down at my socks. I could hear the wind in the branches of the gum tree.

"He took our shoes," I said.

Kannemeyer blinked.

"We'd left them outside," Jessie said. "My boots and Tannie Maria's veldskoene."

Kannemeyer frowned at us, and took a breath like he was about to say something, then shook his head. He turned away from us and toward Reghardt.

"Warrant Officer Snyman, where's the police photographer?" he asked.

"Not answering his phone," said Reghardt. "But the LCRC will send out a forensics team first thing in the morning."

Kannemeyer said, "I want crime-scene pictures before the coroner and EMS get here."

"Maybe," said Reghardt, looking sideways at Jessie then back at Kannemeyer, "Jessie here can take the photographs."

Jessie pulled out her camera. Kannemeyer frowned at us both again. Then he gestured for her to go inside.

"Do only as we say. No walking around."

He followed them in. At the doorstep he said to me, "You. Stay right here. Don't . . ."

Then he sighed and turned away. I watched from the doorway as Piet showed the others the story of what had happened. Jessie photographed whatever he or Kannemeyer pointed to.

Piet acted out pieces of the story. Reghardt did the lighting effects with a bright flashlight. Piet showed how Lawrence had walked into the room, wiped his feet on the doormat, but still left small tracks on the floor. He pointed out the little patch of smudged mud where his right foot had kicked forward when he lifted his right arm to protect his eyes from the flashlight. And the bigger smudge of slipping heels as he was shot and fell onto his back.

"Look here, at these marks in the dust," Piet said, "the killer had plastic bags over his shoes."

Reghardt held the flashlight low on the ground, and Jessie took pictures from all angles.

"His feet were this big," Piet said, holding his hands apart.

"About a size ten," said Kannemeyer and Reghardt nodded.

"His steps were like this," said Piet. "Legs longer than mine, but not so long as yours." He held his hand up to Kannemeyer's shoulder. "He was maybe this tall."

Piet carried on showing the movements of the murderer. "He stepped forward, like this, when he shot the gun."

"Here," he said, crouching beside Lawrence, "is where she touched him."

Jessie photographed the traces of jam on Lawrence's wrist, then Piet led them toward the pantry to continue the story and the photographs.

"Bullets," said Piet, "here, and there, and there through that can of jam, into the wall."

"How many shots altogether?" asked Kannemeyer.

"Five," said Jessie and Piet together.

"Ja. A .38 Special," said Reghardt.

"Get those sock prints in the flour," Kannemeyer told Jessie, "before we go in."

When they'd finished in the pantry, they went into the study, where I couldn't see them, but I heard some pieces of what they said.

Kannemeyer's voice: "Dust the filing cabinet and desk for prints."

A little later, I heard Reghardt say, "No prints. Looks like he had gloves. We'll see what LCRC says."

When they were done in there, they went out the back door. I sat down on a cane chair on the stoep and looked out into the rain-washed night. There were lines of moonlight across the dark clouds, like veins.

The wind had stopped now, and I heard a rough croaking sound. Then the noise got stronger, and more rhythmical. It was a frog calling. In the dim light I could now see the pond with the reeds around it. Where the ducks used to swim. More and more frogs joined in the chorus. The ducks were dead, but the frogs were alive and singing. Each one calling for a mate, after the rain. Calling and calling. I wondered if every one of them would find a mate. Or if some would just keep on calling till they died.

TWENTY-EIGHT

Piet's totally awesome," Jessie said to me, coming back before the others. "The things he sees!" She came around the front of the house, her socks brown with mud. "He found our tracks under the gum tree. And also the tire prints of the four-by-four where it turned around. The tire marks were quite clear because the ground was soft but protected from the heavy rain by the big tree. He said they were Firestones. He got very excited about something he saw, jumped about like a springbok and made me take photographs from this side and that of one of the tire prints. Then he took Kannemeyer aside and spoke to him about it, but I couldn't hear what they were saying."

The three men approached the stoep.

"What did Piet see in those tracks?" Jessie asked Kannemeyer.

He shook his head and said, "How did you get here?"

"We came on my scooter," Jessie said. "It's up near the entrance gate."

"You have no business being here," he said to us both. "You could have gotten yourselves killed. Warrant Officer Snyman, take them to the station to sign statements. Then take them home. Konstabel Witbooi and I will carry on here until the coroner arrives."

"We can go on my bike," said Jessie.

"You can't ride without shoes," he said.

I took a deep breath.

"Detective," I said, "there were some things we . . . noticed, that might help with the . . . um . . . investigation. We found drops of pomegranate juice, by the sink. And a shopping bag, not folded up. She usually folds them, in little triangles . . ."

His face was going red.

"And the table, it was only partly wiped . . . ," I said.

His mustache was twitching.

"There's a lettuce in the fridge. Its sell-by date shows—"

"Enough!" he said. "You shouldn't even be here. This is a crime scene, not a a a . . . blerrie . . . shopping list!"

"But, Detective . . . ," I said.

"Warrant Officer Snyman," he said. "Take them away."

He was a lot bigger than me, but I just stood there, looking up at him.

"Detective," I said, "maybe we can help."

His cell phone rang and he walked into the darkness as he answered it; he went and stood down by the duck pond to speak.

Kannemeyer didn't want to hear what I had to say, but Piet had been listening. He nodded at me and went inside and looked at the sink and the table and inside the fridge. He called for Jessie to come and take photos. I heard her explaining to him and Reghardt what I had been trying to tell Kannemeyer.

Kannemeyer stomped back onto the stoep as they came out again, and Jessie said, "Let's go, Tannie M."

As we were climbing into Reghardt's car in our muddy socks, we heard that jackal calling for its mate. I looked across at the dark veld, but could see no animals there. There was someone crossing the lawn, coming toward the house. A woman wrapped in a thin blanket. She reminded me of a wild buck, a kudu, walking so gracefully and holding her neck and head up like that. Moonlight shone through a gap in the clouds and her face glowed like a polished black stone. Her hair was braided in neat rows across her head.

"Lawrence?" she said.

Detective Kannemeyer put his forehead down into his hand for a moment, then stood up straight, stepped off the stoep, and walked toward her.

The jackal called again. A long and lonely cry. But it got no reply.

TWENTY-NINE

It was very late by the time I got home, and I was tired, but I struggled to fall asleep. There were toads in my garden, singing like crazy after the rain. And the clicking stream frogs were at it too. Behind my house, toward the mountain, is a small spring and a stream that flows when it rains. But it wasn't the frogs keeping me awake. It was the things going on in my mind. I could see Lawrence's body lying there. And Kannemeyer's cross face. And that beautiful woman walking like a kudu. And Kannemeyer stepping toward her.

I got up and made myself a cup of hot milk with honey and cinnamon and sat at the kitchen table in my nightie. Questions were swimming around in my head:

Who is the murderer?

Did the same person kill Martine and Lawrence?

Did Martine drink pomegranate juice with the murderer?

I found a pen and paper and started to write some of my questions down:

Why was the shopping bag not folded?
Where are our shoes?

I also wrote a list of people we should interview. I'd take it to the office in the morning, to discuss with Jess and Hats. Jessie and I had agreed to meet first thing, and Hattie is always at the *Gazette* on a Saturday morning. It's when she does the books.

As my thoughts emptied out onto the paper, I could feel the tiredness fill my body. I headed back to bed.

I lay down and listened to the rough mating call of the toads and the rain that was falling again, dripping through the leaves of the tree outside my window. I breathed in the smell of wet earth and camphor leaves. Hey, I thought, it's not pomegranate season yet . . .

But as I fell asleep, the last thing I saw in my mind was not a pomegranate but Detective Henk Kannemeyer, in his white shirt with the top buttons open, stepping off the stoep. But in this picture, he wasn't going toward the woman who was calling the dead man's name. He was walking toward me.

THIRTY

I woke up with the birds the next morning and after breakfast I drove into town. I opened the windows of my little bakkie and breathed in the fresh air. It was nice and cool for a change. The sky was extra clean after the rain and you could see far across the hills to the blue folds of the Langeberge. The veld was washed and green.

At the *Gazette* office, Jessie was at her desk. She was hanging one shoe from the tips of her toes, and smiling to herself. When she saw me her smile got even bigger. Her eyes had a sparkle in them like they had also been washed by the rain. Over her tank top she was wearing a short-sleeved cotton shirt. A faded brown color.

"Tannie M," she said, "Hattie's just gone to the bank. I told her all about last night."

"Was she cross?"

"Uh-uh. More worried, I think."

"You're not looking worried," I said.

She didn't answer but her hand went onto her shoulder and stroked her gecko tattoo. The shirt was too big for her; it was a man's shirt. She cleared her throat, and started typing on her computer. I patted the letters on my desk.

"I'll get busy with these until Hattie gets back," I said.

I prepared a cup of coffee and a beskuit for each of us, then I settled down to work. I finished typing the letter and meatballs recipe for Marco with the blue plates, and then I looked through my new pile of letters. I recognized a brown envelope, although this time there was no smudge of mechanic's grease on it.

I dipped my beskuit into my coffee, and had a bite before I opened the letter from Karel.

Thank you, Tannie Maria,

I did it! I sent that text message. I had to buy myself a cell phone. But they are selling them at PEP for 140 rand. So I bought two. One for Lucia. I got my friend to give the phone to her and we sent fifteen text messages back and forth before I even saw her. We went to the Movie Club and watched As It Is in Heaven. *I enjoyed it though I didn't really understand it. When the movie got sad, she started shaking like an engine that needed tuning. I put my arm around her and at first she shuddered like her starter motor was faulty, but soon she was purring along nicely. When she stopped crying I kept my arm around her.*

Afterward we went out for a burger and a salad and I said almost nothing and she ate a few of my chips off my plate and we held hands under the table.

We didn't kiss good-bye, but she gave me a smile that made my heart vroom like a V8 engine. When she got home she text-messaged me and we stayed up late that night sending messages to each other. And I also wanted to thank you about the egg. I know what you mean, because if you pour cold water into the radiator when the engine is hot you can crack the engine casing. I am wondering if there is something else easy that I can make, now that I know how to do the egg.

Dear Karel, I wrote.

Well done! Now you could make a Welsh rarebit. Which is not as fancy as it sounds. It's just a cheese sauce, really. It is delicious when you pour it over a sliced boiled egg on toast.

Parmalat has a special on mature Gouda at the moment, which will be very nice for this sauce.

I gave him the recipe my father used to love. The one made with beer and mustard. We heard Hattie arriving. When she parked she revved her car like a Harley-Davidson. We listened for the bump, but she didn't hit anything this time.

She stood in the doorway of the office, looking at me with her mouth all tight.

"You two!" she said at last. "Honestly. You're lucky to be alive."

She came and gave me a hug.

"Okay," said Jessie, "let's write up what we know."

There was a big whiteboard that we sometimes used for lists and plans. Jessie wiped the whole thing clean with a cloth. Hattie's mouth opened and closed a few times but she didn't stop her. Jessie wrote "Crimes" and "Clues" as headings. Under "Crimes" she wrote "Murder of Martine," and "Murder of Lawrence."

"Here," I said, giving Jessie my list from the night before. "Some questions we need answers for, and people we could interview."

She wrote a heading: "Questions." And then another: "People."

I turned on the kettle.

"Hold your horses, girls," said Hattie. "You can't be serious."

"Tea?" I asked Hattie.

Jessie was writing up my list on the whiteboard.

"It's all become far too dangerous," said Hattie.

"Since when do journalists run from danger?" said Jessie.

"Two murders! This really is a police matter," said Hattie.

"We could help the police," I said. "We should cooperate with each other."

"Fiddlesticks," said Hattie. "Jessie told me they weren't interested. The detective was quite rude."

"Well, yes, he was," I said. "But I suppose we shouldn't have been there."

"You defending him now?" said Jessie with a wink.

"He was worried about me—about us," I said. "He said we could've been killed."

"And jolly right he was. Enough of this silly nonsense, ladies. The police will give the *Gazette* their reports when they are good and ready."

"I have gotten some reports from the police," said Jessie, "sort of."

She was swinging her sandal on her toe again.

"Is this from Reghardt?" said Hattie. "What *is* going on with the two of you, Jessie? Enough to give up police secrets?"

"Not on purpose, really. But he does talk on the phone, and even when he's outside, if I stand at the bathroom window . . ."

"Goodness, Jessie!"

"Oh, Hattie. It's my job to find out things. Remember, Maria, I told you last night about the tire tracks of the four-by-four that Piet was looking at?"

"Ja," I said, passing her coffee.

"Well, I heard Reghardt talking to the LCRC about them. Early this morning."

"That's the Oudtshoorn people who come and do forensic tests," I explained to Hattie.

"They were Firestone tires, which you find on a lot of four-by-fours," continued Jessie. "But tires wear differently. Like every animal has its own track, depending on how it walks. If you are a really good tracker, like Piet is, you can see the differences."

"So . . . ," said Hattie.

Jessie took a sip of her coffee.

"Piet thought that last night's car tracks were exactly the same as the ones he saw after Martine's murder," said Jessie. "The LCRC will be taking tire impressions to be sure."

"Gosh. Does this mean Anna and Dirk are both off the hook because they were in the hospital?" Hattie asked.

Jessie wrote a heading: "Suspects." Under it she wrote: "Dirk?" "Anna?"

"Maybe they escaped . . . ," I said.

"No, my ma said they were there the whole night. Sedated. No way either of them could drive a car with their injuries anyway. And Anna's in a plaster cast—she can't walk."

"So it couldn't have been them," said Hattie.

"Not last night, no. It may take a while to get the results back from the LCRC because tire tracks have to be sent to the Cape Town lab and there's often a long waiting list. The fingerprints they do themselves, so it's quicker. I called LCRC this morning just to get a sense of police procedure, nothing to do with the case, of course. But in the meantime, the police trust Piet and they're going to look for other suspects. If they catch the guy who killed Lawrence, the tire tracks would link him to Martine."

"Hmm," said Hattie, "sounds like the police know what they are doing."

"But there are lots of things the police aren't looking at," I said. "And we can't just sit on our hands and watch."

"Yes," said Jessie, adding "To Do" to the headings on the whiteboard. "And there are some clues that they missed."

"They sometimes don't pay attention to small but important things," I said, "like food."

"What's all this about lettuce and pomegranate?" asked Hattie, pointing to what Jessie had written under "Clues" on the whiteboard. "Jessie spoke to me about it earlier, but I don't get it."

"The Spar doesn't have fresh lettuce on a Monday," I explained, "so the sell-by date on the lettuce tells me it was bought on Tuesday, the day of the murder. The unfolded plastic bag, the missing slip, her broken arm—it all makes me think someone else shopped for her. And, who knows, it might have been the murderer. Pomegranates are not in season yet, so I'm thinking he bought her pomegranate juice. This might have been what they drank together. Maybe he put a sleeping drug in her drink."

I wished I could've explained things so nicely to Kannemeyer last night.

"Piet was unscrewing the sink at Martine's house," said Jessie, "so maybe they'll find some juice to send off for testing."

"Hmm," said Hattie. "It could've been her husband, shopping for her."

"Ja, Mr. Nice Guy," said Jessie. "I'll speak to my friend Sanna, who works at the AgriMark with Dirk. Martine died sometime in the morning and they usually only take off at lunchtime."

Jessie added Sanna's name up on the whiteboard, under "People."

"You think he might've left early, to shop, and knock off his wife?" said Hattie.

"Who do you think we should interview first, Harriet?" said Jessie.

Hattie studied our notes on the whiteboard.

"I'd say start with the woman who showed up last night, calling for the dead man."

"I found out her name. It's Grace," said Jessie, writing it on the board. "I'm not sure of her surname. She's a domestic worker at the Van Schalkwyks'."

"And of course you should talk to Dirk and Anna. And your friend at the Agri. Maybe the people Martine worked with too . . . I don't see any of their names up there. And what about the people who look after her boy with cerebral palsy? Any other friends, family, religious contacts? Look into her past a bit, see if anyone pops up there."

"That's quite a list," said Jessie, scribbling Hattie's ideas onto the whiteboard.

"If you *are* going to investigate, you might as well do it properly, for heaven's sake."

Jessie had a sip of her coffee and winked at me.

"Some of these people might not talk to us just like that," I said. "They might need some convincing."

"Ja," said Jessie, "I think that vetkoek idea of yours was good. With curried ground meat."

"Mmm," said Hattie, because even English people who don't

eat properly know how convincing a vetkoek with curry can be. "Okay, you two, find out what you can. But be jolly careful. And any articles, you run by me before posting." She looked at Jessie. "And don't let the other *Gazette* work fall behind."

"I'm finishing my stories right now," Jessie said, turning back to her computer. "The article on the Philipstown Quilting Festival and Car Wire Derby is almost done, and I'm going to the Ladismith school fete this afternoon." She grinned. "Looking forward to it."

"I'll take these home," I said, picking up the rest of my letters. "I need to pick some things up at the Spar and then get cooking."

"Can you fetch me here at five, Tannie M?" Jessie asked. "And we'll go straight to Lawrence's woman, Grace. My scooter's still on their farm."

"Sure," I said.

"Then we can go on to Dirk and Anna at the hospital. You'll make vetkoek for them too? And maybe a couple of extra ones . . . ," she said.

"Of course."

I was at the door already. I had a lot of cooking to do. Starting with that Welsh rarebit.

THIRTY-ONE

As I drove past the Dwarsrivier B and B, I slowed down. I was feeling bad about those children—I had promised them cake. Maybe I could find a cake recipe without butter and eggs.

I noticed three white 4x4s parked in that street. I pulled over and got out to look at their tires. The first one was a Toyota bakkie, the same one that Jessie had told me was Dirk's when we'd visited the B and B. The tires were Firestones. They were dry and dusty on top, where the car had protected them from the rain. I was no expert, but it didn't look like it had been driven since the rains.

The next 4x4 had very muddy tires, but they weren't Firestones. The third one was a cream 4x4 bakkie. The tires were Firestones. They were clean. Very clean. Had they been recently washed? As I was peering under the car a man came out of the B and B. He had a red face and a big bushy beard and eyebrows like hairy caterpillars. The caterpillars dived together on his forehead as he frowned.

"Hey!" he said. "What are you doing?"

"Ag, I just dropped something," I said. "Good morning. I'm Tannie Maria."

"I'm late," he said, climbing into his car.

"Are you one of the Seventh-day Adventists?" I said.

He slammed the door and roared off. Much too fast.

People in Ladismith never rush. They always have time to at least say, Good morning, how are you? They usually want to say a lot more, and it's not difficult to spend the whole day in town talking to people, even ones you have just met. That man must be from out of town.

Where was he racing to? I suppose with the end of the world coming, there must be lots of things to get done.

As I got back in my car, I wondered what I would do if I thought the end of the world was coming. I don't believe in God or church or anything, so I don't think I'd spend my time praying or ascending. I would probably cook something nice. But what would I cook? And who would I invite to eat it with me?

My mind went to the lunch I had with Detective Kannemeyer. That was a really good roast. And the cake was excellent. Still, I'm not sure I'd make that meal as my last.

In the block before the Spar I saw five more 4x4s. And three of them were white. I parked and as I walked past them, I checked their tires. Two of them had Firestones and both were muddy. I sighed. I could spend my whole time just looking at tires and what would it prove? And I had shopping and cooking to get on with.

I popped into the shoe shop and bought some olive oil from Elna le Grange. Her brother has an olive farm near Riversdale, and she told me his wife was expecting a baby. She wanted to chat some more, but I kept moving. I went to the library and asked Tannie de Jager, the librarian, to find a delicious vegan cake for me on the Web's Google. It was so quick—it was printed out before she had even finished telling me how celery helped her arthritis. A recipe for a vegan walnut-and-date cake. I thanked her and folded it into my bag.

Just before I got to the Spar, I saw the manager—the guy with the chocolate-milk mustache—getting into his little blue Golf. We should talk to him too. He was Martine's boss. But he drove off before I could get close enough to say hello.

There were not a lot of people in the Spar, so my shopping

went quite quickly. I got dates, walnuts, and the other ingredients for the vegan cake. I had enough flour for the cake and vetkoek, but I did need some of the ingredients for the curried ground meat. I usually grind my own meat, but I saw they had some frozen wildsvleis ground meat, and time was tight, so I bought that. It was unusual to see game meat in the summer. But I guess they keep it frozen from the winter hunting season.

I chose Marietjie's till. I knew she was a talker, but this time it was what I wanted.

"How are you, Tannie Maria?"

She was a coloured girl, with a round, pretty face. Her hair had been straightened and smoothed into a swirl around her head.

"Can't complain," I said. "Lovely rain."

"Ooh, ja," she said as she scanned the wildsvleis.

"Your manager isn't here much?" I said.

"He's the regional manager of all the Spars in the Karoo," she said, like she was all proud of him.

I looked at my watch. "It's a bit late on a Saturday to be going to other branches."

"Oh, maybe he's just leaving early. On the weekends he likes to go to his place on his game farm in the Touwsberg." She packed my groceries into a plastic bag. "With his wife," she said, as if I might be getting funny ideas.

"Were you friendly with Martine—Mrs. van Schalkwyk?" I asked.

"Ooh, wasn't that terrible what happened to her," Marietjie said. "I never liked her husband. Or do you think it was suicide? I hear she was depressed."

"Do you think she was depressed?"

"Oh, I don't know. Mr. Cornelius says she was. She kept to herself, you know. Stayed in the office mostly."

"Is that her office over there?" I asked.

"Ja, she shared it with Mr. Cornelius."

"Thanks, Marietjie. Bye-bye."

"Totsiens, Tannie. Enjoy your day further."

On my way out, I went past the office. It had a big window looking out onto the shop floor. There were silver lines on the window, like thin mirrors. I knocked on the door, and tried to open it, but it was locked. Then I pressed my face to the glass and looked between the skinny mirrors. I could see a big desk with papers scattered all over it, and an empty pie wrapper. And over in the corner, a small empty desk with a neatly stacked in-tray and out-tray. I could guess which one belonged to Martine.

On the way home I counted another five white 4x4s. I had never really noticed them before, and now they were just everywhere.

I was hungry for that rarebit, but before I prepared it I made the dough for the vetkoek. I like to make it the old-fashioned way, with yeast. While the dough was rising in the sun on the stoep, I sat beside it and ate the Welsh rarebit. I'd put a sliced egg on the toast before pouring the thick cheese sauce on top. The flavors of the beer, mustard, cream, and mature Gouda blended into one creamy, tangy taste.

I gazed out at my garden and the veld, clean and green after the rains. It looked like new shoots were starting to grow already. The afternoon was warm, but not crazy hot. My chickens were pecking the ground in the shade of the lemon tree.

While the vetkoek dough was fattening up in the sun, I prepared the curry. I fried the ground meat in butter till it was a lovely deep brown, then added onions, ground turmeric, coriander, and cloves, then the tomatoes and my green tomato chutney. I left it to simmer.

I fetched the dough from the stoep, gently knocked it down, and worked it into balls. I flattened the balls and rubbed each one with oil and left them to rise.

When the oil was very hot I deep-fried the vetkoek, three at a time, to a golden brown, and drained them on empty egg boxes.

Of course, I had to have one while they were still hot. I cut it in half, spooned in the warm curry, and ate it right there at the kitchen table among the flour and the chopping boards. It was good. No—it wasn't good. It was perfect.

Cooking vetkoek and curried meat is an art that South African tannies have spent generations getting just right. As I sat there enjoying the food, I was grateful to them all, especially my own mother, who taught me how to do it. There in my kitchen, eating that vetkoek and curry, I had the sort of feeling I'd expect you should have when you go to a church you have faith in.

I said I didn't believe in anything, that my faith went out the window, but maybe this wasn't true. I believed in vetkoek with curry, and all the tannies who made them. If the end of the world was coming, this was the meal I'd make.

THIRTY-TWO

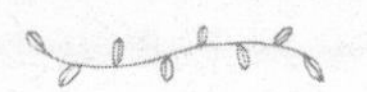

Two Tupperwares (each holding four vetkoek) and Jessie and I all traveled in my sky blue bakkie to the scene of the crime—Dirk's farm. We were going to visit Grace. We parked in the shade of some rhus trees, and took one of the vetkoek Tupperwares with us. We walked past the empty farmhouse and the big gum tree, which were all wrapped up with crime-scene tape. I was wearing my khaki veldskoene. I looked at the place at the back door where I had last seen my brown veldskoene. I worried about those old, faithful shoes of mine. I hoped they were okay. We headed down toward the cottage at the bottom of the farm. Lawrence's cottage.

"Look," said Jessie, as we passed the little pond. "There are still duck feathers."

They were stuck in the reeds all around the water. A frog looked up at me with golden eyes.

"Looks like a kraal over there by the apple trees," said Jessie, as we walked on. "But I don't see any animals."

"There are some other fruit trees too," I said. "There, behind those thornbushes. Let's go have a look."

The shadows were long, but the day was still hot, so I wasn't moving as fast as Jessie.

"Tannie M," she said, arriving first. "It's a pomegranate tree!"

"I thought so."

"The fruit is still totally green."

She touched one—it was tiny and hard.

"Even the baboons wouldn't eat this," I said, catching up with her.

"Ja, they're not in season yet, like you said. I wonder where that juice came from. Maybe Liqui-Fruit or something."

"Maybe, but I've never seen Liqui-Fruit pomegranate. And it tasted really fresh. Not like box juice."

We walked down to the cottage, on a little stony path, and knocked on the wooden door. We could hear movement inside, but no one opened up. The steps were clean and polished and there were small flower beds on either side of the door, with red roses, pink geraniums, and orange botterblomme. The roses were in good shape. I've never grown roses myself—they are too much work for something you can't eat. It takes years of pruning to get them flowering so nicely.

We were just thinking about knocking again when the door opened. The woman wore a blue African-print dress and was drying her hands on a dishcloth. She was just as beautiful in the late-afternoon light as she had been in the moonlight. Her cheekbones were high, her skin was glowing, and she smelled of cocoa butter.

"Hello, Sisi," said Jessie. "This is Tannie Maria, and I'm Jessie."

I smiled at her.

"Nice roses," I said. "Have you got the green thumb?"

She shook her head.

"Lawrence," she said.

"Grace, we work at the *Karoo Gazette*," said Jessie, stepping forward and handing the woman a card. "May we come in?"

The woman took the card but did not look at it. Her gaze darted behind her and then back at us.

"We were here last night," said Jessie, "when Lawrence was shot. We are so sorry."

The woman looked down at her feet and a lump moved up and down in her throat as if she was swallowing her sadness.

"We've brought some vetkoek," I said. "With curry."

She looked up.

"Curried ground meat?"

"Let's have a bite to eat," I said, showing her the four plump vetkoek, wrapped in wax paper.

"It's messy in here," she said, but she stepped back to let us in. "I'm sorting his things."

In a tiny kitchen were open boxes packed with all sorts of stuff. I could see plates and enamel cups and a ceramic dog. We followed her into a small living room. She went to close the bedroom door, and I saw a battered suitcase on the double bed before she closed it.

"You're packing up?" said Jessie, as she sat in an armchair.

The woman sat down on a wooden chair with her back straight and her legs together, her knees slightly to one side.

"Shame," I said. "This must be very hard for you, Mrs. . . . ?"

I sat on the couch next to a neat pile of clothes and a box with tools sticking out of it—a small garden fork and a sheep-shearing knife.

"Zihlangu," she said. "My name is Grace Zihlangu. I am not married."

"Lawrence was your boyfriend?" asked Jessie.

Grace nodded. She looked around the room at the piles of Lawrence's things. Then she sighed, and her body seemed to fold in on itself. It was time for the vetkoek. I opened the Tupperware and gave one to her, Jessie, and myself, each with our own napkin.

"Thank you, Mama," Grace said. Xhosa people are like Afrikaners. Everyone is family: Auntie, Mother, Sister . . .

"Are you leaving, Sisi?" asked Jessie.

Grace didn't answer. Instead she took a bite of her vetkoek. After a few bites, she was sitting up straight again. We didn't talk while we ate, but Grace was studying us as she chewed. The afternoon light streamed in through a sash window. I could see tiny dust particles in the air, but the glass on the window was sparkling clean. There were cracks in the walls of the cottage that had been repaired and whitewashed. The coffee table in front of me and the other surfaces I could see were all very clean. Nothing half wiped.

"That's the best vetkoek and curry ever," said Jessie. "Awesome."

When Grace had finished eating her vetkoek, she wiped her mouth and fingers with the napkin, then she took ours and threw them all in the kitchen trash.

"I want to leave here," she said as she sat down again. Ready to talk. "Go to Cape Town."

THIRTY-THREE

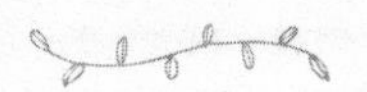

"Do you have family in Cape Town?" asked Jessie.

"In the Eastern Cape," said Grace. "I am going there for Lawrence's funeral. But I want to go to secretary training college in Cape Town. I have a friend there."

"You were working in Martine, Mrs. van Schalkwyk's house?" I said.

"Yes. Twice a week. Wednesdays and Fridays."

"So you weren't here on the Tuesday, when she . . . ," I said.

"No. Monday, Tuesday, and Thursday I work for Mr. Marius in town."

"What did you think of Mrs. van Schalkwyk?" Jessie asked.

"I liked her. It was a very bad thing that happened. She was a good woman. I was happy to work for her. I wish I could work for only her, and not . . ."

Jessie raised an eyebrow, but Grace did not say more.

"Is the work too hard at Mr. Marius's?" I asked.

"I am not afraid of hard work," Grace said. "No. He's just, you know . . ."

She stroked her hands across her skirt.

"Does he harass you?" said Jessie.

"He looks at me in a way I do not like. He is not a good man. Mrs. van Schalkwyk also does not like him. Did not like him."

"How do you know?"

"Maybe two weeks ago, he said he wanted to see the Van Schalkwyks and he drove me home at the end of the day. He knocked on the door. Mr. van Schalkwyk was not home from work yet, and Mrs. van Schalkwyk told him to voetsek. She closed the door in his face. He was not happy. He drove over the roses next to the road. Lawrence's roses."

"What did he want?" Jessie asked.

"I don't know," Grace said. "I was walking to my house. I could not hear everything."

"What kind of car does he drive?" I said.

"A big white one, like Mr. van Schalkwyk's. There's writing on one side: Karoo Real Estate."

"An estate agent?" said Jessie.

I nodded. He was one of the advertisers in the *Karoo Gazette*—the one who gave Hattie a headache.

"Yes. There are pictures at the office in his house. Houses. Veld. And photographs taken from the sky."

"Did Martine have other visitors?" Jessie asked.

"Her friend Anna did visit. They laughed together. It was nice. That husband of hers did not make her laugh."

"Did he hit her?"

"I did not see him, but I saw the bruises." She shook her head. "The broken things in the trash."

"Any other visitors?" said Jessie.

"A man came around. Maybe a month ago. When his tea was finished, she said he must go. Her husband wouldn't like him there, she said. He came around once more, on a Friday, but she is at work on that day, so he went away."

"Do you know who the man is?" said Jessie.

"John. I have seen him in town some mornings. He sells farm things from a wooden table. Eggs, vegetables, plants."

"At the market?" I asked.

Grace nodded.

"What did Martine speak about with him?" Jessie said.

"I do not know. I don't listen."

I looked down at the last vetkoek and asked, "Nothing else you heard, by mistake maybe?"

"I was cleaning the room next door. She said the old days were over. Then he was talking about frucking. He was cross, I think."

"Frucking?" said Jessie.

Grace bit her lower lip, and looked down at her fingernails.

I helped her out with a different question:

"If Mrs. van Schalkwyk wiped a table, would she wipe just half of it clean?"

"Oh, no!" she said. "She is not that kind of person. She is like me. She would never do that."

"Have the police come to interview you?" I asked.

"I spoke to them that night, the night Lawrence— But I heard nothing. Just the thunder and the rain. I did not wake up when Lawrence got up. I don't know why I woke up, but when I did, I waited. I waited and he did not come back. I called and then I went to look for him." She rubbed her hands down the sides of her arms. "I told the police there is no one who wants to kill Lawrence. He was a good man. He was just doing his job."

"I am sorry," I said. "We think maybe the same person killed him and Martine."

"I am afraid to stay here. I want to go. But I have not got enough money. I must ask Mr. van Schalkwyk and Mr. Marius for help."

"Did Lawrence work here every day?" Jessie asked.

"Yes. It used to be a sheep farm here, but they stopped that long ago, before I got here. They sold a lot of land and a lot of workers did lose their jobs. But they kept Lawrence, to look after the place. The garden, the fruit trees. He is good at his job."

"The day of Martine's murder, was Lawrence here?"

"Yes. The police asked him about that day. I was here when they were talking to him."

"What did he tell them?"

"He told them he saw Mr. van Schalkwyk come home that

morning. He waved to him but the meneer didn't wave back. The police asked if he was sure it was him, and he said yes."

Jessie leaned forward in her armchair as Grace continued to speak.

"They asked if he was close by, and he said no, he was down at the bottom by the trees." Grace waved her hand toward the window. "He was clearing the dead branches and chopping wood. Then they said, so how could you be sure? They told him that Mr. van Schalkwyk said he did not leave work. The workers at the Agri said he was there all morning. Lawrence said, maybe he was not sure, but it was Mr. van Schalkwyk's car. They said are you sure it was his car, or could it have been the same kind of car as his? Lawrence said it looked like the meneer's car, but maybe it wasn't."

Grace rubbed the fingers of one hand over the knuckles of another. I nodded and she carried on talking.

"When the police had gone I asked him if it really was Mr. van Schalkwyk, and he said that he didn't want to be the one to get the meneer in trouble. I said to him, a woman is dead now and he must tell the truth, but he was just quiet and shook his head. He was not a bad man, Lawrence, but he was not strong."

"Did you love him?" I asked.

"Lawrence?" she said. She looked at the neatly folded pile of men's clothes on the couch and at the closed bedroom door. "No."

I picked up the Tupperware and offered her the last vetkoek.

THIRTY-FOUR

I sat in my bakkie outside the hospital, watching the sunset as I waited for Jessie.

Tidy flower beds lined the long white hospital building. The plants were nicely looked after. I knew it was the same inside the small hospital: The patients were well cared for—even if the food was no good. Hospital food is terrible. Which is why the vetkoek might work very well with Anna and Dirk.

The hospital was on top of a low hill at the foot of the Klein Swartberge, Small Black Mountains. The brown hills rolled toward the Rooiberg, Red Mountain. And in that light it really was red. It looked like a big animal that had lain down to rest and didn't want to be disturbed. I wondered if it was a good idea to visit Dirk in the hospital now.

The sky was going that light greenish-blue color like you see on old copper pipes, and there were strips of pink and orange clouds.

I could hear the sound of Jessie's red scooter. But also some other wild sound, like distant thunder and rattling windows, that was coming from inside the hospital. Jessie buzzed up the hill and parked next to me. We walked to the hospital entrance.

"What's that noise?" asked Jessie.

We went inside, me with my Tupperware and she with her helmet. The roaring and clattering stopped and started again as we moved toward the sound. The doors of the small wards were open and we could see some of the patients. We passed a yellow-faced man propped up in his bed, a young woman sitting by his side, staring at a vase of flowers. An old woman smiled a wobbly smile at us, as if we might be coming to visit her. Then, in a room of her own, we saw Anna.

"Haai, Tannie!" she called.

She tried to wave at us, but her hands were chained to the sides of her bed. Her left leg was in a plaster cast and her right was bandaged on the calf. There was a wheelchair beside her.

That strange sound was getting closer. It was like an angry animal crashing its way through the bushes.

"They've locked me up!" Anna said, jangling her chains.

"Ooh, gats, Anna, you under arrest?" said Jessie from the doorway.

"Ja, that too," said Anna. "But they chained me to the bed because I found Dirk and pulled out his drips!"

The wild sounds were even louder now. I looked down the corridor just as the creature came around the corner.

"Ooh, gats!" said Jessie again.

It was Dirk, in a pale green hospital gown, roaring like a wounded beast, and he was dragging with him a number of noisy things. Chained to his ankle was a bar of metal that looked like a piece of a hospital bed, and clinging to his legs were two men in white uniforms. Dirk's arms were bandaged, one of them in a sling, and the orderlies were trying to slow him down without hurting him. You see what a good hospital it was.

A nurse was running after them, and they were all shouting at once. She had a needle and syringe that looked big enough for a horse, but Dirk wasn't staying still long enough for her to jab him. Dirk kicked off the man who was attached to his right leg. The guy went flying across the corridor, and then jumped up and threw himself back onto Dirk. The staff there was very dedicated.

Jessie and I tried to block the door, but Dirk and his circus pushed right past us. From the back of Dirk's gown you could see his bottom had the same wiry hair as his head and sideburns. Anna sat up, ready to fight, rattling the chains on her wrists, as Dirk clattered toward her bed. Jessie ran forward and squirted Dirk in the face with her pepper spray before he got to Anna. He coughed and spat but still reached Anna's bed. He pulled her drips out with his teeth. It was hard to breathe with that burning pepper smell, and my eyes were streaming. Dirk was kicking at Anna's bed, trying to push it over, but now the nurse had him trapped and she plunged that big needle into his thigh.

Dirk barked like an angry baboon, but it was too late. His body slumped against Anna's bed. The orderlies managed to get her wheelchair under him before he hit the ground, and his head fell forward onto the bed and rested on Anna's thigh.

He was the only one looking peaceful, sleeping there on Anna's lap while the rest of us cried and coughed.

THIRTY-FIVE

"We brought you a vetkoek, Anna," I said, "with curried ground meat. I hope the pepper spray doesn't make it taste funny."

The orderlies had carried Dirk off and moved Anna to another ward. It was dark outside now and the room was brightly lit.

"Ooh, dankie, Tannie," she said.

They had taken the chains off her arms and she reached out for the vetkoek.

She had bruises on her arms, a plaster cast on one leg, and a bandage on another, but her eyes were shining and her cheeks glowing. None of that black lost look from when I'd last seen her.

"I think the fighting might be good for her," I said to Jessie. "Makes her strong."

"Ja, Dirk too," Jessie said. "He's not such a big man, but look how he dragged those guys and half a bed with him."

Anna wasn't listening to us. She was gobbling that vetkoek like she hadn't eaten all week.

"Should we even tell them that they are probably both innocent?"

"Maybe the revenge stuff is helping them with their loss."

"If it doesn't kill them," I said.

Anna wiped her mouth with the napkin, and eyed the Tupperware. But she had some questions to answer before she got another one.

"That day Martine died, did you shop for her?" I asked.

"No," she said, frowning, "not that day."

"Did Dirk ever do the shopping?"

"That vlakvark never shopped a day in his life. Anyway, she got her stuff after work at the Spar."

"Her arm was broken, remember, she couldn't drive herself to work," said Jessie.

"Maybe he felt guilty," I said, remembering Martine's first letter to me.

"Pfah!" Anna said. "He feels nothing."

"Did Martine like pomegranates?" I said.

"Ja," said Anna, "but what she was really crazy about was pomegranate juice. Now and then the Spar gets bottles of frozen juice from Robertson. Martine would invite me over to share it. I only drank a little glass, because she enjoyed it so much. I loved to watch her drink it."

I wasn't going to tell her Martine was drinking pomegranate juice with someone else in case it gave her a jealous attack.

Anna smiled, and her voice went soft as she said, "She'd close her eyes when she drank, and I could look at her without feeling shy. I let all my feelings and thoughts go free when her eyes were closed." Anna closed her eyes herself. "I loved Tienie, you know, even though she was an English. My great-grandmother—Anna Hermina Stefanus Pretorius—died in the concentration camps in the Vaal. The English burned our farms down to nothing."

The Anglo-Boer war was a long time ago, but when Anna opened her eyes, she was glaring at us like it had happened yesterday. I even felt guilty that my father was English. I wanted to explain to her that my pa had some Scottish and Irish ancestors. My great-ouma was related to the Irish hero Robert Emmet, who was hung, drawn, and quartered by the British.

Anna ran her thumb softly over her fingertips and stared past my shoulder, as if she was looking back into time, and said, "But Tienie was different, I tell you. She made me feel like I was a child again, playing by the river. In the days before I knew life had troubles. She was like the taste of that clean water. Sweet and fresh."

She looked at Jessie and said, "I loved her. But I'm no fool. I knew she didn't love me in the same way. But she loved me in her own way." Her gaze drifted off to something inside her own mind. "When she saw me she would get that little smile of hers and her eyes would light up, and my heart would slaan 'n bollemakiesie, y'know, somersault. And when we spent time together drinking coffee, or looking at the ducks splashing about, it was like I was in a stream of happiness."

Now she looked right at me.

"I hoped that one day she would move in with me. She would never go hungry. If the rains fall, and the price of mielies does not fall, I'd even have money for her nice clothes. The expensive thing is her son in that home. I said he could come live with us, but she said he needs special care. She loves that boy." Anna got that dark lost look again. "Loved . . . She is dead . . . How can something so big in your heart just be gone?"

She shook her head and put her hand on the center of her chest. Then she looked past us again, and a bright fire came into her eyes.

"That bastard's not gonna get away with this," she said. "I'm going to make him pay. I'm not afraid. If I die, I go straight to Tienie. We'll be together, with no more worries about men or mielies—"

"Anna," I said, "Anna." She blinked like she had just woken up. "Listen to me. Last night someone went to the Van Schalkwyks' house. Lawrence, the guy who works there, went up to see what was happening. He was shot. Dead."

"Ag, no," she said, covering her mouth with her hand. "Poor Lawrence."

"We think it was probably the same person who killed Martine. Looked like the same tire tracks."

Jessie said, "Dirk couldn't have done it. He can't drive with his arms messed up like that, and he was here, drugged, all night."

Anna looked at her own drip and tapped her fingers on her plaster cast.

"Maybe someone else shot Lawrence," she said. "Dirk still might have killed Martine."

"Maybe," I said.

"But maybe not," said Jessie.

I saw the doubt wrinkle Anna's forehead. Her face became smaller and her head sagged onto her chest.

"I miss her," Anna said, and then she looked up at us with her brown eyes, her eyelashes wet. "You can't understand how much I miss her."

THIRTY-SIX

We left Anna alone with her missing and a vetkoek, and found Dirk's ward.

He was lying on his back, snoring. His sideburns looked like wild veld bushes. A bit of dribble was coming out of the corner of his mouth. Beside his bed was a TV and a white table with a tray of hospital food that hadn't been touched. His left arm was in a sling across his chest, and his right was bandaged from the shoulder to the palm of his hand, his fingers sticking out. A foot was handcuffed to the rail on the bed.

In another bed in the ward was a teenager wearing earphones. A sign above the boy's bed said Nil by Mouth. I smiled at the boy because I felt sorry for him, but he didn't look at us, his eyes glued to the television.

"Dirk?" said Jessie.

His snores sounded like a warthog grunting.

"Oom van Schalkwyk," I said.

Uncle van Schalkwyk jerked his foot, but didn't open his eyes. That horse medicine must be keeping him asleep. I wished I had smelling salts to bring him around. Then I remembered my vetkoek and unwrapped one and held it close to his face. He sniffed and opened one of his eyes a crack.

"Vetkoek?" he snorted.

His nose twitched and he opened both his eyes and stared at

the line of brown where the curry reached the edge of the vetkoek.

"Mama?" he said.

"Sit up, Dirkie, and eat your vetkoek," I said.

"How do you get these beds up?" said Jessie, picking up the control buttons.

The television next to his bed suddenly blasted us with an advertisement for Five Roses tea. Dirk blinked. Then the TV went off and his bed shot up, into a sitting position.

"Hey!" he barked.

Dirk peered at us with soggy eyes.

I handed him the vetkoek, which he managed to get to his mouth with the fingers on his bandaged right hand. His eating was a bit messy, so I tucked the napkin from his food tray into the top of his hospital gown.

"Lekker . . . Thanks, Ma," he said. "The food in this . . . hotel is kak."

"Dirkie," I said. "Did you go shopping for Martine this week? On Tuesday—the day she died?"

"Martiiiiine," wailed Dirk, setting his vetkoek aside, and starting to cry. "She's deeeead."

"Did you shop for her?" I asked.

"No," he sobbed. Bits of ground meat fell out of his mouth, rolling across the napkin and onto his sling. "I never shopped for her. Never. I was a bad husband. Bad."

"Did you kill her?" asked Jessie.

"No," he said, looking up at us with big red eyes like those hunting hounds. "That woman, that rat, she did it. They found her fingerprints."

"Dirkie, listen to me," I said. "We don't think Anna did it. It might be someone else who killed her. Someone shot Lawrence last night."

"Lawrence?" said Dirk. "Dead?" I nodded. Dirk looked up at the ceiling as if he might find an explanation up there. "Ag, no. I liked Lawrence . . ."

Dirk's eyelids drooped and then he stretched his eyes wide open; he was fighting with the sedative.

"We think the man who killed Lawrence was probably the same one who killed Martine," said Jessie. "Can you think of anyone who might want to hurt Martine?"

He looked down at his hand, seemed surprised to find half a vetkoek there, and took a big bite. He wiped his mouth with his bandaged upper arm.

"She was a good woman," he said. "I was a bad husband. I broke her arm."

"Was there anyone, a man, who . . . ?"

"I'll kill him," he slurred. "I swear I'll kill them both. Him and that dyke."

His eyelids were getting heavy again. Then suddenly they popped open, as if he had seen a ghost. The teenager was also staring, his eyes wide and his jaw hanging down. We turned around and saw a woman standing in the doorway. She looked like she had stepped out of a 1940s movie. She was wearing a short, stylish black dress that showed off her round breasts and long legs, and black suede high-heeled shoes. Her hair was sunshine blond, pinned up at her neck, and her lips were the bright red of cherries. She had a little smile on the corner of her mouth.

"Dirk van Schalkwyk," she said. His head swayed with the movement of her hips as she walked toward us. "You are a sight!"

She spoke with an American accent, but from the South, I think, like those people from *Gone with the Wind*. But she'd said Dirk's name in the proper South African way.

"You're Martine's cousin," said Jessie, "the fashion designer from New York."

The excitement, the vetkoek, and the horse sedative were finally too much for Dirk, and he passed out.

"You got me, sugar," said the movie star, over the sound of Dirk's warthog snores. "Is there anywhere around here a girl can get a decent martini?"

THIRTY-SEVEN

"Candice Webster," said the cousin, offering her hand, "but call me Candy."

"Jessie Mostert," said Jessie, shaking it, "and this is Tannie Maria van Harten."

She shook my hand too. Her grip was firm but her skin very soft.

"You girls friends of Dirk's? I sure could use some help with the funeral."

"More of Martine's," said Jessie. "Let's go out for that drink."

We left Dirk snoring and the teenager with his nil by mouth still hanging open.

"Dirk's an idiot," Candy said, her heels clacking as we walked along the hospital corridor. "That fella couldn't organize gravity to drop an apple. If he wasn't so incapable, I'd think he was the one who killed her. If she's going to have a decent send-off, it's up to me. Luckily I was in South Africa when I got the call. I've got a boutique in Cape Town."

"Hasn't she got other close family?" asked Jessie.

"Her father's a miser and her brother's a creep. Don't give a dried-apple damn about anyone. Turns out they're in this area anyway, so at least they may turn up for the funeral. I thought we could have it on Wednesday."

"I'm sure we can help out," said Jessie. "Follow me down to the Ladismith Hotel. They serve a good martini."

We were in the parking lot now. Candy opened the door of a little red MG that looked like it had come out of an old-fashioned movie.

"Awesome car," said Jessie.

"Yeah. Cute, ain't she," said Candy. "Rental."

"We'll meet you there, Tannie M."

I shook my head.

"Sorry," I said. "It's been quite a day. I need to go home and rest. I'll catch up tomorrow."

Jessie gave me a hug and Candy kissed the air next to my cheek. The red MG followed the red scooter down the hill, and the one remaining vetkoek and I rode behind them in my little blue bakkie. They turned off to the Ladismith Hotel and we headed right out of town and then along the dirt track that led to my home.

We sat together at my kitchen table, just the vetkoek and me, then just me.

THIRTY-EIGHT

I sank into a heavy sleep and only woke up when the sun was big and bright. It's not good to start the day so long after the birds, but I just needed the rest. And it was Sunday after all.

I put on my dressing gown and let my chickens out. They went running to their twenty-four-hour buffet, the compost heap. The morning sunlight showed off the gold and the red in their feathers.

I sat on the stoep and had my morning coffee and beskuit. The rusk tin was running low.

"I should make some more rusks," I said to my coffee, "and bake that vegan cake I promised to the kids."

I dressed and ate farm bread with boiled eggs, followed by apricot jam. Then I got going on the date-and-walnut vegan cake. I made enough batter for a small cake on the side that I could taste without cutting into the children's one.

I also prepared two big trays of buttermilk beskuit dough. I needed to fill my tin at home, and the one at the *Gazette*, and I also wanted a third tin for the bakkie, as company and padkos. It's always good to have food for the road.

When they were ready, I took out the cakes and the trays from the oven, cut up the sweet bread into rusks, turned the oven to low, then put them back in to dry out. As soon as my baby cake had cooled, I sat down at the kitchen table to eat it.

"Hmmm, not bad at all," I said, after my first bite. "Okay, maybe it would be even nicer served with cream, but it's definitely not the end of the world." I ate half the little cake, very easily. "Those Seventh-day Adventists must have some other reason for wanting to run up into the mountains. I wonder if I might find out a bit more about that," I said to the bigger date-and-walnut cake, "when we deliver you to the kids."

While the beskuit were drying out in the oven, I made a jug of watermelon juice so I could sit outside on the stoep without drying out myself. The sun was high and the shadows in my garden were small. I looked out across the veld onto the Rooiberg. The mountain slopes were a reddish-brown, sprinkled with brown and green bushes. In the place where the top of the red mountain met the blue sky, I could see wobbly lines. It was so hot, the mountain was starting to evaporate.

I just sat for a while and listened to the sounds of my garden and the veld. My chickens were quiet, but the birds were calling to each other. The bokmakieries have the prettiest call. They've got more tunes than all the other birds put together. Now and again I could hear a car on the road that goes to and from town. Maybe people driving back from church, home to their Sunday lunch.

But the loudest sound, bigger than all the noises put together, was the silence.

Sometimes silence scares me because it makes me feel so alone. But today I was enjoying it. There had been so much noise the last few days that I was thirsty for the quiet. I was drinking it, alongside my watermelon juice.

I could even hear myself breathing, and feel my own heart beating. Then I heard a buzzing sound, and I looked around for a big insect, a bumblebee maybe? I saw nothing, but the noise got louder. A scooter. It traveled up the dust road toward me, and I saw Jessie pull up and take off her helmet and shake out her black hair. I waved to her. It was too hot for jumping up. She would come to the shade of the stoep.

She sat down in the chair next to me but did not speak. Her face was pale, like someone had squeezed all the flavor out of it.

I poured her a glass of watermelon juice, but she did not even look at it.

"Jessie," I said, "are you all right, my skat?"

She opened her mouth and took a big breath and then her whole body started to shake.

"Oh, Tannie Maria . . ."

THIRTY-NINE

Jessie closed her eyes but tears leaked out from under her eyelashes and rolled down her cheeks. I put my arm around her and she leaned into me and cried on my apron and I patted her head and stroked her hair.

"Ag, moederliefie," I said.

When she had finished crying, I said, "Listen to the bokmakieries."

They were making such lovely sounds again. As Jessie rested her head on my shoulder, I watched one fly from the thorn tree to a gwarrie tree; it lifted up its yellow throat and made a beautiful bubbling sound, like a stream that could sing.

"Have some watermelon juice," I said. "Crying like that. In this heat. You must be all dried out."

She sat up and had a big sip.

"Ag, Tannie Maria . . . ," she said.

Then she swallowed again, even though there was nothing in her mouth except for my name.

"What is it, Jessie girl?"

"I'm such a fool," she said.

Then I knew it was a love problem she had. Only love could make a fool of a clever girl like Jessie.

"Reghardt?" I asked.

She nodded and sniffed.

"We were at school together, and he's always been a bit into me, y'know, but I just wanted to stay friends. When I was in Grahamstown, I missed him. I missed my mom and family and everyone, but I really missed him. We've seen each other a bit since I moved back home. But I told him I'm not really ready for a boyfriend. I like my independence."

She had another sip of juice and then she hugged herself, her hands cupping the tattoos on her upper arms.

"Then the other night, after the shooting, after we dropped you off, I went home with him. He was being so nice, and I was a bit freaked out, and . . . The thing is . . . I've never actually been all the way with a guy before . . ." She looked out across the veld. "But it was nice. Really nice. I really opened up to him, if you know what I mean."

I nodded, but I wasn't sure if I did.

"It was really special. Awesome. He acted like it was too. But then . . ."

She looked around the table like she was looking for help. There was just my plate with crumbs of cake on it . . . No help at all.

"Last night he was in the bar," she said, "with his pa and the guys, watching rugby. He hardly said hello, and I was a bit like, ja, well, whatever, but I thought he'd come over at halftime, and anyway I was busy interviewing Candy."

I wanted to know what Candy had said, but that could wait.

"Then at halftime he didn't come over, though he did sort of wave at us. Some guys sent over drinks. Martinis. Candy drank most of them. I was tired, and went home at about eleven. Reghardt waved good-bye to me. Didn't kiss me or walk me out or anything. When I got home, my sister was still up and I spoke to her and she told me what I should've known already."

Jessie found a napkin on her lap and blew her nose.

"I'd forgotten what a racist little town we come from," she said. "Reghardt wouldn't want his father and friends to see him with a coloured girlfriend."

"Ag, no, Jessie," I said.

But as I said it I knew it could also be true.

"I was just his loslappie . . . Just a loose rag for him to use and then throw away."

I didn't know what to say. Then I remembered the cake. I don't know why it took me so long to remember there was still half a baby cake inside.

"Just wait here a second, my skat. I'll be right back."

The kitchen smelled of the slow-drying buttermilk rusks. I made a quick cup of coffee and brought it out with the date-and-walnut cake for Jessie.

She took a mouthful, and washed it down with a sip of coffee. But it did not cheer her up.

"It gets worse," she said. Her throat moved up and down even though she wasn't eating anything. "This morning I drove past the Ladismith Hotel. And I saw Candy's red sports car there. I went inside, thinking maybe she had slept at the hotel. Although she'd told me she was staying at the Sunshine B and B. Anyway, in the hotel there I saw Jannie. He was on bar duty last night. He told me that Candy didn't stay at the hotel."

Jessie's throat was doing that swallowing thing again. But she wasn't swallowing any more cake. Maybe without the eggs and butter it just wasn't comforting enough. I should have served her piece with cream.

"He told me Candy left with Reghardt," Jessie said, "their arms around each other. He gave me a wink and said, 'That girl was flipping sexy, he definitely scored.' "

Then Jessie started to cry again, but all her tears were used up, so it was more of a bumpy coughing.

I didn't know what to do. I know I write a love advice column, but a letter is different from having someone right there. I just wanted to make her pain go away. It didn't seem worth it to me—this love business. Look how it can break such a strong girl. How it makes a clever girl feel a fool.

I gave her a hug and kissed the top of her head. Soentjies.

Little kisses, like my mother used to give me when I hurt myself.

"That's what you need," I said. "Soentjies."

When her body had stopped shaking, I put my hands on her shoulders and stood her up.

"Come inside, Jessie," I said. "We are going to bake those little cookies—soentjies."

I led her into the kitchen.

"Pass me that big block of butter from behind you," I said, opening the cupboards to get superfine sugar and flour and cornstarch. "We'll be needing butter. Lots of butter. Put it in the warming drawer to soften it."

She did as I told her, though she moved slowly, like a floppy rag doll.

"Now use a little bit of this butter to grease this tray," I said, laying all the ingredients out on the table. "There's a good girl. Now beat the butter. Ja . . . and slowly add the superfine sugar. Keep beating it . . . Nice."

I could see some strength coming into her arms when her hands were busy. I needed to get her mind busy too.

"Now sift all these together . . . Ja," I said. "So, did you learn anything? That might help our case? From . . . the cousin."

Jessie's hands were covered in flour and butter.

"Well," said Jessie, "she did tell me quite a lot."

"Yes?" I said, breaking three eggs and whisking them in a bowl.

"That guy Grace told us about," she said. "The one called John. Candy says he could be Martine's old boyfriend, John Visser. He's an organic farmer."

"Now add that flour to the butter mixture, while I add this. Ja, keep stirring."

"He wanted to marry her but she said no. Candy thinks that he wasn't stable enough for Martine."

"Okay, now get in there with your hands. Knead the dough. So she went for that Dirk instead?"

I moved the rusks from the oven to the warming drawer and turned the oven up to 350 degrees, to be ready for the soentjies.

"Dirk is financially secure, and he seemed like a solid guy when they married. Candy didn't know Dirk beat Martine. She was pretty freaked when she heard, and upset that Martine hadn't told her."

I thought of my time with my own husband, and of Martine's letter to me. She'd made her bed and she would lie in it, she'd said.

"You don't want other people to know your man is beating you," I said. "It feels like it's your own fault."

"Candy said Martine was very proud," she said. "Not one to ask for help."

I put the superfine sugar back into the cupboard and took out the confectioners' sugar. Next to it was some peanut butter. I thought it might make a nice addition to the usual soentjie recipe.

"I think we'll try adding some of this," I said, putting the jar next to Jessie. "What do you think?"

"Yum," said Jessie, her eyes bright now. "They come from an interesting family. Martine and Candice's fathers were brothers and they were both mega wealthy. The grandfather had a gold mine, literally. Candy's father set her up in business, and left her a small fortune."

"Mmm?" I said, spooning in the peanut butter.

"But Martine's father is on this mission that his two children should learn to be independent, so he hasn't given them a cent." She worked the peanut butter into the dough. "He and Martine had some kind of argument a while back, after her mother died, and they haven't been in contact. Martine's brother hangs around their dad, hoping for some crumbs, but no luck. Yet. The father's in his eighties and pretty sick. He's in a wheelchair."

"Now roll them into balls, like this," I said. "Then flatten them with a fork."

"And how's this?" Jessie said, quickly making lots of little dough balls. "Martine's brother doesn't even know about her boy! You know, the special needs one in that home."

The cooking and talking had brought the rag doll Jessie back to life. She smacked a row of cookie balls with a fork, *bam, bam, bam,* and popped them onto the baking tray.

"I wonder why," I said. "You think she was ashamed?"

"Candice thinks it's just that she was very private, and not that close to her brother. Sounds like there were some family secrets. Didn't get the details."

"Martine didn't have much money, or she would've left Dirk," I said. The tray was now full of little flattened cookies, and I put them into the oven. "But she said she was making a plan . . . I wonder what she was up to."

"Her last few bank statements don't show much happening. Just small withdrawals and her salary."

Jessie wiped the messy part of the table. Then she looked at me and wiped the whole table clean.

It wasn't long till the soentjies were ready. We made a glue of confectioners' sugar and lemon juice that we used to kiss each soentjie together with its mate. Then we put them on a plate and took them to the stoep with a big pot of rooibos tea.

Now that it was cooler, my chickens were up and about, scratching through the compost. The shadows were long on the hills and the afternoon light made all the prickly trees and bushes look soft. I couldn't hear the bokmakieries, but there were other birds calling.

The soentjies were delicious. Crisp, nutty, and buttery. At last Jessie had something worth swallowing.

"Jislaaik, Tannie, these are awesome," she said, after she had eaten five of them.

It was good to see a smile back on Jessie's mouth.

I'm your man, sang her phone.

She took her BlackBerry from its pouch on her belt, and the smile fell right off her face as she looked at the name of the caller.

"Reghardt," she said, pressing a button that stopped the song in midsentence. "I'm going to change that ring tone right away."

The phone rang again, and again she didn't answer.

This time it sang, *By the rivers dark.*

FORTY

Jessie left without her smile, but with a Tupperware full of soentjies. By the time I'd tidied up, it was cool enough to work in the vegetable garden. I missed my brown veldskoene, but put on the khaki ones and my straw hat.

"I hope she'll be okay," I said to the lettuce, as I pulled up the weeds. "I'm sure she will be. She is young and pretty." I tidied up around the tomatoes. "She'll find someone else."

I fetched a spadeful of the dark compost from the bottom of the heap. My rust-brown chickens were pecking in the grass nearby, and they came to inspect the soil for fresh food.

"Come and eat the goggas that are eating my vegetables," I said to them, but they ignored me.

I spread compost between the plants with a small garden fork, and pulled off a slug that was sitting at the heart of a purple lettuce.

"*Kik kik kik kik,*" I called and the chickens came running.

I threw the slug at them and the fastest gobbled it. They all came wandering through the veggie patch, looking for things to eat. I put compost around the marigolds and wild garlic. Together with the chickens, these plants helped me keep the insects away.

"She'll be just fine," I said to the chickens. "Jessie. She'll find someone to love."

One of the hens came and stood quite close and looked up at me with bright eyes, its head cocked on one side.

"Me?" I said, stabbing the fork into the soil, mixing in the compost. "I'm fine too."

I left the salad vegetables and headed across to the beets and potatoes. The hen followed me.

"I'm just fine."

At sunset, I closed the chickens into their hokkie, washed the garden off me, and put on my nightie. I made a sandwich with leftover ground meat curry, and ate it on the stoep, watching the night go dark and the sky fill up with stars.

"I *am* just fine," I told my curry sandwich, just before I ate the last mouthful.

The birds had gone to bed, so I listened to the toads and frogs a little. When I went to bed, they were still at it, singing with their hearts in their throats.

The next morning I woke before the birds, and watched the sun coming up over the Groot Swartberge. I had an empty feeling, like something was missing . . . Probably because it was breakfast time.

I let my chickens out and fed them (mielies), then fed myself (scrambled eggs and bacon, toast, appelkooskonfyt, and soentjies). I rattled into town in my little blue bakkie, with two tins of buttermilk rusks shaking beside me. One for the car, one for the office. The vegan date-and-walnut cake was wrapped up nicely in wax paper in a Tupperware. There were three big black birds on the telephone poles beside the road, and as I got closer they took off. Crows. They flew up and up, high into the air. I don't trust those birds, I don't know why.

I pulled up outside the Dwarsrivier B and B. I walked in the sun along the pavement, past Dirk's bakkie and the 4x4 of that rushing man. The flat beige walls of the building gave off a glare in the bright light. The front gate was in the shadow of a jacaranda tree. Two women were sitting in the garden on a bench under a Karoo willow, drinking tea and talking. They were turned away from me, so I decided to just have a little rest there where I stood.

"I just don't want to spend my last few days on earth with him," said the taller woman, twisting her long red hair into a rope and holding it up on top of her head.

"But, Emily, you can't just ditch him," the other woman said. "He's your husband, and our leader."

She was shorter and rounder, with curly gray hair.

"I don't care. I'm entitled to some fun. You can have him, Georgie."

"Ooh-woo!" Georgie squealed and fanned herself with a piece of paper. "What would Joel say?"

"Have them both. Your days of carnal pleasure are numbered."

"When we ascend, our pleasures will be infinite," said Georgie.

"Carnal, I said, carnal."

"Ooh, Emily, you are a hoot."

"No, I'm serious." She let her rope of red hair drop onto her back. "I can't tolerate another day with that egotistical maniac. Somehow, realizing that it's all ending just makes everything clearer."

"But where will you go?"

"I've got a little money saved and there are some things that I've always wanted to do . . ."

"But what if you aren't back in time to ascend with us?"

"And what if I'm not?"

"But, Emily, if Emmanuel finds out, you know what he'll do . . ."

Just then a man came out, that rushing one with the big beard.

"Get in here," he shouted from the front door. "You're late for breakfast."

"Ooh-woo," said Georgie, her hands flying into the air like startled birds.

"Coming, dear," said Emily, and the two women stood up.

The man saw me at the gate and frowned and turned away.

I took a deep breath, held my Tupperware in front of me, and stepped inside. I followed them into the dining room. The Seventh-day Adventists were all seated at a long table having breakfast. The big mama who ran the place, her hair now nicely curled, was sitting at another table with her daughter. A young coloured woman was bringing them a tray of hot sausages, bacon, and eggs. The mama grunted her thanks, and the woman rushed off and came back with toast, margarine, and jam, which she took to the long table.

The skinny little boy who'd wanted cake was pouring from a box of soy milk into a bowl of muesli. I have never tasted soy milk.

"How does a bean make milk?" I said.

Emily with the long red hair looked up at me and smiled, but didn't say anything.

"Hello," I said. "I'm Tannie Maria."

"I'm Emily," she said.

No one asked me to sit down or join them for breakfast. These people were definitely from outside Ladismith.

"I have made a vegan date-and-walnut cake," I said, patting my Tupperware, "for the children."

Emily frowned at me, not understanding.

"Vegan," I repeated. "Like vegetarian but no butter, eggs, or anything."

"Oh, vegan," she said, but she said the *g* hard, like egg, instead of soft like vegetable.

"Did any of you know Martine? Martine van Schalkwyk?" I said.

"Isn't she the one who worked at the Spar?" said Emily.

Georgie nodded and said, "A sweet soul."

A pale lady sitting next to Georgie shook her head—she was the same lady who stopped me from feeding the children last time.

"She didn't join us," she said. "We don't know her."

The man at the head of the table was still frowning. He got up and left the room, the toast on his plate only half eaten. Perhaps it was the smell of the meat and eggs on the other table.

Everyone else seemed to be enjoying their vegan food okay. When the kids saw me open the Tupperware, they jumped up and crowded around me.

"Ah, please, Mom, can we have some?" said the skinny boy, talking to the pale lady.

"Oh, all right. As soon as you've eaten your cereal. Thank you, um—Tannie," she said, taking the Tupperware from me. "That was kind of you."

"If you don't mind me asking," I said, "when is the end of the world coming exactly?"

Emily laughed and said, "Last May the twenty-first."

The pale lady gave her a little frown.

"We don't talk about exactly anymore," she said. "But we think it will be around the twenty-first of December."

"Three weeks from now?" I said. "That doesn't leave much time."

She shook her head as she spread marmalade on her toast.

"You don't look too worried," I said.

"Oh, we'll all be fine," she said, and bit into her toast.

Georgie's little gray curls bobbed up and down as she nodded in agreement.

"We'll be ascending," Georgie said.

"Who will be ascending?" I asked.

"We believers!" the pale lady said.

She smiled. Her eyes were blue and shiny. Full of faith. Her teeth had marmalade on them.

FORTY-ONE

In the *Gazette* office, I put down the tin of beskuit and turned on the kettle.

"What do you believe in?" I asked Harriet and Jessie.

Jessie looked up from her computer but didn't even smile when she saw me and the rusks. Her ponytail wasn't as neatly tied as usual. Hattie was at her desk, every hair in place.

Hattie and Jessie didn't answer, and I prepared the cups—tea for Hattie and coffee for Jess and me.

"We've got till the twenty-first of December," I said. "To believe in something."

"Oh, darling," said Hattie. "You've been talking to those Seventh-day Adventists, haven't you?"

"The end of the world is nigh," said Jessie, sounding like she didn't really care if it was.

"Oh, honestly," said Hattie. "Those people are quite batty."

"But we are all going to die," Jessie said. "If not on the twenty-first—one day."

"I suppose so," said Hattie, getting up to help herself to her tea. "Maybe that's why I go to church. In case of life after death. But to be totally honest, I'm not sure what I believe . . ."

"I'd like some kind of life before death," I said.

Jessie looked up from her computer. Harriet lifted an eyebrow.

"Are you all right, Maria?" said Hattie.

"Sorry, ja, I'm fine. I don't know what I'm talking about. I have a good life."

I gave Jessie her coffee, then offered them both buttermilk rusks. I was pleased to see Jessie was not so miserable she couldn't take a beskuit. Hattie of course shook her head.

"I'll have one at lunchtime," she said. "I hear from Jessie you two had a busy weekend."

"I told her about Dirk and Anna," Jessie said. "And what I learned from Candy."

"There are a few leads we need to follow up on," said Hattie.

There was the sound of clip-clopping, like a little horse was coming up the pathway. The door was open and a head popped around. It came with orange lipstick, long black eyelashes, and a straw sun hat.

"Oh, fantastic," said Candy. "Y'all are here!"

She pushed the door open, and trotted in on her purple high heels. Today she wore a lilac cotton dress that made you feel cool just looking at it. Her blond hair was loose, swinging at shoulder length. Jessie sank down into her chair, her back hunching forward.

"Hattie," I said, "this is Candy, Martine's cousin."

Candy took off her hat, fanned herself with it, and hung it on the back of Jessie's chair. Then she sat on a stool beside Jessie's desk.

"The funeral's at ten on Wednesday morning," Candy said. "I've got myself a priest and a venue, but I need a caterer. And I could use some help inviting people."

"We could put a funeral notice into the *Gazette,* for tomorrow's edition," said Hattie.

"Yeah, that would be terrific," said Candy. "We should do some personal invites too. I was thinking . . . after what Jessie told me about looking for the murderer, that inviting people in person would be a good way to give them the once-over. We could go together."

Jessie was pale and studying her hands. I was looking at Candy's orange toenails.

I didn't want to upset Jessie by doing anything with Candy. On the other hand, Candy didn't know about Jessie and Reghardt, so hadn't meant to hurt her. While Jessie and I were caught up in our thoughts, Harriet gave our visitor a cup of tea and wrote down the details of the funeral. At least one of us remembered her manners.

"Thanks for a fabulous evening, Jessie," said Candy, sipping her tea. "Sorry I got carried away. I reckon I'm still in shock about my cousin. You have some real sweet guys in this town, by the way. Real sweet. Why, one of them—"

There were footsteps up the pathway. A man knocked and stepped inside. Reghardt. Jessie jumped up.

"Why, Reggie!" said Candy, smiling at him. "Just talking 'bout you."

Reghardt's mouth opened and closed like a fish. Jessie gave him a look that would spear a fish, and then pushed past him.

"Jessie . . . ," he said, following her out.

But by the time the rest of his words actually left his mouth, her scooter was buzzing off. Reghardt came back and hovered in the doorway.

"Nooit," he said. "She's gone . . ."

"Need to see a man about some flowers," Candy said, looking at her watch.

She patted Reghardt on the cheek as she trotted past. He turned bright red, and did that fish thing again.

"Reghardt," I said, "I was wondering. Did you find anything in the pipes, at the Van Schalkwyks'? Pomegranate juice?"

"Ja," he said. "I mean no, I can't tell you these things. Not yet. Sorry, Tannie. The lieutenant . . . It's police business, you know."

"Will LCRC test it themselves to see if there are sedatives in it, or must they send it to Cape Town?"

"No, man, Tannie, I can't tell you, sorry. You can ask the press liaison officer. But there's nothing to report . . . yet. Do you know where Jessie's gone? Is she coming back?"

"I can't tell you, sorry," I said.

"I'll go and see . . . ," he said.

He nodded politely at us both and then left. Hattie walked to the door and looked out.

"What in goodness gracious was that all about?" she said.

"Chicken pies and milk tarts," I said. "Tannie Kuruman's melktert is the best. She could do the catering."

"What?" said Hattie.

"For the funeral," I said.

Hattie stood at the door, looking down the path and shaking her head.

FORTY-TWO

"Heavens," said Hattie, straightening her skirt as she sat down at her desk. "Why did Jessie rush off like that?"

"She'll be back," I said.

It didn't feel right for me to explain to Hattie about Jessie's love life. I put on the kettle and made tea for us both, then I sat down at my desk with my letters. I opened a plain white envelope with a Ladismith postmark.

Dear Tannie Maria,

Two things are bothering me that maybe you can help me with.

The first is—I am wondering what really matters. Really. Family? Duty? God? Friends? Food? Love?

The other is—do you have any good camping-food recipes? Without meat or fridge food. I have some lentils and cans of tomatoes.

Yours in hope,
Lost Lucy

Now that was a short letter with a tall order. I watched the morning sunshine move across the wall above Hattie's desk as I sat thinking. My biggest problem was that I have never actually been camping myself.

And I was no expert on most of the things she asked about. I didn't have a family. My duty died with my husband. God was a stranger to me. I had friends, Hattie and Jessie, and I'd cooked and eaten a lot of good food. But what did I know about love? How could I know what really mattered?

"Hats," I said, "remember that time two years ago, when it had rained and rained and part of my road got washed away and a river ran across it?"

"Oh, yes—you were cut off for almost two weeks."

"You came and stood on the other side of the river close to my house."

"But you were stubborn and wouldn't let me throw you fresh food."

"Hattie, those tomatoes landed in the water, and I couldn't risk watching more good food floating down the river. I was eating just fine with my dried and canned foods. And some fruit and vegetables that lasted nicely."

"I didn't believe you. But when the river went down I came across and you fed me that delicious meal, the butternut squash and beet stew."

"With that fresh bread I baked."

"And even some apple crumble. Wasn't it after those floods you planted your veggie garden and got your chickens?"

But I didn't answer. I was busy writing to Lucy. Now that I thought about it, I had lots of camping recipes.

Dear Lucy, I wrote.

In the end what matters most is love and food. Without them you go hungry. And you need them to enjoy all of the other things you wrote about.

Then I gave her two camping recipes. The first one was pasta with a lentil Bolognese made with canned tomatoes and fresh onions, garlic, ginger, and lemon rind. The other was the stew I'd made for Hattie. As I typed the recipes out, I heard footsteps up our pathway. I was hoping it was Jessie, but I knew it wouldn't be.

Candy walked right in and said, "Hell, I've just seen him, at a table piled with fruit. Oh, my hat."

She took it from the back of Jessie's chair and arranged it on her head. I fanned myself with an envelope.

"Martine's ex—John. He's at the market," she said. "He didn't see me." She looked at me. "Let's go talk to him together."

"You go ahead," said Hattie, nodding.

But I wasn't jumping up. I didn't want to hurt Jessie. She was my investigating partner, and to go with Candy after what had happened . . . But Candy knew John, and she was like a vetkoek in the way she might get a man to talk.

"I guess I could just talk to him alone . . . ," said Candy, tapping a foot on the wooden floor.

Her orange toenails matched her lipstick exactly. I put down my letter and stood up.

There was a murderer to be found.

FORTY-THREE

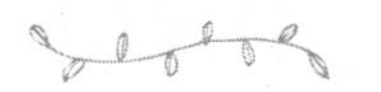

We flew up the road in Candy's red MG, the wind so strong my eyelashes were blowing back. I was holding her straw hat in my lap where she'd dropped it. And then, just then, Jessie came by on her scooter from the other direction. She passed us, and must have seen us, but she didn't turn her head.

There was a row of market stalls in the parking lot, close to the pavement. For a hundred rand a day, locals could rent a wooden trestle table, with a big umbrella. The umbrella was on a stand with a heavy concrete base. The umbrella shade was smaller than the table, and it moved around as the sun moved, so the wares were usually piled up on just one part of the table and then shuffled around to follow the shade. You could buy colorful hats or ugly handbags or cheap plastic things that broke before you got home. But some of the tables had good fresh produce from the farms nearby.

"That's him," said Candy.

We pulled up in front of a stall made of a double trestle table loaded with fruit and vegetables. A good-looking man with curly brown hair, a leather hat, and a denim shirt stood in the sun, between two umbrellas. He had organized his tables so the green and leafy things were in the shade, and the melons, tomatoes, and pumpkins were in the sun. He had also set his umbrellas so that there was some shade for his customers to stand in. Which was considerate of him. Or maybe just clever business. I recognized the man and his table. He had lived in the Ladismith area quite a few years, but he still behaved like an out-of-town type. He was there to sell, not to chat. I wondered if he would talk to us now.

Candy had parked so that he was on her side of the car. She did not look at him as she got out, but she knew he was watching. She moved slowly, as if someone was taking pictures of each pose: the red car door opens—out come her purple heels and long legs; she stands up, adjusts her sunglasses, shakes her blond hair; her hands tug on the hem of her lilac dress; the cloth tightens on her hips and breasts.

The man's eyes were photographing every image. I got out too, carrying Candy's hat.

"Look at these fine mangoes, Tannie Maria," she said, crossing the pavement, heading to his stall.

He had a nice selection of fruit and vegetables. I picked up a mango and smelled it. Sweet like honey. Some of the mangoes had little bumps on them. But that's what you get when you grow food in your garden. It doesn't always look as good as the store food, but it tastes a lot nicer. A pile of fat black grapes sat next to the mangoes.

"Can I taste one?" I asked, looking up at the man.

He was about the same height as Candy in her heels and was still watching her from under his leather hat.

"Go ahead," he said.

Ooh, it was good: sweet and juicy.

Candy was also tasting a grape, but she was taking longer about it. She rubbed it against her lips, touched it with the tip of her tongue, then licked the grape slowly. By the time she popped it into her mouth, I thought the man was going to burst. She smiled and then lifted up her sunglasses and looked right at him, as if noticing him for the first time.

"Why, isn't that John? John Visser."

The man swallowed and wiped his mouth.

"Remember me, sugar? Martine's cousin, Candice."

"Candy?" he said.

"I suppose you've heard," she said, "about Martine."

He frowned, and moved a cabbage into the shade.

"Ja. Terrible."

"I was wondering how to get ahold of you. The funeral's on Wednesday at ten in the morning."

"Terrible," he said again, his arms now at his sides. "That man."

"Her husband?"

"Yes."

His hands became fists.

"You think he did it?"

"He didn't treat her right."

"Did you see much of Martine?"

He opened and closed his fists.

"He was too jealous to let anyone near her," he said. "But I kept in touch . . ."

"When did you last see her?"

"Couple of weeks back. She should never have married him."

"Did you visit her at home?"

"What's this, an inquisition?"

Candy smiled. She took her hat from me, and arranged it nicely on her head.

"This is a family friend, Maria," she said. "John Visser. An old . . . friend of Martine's. Maria is helping out with the funeral arrangements. John is a farmer. Still organic?"

He nodded.

"Nice," I said, patting a pumpkin. "I've got a little garden myself. My chickens and my wild garlic keep the goggas away."

"So you're also an organic farmer," he said.

"I never thought of it like that," I said. "But I don't use poisons for the insects, and I pull up my weeds by hand."

"And your fertilizer?" he asked.

"Vegetable compost and chicken poo," I said.

"Excellent," he said, bringing his hands together in a silent clap. "Then you're organic. Most home gardeners are. Until they get bombarded by crap from the agricultural companies. They've wrecked subsistence farming across Africa with their products. Pesticides, herbicides, chemical fertilizers, and now the GM seeds. Criminal. Just criminal."

Candy smiled.

"Can't just let nature take its course," she said.

"Not where there's money to be made. Profit. That's all that matters."

"Money money money."

He lowered his voice and leaned across the table.

"It may be more than that," he said. "Control. These guys are evil. They have a plan."

"I'm sorry things didn't work out with you and Martine," Candy said.

He stepped back and picked up a tomato.

"She made the wrong decision there," he said, throwing the tomato in the air and catching it.

"Maybe," said Candy.

"Look how things turned out," he said.

He held the tomato in his fist at his side. He was squeezing it. Red juice dripped out between his fingers.

"These grapes," I said, "how much are they?"

"Fifty rand a box," he said, dropping the squashed tomato.

I didn't like to see food treated like that.

"I'll take a box," I said, "and a package of tomatoes."

"I'll have three of these mangoes," said Candy.

"I'll get a fresh box of grapes from my bakkie," he said, "I'm keeping them cool under shade cloth."

He wiped his hands on his jeans. I followed him across the parking lot, while Candy picked out her mangoes.

"Bit early in the season for grapes," I said.

"These are early ripeners," he said. "But I've got a greenhouse. Bit of a cheat, I suppose. I set it up to keep out the porcupines and baboons. Then I realized I can regulate the moisture and temperature, and sometimes I can get fruit out of season."

His car was a big white 4x4 bakkie. The tires: Firestone.

"Do you have any pomegranate trees?"

John acted like he hadn't heard me as he unloaded a box of grapes. I saw a sticker on the back of his car. It was big and red and said: No Fracking Way. Fracking? Where had I heard that before?

"What is fracking?" I asked.

"She loved pomegranates," said John, talking quietly to himself. "I planted a whole field of them for her. But it did me no good."

He carried the grapes across to the table, mumbling something I couldn't hear.

As I paid him, I asked again: "What's that sticker on your car about fracking?"

"Those fracking mining bastards, Shaft. They won't stop till they've got all the coal, oil, and gas out of the earth. Fracking is how they search for natural gas. They blast through layers of deep-strata rock. Toxic chemicals. It would totally mess up our groundwater. And they want to take water from our deep aquifers. A disaster for the Karoo if they go ahead. Total disaster. We've got a very fragile ecosystem here."

"They want to do it here, in the Klein Karoo?"

"Mainly the Groot Karoo," he said, packing Candy's mangoes into a brown paper bag. "But they've started investigating here too. I hear they are buying up land in likely areas. They've scoped out everything from the sky. With their infrared satellite devices. After last year's drought, a lot of the farmers are struggling, selling their land cheap . . ."

"Did you talk to Martine about fracking?" I asked.

He started rearranging the watermelons on the table.

"Those mining companies are the scum of the earth. We've got to stop them." He looked up at the sky. "Looks like it might rain. Think I'll pack up for the day."

There were a few clouds building up, but it was a long way from rain. He started packing his melons and cabbages into cardboard boxes.

Candy said, "It's at the NGK church. The funeral. On Wednesday. Could you be a pallbearer?"

"Terrible," said John to himself, shaking his head as he walked away, carrying a loaded box.

I reckon that fella's one sandwich short of a picnic," said Candy as we got back in the car.

"Maybe he's got a few sandwiches extra," I said.

I wasn't quite sure what I meant, but I knew it was time for lunch.

FORTY-FOUR

We went to Tannie Kuruman's café, where we killed two birds with one stone: We ordered two of her delicious chicken pies, and while they were being heated up, we spoke about the catering for the funeral.

"What do you reckon we should provide?" Candice asked Tannie Kuruman.

Tannie Kuruman adjusted the little red doek on her head, and looked at Candy's purple heels and lilac dress and then at her face. It was quite a way up for Tannie to look, what with Candy's height and heels, and Tannie K having more width than height. She folded her arms, and then looked back down again at Candy's orange toenails. Maybe she was struck dumb by the look of Candy, or perhaps she couldn't understand her American English.

So I repeated what Candy said in my own words: "What kind of kossies shall we give the people? At the funeral?"

Tannie Kuruman cleared her throat and spoke, "What about my little pies? I can do the chicken ones."

"Ja," I said, "and maybe some of those sausage rolls you make."

"Ooh, ja, and the melktertjies. Little milk tarts." She looked at Candy when she translated. "And small koeksisters . . . Cake sisters?" She pointed through the glass counter at the twisted plaits of dough, fried and dipped in syrup. "Those."

Candy smiled. "Sugar, I know what koeksisters are. That sounds just peachy. Whatever you two decide. Just send me the bill."

"Well, for thirty rand per person I can do something simple. Or for fifty I can make it more special. How many people?"

"Special is good," Candy said. She looked at me. "Sixty people, you reckon?"

"That should be fine." Funerals were not so popular in Ladismith as they were in the old days. "Can you maybe have some pies and puddings without meat or dairy?" I said. "In case some of those Seventh-day Adventists come . . ."

"Ja," said Tannie K. "I've fed them before. Those children look a bit skinny to me, you know . . ."

Our chicken pies smelled wonderful, and we took them outside and sat on a bench in the shade of a jacaranda tree and looked out on to Church Street. Candy was nibbling on her pie, but I took a big bite of mine so that I could get the crust and the filling in one mouthful. Just then I heard a scooter. It was Jessie—turning in toward the café. Maybe she was coming to pick up lunch. Candy waved at her, and she saw us there on the bench, together, with our pies.

The look on Jessie's face made me stop chewing.

I wanted to spit out my mouthful and call to her. Tell her that she was my investigating partner, and the person I most liked to eat with. I chewed very fast but by the time my mouth was free, she had turned around and sped off.

That fast eating meant my food was quickly gone, which wasn't clever because it left me hungry. But then Candy's cell phone rang and she gave me the remaining half of her pie.

"It's good," she said, "but I'm done."

"David! Sugar!" she said into the phone, then more quietly, "What are you wearing?" She laughed. "Did you get my message? Yeah . . . Wednesday. How's my uncle Peter doing? . . . Really? I didn't think he was capable of tears. Are you sure it's not an eye infection? And his health?" She stood up and walked away from the bench. "This afternoon . . . No, her lawyer's here in Ladismith . . . Yeah . . ."

Then I couldn't hear what she was saying anymore. When she came back she pulled a face.

"David," she said. "Martine's brother. I hope he gets a decent suit for the funeral. He has absolutely no fashion sense."

I brushed the pastry flakes off my hands, and stood up. Twice I'd heard her speaking badly about this man, her cousin, but she sounded friendly enough to him on the phone. Maybe that's how family politics go.

"Hell, sometimes I wonder about David," said Candy, as we walked to her car. "He's been wanting to get his hands on his old man's money for a long time. My uncle's such a miser, but he's had stomach cancer for the last year, and the doctors say he's too old for an operation. David's been circling the old man like a vulture, making himself useful, he says. Taking him on holidays. They're at Sanbona now. You know, that luxury game lodge . . ."

We got into the MG. The seats were hot.

"Did he visit her last week?" I asked.

"He says he didn't," said Candy, starting up the sports car, driving out. "They were gonna go and see her. But they hadn't gotten around to it."

"Was he close to her?"

"The only thing David's really close to is his cheap suits. And his longing for an expensive life. But he was her brother. I can't believe he would, you know . . ."

"But with Martine dead, he'd get all his father's money," I said.

"That's what he thinks," said Candy.

Then the wind was moving too fast for us to talk anymore.

Candy dropped me and my grapes and tomatoes outside the *Gazette* office.

"Martine's lawyer asked me to come and see him," she said, looking in the car mirror as she put on orange lipstick. "About her will, I reckon. And I'd better stop in and talk to Dirk about the funeral."

I couldn't see Jessie's bike outside, but I went in to look for her anyway. I put the fruit on my desk.

"Jessie's not feeling too well," Hattie said. "She says she'll work from home. How did it go with John?"

"Interesting," I said. "And Tannie Kuruman will do the catering."

I told her about our discussions with John. Then I called Jessie on her cell, but couldn't get through. I tried her home and no one answered.

"I'm a bit worried about Jessie," I told Hattie.

"Mmm," she said. "She has been acting strange."

Hattie didn't know the whole story, but I still felt it wasn't for me to tell her about Jessie's private life.

"How about a cup of tea?" I said.

I sat down at my desk with my tea and a beskuit so I could have a quiet think. Then the office phone rang.

"That was Nurse Mostert," Hattie said, as she put down the receiver, "Jessie's ma. She wants us at the hospital. Right away."

FORTY-FIVE

Let's go in my car," Hattie said when we were outside.

"No," I said, quickly getting into my little blue bakkie. "Do you think Jessie is okay? Why didn't her ma say what the problem was?" We drove up the hill toward the hospital.

"I couldn't really hear her properly. I'm sure Jessie's fine. Does this window not open any wider?"

"Sorry," I said, "it sticks. Here, I'll turn the fan on you."

I wound my window all the way down and a warm breeze moved through my bakkie. I suppose we should've gone in Hattie's car, but I just couldn't face Hattie's driving when I was so worried already.

"I hate it when a hospital phones you but won't tell you what the problem is," I said as we drove up the hill. "It happened with my mother. They say it's to make sure you don't have an accident on the way. But that's nonsense, I think. Worrying can be worse than knowing."

"There's no shade," Hattie said, as we pulled in to the hospital parking lot. "Your car is going to get so hot." A police van and a cream 4x4 had taken the only shade under the big rhus tree.

The cicadas were screeching. It seemed to get louder and louder as we walked toward the hospital entrance. We passed the 4x4. Firestone tires. Klein Karoo Real Estate written on the side in black letters. It sounded like the cicadas were in a jakkalsbos in the flower bed at the hospital entrance.

As we were going through the doors a man walked out so fast he bumped into my shoulder.

"Mr. Marius!" said Hattie, and he turned around.

He was not any taller than Hattie, but he glared down his nose at her. His hair was black and slicked into a side part and he had a slim mustache curled around his lips. His mouth looked like he was eating something bitter. He stared at us both through narrow eyes then pointed a finger at me and then at Hattie.

The noise of the cicadas stopped. I could hear him breathing through his nose.

He opened his mouth and I thought he was going to speak, but instead he spun around, marched across the tar to the 4x4 bakkie, revved the engine, and sped away. The cicadas started screeching again.

"There you are!" said Nurse Mostert.

She was a short woman with a round face and a nice shape. She reminded me of a vetkoek, wrapped in a clean white napkin—that smart nurse's uniform.

"Is Jessie okay?" I asked.

"Jessie?" she said, looking at Hattie, then back at me. "No, no, this is not about Jessie. It's Miss Pretorius and Mr. van Schalkwyk. Fighting again. We've had to get in police guards now. I was hoping you could talk to them. Get them to stop this nonsense."

We followed Jessie's mom down the corridor as she spoke.

"They caught Miss Pretorius trying to pour Dettol into Mr. van Schalkwyk's drip while he was sleeping. We uncuffed her to let her go to the toilet, and that's when she sneaked off—in her wheelchair! Then in the middle of the night he somehow wheeled his whole bed to Anna's ward. I don't know how he managed, but it looks like he used the drip stand to push himself along—like he was pulling a boat down a river. The bed got stuck in the door, but there was some kicking and throwing of things before we separated them again."

"Honestly," said Hattie. "Like children."

"But more dangerous. We can't watch them twenty-four hours a day. So we called the police. Reghardt said maybe you guys could talk some sense into them. Where is Jessie?"

"She's not feeling well. She went home," Hattie said.

"I couldn't get her on her cell," said Nurse Mostert. "I hope she's okay."

"Nothing serious," said Hattie, "just a bit of an upset stomach. But when you phoned and told us to get up here, we thought that maybe Jessie . . ."

"Ag, shame, I'm sorry. No, it's just that the detective arrived just as I was calling you so I didn't have time to explain everything."

"Kannemeyer?" I asked. "He's here?"

"Ja, he wants to take statements from them, so they can do legal injunctions or something."

"Interdicts?" I said, remembering my conversation with legal aid.

"Ja, to keep them so many feet away from each other."

"Mr. Marius—what was he doing here?" asked Hattie.

"Visiting Mr. van Schalkwyk," she said.

We were at Anna's ward now and I could see Detective Kannemeyer standing by her bed. My hair must have looked terrible. I hadn't fixed it since riding around in Candy's car. I ran my hand across it, but I really needed a mirror.

"I'm just going to use the bathroom," I said to Hattie.

But it was too late—Anna had seen us.

"Tannie Maria!" she called. "Come and explain to the policeman what *no* means."

I took a big breath and went inside.

"Nee, no, hayi khona, blerrie hell," said Anna.

The detective was looking smart in a cream cotton shirt and maroon tie, as if he had been sitting in an air-conditioned office instead of a sports car in the wind and sun. He nodded at us and stood back while Nurse Mostert put a pillow under Anna's foot—which was sticking out from the plaster cast—and turned a knob on the drip beside the bed.

Anna's hair was even more ruffled than mine, and her green hospital gown was wrinkled, but her cheeks were rosy. She smiled and patted the side of her bed, calling us closer. The nurse winked at me and left.

Detective Kannemeyer cleared his throat. In his hand he had a clipboard with paper and a pen.

"Miss Pretorius says she won't press charges against Van Schalkwyk," he said. "She won't even give a statement about what happened."

Anna pressed her lips together.

"But, Anna," I said, "then Dirk will blame you for everything."

She shook her head, raised her eyes towards Kannemeyer, and did a rolling movement with her hand.

He sighed and said, "Van Schalkwyk's also doing nothing."

"It was all just an accident," said Anna.

"That's what he says too," Kannemeyer said. He tapped his clipboard with his finger. "You will both be booked for disturbing the peace and shooting your firearms. And the hospital will be pressing charges with that Dettol nonsense. And you aren't off the hook for your original homicide charge—"

"Did you maybe bring me some vetkoek?" said Anna to me.

"Sorry," I said.

"Tannie Maria. Mrs. . . . ahm . . . ," Kannemeyer said, looking down at Hattie.

"Harriet," she said, "Harriet Christie."

"Tannie Maria and Mrs. Christie, I hope you can talk some sense into this woman. Get her to understand the seriousness of her crimes."

"Cake?" Anna asked.

"Not even a grape," I said. "I'm really sorry."

Kannemeyer looked down at the paper on his board. It was blank. He patted it against his thigh and walked toward the door. Before he left the ward he remembered his manners, and turned around.

"Good afternoon, ladies," he said.

FORTY-SIX

What's going on, Anna?" I said. "Why aren't you pressing charges?"

Anna snorted.

"Nothing's going on," she said. "Nothing to do with anyone else. It's between me and Dirk."

"But, Anna, we told you," I said. "He probably didn't kill Martine."

"Maybe he did, maybe he didn't. But even when she was alive, that man was a stinking pig's ass. And he was always in the way." She leaned back into her cushions. "She should've been with me."

"Mr. Marius was just here," I said. "Visiting Dirk. Did Martine say anything to you about him?"

"Who?" said Anna, staring off at a place inside her own head.

"The real estate agent," said Hattie.

"She didn't like him," said Anna. "They had a fight or something."

"Was Martine selling or buying property?"

"I dunno," said Anna. "She didn't say what it was about. She was a private one, Tienie. Kept her stories to herself. But when she laughed with me, she opened up like a veldvygie in the sun."

"Did she say anything to you about John Visser?" I asked.

She blinked and looked around the room as if she had just arrived.

"Her ex-boyfriend?" I said.

"She had a boyfriend? I'll kill him!"

I looked at Hattie and shook my head.

"I'm going to see Dirk," I said. "You try to talk some sense into her. Keep her out of trouble."

I don't know if sense is something you can talk in or out of someone. You either have it or you don't.

Warrant Officer Reghardt Snyman was on guard outside Dirk's ward.

He said, "Is Jessie here?"

I shook my head.

"She's not feeling well," I said.

"She's not answering my calls. I asked Nurse Mostert to call you guys. I thought maybe you could . . ."

He waved his hand toward Dirk, cuffed to his bed.

"We'll do our best," I said.

"Tannie Maria?" said Reghardt, his eyes wide like a puppy's.

I waited while he looked around the hospital corridor for what he wanted to say. The floors and the walls were very clean and shiny. Not an easy place to find words.

"Never mind," he mumbled.

Nurse Mostert was next to Dirk's bed, adjusting the sling on his left arm. Dirk's face looked like a lawn mowed by a drunk man, the scraggly grass growing into his bushy sideburns. But his sling and his bandages were very neat and white.

"We'll give you a shave and clean you up just now," Nurse Mostert said, as if she could hear what I was thinking.

Dirk frowned at me, like he wasn't sure who I was. I suppose he was under the influence of horse sedative when we'd last met.

"This is Tannie Maria," said the nurse. "She's come to talk to you."

She made a note on his chart and left us alone.

"Oom van Schalkwyk," I said. "You and Anna must stop this fighting. It's not going to help catch the murderer."

"She killed Martine."

"No, Dirk. I don't think so. It was probably the man who shot Lawrence."

He narrowed his eyes at me, and said, "You know, I had a dream about that. My mother. She gave me vetkoek, and told me about Lawrence and the man who killed them both." He looked up at the ceiling. "My mother died a long time ago. She made the best vetkoek." He took a tissue from next to his bed and blew his nose. "It turns out it was true. About Lawrence."

"Yes, it's true. And Anna was here in the hospital the night he was shot. She didn't do it."

"That blerrie Anna. She was no good for Martine. I could always tell when she'd been visiting. Martine would close me out, like I wasn't there. Lock her door—to me—her own husband! Anna started taking her away from me before she died . . ."

The hand at the end of his bandaged arm bunched into a fist.

"Maybe she shut you out because you treated her so badly," I said.

"What?!"

His face went red.

"You hit her," I said.

"Who do you think you are?"

His cheeks were swelling up now, like a balloon. I just stood there and looked at him.

He sighed and some of the air went out of that red balloon.

"You are right, Tannie," he said. "I was a terrible husband. Now it's too late . . ."

"Anna was a good friend to her. If you care about your wife, you'll treat Anna with respect."

"I know people think it was me who killed her. I go crazy sometimes." He sat up, and leaned toward me. "But it wasn't me. I didn't kill her. You've got to believe me."

"I don't think it was you. And I don't think it was Anna either."

"Are you with the police?"

"No, I'm investigating for the *Klein Karoo Gazette*. We got involved when Martine wrote to us, before she died."

"Who was it, Tannie? What bastard killed her?"

"We don't know yet. But if you stop fighting Anna, maybe you can help us work it out."

"I dunno who'd do such a thing to Martine. It makes me blerrie crazy."

He waved his bandaged paw about. I pulled up a plastic chair and sat down next to him. He was ready to answer questions; I just hoped I could remember them all.

"Lawrence said he was sorry—he didn't mean to get you into trouble," I said. "What did he mean by that?"

"Trouble? Oh, ja, Lawrence told the police I was there on the morning Martine was killed. But that was rubbish. I was at work right up till lunchtime. Everyone at work saw me there. I don't know why he said that."

"Maybe he saw someone who drove a car like yours?"

"Ja, could be . . . He wasn't one to sommer talk nonsense, Lawrence."

"The murderer might have thought Lawrence had seen him."

"You think that's why he got shot?"

"Could also be because Lawrence walked in on him when he was at your house that night."

"What was the bastard doing at my house?" he said.

"Going through papers in Martine's study."

Dirk rubbed his scratchy chin with his hand.

I asked, "That Mr. Marius, what was he doing here?"

"He's got someone wants to buy our land." He swallowed. "My land."

"And are you selling?"

"Ag, I dunno. Now he's offering twice what it's worth, so I'd be blerrie stupid to say no. But Martine didn't want to sell. She said Marius was up to no good. With her gone, I dunno . . . Marius wants me to sign an agreement. But it's too soon. I haven't spent any time at home since . . ."

He looked around as if he had lost something. His gaze fell on the water jug beside his bed.

"Can I pour you some water?" I said.

He shook his head, but kept looking at the water jug, as if it made him sad.

"Who's the buyer?" I asked.

His face was confused, like he'd forgotten what we were talking about.

"The one who wants to buy your land," I said.

"Dunno. Marius wants to keep it quiet . . ."

"Was Martine religious?"

"She was a good woman. Righteous."

"Did she have anything to do with the Seventh-day Adventists?"

"The what? Oh, those people. The end of the world and that. Jinne, I don't know. She did once say . . . I didn't always listen. I wasn't a good husband."

"Did you know Martine's friend John Visser?"

"That useless piece of kak. What do you mean, her friend?" His face did that red balloon thing again. "Did you see them together? Where?"

"No, no, I'm just asking. I hear they were together long ago."

"She threw him away. Long ago. And you know what? *He's* got a white bakkie! I've seen it. It looks a lot like mine. It was him . . . I'll kill him!"

FORTY-SEVEN

When we opened the doors of my bakkie in the parking lot, waves of heat came out. I smoothed my dress under my legs so my skin didn't touch the seat.

"Goodness gracious," Hattie said. "You should get an air conditioner, Tannie Maria."

"They cost more than I paid for my bakkie," I said.

"This heat can kill you," she said. "Next time we go in my car."

I dropped Hattie back at the *Gazette* and picked up my grapes and tomatoes and headed home. The brown hills had a hazy mist around them, from the dust and the heat. There were wobbly lines on the road that looked like puddles of water—mirages. It's funny how dry heat can make something that looks like cool water. It's like the air is longing for something so much that it just makes it up. That's the problem with wanting something too much: It can make you crazy.

By the time I got to my own driveway, my dress was stuck to the car seat. I was looking forward to a nice glass of lemonade and ice. I parked in the shade of the rhus tree, and peeled myself out of the bakkie. I took the grapes and tomatoes with me. The tomatoes were sweating in their bag.

"I'll take you out now-now," I said.

It was quiet. Too quiet. Maybe the birds were too lazy to

sing in this heat, I thought, but what about the insects? When I walked up the pathway, my footsteps sounded loud.

My chickens, where are my chickens? I thought. They weren't scratching in the compost heap, and I couldn't see them lying in the shade.

Then I stood dead still. There was something brown lying on the doormat on my stoep. What was it?

I took a step forward.

My brown veldskoene.

For a moment I was pleased to see them again; my khaki veldskoene and I hurried forward to welcome them back after their long walk home. Then I remembered when they had disappeared. The night of Lawrence's murder.

Each shoe was sliced in half, like it had been sawn with a bread knife.

I dropped the box of grapes. I heard a rough cry that I thought was my own, but when I looked up I saw a crow flapping across the sky. I wanted to get under cover. I stepped around the splattered grapes and dead veldskoene, and opened my front door. It wasn't locked. I hardly ever lock it. I closed the door behind me and tried to lock it but the key was gone. The house was very quiet. Just the sound of my heart beating.

I put the tomatoes on the kitchen table and went to the phone. I wanted to see Henk Kannemeyer. I phoned the police station and asked for him. The man I spoke to had a thick, sleepy voice.

"He's not here," he said. "Can I help you, Mevrou?"

"Send a police car to my house."

I gave my name and address. He took a long time to spell it and write it down.

"What's the problem, Mevrou?"

"I need the police."

"Has there been a break-in at your house?"

"I'm not sure. My key's missing."

"You've lost your keys?" he said.

"A murderer was here."

"Was someone murdered?" he asked.

"My veldskoene," I said. "Cut in half."

"Your veldskoene were murdered?" the man said. "Lady, is this a joke?"

"No," I said. "I need Detective Kannemeyer. Doesn't he have a cell phone?"

"We don't just give the detective lieutenant's number out."

"Piet, is Konstabel Piet Witbooi there?"

There was silence.

"I need to talk to him. This is serious."

The phone went quiet. I wasn't sure if he'd put the phone down or had gone to call Piet. Then I heard a background noise, so I kept hanging on.

At last a voice came on the line: "Hallo. Konstabel Piet Witbooi."

"Piet, it's me, Tannie Maria. My brown veldskoene, from the night Lawrence was shot. They are on my doorstep. Cut in half."

"We're on our way."

I called Jessie on her cell. No reply. I phoned her house and a girl answered, one of her sisters or cousins. She had a big family.

"Maria van Harten here. Can I speak to Jessie, please?"

"Jessieeeeeeee!" she shouted.

I heard her footsteps as she walked off. *Thump. Thump.* My heart was going faster—I was holding my breath.

"She doesn't wanna talk, Tannie," reported the girl when she came back. "She says she's not feeling well."

"But she's okay?" I said, breathing out.

"Jaaaa," said the girl.

"Go and look on your doorstep—tell me if there's anything there," I said. "Some boots."

"Huh?" said the girl.

"Just be a good girl and go look," I said.

She tramped off and then came back.

"Nothing there, Tannie."

The phone went dead.

I heard a tapping sound, and I nearly jumped out of my skin.

It was a little bird. Pecking at its reflection in the window.

Fighting with its own shadow.

FORTY-EIGHT

Piet," I said, "thanks for coming."

I was glad to see him. He was with a young policeman who introduced himself as Sergeant Vorster. Vorster had soft, curly hair and smooth brown skin, like a baby's. Piet was wrinkled like an old man but he moved like a youngster. He stepped around the grapes, and bent low to peer at the veldskoene on the doormat from this side and that; he studied the dust on the stoep. With his hand he directed Vorster back, out of the way.

Lemonade, I thought. I should pour us all lemonade and ice. That's what I had come home for, not this shoe-killing business. Vorster answered a call on his cell phone.

"Ja," he said, "we're here." He put his phone away. "Lieutenant Kannemeyer is op pad. On his way."

"Excuse me," I said.

I needed to freshen up. A clean dress at least. This one was all sweaty. I grabbed that nice dress with the purple roses from my bedroom closet—I hadn't worn it in a while, but I liked it—and popped into the bathroom. I took off my sticky dress and dropped it in the laundry basket. No time to shower, but I washed my face and wiped myself down with a washcloth. I heard a car arriving, and a door slamming.

I slipped the purple-rose dress over my head and pulled it down. It was tight and wouldn't come past my shoulders. What was wrong with it? It had never done this before. I pulled harder. No luck. So I tugged to get the dress back off but it wouldn't move. My arms were stuck up in the air. I heard footsteps on the stoep.

I hopped up and down, tugging on the cloth. Nothing moved. I was stuck.

"Konstabel Witbooi," Kannemeyer called at the front door. "Can I come in?"

I twisted and wriggled inside that dress. My mouth was full of cloth, so I couldn't breathe so well. Piet and Kannemeyer were in the house, talking. I heard a van driving off. Vorster, leaving. My arms were getting tired and I felt dizzy. I leaned against the wall to catch my breath.

I strained against the dress and felt it tear. I helped it to tear some more, then I pulled it off and I was free.

Whew. I sat down on the toilet lid. First my veldskoene cut up, now my dress torn.

I looked at myself in the mirror. My face was as red as a tomato, and I was sticky again from the fight with the dress. I did another face-and-body wipe with the cloth.

There was a knock on the bathroom door.

"Sorry, Mrs. van Harten." It was Kannemeyer's voice. "Just want to know you're okay."

"Fine," I said. "Coming."

I dug out my dress from the laundry basket. As well as being sweaty, it was now totally rumpled from being bunched up in there. I tried stretching it out, but it was no good. Piet and Kannemeyer were right there; there was no way I could get to my bedroom. I held up the purple-rose dress. The torn bits were only at the back. I pulled it on. This time it fit nicely and I did up the zip. When I turned around I could see two big rips in the mirror, but from the front it looked fine. I brushed my hair and put on my lipstick. I took a sip of water, but it didn't do the trick. Lemonade, I needed iced lemonade.

I stepped out of the bathroom and stood with my back to the

wall. They were standing close by, looking at my sash window.

"This doesn't lock," said Kannemeyer to Piet, frowning.

"Detective," I said. "Lemonade?"

He looked at me and smiled; his mustache went up at the tips. I walked sideways like a crab, so they couldn't see my back.

"It looks like he didn't come farther than the doorway," said Kannemeyer.

He had my brown veldskoene inside a clear plastic bag. Like a tiny body bag. I carried on crabbing past the dish rack, where I picked up three glasses.

"Was your door locked?" asked Kannemeyer.

"No," I said, "and the key was in the front door. Now it's gone."

Kannemeyer shook his head and tugged at a mustache end.

"Can you go and stay somewhere else for a while?" he asked.

I was working my way across to the fridge.

"It's okay," he said. "Konstabel Witbooi has checked the floors, you can walk there."

"I don't want to leave," I said, opening the fridge behind me.

Kannemeyer frowned. I felt on the fridge shelf behind me for the jug of lemonade. Piet came forward and picked up the jug and gave it to me. I filled our glasses and then managed to crab my way along to an armchair not far from the kitchen table. Ah, at last, cool lemonade. Piet swallowed his down, but Kannemeyer didn't pick up his glass.

"I don't think you realize how serious this is, Mrs. van Harten. Konstabel Witbooi has looked at the tire tracks and the shoe prints. This is the same man who killed Lawrence. Maybe Martine too. It's no joke."

"This is my home," I said.

"Just for a while, till we catch him."

"How will you do that? Have you got leads?"

"You're not safe here. Your windows don't even lock."

"Any suspects?"

"Maria. Those shoes—cut up like that—are a threat to your life."

I took a sip of my drink, and looked down at the khaki veldskoene that were safe and whole on my feet.

"We must be getting close," I said, "or else he wouldn't be threatening me."

"Getting close? What do you mean you're getting close? I told you to stay out of this."

"Have some lemonade, Detective."

He paced up and down.

"You've been getting yourself into trouble again. And look. Look where it's gotten you. I hope this is a warning to you."

I had another sip; I looked at a place on my ceiling where the paint was flaking. I was wondering about who we had been irritating apart from the detective.

"Detective Kannemeyer, do people know about Jessie and me being at the house the night of Lawrence's murder?"

"I didn't tell anyone but I'm sure half the town knows by now. Mevrou Gouws at CBL Hardware was spreading the news."

"If the man wanted to murder me, why kill my veldskoene? He's trying to scare me off. It must be someone who thinks I know something . . ."

"This. Is. Not. Your. Investigation."

"No, it's yours. But if you want to find the killer, you should listen to people with things to tell you."

Kannemeyer sat down at the kitchen table. He ran his hand across his hair and drank half of his lemonade. It seemed to cool him off a bit.

"Okay," he said. "Tell me what you know."

"I think you might need a pen and paper," I said.

He took out a pen and a small notebook. He nodded at Piet, who also sat down.

"Help yourself to more lemonade, Piet," I said.

He did, and he filled up our glasses too while I told them everything I knew about Grace, John, Mr. Marius, Martine's brother, Candice, and even the Seventh-day Adventists.

When I'd finished I said, "Now maybe you could tell me your news."

Kannemeyer shook his head.

"You don't give up, do you? This is a police matter. But what I will tell you is that you were right about the pomegranate juice. There were sedatives in it. We are asking the Spar to try and remember who they sold the juice to."

"There must be a lot of people. The cashiers won't remember."

"Not so many. There were only six liters in the crate that came in last week."

"And, like I told you, maybe John is able to ripen pomegranates early. Maybe he's got his own supply of frozen juice too . . ."

"We will check it out. But please stay out of it, Maria. Please. We don't want you getting killed as well."

My last mouthful of juice had little bits of lemon in it. I chewed them.

"Jessie could be in danger too," I said.

"Did her shoes also come home?"

"No. Well, not when I phoned her house earlier."

"We need to get you somewhere safe," he said.

"Detective, I'm not running away. Who would feed my chickens?"

"We could post someone here for a while. In case he comes back. The policeman could feed your chickens."

"And who will feed the policeman? I'm staying here."

FORTY-NINE

I am worried about my chickens," I said to Piet. Kannemeyer had gone. "They're usually in the front garden."

Piet put the three glasses in the sink, and went outside. I found an old cotton shirt of my husband's to cover the rips in my dress, then I followed Piet into the back garden. He was squatting beside the chickens, making little birdie noises. They were huddled under a cancer bush behind the house. The red flowers on the kankerbos looked like big drops of blood. When the chickens saw me, they came running.

One, two, three, four, five. They were all there, and they were fine.

"*Cluck cluck cluck,*" they said.

"*Kik kik kik,*" I said, and they followed me back to the stoep.

I looked at the grapes that I had dropped on the ground.

"Sorry," I said, and I bent down to sort through them.

I threw the squashed ones into the garden for the chickens to eat. The other grapes were fine and I washed them and put them in the fridge. The chickens were still waiting around so I chucked out a handful of crushed mielies for them and I watched them peck at the yellow pieces on the grass. Piet walked around the garden and the driveway looking at tiny things like ants and dust.

A little later, a police van came and fetched Konstabel Piet and dropped off Sergeant Vorster. Vorster sat on the stoep and watched the light changing on the Rooiberg. The shadows were growing on the hills and there was a cool breeze blowing away the heat that had been sitting so heavy on us all day. We had finished the lemonade, but I took him some coffee and beskuit.

"Thank you, Tannie," he said.

"Shouldn't you be undercover?" I asked him.

He frowned.

"You know," I said. "In plainclothes, and hidden away. In case he comes back."

He shook his head.

"I'm here to protect you," he said, and took a sip of coffee.

I prepared the bed in the spare room. I would make a simple supper of Welsh rarebit. I went out to the chicken hokkie and collected some eggs. When I passed Vorster on my way back, I thought I'd better check with him about supper. Maybe he was a Seventh-day Adventist or something.

"Do you eat eggs and cheese sauce? For supper."

"I'm going home for supper. Detective Lieutenant Kannemeyer's doing the evening shift from seven o'clock."

My kitchen clock said it was five o'clock. I put the eggs in a bowl on the kitchen counter. I decided they could wait till breakfast. I suddenly felt like making tomato-lamb stew and a honey-toffee snake cake. The yeast dough for the cake takes a while to rise, but if I put it in the evening sun right away it would be okay. The lamb in the bredie should stew all day. I looked at the clock again, but it didn't give me any more time, in fact it was getting less. I had some slow-cooked lamb stew in the freezer. I could just add the tomato and the bredie spices. I had to work fast to get the slow meal on the road. Once the lamb was defrosting in the cast-iron pot on the stove and the cake dough was rising on the stoep, I boiled the potatoes and scalded and peeled the tomatoes and found the spices. I was glad I had allspice and mace, because I really like them in my tomato bredie. I added the ingredients to the lamb in the pot. When it was simmering sweetly I wrapped it all up and put it in the hotbox to carry on cooking slowly.

I was on the stoep, checking on the honey-cake dough, when I heard the car coming. My hands were full of flour and I had my apron on over my dress and shirt, but I wasn't going to change again. I brought the cake dough in, tidied my hair a bit, and put on the kettle. Then I rolled the cake dough into a long fat sausage, and twisted it into a loose spiral on the baking tray.

He knocked on the door, although it was open.

"Something smells good."

The tips of his mustache were sharp, as if they had been waxed. He had changed into jeans and a white cotton shirt. It looked soft and faded, like he had worn it a lot. His gun was on his hip, and he was carrying a small suitcase and some plastic bags.

"Coffee?" I said, as I poured the almond-honey sauce over the cake.

"Please," he said. "Milk and one sugar."

He put the bags on a kitchen chair, and his suitcase on a couch in the sitting room. He drank his coffee standing up while he studied the front door. I could smell the cardamom in the honey-toffee cake as I put it in the warming drawer to rise.

"You'll need to get a new lock put in," he said. He took some tools out from one of the plastic bags, and fixed a big bolt on the front and the back of the door. "That will have to do for now. Here's the padlock and keys for the front bolt."

He put them on the table, next to a bag of flour. He fixed a smaller bolt on the window with a broken lock. I didn't tell him that I liked to leave my doors and windows open.

"Are you hungry?" I said.

"I brought some pies," he said, pointing to a package on the chair.

"Oh, okay," I said, washing my hands. I dried them on a dishcloth. "I've made tamatiebredie, Detective."

"Call me Henk."

"And honey-toffee snake cake," I said.

I couldn't get my tongue to say his first name.

"Sjoe. I guess I could have those pies for lunch tomorrow."

He pointed to my face.

"You've got some flour there. On your cheek."

I wiped it with the back of my hand.

"You missed it," he said.

I tried again.

He shook his head and came closer to me. I could feel the warmth coming off his body, like he had just come out of the oven. He was a lot taller than me. I could see the red and copper hairs on his chest. His hand brushed my cheek, next to my mouth.

"There," he said.

He smelled like fresh-baked cinnamon bread and honey. He stepped back. My mouth felt dry. I poured myself some coffee, my hands shaking. When I picked the cup up, the coffee spilled onto my hand.

"You all right?" he said.

I put the cup down, and wiped my hands on my apron.

"It's been quite a day," I said.

"Sit down," he said.

I sat. I put my elbows on the table and rested my forehead on my hands.

"Have you got some brandewyn?" he said.

I pointed to the top cupboard. He found the brandy behind the vanilla extract and poured some into a glass, then stirred in a spoon of sugar and put it in front of me. The brandewyn was sweet and warm and made a small fire inside my belly.

"For the shock," he said.

He was talking about the veldskoene on my doorstep. And yes, that was scary. But the thing that was making my whole body shake was the shock of a man touching my face. With gentleness.

FIFTY

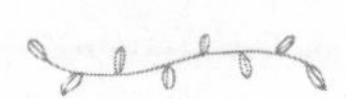

Maybe it was the brandy, because I hardly ever drink, but that whole night felt like a dream.

Henk Kannemeyer wiped down the kitchen table and found plates and knives and forks, which he laid out nicely. He checked the rice on the stove, and when it was ready he put it on the table.

"I can smell that bredie, but I can't see it," he said.

I pointed out the hotbox, and he put the bredie on the table, and dished up my plate and then his.

"Eat," he said.

I was staring at the plate and the table with wide eyes. I had never seen a table laid and a plate dished up by a man before. It looked fine. The smell of the tomato stew came swimming up to me, and I ate.

"When must the cake come out?" he said.

I couldn't believe I had forgotten the cake. I had remembered to put it in the oven but not to take it out. I looked at the clock.

"In two minutes," I said.

Then I forgot about it again. But he remembered it.

When we'd finished our dinner, he put the honey-toffee snake cake on the table, together with small plates and cake forks. He had chosen the salad plates instead of the cake plates but it didn't matter.

"You are a fine cook, Maria. I haven't had food as good as this in a while."

He smiled at me. But his eyes looked sad.

Then the brandy made me ask, "Do you not have a wife, Detective?"

The sadness in his eyes turned to pain, and he looked away.

"She was a really good cook," he said, then he swallowed. "She died four years ago. Four years and three months."

"I'm sorry," I said.

But I was not really sorry at all. I felt so pleased that he had no wife that my heart did a little dance. Then I felt terrible that I was glad. I could feel his pain even from across the table.

"I'm sorry, Henk," I said again, and this time I meant it.

I cut a big piece of cake and put it on his plate. The honey-toffee had seeped nicely into the top crust, and the almonds were toasted and caramelized. When we had finished our cake we just sat and listened to the frogs.

He sat still, looking at the table, while I tidied and washed up.

It was a quiet evening. But although we didn't talk much, it felt like a lot was said.

Then the strangest thing happened, while I was standing there at the sink, with my hands in the soapy water, and the big man at the table behind me, and my tummy full of good food and brandy. I felt a new kind of happiness. A different kind of happy from when I bake a good cake, or see my chickens, or get a visit from Hattie.

I was getting a taste of something I had always been hungry for but never knew how to cook. Maybe I was going to have a real life before death after all.

Detective Kannemeyer went around the house locking up. The sash windows in my bedroom allowed an opening at the top, and I was glad to see he left a gap for fresh air.

He laid a sleeping bag out on the couch.

"There's a bed for you in the spare room," I said.

"I can hear better from here," he said. "He might try the front door."

He went outside and walked around the property with a flashlight. I brought the bedding through from the spare room, and made up the couch with sheets and pillows. On a warm night like tonight, a sleeping bag can get too hot, and a sheet can be just right.

I brushed my teeth and put on my nightie, bathrobe, and just a little bit of lipstick. Then I went to say good night.

"I'm a light sleeper," he said, "but if you hear anything—anything at all—wake me."

When I lay down, my head felt very light. It might have been the brandy evaporating. My door was a little open and I heard him walking to the bathroom and wondered if he had brought his toothbrush and pajamas.

I heard him lie down on the couch. I listened to the frogs sing and an owl calling and its mate answering. Then there was a low growling sound. I sat up. I wasn't very frightened—it sounded like an animal, not a murderer. I got out of bed and walked toward my door. The growling got louder. It was inside the house! I was about to call Kannemeyer when I realized I knew that sound. The sound of a man snoring. I tiptoed to the living room. Henk was lying fully clothed on top of all the bedding, his mouth slightly open, snoring evenly. I stood for a moment and watched the rise and fall of his chest.

He twitched and then he was sitting up, a gun in his hand.

"Maria?"

"Sorry," I said. "I heard a growling sound, but it was you snoring. I'd forgotten . . ."

"Ag, sorry," he said. "I'll lie on my side."

"No," I said. "Don't. I like it."

He laughed. A deep, warm sound, even nicer than the growling. He was still looking at me.

I realized that the moonlight was behind me. My nightie was made of thin cotton.

I blushed. My face was burning. I walked backward, bumped into the wall, then hurried back to my room.

I closed my bedroom door and jumped back into bed. Even my husband had never seen me naked. Even when we were, you know, intimate, I kept the sheets on me. Henk Kannemeyer had seen me. The full shape of me, against the moonlight.

My whole body was blushing. My breasts, my thighs, were so hot I had to touch them just to make sure I was not really on fire.

FIFTY-ONE

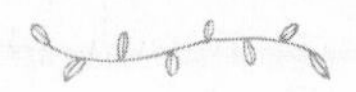

I was hot, and could not sleep, even when I threw off my sheet and lay there in just my nightie. I wanted to open my window wide, but I didn't want to make a noise that Kannemeyer would hear.

I listened to the sounds of the night and Kannemeyer's soft growl. It was not loud, but I could feel it in my whole body. After a while the snoring stopped. The frogs were still carrying on. A cool breeze came, but it didn't bring sleep. Then the frogs finally went quiet and it was just the crickets, and now and then the sound of a faraway truck on Route 62. And then, at last, there was nothing. Just the silence.

I fell into the deep silence of the Klein Karoo.

I woke, tangled in my nightie. The sun was bright and the birds had finished saying good morning to each other long ago. I closed my door and put on my veldskoene and my brown dress. It wasn't that pretty but it fit. I went to the bathroom to freshen up. I brushed my hair and put on my lipstick before going into the living room. It was empty. The sheets were folded neatly on the couch.

The front door was unbolted and I stuck my head out.

"Good morning, Mevrou," said Vorster.

"Hallo, Sergeant Vorster," I said. "Where's Kannemeyer?"

"At work."

"Coffee?" I offered.

"Please."

Of course he went to work. I looked at the kitchen clock. Eight o'clock. I looked around for a note. Why should he leave me a note? He's a policeman not a . . . whatever I was imagining. Surely as a police guard he would say good-bye, or check on me.

Then I remembered my bedroom door. It was slightly open that morning and I was sure I'd left it closed. He'd have knocked and when I didn't answer he would have checked to see that I was okay.

He had seen me, in the full light, hardly dressed, there on the bed.

I felt sick. The moonlight may have shown him my shape, but the sunlight would have shown him the worst truth of me. The uncooked dough of my legs. My hair all messed up. My breasts without a bra.

I made coffee and took Vorster his cup on the stoep along with some honey-cake. I sat at the kitchen table and dipped a rusk into my coffee, but I did not feel like biting into it. I put the soggy rusk onto the saucer. It was breakfast time, but I wasn't hungry.

"Maybe I'm coming down with something," I said to the rusk. "My belly feels strange."

I drank my coffee and threw out some mielies for the chickens. Then I packed most of that snake cake in a Tupperware for Jessie, and headed into town.

Hattie was in the *Gazette* office, but no Jessie. I put her cake in the fridge.

"Golly, Tannie Maria," said Hattie, "you look terrible."

"I know," I said.

"Have you got Jessie's sickness?"

"Maybe," I said. "How is she?"

"She's not coming in today, but she can't be too bad because she's done a lot of work from home. She's written an article on fracking. I've just posted it on our website. There's also a nice piece about Grace Zihlangu, Van Schalkwyk's domestic worker. Both articles are rather provocative, but that's our Jessie."

Hattie put on the kettle at my desk.

"Let me make you some tea for a change," she said. "Here's some mail for you. That letter on top was stuck under the door this morning."

Who would have made a hand delivery? I picked up the small white envelope. TANNIE MARIA it said. In capitals. Underlined. Nothing else written on the front or the back.

Inside, a lined sheet of paper was folded into four. I sat down and spread it out in front of me.

Dear Tannie Maria,

Please will you help me. I don't know what to do. It's like this. There's this girl. Even when I was young I knew she was the one for me.

I sighed. There was no escaping this love sickness. Hattie added milk and sugar to my tea and handed it to me.

"Thank you, skat," I said.

She offered me beskuit, but I shook my head.

"Good heavens," said Hattie. "What's wrong, Maria?"

"I think it's my tummy," I said.

"I've never seen you like this."

"It kind of hurts," I said.

"It does sound like Jessie's problem."

"I'll be okay," I said.

Hattie took her tea to her desk and I went back to my letter.

We've always been just friends. Then she went away and came back and she was all clever but she was still my same girl and this time it seemed like she was interested in me, in that way, you know. But she said she didn't want a boyfriend and she wanted to be independent and all that. But then one night it just happened. She was in my arms, and—you know.

I had a sip of my tea. It wasn't bad. Harriet was much better at making tea than coffee.

I don't have the right words. I can just say it was awesome. I thought it was special for us both, I really did. I remembered her independence story and I didn't want to pressure her so I thought I'd let her phone me but she didn't. Then the next night I was out with the guys watching rugby and she came in with a friend and said hello but was not very friendly, so I thought okay, maybe she doesn't want it to go public about us. I really wanted things to work out between us, so I was happy to do whatever she wanted. She didn't invite me over to sit with them. They were getting stacks of drinks from other guys. I just watched the rugby.

The phone rang and Hattie got it.

"Harriet Christie," she said. "Hello, Mr. Marius."

Then she was quiet for a long time as if he was talking and talking. She would say "But—" or "Mr. Marius—" like she was trying to speak but he wouldn't let her. I got on with my letter.

She didn't really say good-bye when she left. But I still hoped she would be my girlfriend and we would work something out. The next day I phoned her a few times, but she didn't answer my calls. Then on Monday I went to see her at work. She looked at me like she hated me and walked out.

I don't know what to do. I suppose I should give up on her because it obviously didn't mean anything to her and she doesn't want to be seen with me. But I somehow can't give up.

Can you help?

He did not sign it. But I could guess who it was from.

FIFTY-TWO

Mr. Marius," said Hattie into the phone, "if you will just let me get a word in—" Her face was pale, with spots of pink high on her cheeks. "This is an independent newspaper. Sponsorship does not mean you own us—"

Mr. Marius blasted so loud that even I could hear him. Not the words, just the sound—like an angry monkey. Hattie held the phone away from her ear.

"We have journalistic standards—," she said when there was a pause in his noise.

Then I heard the monkey again, this time the words he was shouting too: "You'll be sorry!"

Hattie looked at the receiver.

"Fiddlesticks," she said. "He slammed the phone down."

I clicked my tongue.

"So rude," she said, tapping the pencil on her desk, and her foot on the floor.

She picked up her tea and had a sip. I could see from her face that it was cold, so I put the kettle on.

"It's Jessie's articles," she said. "About fracking and on Grace. Too political, he says. He wants them removed from our website and not printed in the paper."

"I don't like that man," I said.

"He's the chairman of the Ladismith Chamber of Commerce," said Hattie, and sighed. "We can't lose their support."

Hattie was like a tall strong tree. Now she was bent over, as if a storm wind was blowing her. But she was not broken.

I gave us each a fresh cup of tea, and put extra sugar in hers to get the color right on her face.

"Do have a look at the website," she said. "Tell me what you think of Jessie's articles. I'm going to phone around a bit, talk to some of our other sponsors."

I sat down at Jessie's computer, clicked on the picture of the *Gazette*, and the website opened up. Websites are confusing for me, like a shopping mall with bright lights instead of a nice corner shop. But I found my way to Jessie's articles.

Jessie writes much more smartly than she talks, but her articles are not difficult to read. They are always alive and full of stories and quotes. The one about Grace was called "At the End of the Day." She was telling Grace's story, but she was also talking about domestic workers all over. How hard they work, with so few rights. She made you care about this one woman, Grace, and her loss and her dreams. She didn't say it right out, but it was obvious Jessie thought that if Grace's employer did not help her out, he must be a really mean man. I suppose Mr. Marius might read this as an insult to himself.

"Oh, bollocks," said Hattie, putting down the phone. "The manager of the Spar, Cornelius van Wyk, agrees with Mr. Marius. He complains that our journalists are doing investigations instead of just reporting. He says the chamber could withdraw sponsorship."

"Oh, Hats," I said.

"I'm going to phone Mrs. van der Spuy, she's the secretary," said Hattie.

Mrs. van der Spuy owned Mandy's Furniture Shop on the corner.

"Ask her if she's got some honey," I said.

She had her own hives.

I started reading the article about fracking. It was called "No Fracking Way"—the same as John's car sticker. It wasn't as personal as the article about Grace, but it did have some nice quotes. Some guy who swam with polar bears had a lot to say. He described how damaging fracking had been in other parts of the world. And told of how bad it could be for the Karoo and the whole of South Africa. The fracking chemicals could poison our water supply and our giant pools of underground water. And the government was supporting the mining companies, like Shaft, because they had so much money.

"Oh dear," I said.

Jessie also spoke about climate change and renewable energy—like the sun, or the wind—that could do a better job than gas, oil, and coal. But it's harder to make profits from renewable energy, because nobody owns the "rights" to the sun and wind, like they own rights to gas and coal. It sounded like it was all about money, not about what was good for the Karoo.

I didn't understand everything she was saying, but I understood enough to get me worried about poisoned water, and what this would mean for the people and plants of the Klein Karoo. And the bokmakieries and the jackals and the frogs. It also made me think that John was maybe not as crazy as he seemed. Fracking was worth getting cross about. I wasn't sure why Marius was so upset by the article. If he cared about the Karoo, he should want people here to know the dangers of fracking.

"She's got honey," said Hattie, standing up and helping herself to a beskuit. "Mrs. van der Spuy. And she still supports us, thank heavens. She says I should come to the next chamber of commerce meeting. Marius or Van Wyk may withdraw their own adverts, but the chamber of commerce funding can't be cut off without a majority vote from all the businesses."

"They can't all be as crazy as Marius," I said. "Do you think Shaft might be buying his support?"

"Who knows? That chap would take money from the devil. If he's not the devil himself."

"These are good articles, Hattie."

I turned off Jessie's computer.

"It's going to print, as is," she said.

Hattie was standing up straight again, like the wind had passed. But I felt the storm wasn't over.

FIFTY-THREE

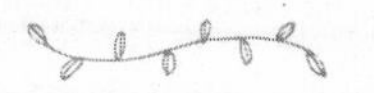

I went back to my desk and picked up that hand-delivered letter.

"I think it's time for Jessie to come back to work," I said.

"I do wonder what's going on with her," Hattie said.

"She's got a broken heart," I said. "But it can be fixed."

I phoned the police station and asked for Reghardt but he wasn't there and they wouldn't give me his cell number.

"Reghardt?" said Hattie, raising her eyebrow. "I have his cell number. Is he the heartbreaker?"

"He's also got a broken heart," I said.

There was a knock on the door.

"Hey y'all," said Candice, stepping in.

She had leather sandals on so we had not heard her usual clip-clopping. She wore a cream dress that fit her just right. She smelled of lemon blossoms and her lipstick and her toenails were a pearly pink. She probably looked good in her sleep.

"Maria?" Candice said.

"Sorry, I was just thinking," I said. "What did you say?"

"The funeral's all set for tomorrow. How's it going with y'all? Can I help out any?"

"That night you went out with Jessie and got drunk," I said. "Where did you sleep?"

Harriet frowned at me.

"Would you like some tea, Candice?" she asked.

"Sure, thanks," Candy said. "I was too drunk to drive. That nice young fella, the policeman, he took me home. To the Sunshine B and B, where I'm staying."

"Reghardt?"

She nodded.

"It's important, Candy, that you tell me the truth," I said. "It will really help our investigation."

"Truly, that's what happened. I wasn't so pickled that I can't remember. We made a bit of a racket getting in and the owner got up."

"So Reghardt went home with you?"

Candice laughed.

"Oh, no! He just helped me to my room. I wasn't walking so well. The owner, Mr. Wessels, stood frowning at us and let Reghardt out himself."

"So nothing happened between you and Reghardt?"

"Hell, no," she said. "He's a sweet little guy, but not my type. And I'm not his. He's got a girlfriend."

"He told you that?"

"Yeah, he seemed real proud of her. Didn't tell me her name."

"It's Jessie," I said.

"Oh hell, damn," said Candice, "does she think . . . ?"

I nodded. Candice sat down and Hattie handed her a cup of tea.

"The poor thing," Candy said.

"Could you give me that number, Hats?" I said.

Reghardt answered on the first ring.

"Jessie?" he said.

"It's Tannie Maria," I said. "I got a letter from a young man. I'd like to help him. I was thinking maybe you could give me some advice about what to say . . ."

Reghardt was quiet.

"His girlfriend is ignoring him because she thinks he spent the night with another woman," I said.

"But why would she think that?"

"Because she heard about him leaving a bar with his arm around another woman."

"What?"

"One who was beautiful and drunk."

"Oh, that. She was too drunk to drive."

"Ja."

"So I, I mean he, took her home."

"Ja, and . . . ?"

"And? And nothing. Oh, no—she thinks . . . Ag, nee."

"She's really upset. The man is someone special to her."

"He is?"

"I don't think he should give up on her."

"You don't?"

"What should I tell him to do?"

"Maybe he can ask her friends to tell her the truth. Do you think they'd do that, Tannie?"

"If she's feeling really hurt, she might be ignoring her friends too. I think he must write her a letter telling her what happened and how he feels about her. And then he must go around to her himself. If she won't see him, he can leave the letter."

"Ja, that's good advice, Tannie. You should tell him that."

"It won't do any harm to give her some koeksisters. She really likes koeksisters."

Just as I put the phone down it rang again and I picked up. It was Nurse Mostert from the hospital.

"They've gone," she told me. "Anna and Dirk. Just now they were eating breakfast and, next thing, they've disappeared."

"What about the police guards?"

"You won't believe this, but they made friends with each other. Dirk and Anna. Stopped fighting. So the police left."

"And Dirk and Anna weren't discharged?"

"No. And another thing. An ambulance, it's been stolen."

"You think they took it?"

"Who would drive? Her leg is in a plaster cast. His arm is in a sling . . . I can't understand it. I phoned the police. But I also thought I should tell you."

"What is it?" asked Candice as I hung up.

"It's Dirk and Anna. Disappeared. And so has an ambulance."

"In their condition . . . ," said Hattie.

"They've got one good pair of arms and legs between them," I said. "If they worked together, they'd be a whole person. But could they steal an ambulance?"

Hattie laughed.

"Honestly. Those two, working together?" she said.

"Nurse Mostert says they made up. They're friends now."

"Where would they go?" said Candice.

"Looking for revenge," I said. "And I think it's my fault. They listened to me for a change . . . Candice, can we take your car? It's faster. Let's go to John's farm."

"You think they blame him for Martine's murder?" said Hattie.

I nodded and asked Candy, "Have you got a cell phone?"

"Yeah."

"Hattie, we'll call you when we get there, but phone the police in the meantime. Tell Kannemeyer the story and ask him to send a van out to John's."

The top was up, so we didn't have that wild wind, but the car was going fast. Very fast. It was okay though—Candy was a good driver. As we shot out of town, I looked at the yellow and purple flowers that were coming up all over the veld. Candy saw them too.

"Beautiful," she said.

"It's the rain," I said. "They come out after the rain."

"Beautiful," she said again.

"Are you just born with beauty?" I asked, looking at her

smooth peach skin and golden hair. "Or can it grow on you like flowers? How do *you* do it?"

She smiled.

"Beauty is my career."

"I couldn't wear your kind of clothes," I said.

"No. You'd have to find the right clothes for you. That show off your best parts."

"Hah. I've got no best parts."

"Nonsense. Your face, your hips, and your breasts are in a perfect ratio. Excellent curves. And your hands and ankles are real cute. I know just the style for you. If you like, I'll get my shop to send up something. What are you, a fourteen? And shoes. A six?"

I nodded and looked down at my brown dress and khaki veldskoene. They were very practical, but even I could tell they weren't the best style for me. My dress size used to be a ten, before I married, then a twelve, and now it's fourteen.

"I can't wear those fancy New York clothes," I said.

"It's on the house."

"It won't help . . ."

"Oh, nonsense. You're lovely. And you've got good skin, even though it's so hot and dry here. What do you use?"

"Olive oil."

"And as we get older we've got to watch the exercise and diet a bit more."

"Is that your secret?"

"Secret? I've got no secrets."

We were passing a grove of bright green spekboom trees.

"I guess there is one secret I've learned," she said. "Clothes, skin, makeup can all help. But if a woman thinks she looks good, she glows with her own special beauty."

"Ja, maybe, but even if she's thinking and glowing and all, will a man see her beauty?"

"Men aren't as dumb as they seem, Maria."

"Look," I said, "a bokkie."

"What?"

"A little buck, there, in the shadow of the spekboom. By those big rocks. A steenbokkie."

But she couldn't see it. It's easy to see bright flowers, but you need the right kind of eyes to see a brown animal in the shade.

Maybe I would find a man with the right kind of eyes.

FIFTY-FOUR

"There's the sign," I said. "Wild Things Organic Farm."

Candice swerved onto the dust road. A mongoose dived into the bushes. We headed up toward the farmhouse that was on the foothills of the Swartberge. The veld looked green and healthy here. There was long grass and flowers growing between the bushes and trees. A line of sweet thorn and other trees ran down from a kloof, so there was probably a riverbed. There were also those old gwarries and spekboom trees all over the veld.

"Slow down a second," I said to Candy.

We were passing a grove of trees, with a strange fence around it.

"Pomegranate trees," I said. "But the fruit is small and green."

"Looks like an electric fence," said Candy. "Attached to solar panels."

She was right—there were two panels at the bottom of the field, catching the sun.

"What's that barking sound?" she said.

"Baboons," I said, hoping it wasn't Dirk and Anna we were hearing.

But it was baboons. As we turned a bend in the road, we saw them running out of a greenhouse. They were galloping out, their arms full of stuff, like rude customers at a summer sale. One baboon was sitting on the glass roof eating a bunch of black grapes.

Ahead of us was the farmhouse.

"There's the ambulance," said Candice.

"Your phone?" I said.

We parked next to the ambulance. Candy handed me her phone and I called Hattie.

"The ambulance is here," I said.

"Goodness! Is everything all right?"

"I don't know yet. We're going in now. Are the police coming?"

"Finally got through to Kannemeyer. He's leaving now. I'll call him again to confirm that the ambulance is there. Maria, please do be careful."

Candy and I got out and walked to a wheelchair that was on its side at the foot of the stoep stairs. It looked like Anna's wheelchair. But where was she?

The stoep was big and wide, with a corrugated-iron roof and wrought-iron broekie-lace around the edges. One of those really old farmhouses. It had been nicely whitewashed but there were some dusty cracks where the thick mud-brick walls needed repairs. A skinny woman in denim overalls was standing on the stoep, looking in through the doorway.

"Just leave him alone!" she shouted.

Candice trotted past her, and I followed.

"Careful," she said to us, "they're crazy."

"Stay away!" called Anna, as we walked inside. "Or we'll kill him."

"Anna," I said.

"Dirk," said Candice, her hands on her hips.

Anna and Dirk looked up at us as if they were two dogs that we had caught up to no good. But they did not let go of their prey. John was lying facedown, with Dirk sitting on his back, pinning him to the floor. Dirk's eyes were wild, and his arms were still in a sling and a bandage, but he had a good grip on

John with his legs. His hairy bum peeped out from the gap in the green hospital gown. Anna was sitting beside John on the floor, her gown neatly closed. The leg with the bandage was tucked under her and the plaster-cast leg stuck out straight in front. With one hand she was pressing a long metal pipe across the side of John's neck and in her other was a big syringe jabbed just beneath his ear.

The metal looked like the stand that supported a hospital drip. Anna's cheeks were pink and her hair was wild. Wild Things Organic Farm, I thought.

"What are you doing, Anna?" I asked.

"Eep," said John.

Anna sniffed, and tightened her grip on the pole and the syringe.

"It's got air in it," said the woman at the door. "She said she'd inject it into his bloodstream and kill him if I came inside or phoned the police."

Candice pulled up two chairs and we sat down. The woman stepped inside. She found a third chair and the three of us sat in a line, facing them in our front-row seats.

"Are they escaped lunatics?" the woman asked us.

Candice nodded. I shook my head.

"We know he did it," said Anna. "He just won't talk."

"Did what?" said overalls girl.

"Killed Tienie," said Anna.

"Slept with my wife," said Dirk at the same time.

"What's going on, John?" said Overalls.

" 'Elp," John squeaked.

"These three people were in love with the same woman," said Candice. "Martine. She was murdered. The two of them are blaming John."

"Lawrence saw your car that day," said Dirk. "That's why you killed him."

"Martine?" said Overalls. "That woman in the photos? You were still seeing her?"

John wheezed.

"I found photos of this woman," she told the two of us in the front row, "that he kept in a book by his bed. After we'd been together for a year!" She turned back to John. "You promised me you'd never see her again."

John's tongue was sticking out between his lips.

"Did you see her again, John?" asked Overalls.

John looked like he was trying to shake his head, but he was not in the right position for it.

"Anna," I said, "how is he going to talk if you keep squashing his neck like that?"

Anna released her grip on the pole, but kept the syringe in place. John sucked some air in.

"Help," he said.

Overalls folded her arms.

"Did you?"

"I did nothing wrong," said John.

"You called out her name, John. At just the wrong time. I pretended I didn't notice. Martine, you said, when you should have been calling Didi. My name. Didi."

"Did you visit Martine?" I asked.

John sniffled. Anna pressed the pipe down again, and he made a noise like a choking chicken. She released the pressure.

"Please don't kill me," he said.

"The truth, John," said Didi.

"I did go see her. Not because I loved her. But because of the fracking."

"I knew it!" said Dirk.

He bounced his weight on John's back and I thought I heard something crack.

"No!" John said. "Not that. Hydraulic fracking. The mining companies are doing it to look for gas. They are buying up farms and I think Marius is working for them. For Shaft. He wanted to buy your land, and I was telling Martine that she mustn't sell. Fracking will destroy the Klein Karoo."

"Ja, it's very bad, fracking," I said. "You'll see Jessie's article in tomorrow's *Gazette*."

"So you still love her," said Didi.

"No. I love you, Didi. She was in my past. Help me here."

"Did you ever take her pomegranate juice?" I asked.

"No," he said. "No."

"Do you have pomegranate juice?" I asked Didi.

"It's not the season," said Didi. "They ripen in March."

"Nothing frozen?" I asked.

She shook her head.

"What about in that greenhouse, where you make things ripen early?"

Didi looked at John.

"You have a pomegranate tree in there, John, haven't you? Are they ripe?"

"No," said John. "Green. Please. Let me up, I can't breathe."

"That Mr. Marius," said Dirk, shifting his weight to turn to Anna. "Do you think he did it because Martine wouldn't sell?"

John moaned under Dirk's movements.

"Dirk," I said, "you and Anna need to be in the hospital getting better. The funeral is tomorrow."

"I don't trust that Mr. Marius," said John. "If he's working with Shaft . . . And he wanted that land for fracking . . . What would he do to a woman like Martine who stood in his way?"

Anna loosened her grip on the pole and took the syringe needle out of John's neck. She was gazing into a corner of the room. She said something under her breath that was hard to catch. But Dirk and John heard her, and they both nodded. I knew what it was because I'd heard her say it before: "I'll kill him."

Dirk climbed off John, and sat down in an armchair. Anna pushed the pole aside and poked the syringe under a chair cushion. She used her arms to pull herself a little away from John, and stretched the leg under her alongside her plaster cast. John turned himself onto his back and stroked his ribs.

"That blerrie fracking donder," said Dirk.

"We'll get him," said John.

John looked at Anna and then Anna looked at Dirk. These were very different looks from the earlier ones of hatred and fear. They were like naughty children now, hatching a secret plan.

There was the sound of a car racing along the dirt road toward us.

"It's the police," I said.

"How about some tea?" said Didi, getting up.

The show was over. I went to help her in the kitchen.

Then they were at the door. Kannemeyer and Piet. Kannemeyer cleared his throat. Candice stood up, and gave him a sunshine smile. One of those smiles that showed off her long legs and pearly toenails.

"Well, hello, big guy," she said.

She wasn't talking to Piet.

FIFTY-FIVE

Kannemeyer smiled at Candy then frowned at the rest of us. He gave me an extra-big frown.

He said, "All right, what's going on here?"

"Niks nie," said Anna, wiggling the toes on both her feet.

"Nothing," echoed John, sitting up, holding his ribs.

Dirk just said nothing.

"These beskuit look good," I said to Didi as I carried them to the coffee table in the living room, along with the cups. "Did you make them?"

"Organic muesli rusks," she said, putting her tea tray down on the same table.

Kannemeyer looked at me as if it was all my fault and shook his head.

Piet was moving between us like a mongoose through the grass. He looked at the back of John's neck. There was a spot of blood on it. He found the syringe under the cushion, but he didn't touch it. He put his hands on the cushions on our front-row seats.

"Please help yourself to milk and sugar," said Didi, pouring from the teapot.

Candice added milk to one cup, and milk and two sugars to another.

"Coffee," said Dirk, adjusting his green robe to be respectable.

"Ja, coffee, please," said Kannemeyer.

Anna and John also grunted agreement. Didi put down the teapot and went into the kitchen to prepare coffee.

Candice took a beskuit and the sweet tea to Kannemeyer. He thanked her. I watched him sip from his cup and look at her as she smiled and drank her own tea. It was hard not to look at her. She knew how well that little cream dress fit her, and she was glowing.

Piet pulled Kannemeyer aside to tell him what had happened. I could see from the story of Piet's hands that he had a good idea of the truth.

I also wanted coffee, but it seemed rude to leave all that tea, so I poured myself a cup and went and stood by the kitchen door. It was open and I looked out onto a wild garden with big camphor trees. I wasn't hungry, but I went back to the living room to get a rusk—just for the company. Kannemeyer was listening to Piet and watching Candy. I went out the kitchen door, and stood with my rusk and tea in the shade of a camphor tree.

I stood between a buchu shrub and a bitterbos plant. The sky was big and bright blue. Too bright. I was feeling blue, but not that bright kind of blue, the other kind.

I drank some tea and looked down at the greenhouse. The baboons were gone. I finished the tea and put the cup down next to a slangbos.

"We've got a murder to investigate," I told the rusk, which I hadn't eaten.

It looked good, but not as good as my mother's muesli beskuit, and I still wasn't hungry.

We marched out into the sun, the rusk and I, in the direction of the greenhouse. I trampled some heart-seed love grass with my veldskoene. The vetplantjies and vygies were all flowering after the rain. I stepped on a little mouse-fig succulent and its iridescent petals were crushed under my heel.

I was sorry I had stepped on the mouse fig, and I placed my feet more carefully. I found a narrow dirt path and followed it down to the greenhouse. It was not a long walk, but it was hot. I was glad to reach the shade of a rhus tree that stood at the entrance to the glass room.

"Blikemmer," I said to the rusk. "What a mess."

You could tell a troop of baboons had run wild there. Pots of soil were knocked over and plants were broken. There were squashed red and green things on the floor that were maybe once fruits or vegetables. In the corner I saw what I was looking for.

"A pomegranate tree," I said to the rusk, "but there's no fruit on it. Not even tiny green fruit."

I walked between some blobs of red and purple. Tomatoes and grapes, I think.

"But there was fruit on it," said a voice.

I jumped and looked down at the beskuit in my hand. For a moment I thought I had finally gone crazy, and my rusk was talking back to me. But then Piet was by my side.

"Jinne, Piet, you walk like a cat," I said. "I didn't hear you."

Piet ran his fingers over the tips of a pomegranate branch. "You see—it was plucked here."

"Was it ripe?" I asked.

He shrugged.

"Those bloody baboons," I said.

"Let's ask them," he said.

He pointed to a tomato-colored paw print on the floor. I walked behind Piet as he followed their tracks out of the greenhouse, then across a field and into the dry riverbed. Even I could see their prints there in the sand. I stood in the shade of the sweet thorns and wild olives, and looked up towards the kloof, where Piet was pointing.

The trees were flowering, and the air was full of bees and the sweet smell of blossoms. Piet walked ahead of me, up the sandy bed. He stopped often to look at ants so I could catch up with him. I also stopped to watch the ants so my breath could catch up with me. There were lines of them marching along, carrying pollen and flowers.

We walked up the dry river toward the mountain. I was glad I was wearing my veldskoene. They know how to walk on the sand and stones. We came to a big gwarrie tree. Piet nodded to it as if he was greeting an old woman, then he crouched on his haunches in its shade. I stood beside him in the cool, and let my breathing slow down. He rested his hand gently on one of its branches. His pale brown skin was rough and dry, like the dark skin of the gwarrie bark, and his face was wrinkled like its leaves. Gwarries grow very slowly, and the trunk of this one was thick—it must have been a few thousand years old. Piet's people, the Bushmen, had been around many thousands of years. He said something I couldn't hear to the tree before we stepped out again into the patchy shade of the riverbed.

Piet tapped his ear, and I listened. Baboons were barking from inside the kloof. Soon we were in the shade of the mountain—close to the ravine. Piet pointed up at a giant fig tree in the kloof, its gray roots wrapped around big stones.

The baboons were having a picnic in the tree. As we got closer, they moved farther up its branches. Two young ones were chasing each other, fighting over some grapes. A baby baboon was attached to its mama's belly, holding a red tomato in its mouth.

Piet looked around the base of the tree. He found a piece of melon rind, and some green leaves, but they had not left much else.

Piet pointed out a big baboon. The baboon was holding on to something in one paw and scratching his tummy with the other. He showed us his teeth. I think he wanted my rusk. I gave the rusk to Piet. Piet chewed on it and looked up at the baboon. The baboon grunted and bared its teeth again.

When he had finished eating, Piet picked up a white stone from the riverbed.

He took a few steps back and shouted, "Jou skollie!"

Then he threw the stone at the big baboon and it hit him—*thwock*—on his hairy belly.

You could see the baboon didn't like being called a scallywag, because he barked very loudly and threw something down at Piet. This was followed by a noisy storm of barking and a rain of food flying down at us. Something hard hit me on the head. It hurt.

"Bliksem," I said, rubbing the spot.

The baboons jumped from the tree onto the mountain cliffs and made unhappy grunting barks. We had really messed up their picnic. In the sand around us were grapes and melon rinds and tomatoes. On his face Piet had tomato splatter and a smile.

There at my feet—the thing that had whacked me on the head—was a half-eaten ripe pomegranate, its seeds red and glistening like jewels.

FIFTY-SIX

"How come I always find you in the middle of the trouble, Mrs. van Harten?" said Kannemeyer.

We were back, on the stoep of the farmhouse. Piet handed him the pomegranate. He looked from the fruit to Piet to me. Inside I could hear John moaning, and Didi fussing over him.

"The baboons," I said, "they took it from the greenhouse."

"Nice work," Kannemeyer said to the pomegranate. "You went baboon chasing?"

"Piet found them," I said, "in a fig tree."

"That woman, Candice, she took Anna and Dirk to go and see the boy in George. Tell him about his ma."

"Oh."

"I told them now was not a good time to go," he said. "But the people around here don't listen to me."

Piet was looking at the ants on the other end of the stoep.

"Could you drive the ambulance back to the hospital?" said Kannemeyer. "With John. He needs to get his ribs checked."

"Did they tell you what happened here?"

"No. But we worked it out." He shook his head. "Of course, no one wants to press charges."

"At least Anna and Dirk have stopped fighting," I said.

"With each other, maybe."

"What are you going to do about that?" I said, looking at the pomegranate in his hand.

"Have a word with John."

"Best when she's not around," I said.

He nodded. He looked out on to the blue slopes of the mountain.

"This Candy woman," he said, "you're friendly with her."

"Kind of," I said.

Now he was calling her Candy.

Piet looked at me, then Kannemeyer, then back at me, like something was about to happen.

"What do you know about her?" asked the detective.

"I told you about her yesterday. She's Martine's cousin."

He hadn't asked me about Candy yesterday. But now that he had seen her, he wanted to know all about her.

"Tell me more," he said.

I shrugged.

"She drinks," I said. Then I felt stupid. "Sometimes. She was upset about Martine."

Kannemeyer smoothed the tips of his mustache.

"Why do you ask?" I said.

"Just interested," said Kannemeyer.

Hattie came to fetch me from the hospital in her Etios. As I got in, she handed me a brown envelope with a Riversdale postmark.

"It was sent priority mail," she said. "So I thought it might be urgent."

I had thought of walking down to the *Gazette,* rather than asking her for a lift, but my legs were walked out and the day was just too hot. At least her car had air-conditioning. I breathed in a big mouthful of cool air as we jerked across the parking lot.

"So, do tell, Maria, what did you find?"

She was on the wrong side of the road, and she scraped lightly against a low wall to avoid hitting an oncoming car.

I gave her the latest circus, baboon, and pomegranate report. She shook her head and clicked her tongue and asked questions in all the right places. Hattie was a good listener, even if she was a bad driver.

"You must have missed lunch?" she said, as we raced down Hospital Hill.

"Ja," I said.

"Me too," she said. "I thought we could go for a chicken pie."

"I'm not hungry," I said.

She slammed on her brakes and pulled over to the side of the road, bumping into the trunk of a jacaranda tree.

"Maria," she said, "are you going to tell me what's going on with you?"

I watched a few purple flowers land on the bonnet of her car. Loosened by the thud.

She said, "The detective called me. He told me what happened. With your shoes."

Some insect in the tree was creaking like a door that needed oil.

"I didn't want to worry you," I said.

"For heaven's sake, don't be an idiot," she said. "Why don't you come and stay with me for a few days?"

"Did the detective put you up to this?"

"The man is worried for your safety," she said. "And I'm worried about more than that. You're not yourself."

Now the insect was creaking double time. Calling for a mate, I suppose.

"I'm tired," I said. "I didn't sleep well last night."

"Now you say you're tired. Earlier you said your tummy was sore, and that you've got Jessie's sickness. Now it turns out she wasn't sick after all. Well, lovesick maybe."

I heard what sounded like another insect replying to the first one. *Creak. Creak-creak.*

"Well, I never . . . ," said Hattie. "Tannie Maria. Are you in love?"

I snorted and folded my arms. Now the insect and its mate were singing together.

"Goodness gracious. It's that big detective, isn't it?" she said.

"Don't be stupid, Hattie."

"He said you had a police guard last night. Did he stay there himself?"

I watched the shadows of the branches moving across the skin on my hands.

"Maria van Harten," she said. "You are blushing." She smiled and nudged me. "What happened?"

"Nothing. Nothing happened. And nothing's going to happen. It's hot here, let's go."

We drove to the *Gazette* office in silence. Well, we were quiet, the car was full of the usual revs and squeals.

Hattie stopped just inches behind my blue bakkie.

"I'll see you at the funeral in the morning," she said. "First thing tomorrow I'm going to chat with Mrs. van der Spuy about the chamber of commerce."

"Good luck with that." I said, as we got out of her car. "Thanks for the lift."

"He's a real hunk," Hattie said. "And he obviously cares for you—phoning me like that."

"He's just doing his job," I said, climbing into my bakkie.

It was as hot as a beskuit oven in my bakkie, but I drove off without opening up the windows. I didn't want to hear anything more Hattie had to say. What she said hurt, I don't know why. Maybe because it gave me hope. Hope hurts.

I rolled my windows down at the end of the block. A warm wind was blowing and fat clouds were gathering in the sky. I hoped for rain. That sort of hope didn't hurt so much.

FIFTY-SEVEN

My chickens and Vorster greeted me when I got home.

"*Kik kik kik*," I said to my chickens, throwing out some mielies for them.

"Lemonade?" I offered Vorster, who was on the stoep.

I poured some for myself too and went and sat on the metal chair in my garden, in the shade of the lemon tree. I watched the shadow of the Rooiberg growing and the clouds beginning to get thick and dark, and I felt lonely. I went inside and made myself a cup of coffee and got a beskuit, picked up that brown envelope and a pen and paper and took them outside to the garden chair.

I looked at the biggest gwarrie tree in the veld. It was the closest gwarrie to me, and stood apart from the others. It had been growing old alone there for thousands of years.

Even with the coffee and rusks and chickens and Vorster, I still felt lonely. I guess I just wasn't the right kind of company for myself.

I ate a bit of beskuit, not because I was hungry but to remind my body that it was real. My mind didn't feel real. It felt a little crazy. I was a fool to have hopes of love at my age. With my body. And a man like Henk Kannemeyer. But still, we could be friends.

I decided to make us bobotie for supper. But first I opened the brown envelope. It was, as I'd hoped, from the egg-boiling mechanic.

Thanks, Tannie, he wrote.

That was a fantastic cheese sauce. Cooking with beer is lekker.

I wasn't sure how full to make the tablespoons in the recipe, but then realized it didn't matter so long as they were the same kind of full as each other. It tasted really good and sometimes I make it for myself with supper. With a fried steak on the side.

Things have been moving along nicely and she is now really my girlfriend. I have met her parents and everything. They don't mind that I don't talk much, they are glad I have a good job and love their daughter.

There, I used the love word. When I am with her I can't stop smiling. She seems to be happy with smiling instead of talking. If there's something important to say, we just use our text messages.

She's coming for supper by me this weekend. It's nice weather for sitting outside and looking at the stars so I thought I'd have a braai. I've got some nice kudu boerewors. It's just me and her, you know, and I want it to be something special. What else can I do? I don't think the Welsh rarebit will fit.

Help.

Karel

I was glad things were going well for him and his girl. I fanned myself with the envelope. The air was muggy, the rain stuck up there in the clouds. I wrote out a nice easy recipe for potjiekos made with boerewors. And also my recipe for farm bread. That bread is so easy to make, and it would really impress his girlfriend. I was going to give him some salad recipes but thought that would be going too far for now.

Writing to him made me feel less lonely. It was nice to have someone who I could lead by the hand from one step to the next.

I prepared the bobotie, then got myself ready. I put on my cream dress with the little blue flowers. Vorster shouted good-bye, and I heard his steps going up the pathway, and a car arrive. I heard

Kannemeyer walking toward my house. I put on a welcoming smile and opened my front door.

It was Piet, standing on the stoep.

I kept that smile on my face.

"Good evening, Piet."

Piet nodded, and said, "Lieutenant Kannemeyer has got a meeting. I'm here tonight."

The phone rang.

"Excuse me, Piet," I said, and went to answer it.

"Tannie Maria!"

"Jess."

"I'm so sorry I've been so scarce, Tannie. I've missed you."

"I've missed you too, my skat."

"Reghardt dropped off a letter, Tannie. Explaining everything. And a box of koeksisters. My whole family ate koeksisters."

"I'm glad, Jessie. I left you some honey-toffee snake cake in the fridge at the *Gazette*."

"Awesome. Thanks, Tannie M. I interviewed the owner of the Sunshine B and B. He told me it was true, Reghardt didn't stay that night."

"That's my girl."

"Just being a good journalist," she said. "Double-checking the facts."

"I also spoke to Candice," I said. "She says nothing happened. He's not her type."

"The nerve," said Jessie. "Who is her type?"

"Have you seen Reghardt yet?" I said.

"I'm meeting him at the Route 62 Café," she said. "I'm walking in there now. I just wanted to thank you, Tannie, and apologize. Oh, there he is. Catch you later, Tannie. Hang on. Nooit—you'll never guess who else is here. Sitting in the corner. It's Candy girl. With Detective Kannemeyer . . ."

FIFTY-EIGHT

It rained on the Langeberge in the distance, but all around me the veld stayed dry. In the middle of the night there was thunder and lightning, but not a drop of water. In the flash of the light I saw her pearl dress, and in the rumble of the thunder was the sound of his voice.

When I arrived at the church for Martine's funeral the next morning, the skies were clear. No hope of rain. Candy was talking to Kannemeyer, her hand on his arm. He wore a blue shirt and a dark tie. She was wearing a pillbox hat with a veil, and a short black dress with pearl buttons all the way down the front. I was wearing my brown cotton dress.

"Sugar. Thank God you're here," she said, trotting toward me in black suede high heels.

"Hello, Candice," I said.

My shoes hurt. They were my smartest but least comfortable pair.

"I need your help," she said.

She pointed toward the church. The Nederduitse Gereformeerde Kerk is a tall white building, not at all friendly looking. I used to come here with my husband, Fanie. Gathered at the far end of the big white stairs was a collection of people.

"I wasn't thinking straight," said Candice. "I told family and close friends to come early, thinking they could help out. But look at them."

Henk had disappeared. There was an old man in a wheelchair. A man stood behind him, wearing a shiny blue suit that looked too small. Anna was in her wheelchair. The leg in the cast was at an angle, resting on a metal platform—an extension of the footrest. She had on jeans with one leg cut off above the cast, the other covering her bandages. She wore a smart black blouse and soft black shoes. Even from this distance I could tell her eyes had that dark look again. I waved at her, but she did not see me.

Didi was there, adjusting the bandages on John's ribs. And Dirk, one arm in a sling, wearing a dark suit, the jacket hanging over his shoulders. His whiskers had been neatly shaved and his face was as pale as his bandages.

"This bunch all need help up the stairs," said Candy. "There's no damn ramp. Thank God Henk Kannemeyer is here. He'll be a pallbearer too."

Jessie appeared at my side in her usual black vest but with smart navy trousers.

She cleared her throat, and said, "I can help too."

"Thank you, sugar. You're real sweet. Tannie Kuruman's having a hard time laying out food in the reception hall, because those people are pestering her." She pointed toward the hall, where I could see Tannie K carrying a silver tray, and pushing her way past a small crowd of people. I thought I recognized some of them. "But our biggest problem is the priest. He's sick, and the lay preacher's gone to Riversdale. Any ideas?"

I looked at Candy, her skin and hair glowing like the pearl buttons on her dress, and tried to speak but the sound somehow got lost.

"Reghardt and I will get the wheelchairs up the stairs," said Jessie.

I swallowed and said, "I'll sort out the food and the preacher."

"You are both angels, thank you. Oh lordy, here comes James," said Candy. "Martine's boy. I must introduce him to Grandpa

Peter and Uncle David. They've never met. In fact, David's only just learned that he exists."

She trotted away from us toward a young boy in a wheelchair, being pushed along the pavement by a man in a white nurse's uniform.

The boy's head was hanging down, his neck soft. Candice squatted down and spoke to him. They were too far away to hear, but we saw the boy lifting his head and his mouth falling open into a big smile.

Candy's dress was a lot tighter and shorter when she was on her haunches. Dirk went tumbling forward to join them, and put his bandaged hand on his son's shoulder.

"The one in the shiny suit and the pink tie must be Martine's brother, David," said Jessie.

He was wheeling the old man toward the boy. The oupa used his hands to speed up his own wheels and left David behind.

Candice stood up and helped the wheelchairs meet, so that Jamie ended up knee to knee with his grandfather. The boy's head lolled to one side. He was still smiling. The oupa wore a starched black shirt, but the skin on his neck and face was pale and rumpled. He was small, like a bird, too small for his clothes.

Grandpa's eyes went wide, like he'd seen a ghost; he kept looking at Jamie. The boy had Martine's blond hair and her sharp nose. The same as his grandpa's nose. Jamie grinned, his head wobbling from side to side. The nurse wiped the edge of his mouth.

Jamie waved his hand toward his grandpa, and the old man reached out and grabbed it.

The light caught the cheeks of the old man, and I saw they were wet.

"He's crying," Jessie said.

Candy dabbed her eyes with a handkerchief and rested her fingers on David's arm. David was now standing behind his father's wheelchair. They were all looking at the boy, who was gripping his granddad's hand.

"Look at Uncle David," said Jessie.

His face was twisted with what looked like anger, hatred even. His look shone like a dark light upon the boy. Then he was smiling with his mouth, but his eyes were empty, like a flashlight switched off.

The boy looked up at David then his head fell down like a wilted flower. Jamie pulled his hands away from his grandfather; they fell curled on his lap, like sleeping mice.

They all turned and moved toward the church. Dirk and Oupa stayed close to the boy. David and Candice were a little behind.

"So he really does exist," said David, as they walked past us. "Well, sort of."

FIFTY-NINE

"Tannie, Tannie," the skinny boy said, as he came running toward me, "have you got cake?"

"Sorry," I said.

I was right; the people outside the hall were Seventh-day Adventists. They were dressed very smartly for church. Ties and fancy hats and all.

"There's food here that we can eat, Tannie. My mother said." He looked hungrier than usual. "We've been saving our food for the mountains, Tannie. We're going camping."

The pale lady who had stopped me from feeding the children came and stood beside the little boy. She was wearing a blue bonnet.

I told them both, "Yes, there will be vegan food, but you need to wait until after the funeral. And we can't have the funeral without a priest. Do you have a priest who can help us?"

"Well," said the lady in the bonnet, "there's Emmanuel, but he's not here."

"Gone looking for Emily, his wife," said Georgie, joining us.

She was wearing a pink hat on top of her gray curls.

"Georgina here is a lay priestess," said the lady.

"Ooh-woo," said Georgie. "No, no. I've never preached outside the Adventists."

"She's done funerals," the woman said. "Two of them."

Georgie shook her head so fast that the small pink roses on her hat looked like they might fly off.

"I'm sure we can organize some payment," I said.

Georgie looked at her friend then back at me.

"How much?"

"A spinach pie now for you, and two hundred rand afterward," I said.

"Ooh," said Georgie. "Done."

More people were arriving now, on foot and by car, dressed in their church best. Candice and David stood at the door, greeting them as they walked in. The wheelchair-and-bandage group settled in at the front. I sat next to some of the Spar workers in the middle. Most of them were still in their work clothes, but Marietjie was all fancied up in a dress and heels. She was sitting next to the manager, Mr. Cornelius van Wyk. I suppose he used some kind of glue on his hair to keep it combed sideways like that. The Seventh-day Adventists sat at the back.

The light was coming into the church from windows that were very high up, and it felt like we were underwater. When the pews were almost full, music started playing, and the pallbearers came in with the coffin. Reghardt, Piet, and Jessie carried one side of the coffin; Kannemeyer, David, and Didi the other. I guessed Didi must have forgiven John. Maybe she wasn't the jealous type. She probably didn't know about the ripe pomegranate. Jessie and Henk sat next to Candy in the front. Grace was near the front too. She wore a blue shweshwe headdress and sat up very straight. Hattie came late and stayed at the back with the Seventh-day Adventists. There was an empty space next to me, and the ghost of my husband, Fanie, came and sat down. I tried to shoo him away, but his heavy presence stayed.

Georgie did a good job with the sermon. She spoke about how our lives all come to an end, and gave us a bit of God and heaven talk. She threw in some stuff about the end of the world too, but didn't invite us to join them in the mountains for the big day. Then she invited family members to speak. Dirk got up, but when he was in front of everyone, the words stuck in his throat so he sat down again. Candy stood up and said some sweet words about her cousin and the kind people of Ladismith.

The bad-tempered ghost of Fanie still sat beside me. No mention was made of the husband hitting Martine or the person who murdered her. Funerals are always scrubbed clean of dirt. We sang "All Things Bright and Beautiful."

And then we sang "The Lord Is My Shepherd" and the pallbearers carried the coffin back down the aisle. Kannemeyer looked sad, his mustache drooping. My tummy felt strange, like it was being kneaded, as he walked right past me. I stood up to join the procession and left Fanie's angry ghost there on the church pew.

The family and all their wheelchairs were behind the coffin: Candice pushing Oupa, the nurse pushing Jamie, Anna wheeling herself, and Dirk walking slowly behind them all. The coffin then the wheelchairs were carried down the steps.

Then we all rolled, hobbled, and walked to the cemetery behind the church. Someone had dug a very deep hole. The wheelchairs parked in the front row on the flatter side of the grave: Anna, Oupa, Jamie. Rows of people stood behind them: Dirk and the nurse; David, Candice, and Kannemeyer; John and Didi; Jessie, Reghardt, and Piet. Even Hattie was on that side, with them all.

I stood on the other side of the grave with the Seventh-day Adventists and some workers from the Spar. Just when I thought we had all settled down, and Georgina was giving Martine some final words of farewell, I saw Jamie's wheelchair rolling forward. The nurse grabbed for it but missed and it hung out over the edge of the grave. Piet dived forward and managed to catch it before it fell. He pulled it back onto safe ground. David took a couple of steps backward.

"Ooh-woo," cried Georgina.

"The brakes were on," said the nurse, gripping the back of the chair. "I don't know what happened."

Grandpa reached out for Jamie and patted him on the knee. Candice crouched down beside him, but the boy seemed okay, humming to himself, making grabs for his granddad's hand.

Priestess Georgie said quietly that we all came from dust and to dust we all return. Men in workers' coveralls used ropes to lower the coffin into the grave. Then they began to cover it with spadefuls of earth. There was a big mound of soil. The service was scrubbed clean of dirt, but there was no getting away from it here.

It made a soft, heavy sound as it hit the lid of the coffin.

Martine was never coming back.

I picked up a handful of soil and threw it in.

I'll do my best, Martine, I told her. *I'll do my best to find who did this to you.*

SIXTY

At the wake, I sat with Hattie by the food. A small circle of men, including Henk, stood around Candy like they were warming themselves at her fire. Her smooth dress fit her curves perfectly. My own brown dress was creased after the long morning.

"So that's Grace that Jessie is talking to?" said Hattie, brushing a tiny flake of chicken pie off her lap.

I nodded. Grace was wearing a dark blue dress that matched her shweshwe headdress. "She looks like a princess," said Hattie. "Maria, are you not eating anything?"

I shook my head. Henk put his hand on Candy's bare arm and leaned in close and said something in her ear. Then he left. He didn't say hello or good-bye to me.

David collected a cup of tea and a milk tart for his father, who was parked next to Jamie's wheelchair, not far from Candy. The old man's hands shook as he lifted his teacup to his mouth. His face was soft and sad. His grandson looked happy as the nurse fed him a vegan spinach pie. He must be a very dedicated nurse to have gotten a vegan pie because the Seventh-day Adventists had rushed in to gobble them up.

"I wonder if he understands his mother's gone," I said.

Candy leaned down and stroked the boy's hair. Jessie joined Hattie and me, her plate piled with koeksisters.

"Grace says Dirk gave her some money," she said.

"Super. Maybe he's not such a pig after all," said Hattie.

"Hmph," said Jessie. "A pig is a pig. He can't buy his way out of that. Anyway, along with Lawrence's life insurance, she now has enough to set up in Cape Town."

"Hmm. So, she was the beneficiary of his life insurance?" Hattie said.

"Oh, stop it, Hattie, she didn't kill anyone."

"It's often the nearest and dearest," said Hattie.

"Did she get anything from Marius?" I asked.

"Not a cent," said Jessie. "Grace tells me he offered her money if she'd 'do something' for him."

"Marius really is a pig," said Hattie. "I visited Mrs. van der Spuy this morning. She tells me Marius is campaigning hard against us. If we lose the support of the chamber, the *Gazette* won't have enough funding to continue."

"Oh, Hats," I said.

"I am attending their meeting tonight. Cross your fingers. Where is that Mr. Marius now? I saw him earlier . . ."

"Hah," said Jessie. "Just now, outside, Dirk, Anna, and John were chasing him. Look at them." She nodded toward where the threesome sat together, with Didi taking care of them. "In bandages and wheelchairs, but they attacked him. Reghardt and Kannemeyer intervened and Marius got away."

I explained to Hattie and Jess what had happened at John's farm, and why Dirk and Anna had stopped torturing John to gang up on Marius.

"Jinne," said Jessie. "A fracker. After Martine's land."

"Goodness gracious," said Hattie. "If Marius works for Shaft, that would explain why he had such a hissy fit about your article, Jess. Well, he'd better watch out for the terrible trio."

"You mean them," said Jessie, pointing to John, Dirk, and Anna with her koeksister, "or us?"

"What I also wanted to tell you," I said, "is that pomegranates are not in season, but we found a ripe one on John's farm. He has a greenhouse."

"So you think maybe he . . . ?" said Hattie.

"He used to be in love with Martine," I said, "and she was crazy about pomegranate juice."

"Does his girlfriend know?" asked Jessie, looking at Didi, who was feeding John a chicken pie.

"Maybe not about the pomegranate juice," I said. "But she knows about Martine. John called out Martine's name at just the wrong time."

Hattie raised her eyebrows, and said, "Hell hath no fury . . ."

"I wonder if the Spar has gotten anywhere with the pomegranate juice?" I said.

"I'll ask my cousin Boetie," said Jessie. "He works there."

Hattie looked around the hall. She was taller than us and had a good view of all the people: Martine's family and friends, work colleagues, Seventh-day Adventists.

Then she looked at us, and said, "Any one of the people in this room . . ."

Jessie completed her sentence: " . . . could be the murderer."

Beneath the chatter of the people, we heard a long low moan.

"What was that?" asked Jessie.

"It's the grandpa," Hattie said.

Grandpa was bent over, clutching his stomach. His cup and plate with the half-eaten milk tart were slipping off his lap, onto the floor.

Candice rushed to his side and we followed, pushing our way through the crowd that was gathering around him.

"Help," said Oupa, his face green. "I've been poisoned."

SIXTY-ONE

We three *Gazette* girls moved in like a team. Jessie stood in front of Oupa's wheelchair, looking like a bodyguard in a movie. Hattie stood behind the chair, like a strong, sharp thorn tree, giving protection and shade. I got there too late to save Tannie Kuruman's milk tart. It was trampled on the floor, sticking to the bottoms of the shoes of the Seventh-day Adventists.

"Call Kannemeyer," I said, but Jessie was already on her cell.

"They're on their way," she said.

"We need an ambulance," said Hattie.

"My car will be quicker," said Candice.

Hattie stood aside to let Candy wheel the old man forward.

Jessie stayed close, clearing a path for them.

"Move it. Move it," she said to the people in the way.

Candice drove the wheelchair like a sports car, but Oupa seemed to handle it. Hattie and I walked in their trail and got left behind. David was following too, but not rushing to catch up.

We watched Candice, Jessie, and the old man zoom away in the red MG.

"You look peaked," said Hattie, patting my shoulder.

"I had a bad night," I said.

"Why don't you nip home and rest? I'll stay and wrap up."

"Thanks, Hats. Funerals make me tired."

I walked the block from the church to my bakkie. The road

was flat, but I felt like I was climbing one of those Karoo koppies.

I drove out of town, between the hills that looked like big animals sleeping under a warm blue sky. I wanted to pull over and join them. But I managed to drive myself home. I even made Vorster a cup of coffee and threw out mielies for the chickens. Then I took off my shoes and lay down on my bed and fell into a black hole of sleep.

I dreamed of nothing.

I woke up and blinked and looked out my window at big gray clouds and realized it was evening. I must have slept for hours.

I heard a clanging sound in my kitchen. I could feel my heart in my chest like a rabbit running. Then I got angry. I did not want to be afraid in my own home. If something was going to happen to me, then let it happen. I was not going to be that rabbit, afraid of its shadow. I looked around for a weapon. All I found was my hairbrush, so I picked that up.

I walked toward the kitchen, barefoot and armed. There was Henk Kannemeyer, putting a frying pan on the stove. I stepped back into the corridor and used the brush on my hair.

"Maria?" he said.

"Coming," I said.

I scooted into the bathroom. I got a fright when I saw myself in the mirror. My cheek was creased from sleep and my eyes were puffy. I did what I could and changed into a fresh blue dress and went into the kitchen.

"Hope you like scrambled eggs," he said, beating the eggs in a bowl.

He was still wearing the blue shirt from the funeral, but the tie was gone and his sleeves were rolled up.

"I'm not really hungry."

Something popped and I jumped. It was just the toast in the toaster. He took it out and put in two more slices of bread, then went back to beating the eggs.

"It's about all I know how to make," he said. "And when I put the chickens in the hok there were some eggs there, waiting."

He opened the fridge. How did this man make his way into my chicken hok, my kitchen, my fridge?

"Have you got yogurt?"

"No," I said.

"Here's some." He added a spoonful to the egg mix. "I couldn't find your cutlery. To lay the table."

"I'll do it."

I dropped a knife and we both bent down to pick it up; our arms touched while we were upside down. I stepped back, holding the knife. I washed it and laid the table.

He put the toast and eggs on our plates and buttered his toast.

"I need to talk to you," he said, looking at me with his storm blue eyes. "About Candice."

I studied my own dry toast.

"This isn't an easy thing to do," he said. "I know you are friendly with her." He put his knife down. "You probably trust her."

"You don't have to do this, Detective," I said.

"I worry about you . . . ," he said.

"You have no—" What was the word? "—obligation. To me."

"Maybe I shouldn't be telling you this . . ."

"No, you shouldn't. You don't have to explain anything to me. You can do as you like."

"Maybe you've already worked it out. About her."

"Yes. I'm no fool."

"So you are being careful?"

I frowned at him as he put the scrambled egg onto his toast. A breeze rattled the sash window.

"I worry for your safety," he said.

"My safety?"

"Maria, Candice could be the murderer."

SIXTY-TWO

"What?" I said.

"I don't want you spending time alone with her."

"What?" I said again. "You had supper with her."

"She has motive, means, and opportunity."

"I don't understand," I said. "I don't believe it."

"She comes into a lot of money. Martine made Candice the trustee for her son."

I rearranged my knife and fork on the table. Got them parallel to each other.

"Martine wasn't rich," I said. "Dirk paid for their son's special needs place. She didn't have enough money to leave her husband."

"Martine's father had money in trust for her."

"Yes, I heard he had lots of money, but that he wouldn't give his children anything. Thought they should be independent or something . . ."

"I'd rather not tell you the whole story, but it may be the only way to get you to believe me." He ate some of his meal and then explained: "Long ago Martine had a miscarriage and was very upset about it. Her father told her she'd only get her money when she had a child. In a funny way he thought this might help, but Martine didn't see it like that."

"So, did her father then give Martine the money when she had her son?"

"No, because when she did have a child, she wouldn't allow her father to see him. So then he removed her from his will, but left her share to his grandson in a trust fund. But as it stands, Jamie only gets the money on Grandpa's death. It's a lot of money."

"I still don't get it," I said. "Even if what you say is true, Candy's very rich. She doesn't need the money."

Kannemeyer shook his head.

"She *was* very rich. She earned well as a model and then her father, Martine's uncle, left her a fortune. But she married a Texas oil farmer who lost most of it on a bad deal. He cheated on her, and she got a bit of money out of the divorce, enough to set herself up in the clothing business. She does okay . . . but nothing like what she'll be getting."

"And the oupa wouldn't mind her stealing from a sick boy?"

"He's happy for Candy to be the trustee. There's more than enough money for them both."

"How do you know all this?"

He tugged at the corner of his mustache.

"When we're not busy getting you bunch out of trouble," he said, "we get a bit of work done."

"But Candy wasn't even here when Martine died," I said. "She's only just arrived."

It felt strange to be defending Candy. But it was one thing to believe she was a man stealer. Quite another to think she would steal a life. Murder her own cousin.

"Her car rental shows she's had the car for a week."

"And it was a man. We saw a man the night of Lawrence's murder."

"Are you sure? She's quite a big woman, and she might have been wearing a man's shoes."

"She doesn't walk like a man."

"You saw a flash of someone in a storm."

"You've seen her, Detective. She does not walk like a man."

Kannemeyer sighed and said, "She might be working with someone else."

"A man who also gains from Martine's death . . . ," I said. "The brother! He's been close by. He was at the Sanbona game reserve last week."

"You don't need to worry about it," he said. "I just wanted to warn you to be careful. I don't want to discuss the murder case with you."

He'd finished his meal and he put his knife and fork together. I opened the rattling window to let in the cool breeze. It washed through the house.

"Is there anything else you can talk about?" I said, sitting down again. "How was your day?"

We could pretend he wasn't my bodyguard, that he was just visiting me. I buttered my toast. My hunger came rushing back, like a lost dog coming home.

"Well . . ." He twisted the tip of his mustache with his finger. He would play the game. "I saw a little bokkie on the way here."

"What kind of bokkie?"

"A steenbuck."

"They are hard to spot," I said between mouthfuls. "They lie so still in the shadows."

"They mate for life," he said. "And I went to the Spar."

"What if their mate dies?"

"No, then they find another. Unless they are too old."

The breeze brought in the smell of damp earth. Perhaps it was raining on the Swartberge.

"What did you buy at the Spar?" I said.

The eggs were delicious. Light and fluffy.

"I wasn't shopping. Things are being stolen off the shelves. Cans and dried goods, lentils, rice, that sort of thing."

"They called you in?"

"The manager thinks it may be staff."

"Why does he think that?"

"Oh, I don't know, probably because it's been going on and on. Something small is stolen every day."

"It doesn't seem worth it to me. They could lose their jobs. Small town like this, it's hard to get another job."

Kannemeyer shrugged.

"I've told them to keep an eye on the shoppers who come in every day. The people who buy their lunch there, chips and pies."

I nodded and asked, "What about security cameras?"

"Expensive. More expensive than cans and rice."

I wiped my plate with the last piece of toast and popped it in my mouth. He started to clear the table and I joined in, putting the washing up in the sink. Then I served him the last piece of snake cake. He smelled of honey, like the cake.

"What about you?" he said.

The cake looked good but there wasn't enough for two.

"I'm full," I said.

"I mean, how was your day?"

"Mine?"

We were sitting again now, at the table. He ate the toffee cake with his fingers. His gray-blue eyes were on me; he was ready to listen.

This was a strange feeling, a man sitting there ready to listen to me. I suppose it was something I'd always wanted and now that I had it, I didn't know what to do with it.

I said, "Funerals make me tired. I don't know why."

"I know what you mean."

"Heavy, like I'm carrying the weight of a dead body."

He nodded. I thought of Kannemeyer's sad face when he was bearing the coffin.

"But it feels like more than that one dead body," I said. "It's like all the other deaths from before are also there."

He looked down at his plate and pressed his fingertips onto the last crumbs. They kept falling off but he pressed his fingers onto them again and again.

I could hear the first drops of soft rain on the stoep roof.

SIXTY-THREE

The next morning I was up before the birds, and made us breakfast. I couldn't very well do scrambled eggs so I made poached eggs—what my mother used to call "calf's-eye" eggs—in a tomato base, with some fried beef sausage. I also baked a quick batch of cheese scones, and a pot of mieliepap. Kannemeyer folded the sheets on his couch, then helped me carry the breakfast outside. There was butter and appelkooskonfyt with bread, and milk and sugar for the maize porridge. And a small plate of John's grapes, which were still black and firm.

We sat on the stoep and while we had breakfast we watched the Rooiberg turn red, and then the tops of the rolling brown hills getting lit up. I had been hungry, but after eating a cheese scone and one poached egg and sausage, I was satisfied. When I was finished with eating and looking at the sun-red hills, I watched Kannemeyer eat. He needed a shave but his mustache looked very smart. He was a man with an appetite, and he ate something of everything that we'd laid out. When he had finished with the warm food, he slowly ate a small bunch of grapes while he looked at my garden and at me.

The birds were awake then, and calling to each other, so there was no need for us to talk. Then we heard a car turning off Route 62, and heading up my driveway.

"That'll be Sergeant Vorster," said Kannemeyer, checking his mustache for crumbs.

"Do you wax your mustache?" I said.

"Sometimes. Just the tips," he said. "With beeswax."

That explained why he smelled of honey.

"I'd better get going," he said.

"The old man, in the hospital," I said, then I shook my head. "Never mind."

I knew he wouldn't tell me and I didn't want to ruin our game.

"Have a nice day," I said.

"See you later," he said, standing up.

He bent over close, with his honey and cinnamon smell, and for a moment I thought he was going to kiss me good-bye. But of course he was bending down to pick up our bowls and plates, which he took into the kitchen. The game was over.

"I'll clean up," I said. "Never mind."

I dished out the rest of the porridge to Vorster.

Kannemeyer drove off and I stood on the grass and fed my chickens and listened to the sound of his car moving farther and farther away.

SIXTY-FOUR

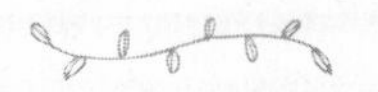

The phone rang. I thought it might be Hattie with news of the meeting last night. But it was Jessie.

"There's a lawyer. At the hospital."

"Is the old man okay?"

"He's alive, but weak."

"Is Candy there?"

"Ja, and the brother. She asked my mother and the police guard if they'd sign a document as witnesses, but they said no."

"I wonder if it's his will," I said. "Can't the police stop it?"

"They're doing nothing illegal," she said.

"We'll have to stop them ourselves," I said.

I parked my blue bakkie next to Jessie's red scooter in the hospital parking lot. We shared the shade of the rubber tree. The day was hot already and the cicadas were singing their same tuneless note.

Jessie was pacing at the hospital entrance. She wore khaki pants and what looked like army boots, and was armed with a pen and paper. I had khaki veldskoene and a Tupperware with some grapes in it. We were ready for battle.

It felt good to have Jessie by my side again. We marched into the hospital together and met Nurse Mostert, her uniform as white and fresh as always.

"Hello, Ma," said Jessie, giving her a soentjie on the cheek.

"I'll show you where they are," said Nurse Mostert.

A woman police guard stood at the entrance to the ward.

Nurse Mostert led us past her, saying, "Oupa Brown, you've got visitors."

But three of them were blocking our way to Oupa.

Candy was in cream again, with her peach skin and her sunshine smile. The brother was still in his shiny suit, crumpled now, as if he'd slept in it. He frowned at us like there was a bad smell in the air, but all I could smell was disinfectant.

I could tell the lawyer by his briefcase and expensive haircut. He didn't smile or frown, he just looked at us as if he was trying to guess our kilograms and centimeters. I think he was deciding if we could be useful to him.

"Maria," said Candy, "Jessie. So glad you've popped by."

"How's your uncle doing?" I asked.

"Much better, as you can see."

But I couldn't see because they were in my way. One on each side, and one at the foot of the bed. I opened my Tupperware and held out the grapes; I used them to wind my way past Candice and toward the old man.

"Some sweet grapes for Oupa," I said.

The brother twisted around and wrinkled his nose at me, and Jessie took the gap and ducked past him. We now stood on either side of the oupa. He looked pale and old, and he seemed to hardly see us. But he reached out for the grapes. The police guard stepped forward and took them away. The old man squawked.

"No," I said.

Those were the last I had of those nice black grapes.

"Sorry, sir, ma'am," the policewoman said. "No food's allowed from outside the hospital. For your own protection."

"Poison," the old man whispered to Jessie. "Someone tried to poison me."

"You're just in time," said Candy, "to act as witnesses."

The lawyer had a piece of paper on a clipboard that he held up.

"We just need you to witness that Mr. Peter Brown is, in actual fact, signing these documents."

I opened my eyes wide, like this was all news to me. Jessie gave me a little wink.

"Do you know what's in this document, Mr. Brown?" asked Jessie.

"Oh, man," said David, "we've been through this twice. Can we just get this over with?"

Jessie ignored him.

"Mr. Brown?" she said.

"It's my will," said the old man. "Some changes."

"Have you read and understood the changes?" she asked.

"I can't find my specs. But Candy explained them to me," he said.

"We just need you as witnesses that he is signing," said the lawyer, putting the pen into the hand of the old man. "Other details are not relevant."

The old man made a long wobbly signature, like the trail of a snail that you sometimes find on the sink in the morning. Then the lawyer gave the pen to Jessie, and tapped the place on the page for her to sign.

"Where?" she said, looking at the page, even though he was already showing her where.

"Just sign here," he said.

She dropped the pen.

"Oops," she said.

The lawyer bent down to pick it up, but it somehow skidded across the room. Maybe someone bumped it with her foot. The air conditioner was making a humming noise now.

"Oh, for God's sake," said David.

While David and the lawyer went after the pen, Jessie read through the page. She was like a reading machine. By the time the lawyer was back with the pen, she was passing the page across to me. The lawyer reached for it, but his arms weren't long enough. I thought Candy might try to grab it from me, but she didn't.

The lawyer got on his cell phone and made a call to someone, telling them to get the hell over here to witness a document.

My reading was slow, and the language was all around about, long lawyer words, but I could see what it was saying.

"My assistant is on her way," the lawyer said. "You can go."

"Hang on," I said.

When I'd finished reading, I looked up at Jessie and we both nodded. I signed and then she did too.

"Stop!" a voice said.

It was Kannemeyer. I hadn't heard him come in, and now he was at the foot of the bed looking down on us all. His mustache was quivering in the way that squirrel tails do when they are all worked up.

"Candice Webster and David Brown. I need to you to come to the station for questioning. Now."

"My clients are not obliged to answer anything," said the lawyer.

Candy put a hand on her hip and cocked her head to one side.

"Why, Detective Kannemeyer," she said. "Just the man I wanted to see."

She gave him a smile, not her usual sweet smile, but a strange small one, as if she was in pain. He didn't smile back.

"Perhaps this can answer your questions for you," she said as she handed him the clipboard with the paper.

I watched him reading the changes to the will. He didn't read as fast as Jessie, but he wasn't as slow as me either.

What the new will said was that all of Martine's share of her father's trust was to go to the care of her son. Anything left over would go to the institution that looked after him. The money was watched over by a board of trustees that included staff from that home as well as Candice. She could not use the money for herself. There was also a paragraph that said that if the old man died in any "unnatural" way, then his son, David Brown, would get nothing from the will.

When Kannemeyer had finished reading, he looked up at Jessie and me, and then at Candy.

She avoided his gaze, and straightened the sheets on her uncle's bed as she said, "Now you can get on with finding Martine's murderer without wasting any more of your precious time on us."

Then the doctor came in. He was a very black man in a white jacket. From Zimbabwe, maybe, with that black skin. His eyes and his teeth were white like his clothes, and they shone when he smiled.

"Having a party here, are we?" he said. "I hope there's no ice cream. We got your test results, Mr. Brown. The good news is, your stomach cancer is still in remission. The bad news is, you're allergic to milk. And you've got a stomach ulcer probably caused by the allergy."

"Yes, yes, I know about the cancer . . . ," said the old man.

"You didn't tell me," said David. "You said you were dying."

"But milk," the old man continued, ignoring David, "I've always drunk milk. It's good for you."

"I'm afraid not," said the doctor. "Although most doctors would agree with you, so they don't even bother to test for a lactose allergy. The truth is, many people can't digest lactose properly and in some this develops into a severe allergy. It may worsen with age, and certainly under stress. The chemo you had would probably have exacerbated the allergy. If you can get rid of that ulcer by cutting out lactose, your stomach cancer has a much better chance of staying in remission."

"So, he wasn't poisoned then," said David, this time addressing the doctor.

"No. Unless a milk tart can be considered poison."

"You see?" said David. "You see? All these years, and this, this is the thanks I get."

"Now, David," said Candy, "nobody said you actually—"

"Nonsense!" said David. "He's said it. The will says it, for

Christ's sake. It's insulting." Little bits of spit were coming out with his words. "After everything I've done."

He marched out and Kannemeyer turned as if to follow him, but then rubbed his hand on his forehead and stayed with us.

"He did give me that milk tart," said the old man.

I couldn't stand by while an innocent was accused.

I wasn't going to let anyone speak badly of Tannie Kuruman's melktert.

"They were very good melkterte," I said, "and a milk tart must have milk in it. There's no getting around that."

SIXTY-FIVE

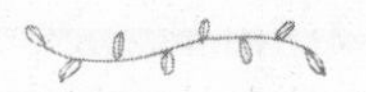

Kannemeyer and I stood on either side of the old man. Everyone else had gone.

"So I find you again, in the middle of the trouble," said Kannemeyer, giving me that frown of his.

But he didn't look all that cross. Oupa was eating the grapes that the policeman had given back to him.

"How come you're following me?" I said.

Kannemeyer smiled and shook his head. That smile of his.

"So are you going to say sorry to Candice?" I said.

"For what?" he said.

"For suspecting her."

The old man popped another grape into his mouth and looked back and forth between us like he was watching a tennis match.

"It's my job to suspect people," Kannemeyer said. "And she might have done all this because she knows I suspect her. The motive could still have been there at the time of the murder."

"Ag, you don't really think she did it?" I said.

He didn't reply.

"She's a good girl, Candy," said the old man. "A good girl."

"I think her feelings are hurt," I said.

"She's used to getting her own way," said Kannemeyer.

"Did you get in her way?" said the old man, offering Kannemeyer some grapes.

Kannemeyer shook his head, and gave his answer to me: "Not in the way she wanted me to."

"They are very sweet grapes," I said.

The old man nodded his agreement.

"I've had a good breakfast," Kannemeyer said, still looking at me.

His phone rang, and he stepped back to answer it.

"Van Wyk," he said. "Ja? . . . Mmm. Mmm. Okay. Ek is op pad."

"Was that Van Wyk from the Spar?" I said.

He was marching toward the door.

"You stay out of this," he said, shaking a finger at me. Then his face changed from serious to sad. "Please."

"It's too late," I said. "I'm already in it."

But he'd left the room, so it was only Oupa and the last grape who heard me. Oupa popped the grape in his mouth.

SIXTY-SIX

As I drove back down Hospital Hill, I wondered about the phone call Kannemeyer had gotten from the Spar. I had some ideas of my own about the Spar thefts. I knew Kannemeyer would say I should leave it alone. But stealing in a small town makes everyone look at each other funny. And the Spar workers were getting a hard time from the manager, which wasn't fair . . .

I was heading to the *Gazette;* I wanted to find out from Hattie how her meeting with the chamber of commerce had gone. But before I got to Eland Street, my arms just decided to turn the steering wheel toward the road that led to the Dwarsrivier Bed and Breakfast. When I got to the B and B, my feet stepped on the brakes and I stopped in the shade of a big bottlebrush tree. It was red with flowers.

I wiped my lipstick off with a tissue and ran my hands through my hair so that it looked a mess. I took the lipstick I kept in my cubbyhole and I walked in through the Dwarsrivier garden gate.

Georgie was sitting alone on a bench in the front garden, as if she'd been waiting for me. She was wearing a white dress with pale blue stripes that went well with her gray hair and made her look a little less short and round than she really was. I wondered where I could get a dress with those sort of stripes.

"Tannie Maria," she said, shifting so I could sit down beside her.

I patted my hair, tidying it a little.

"Thanks for the sermon yesterday, Georgie. You did a good job."

Georgie smiled and dipped her head.

"I just wanted to use your bathroom, to freshen up," I said.

"Sure," said Georgie.

"I'm going to the Spar," I said. "I hear they've put in hidden cameras all over the shop."

"Ooh-woo," said Georgie.

"They've had some thefts—cans and stuff. So now they've got fancy security."

Georgie looked at the grass.

"I don't want them filming me shopping when I'm looking all scruffy," I said.

Georgie patted her gray curls. I went inside and used the ladies' room. I tidied my hair, washed my face, and put on fresh lipstick. When I went out the front again, Georgie had left the garden. I walked past reception to the back, where the rooms looked onto the pool area, and found her talking quietly to some women in a room. They became silent when they saw me at the door.

"Good morning, ladies," I said, looking at all their faces turned to me.

"Hi," said Emily.

She was back with her flock; her long red hair was coiled around her head like a crown.

I wondered which one of them had written me the letter asking for camping recipes.

"Thanks. See you," I said.

I smiled and waved at them.

"Good-bye, Tannie Maria," said Georgie.

"Thanks," said Emily.

My legs took me back out to the car, and my arms drove me around the block, to the *Gazette*.

I went to the chamber of commerce meeting last night," said Hattie, before I even stepped inside. Jessie was at her desk, her face turned away from me. "And I made a little speech about the independence of the press and they voted on whether to keep supporting us."

"And . . . ?" I said, my hand on the front door.

"They voted ten against two."

My face and hand fell.

"In favor!" said Hattie. "Ten in favor of us."

Jessie turned around and I saw her big grin.

"And when Marius had a hissy fit, Mandy's Furniture Shop said they could sponsor the website from now on!"

I gave Hattie a hug, but it was hard because she was bouncing up and down on her toes, and I don't believe in bouncing. I made us tea and coffee and there was still some honey-toffee cake in the fridge, which added to the celebration.

"Marius can go to pot for all I care," she said, waving a piece of cake in the air.

"Ja, fok him," said Jessie.

"Now, now," said Hattie, but she was still smiling.

There was quite a pile of envelopes on my table, and I flipped through them. One had a small brown smudge on it. I wondered if it was another letter from that nice mechanic. But the stain didn't look like grease and my name was typed: TANNIE MARIA. No address. Hand delivered.

"Did someone come by with this envelope?" I asked Hattie, holding it up for her to see.

"It was on your desk when I brought in the other mail," she said. "Thought you'd left it there."

I opened the envelope. Inside was a folded piece of paper, with that same kind of stain, but much bigger. It was a bit sticky and I unfolded it carefully.

The smell hit me at the back of my throat as I saw the dark red shape across the white page.

At the top of the paper, four words were typed:

BACK OFF OR DIE

The folded paper had turned the red shape into a butterfly. A butterfly of blood.

SIXTY-SEVEN

They give people pictures like that when they go to psychologists. They ask them what they see, and then decide what kind of crazy they are.

I felt lots of different kinds of crazy as I sat looking at the butterfly blotches on the page.

I saw a woman trying to run away from herself. Her legs galloping out and her arms reaching away, but she was getting nowhere. Because she was joined at the hip to the same woman running in the other direction.

I wanted to tell her she was also a butterfly, and if she stopped trying to get away from herself, maybe she could fly.

Then I blinked and the women were gone and the picture was of a creature run over in the road, flattened and bleeding. I heard a sound, like an animal in pain.

"Are you okay, Tannie Maria?" said Hattie.

Jessie and Hattie were on either side of me. The animal sound was coming from me. I held up the paper for them to see. My hands were shaking and the shapes on the paper came to life. It looked like fire. A fire that could destroy everything.

"Oh, my goodness gracious!" said Hattie.

"Don't touch it," said Jessie. "Maybe we can get the bastard's fingerprints."

"Oh, Maria," said Hattie.

I had a feeling I was falling, but Jessie and Hattie were standing on either side of me, so I didn't fall because their hips were there holding me up. A woman on each side of me, a butterfly of women.

The picture was still in my hand, still shaking. It looked like a big bird, the ones that rise up from the flames and ashes. Like a dragon. Flying.

Then everything went black.

Just have a sip, Tannie Maria," said Jessie's voice.

I opened my eyes. Hattie was putting my hand around a cup of tea.

I brought it to my mouth. Warm and sweet.

For shock. I'd had a shock. What had happened? I'd been run over. By Fanie. But he's dead, that's all over. I had another sip. I was okay. Alive. I wasn't even in the hospital. I was in the office. My desk at the *Klein Karoo Gazette*. The fan was turning slowly on the ceiling.

I saw the paper on my desk, and remembered.

BACK OFF OR DIE

"Maybe we must shut down for a while," said Hattie.

"We can't just let him get away with it," said Jessie.

"What is that bird," I said, "that comes back from the dead?"

"The police can catch him," said Hattie. "I am going to call them right now."

She put her hand on the phone.

"But will they?" said Jessie. "Fifty percent of murderers don't get caught. And our murder rate is five times higher than the world average. Tens of thousands of murderers get away with it. He's threatening us because he's nervous. We're getting close to finding him. We can't give up now."

"It rises from the flames . . . ," I said.

My brain wasn't working properly; it just couldn't find the right word.

"He knows you two were there the night of the murder," said Hattie. "Maybe we should all three go away, get out of Ladismith for a while."

"Flies up from the ashes . . . like a dragon, but it's not a dragon," I said.

"We could stay on my cousin's farm in Oudtshoorn," said Hattie, looking up a number in her phone book. "Do the holiday edition of the *Gazette* from there. It's a phoenix, Maria, a phoenix."

"You mean just do as the bastard says? Back off?" said Jessie.

"This is a murderer we are dealing with, Jessie," said Hattie, picking up the receiver and punching numbers into the phone. "He's already killed two people. And now he's making death threats. It's just not worth it."

I drank the last of my tea and put my cup down next to the paper. Next to the red phoenix on my desk.

"I'm not running away," I said. "If the end of the world's coming, let it come. But I'm not going to run."

SIXTY-EIGHT

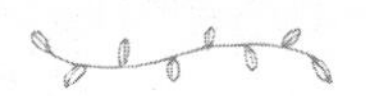

Piet moved around the *Gazette* office like a sniffer dog. Kannemeyer stood behind me. He picked up the phoenix with gloved hands and put it in a plastic bag.

"Only she has touched it," said Jessie.

Kannemeyer wasn't looking at me, but he inspected all around me, and all around my desk. He even looked inside the kettle. He paced the room, then he froze and stared at the whiteboard. He tugged on one side of his mustache as he read the notes we'd made about the case. He shook his head, and turned to stare at me. I knew we were in for a skelling, but I wasn't scared anymore. I had the strength of a phoenix. I could die and come back. I was scared of nothing.

I saw in his eyes not the anger I was expecting, but a sadness. And perhaps fear. Could he be scared of me? His silence was big and heavy and I wished he would speak.

He waved his long arm at the names on the whiteboard and said, "Suspects? Which of these people have you been harassing?"

I tried to answer, but nothing came out.

"We've harassed no one," said Jessie.

"Would you like some tea, Detective?" said Harriet, putting on the kettle.

"Chasing, investigating, whatever you want to call it," he said and now he was looking cross.

"Why don't you sit down?" said Jessie.

"Have you had arguments with anyone in the last few days?" he asked.

I shook my head.

"We prefer not to argue," said Hattie. "Would you rather have coffee?"

"Have you been bothering all these people on your list of suspects?"

"If you sit down, Detective," said Jessie, "we could discuss the case with you. Maybe we can work with you in finding this murderer."

He looked like he wanted to spit, but he sat down. Hattie gave him coffee and Jessie explained the notes on the whiteboard. Kannemeyer listened for a long time while she spoke. Piet was outside now, studying the garden path. Jessie was a very good reporter, and Hattie added a thing or two. I was just watching, as if it were a movie.

"So, what can you tell us?" said Jessie, when she had finished. "Do you have other suspects? Or more information on any of this bunch?"

Kannemeyer turned to me and said, "Is there somewhere out of town you can stay?"

I blinked.

"Tannie Maria," he said. "Your life is in danger. You have had two death threats. And this one is even more serious than the first. We don't have the manpower to give each of you twenty-four-hour bodyguards. You wouldn't need a bodyguard if you had left police matters to the police. I am asking you. Please. Can you move out of town? Just for a while."

I shook my head. His face got red and his mustache twitched, but he didn't speak. Then he stood up and walked outside.

I thought he had gone, but he stuck his head back in the door and said, "Do any of you know where Anna is?"

"Anna Pretorius?" said Jessie.

I shook my head again.

"Not at her house?" said Jessie.

"No," he said. "If you hear from her, tell me."

"Is she in trouble?" asked Jessie.

He stepped into the doorway and looked at each one of us. He took in a breath, like he was going to speak; his mustache lifted up. But then he sighed and closed his mouth. He turned and stomped down the pathway.

Everything went black again; I think I fell asleep for a minute. What was wrong with me? I shook my head fast, like I was shaking water out of my ears. Jessie and Hattie were arguing.

"But, Hattie, the only way we are going to be safe is if we catch him," said Jessie. "If the police manage to do it, that's grand—we can relax—but I'm not going to sit around doing nothing in the meanwhile."

"We've got a paper to run, for heaven's sake," said Hattie.

"Ja. And this is hot news material. Let me look into Marius's links with Shaft. If he's linked to the frackers, it's a motive for killing Martine."

Harriet sighed, and said, "There really is no stopping you. Just don't get yourself in trouble and don't post anything on the website that I haven't checked first."

I needed a proper lunch. That would bring me right.

"I'm going to the Spar," I said.

It made me feel peaceful, just being in the grocery store, looking at those piles of fresh fruit and vegetables. Bananas, apricots, and melons. That sweet smell of ripe spanspek. I peeled a banana and ate it. I started to think straight again so I went to the bakery counter and bought four doughnuts and ate one. I would pay for everything at the till, but I was glad they didn't really have security cameras.

Now that my brain was working, I realized I hadn't come here just for food.

I wanted to know what that call from Van Wyk to Kannemeyer had been about. Was the Spar manager contacting him about the stolen cans? Or could it have been to do with the pomegranate juice?

I got a little shopping cart and did some more shopping. There was still frozen game meat, so I took a couple of packs. I picked up some herbs, tomatoes, and pasta for a nice spaghetti Bolognese. Then I waited until there was no one at Marietjie's cash register and headed over there. I put the cart behind me, to chase others away from that line. Today her hair was pulled into a small bun at the back of her neck. She wore a pink bow around the bun and pink lip gloss, which made her look like a teenager.

"Good afternoon, Marietjie."

"How are you, Tannie Maria?"

"So the police were here today?" I said.

I took the shopping from my cart one item at a time. She rubbed her glossy lips together and leaned toward me. She smelled like cherries.

"Ja. It was me—I got the photo. On my cell phone."

She took it out of her pocket and wiggled it at me.

"Mmm," I said, as if I knew what she was talking about.

"She bought all six bottles. All six."

"The pomegranate juice?"

She nodded.

"Ja. The policeman, the one with that mustache. He knew who she was right away. He just looked at my photo of her in the wheelchair. That's Anna Pretorius, he said. And Cornel—Mr. van Wyk—said he'd definitely seen her here before. And the picture would help the cashiers remember. He really wants to help out, you know."

"And what did the cashiers say?" I said, handing her the ground meat.

"Ag, they're useless. They don't remember anything really. But I have seen her here before. Definitely. I've seen her saying hello to Mrs. van Schalkwyk in the office."

"But did she buy the pomegranate juice last Tuesday?"

"I think so. I'm sure she did."

"What did you tell the police?"

I held the tomatoes back.

"Mr. Cornelius really wanted to help them."

"So you told them it was her."

"Mr. van Wyk did the talking mostly . . ."

"Marietjie, this is serious. You don't want the wrong person being locked up, and a murderer running around."

"But she bought all six bottles of the juice. All six. It's very suspicious, Mr. Cornelius said. She must have bought some before. I didn't say she killed anyone. I just said she bought all six, and now that I look at her, I do remember her, she bought a bottle here last week."

She moved the tomatoes quickly through the scanner.

I didn't look at Marietjie as she packed the food into the Spar bags because I didn't want her to see how cross I was. I studied those plastic bags. I thought of the ones I had found in Martine's trash can. Somebody had shopped for Martine, here at the Spar, on the day of her death.

"Thank you, Marietjie," I managed to say.

"Enjoy your day further," said Marietjie.

SIXTY-NINE

"Yum," said Jessie, when she saw the doughnuts I'd brought back from the Spar.

I put my ground meat in the little *Gazette* fridge and made us all tea and coffee to go with the doughnuts. Then I sat down and I told them what Marietjie had said.

Jessie and I ate up our doughnuts, while Hattie pecked at hers.

"I spoke to my cousin, Boetie, last night," said Jessie. "I think he knows something about the pomegranate juice at the Spar, but he was too stoned to make sense. He's a bit of a daggakop but his ma says he only smokes after hours—so I'll talk to him another time."

"You have to admit, there really is rather a substantial pile of evidence against Anna," said Harriet.

"But it's all nonsense," said Jessie.

"Her prints are on the murder weapon. She's got means, motive, and opportunity," said Hattie.

"So have lots of other people."

I gave Jessie a napkin, to wipe the confectioners' sugar off her mouth.

"Maybe we should warn her," I said. "Tell her to get a lawyer."

"There's no reply at her house," said Jessie. "And she doesn't have a cell."

"I wonder if Dirk would know how to find her," I said.

"Sanna from the AgriMark tells me he's moved back home," said Jessie. "I wouldn't mind another look at his place."

"Ja, we left in a bit of a hurry last time."

"I've got his phone number," said Jessie. "Or shall we just maar go?"

"Let's just pop in."

"My dear girls, I implore you to be careful," said Hattie, standing up and putting her unfinished doughnut on my desk. "And before you go gadding about again, I want your completed copy for this week's website and paper edition."

Jessie and I made a quick job of finishing that doughnut, then we washed our hands and sat down at our desks.

I looked at the envelopes on my desk. I thought about the bloody letter from the anonymous murderer. He didn't deserve a response from me. He certainly didn't deserve a recipe.

I sorted through my letters and decided to open the two that had Oudtshoorn postmarks. This is a town a hundred kilometers east of Ladismith, famous for the Cango Caves and ostrich farming.

The first said:

I'm an ostrich farmer. I know how to make biltong and an ostrich steak, but I need a change. My wife used to do all sorts of lekker things with the meat. But she is gone now. For a while I missed her so much I couldn't think of making anything. Now I ground up some of my meat, but I don't really know what to do with it. Can you help maybe? Thank you.

Before I answered, I read the other Oudtshoorn letter. It was from a woman who had too many sweet potatoes:

Suddenly, after a year of almost nothing, my vegetable garden is just full of sweet potatoes and I don't know what to do with them. I've made some fritters, and even sweet potato jam, but I live alone and haven't got such a sweet tooth myself and my children live far away and don't come and visit all that often. I thought of giving the potatoes away, but I don't really know my neighbors all that well and have been a bit shy since the accident. The scars are not so bad anymore, but still I feel people staring.

I decided to give them both one recipe. A shepherd's pie—made with ground ostrich meat and a mashed sweet potato topping.

Why not meet at the Farmers Co-op on Saturday mornings at 10 A.M., I wrote. *You could swap some meat for vegetables . . .*

"Maria," Hattie said, "I've just gotten an email addressed to you. It's marked as urgent. Here, you can look at it on my computer. I'm popping out for a minute."

She stood up and I took her chair.

Oh, Tannie Maria, the email said.

Thank you so much, the braai went really well. You were right, the bread was easy to make and she was very impressed. She said I was a very good cook. Ha-ha.

Sorry about writing an email instead of a letter but this is an emergency. I wish there was someone else I could ask, but I can't, and I need help.

We, you know, did it, together. And we have done it now three times. It's amazing being so close and breathing her smell and there is no need for words. We feel so good together. Too good. The problem is, I get so excited it's all over for me in two minutes and she doesn't always get a chance to, you know . . .

Is there a medical treatment for me?

Karel, the mechanic (in need of brakes)

Jessie's phone rang: *I'm your man.* She answered it with a smile and went outside to talk. I tried to think of some advice for Karel. But what did I know about good sex? I've always imagined it would be something like a really good cake. That gave me an idea.

I wrote:

> *Here is a way you could slow yourself down. Memorize a good recipe, then say it inside your head if you are getting overexcited. This should distract you enough to make it last longer, but still keep your mind on something delicious.*

Then I gave him a recipe for a chocolate cake. Not the one I made for Kannemeyer but a fluffy chocolate mousse cake, made with dark chocolate. The recipe required a long time to beat the eggs and sugar to make them very thick and frothy, and the cake was topped with cream and berries.

Jessie and I drove along the dirt road to Dirk's farm in my little blue bakkie. It was afternoon now and there were fat clouds above us. But instead of cooling us down, they were just trapping in the heat. We rode with the windows wide open, and what with the sound of the wind and the bumping car, we didn't try and talk. It was good to be riding with Jessie again. Back to the scene of the crime.

The klapperbos were flowering; the little red lanterns looked like Christmas decorations. And there were purple handfuls of reëngrassie popping up between the wire-grass that grew by the side of the road. Jessie pointed out a shiny green sunbird that was landing on an aloe flower, and I slowed down to look at it.

"Whoa," said Jessie, as a mongoose came charging down the road, racing toward us. I put on the brakes, and it darted into the grass.

Then we heard a whole lot of bangs in a row.
"Gunshots," Jessie said.
But we kept on driving, heading toward the farmhouse.
The sound of shooting got louder.

SEVENTY

We drove past the house and the big gum tree and saw Anna's bakkie parked behind Dirk's.

Again we heard: *Bang. Bang.*

Silence.

Over the tops of the cars, we saw Dirk standing in a field, his left arm still in a sling. A revolver was clutched in his bandaged right hand and he was shooting from the hip.

Bang. Bang. Bang.

Then, as we got past his 4x4, we could see Anna was there too, in her wheelchair. She lifted a double-barreled shotgun and fired. *Boom! Boom!* Louder than Dirk's gun.

But they were not shooting at each other, thank goodness. Who or what were they shooting at?

Jessie and I got out of the car and walked toward them. Something lay on the ground. As we got a bit closer we saw what it was . . .

A dead tree lay on its side. They had not killed the tree, it had been dead for a long time. It was gray and bare, and in its hollows were bright cans.

What with his injured arms, Dirk was struggling to reload the revolver, and he took the box of ammunition to Anna in her wheelchair. She had a shotgun resting on her plaster cast and half a glass of red liquid in her hand. She bent down to put the drink on the ground and then helped him load the bullets.

Then Anna broke the shotgun, the used cartridges popped out, and she reloaded.

She waved the shotgun at us, shouting, "Haai!"

Dirk grunted. We stood still.

Dirk shot into the tree. *Bang. Bang. Bang.*

"Kolskoot!" said Anna as he hit an empty baked-bean can.

She picked up her drink and raised it to him before having a big sip. Then she put it down and blasted a tomato can. *Boom! Boom!*

"Come!" she called. "I'm using Dirk's shotgun. He's got my revolver."

The way she said her *s*'s made me think it was not just fruit juice in that red drink.

"We'll just wait," said Jessie.

"There are some roses here that need watering," I said.

There was a row of bushes that were missing Lawrence. The leaves were dry and the flowers wilting. I saw a tap with a hose attached.

Bang. Bang.

Dirk walked toward Anna again to reload, but it seemed the ammunition was finished.

"Blikemmer," she said, throwing the empty box toward the tree.

But it did not travel as well as the bullets.

Anna bent down and slurped the last of her drink and handed the glass to Dirk. Then she propped the shotgun between her legs, leaning the barrels on her shoulder, and wheeled across the bumpy field toward us.

"You got a four-by-four wheelchair there, Anna?" said Jessie, walking to meet her.

I was still watering the roses.

"Nah, it's a piece of crap," she said.

Her white plaster cast was smudged with dirt, and splattered with drops of that red juice. Dirk walked in a wobbly way, holding the glass and the revolver in his right hand.

"Do you like our Christmas tree?" she said, pointing to the fallen tree, decorated with cans and bullets. "Come. Have a drink."

She rolled toward the house. I turned the tap off and followed her to the stoep. Dirk was wandering a bit askew and Jessie herded him toward us.

Before we could catch up with her, Anna ditched the wheelchair at the base of the stoep stairs and dragged herself up the stairs with the shotgun under her arm.

"Eina. Jou ouma se groottoon," she cursed as her plaster cast bumped against the stairs. Your grandma's big toe.

I took the shotgun from her, and put it in a corner of the stoep. Jessie lifted the wheelchair up and we helped her back into it.

Dirk swayed from side to side, but managed to get up the stairs without falling over.

"I gotta pee," said Anna. "Help yourself. That pomegranate juice is blerrie lekker."

Dirk burped in agreement.

"Dirk, get them some glasses for Christ's sake."

He bumped his thigh against the table on his way to the front door.

"Donder," he swore.

On the table were empty bottles of a deep-red juice and vodka. As well as full bottles of vodka and juice.

Dirk brought clean glasses, but even though he concentrated very hard, his pouring abilities were not so good.

"Ag, fok," he said, as the juice dribbled down the side of the glass.

Jessie took over and poured us each a glass of pomegranate juice—no vodka. I closed my eyes and held it in my mouth before I swallowed. It was rich and sweet and tasted of the earth and of my childhood.

Anna came back and slopped a lot of vodka into her and Dirk's glasses before topping them up with juice. She drank hers down like a soft drink. Dirk's movements were awkward as he tried to lift his bandaged arm all the way up to his mouth. He brought his head down to meet the glass. Some of the liquid dribbled onto his sling, but a fair amount went in. The bandages were hospital white not so long ago, but now they were grubby, with pomegranate polka dots.

"Anna, someone at the Spar said you were the one who bought the pomegranate juice," I said.

"Ag, Dirk, jou sissie se vissie!" Anna said. Your sister's little fish. "Don't waste the stuff, man. Here, sit up."

She rolled across and lifted the drink to his mouth and he gulped it down. And burped.

"Not just today, but last week," I said. "The day of the murder."

Anna snorted. She poured herself another drink. She was quite accurate with the vodka, but not all the juice made it into the glass.

"Kannemeyer is looking for you," said Jessie.

"Let him come," Anna said.

"Anna, we are worried about you," I said. "You should get a lawyer."

"Maybe I should get some ammunition," she said. "Dirk. You got more rounds for this shotgun?"

Now I was worried about Kannemeyer.

Dirk was looking out onto the lawn and the empty pond.

"I miss those ducks," he said, in Afrikaans.

Then he started singing, his voice rough and croaky like a big frog:

Ek wonder wat my hinder!
Daar's onrus in my hart,
of daar 'n bange vlinder
sag huiwer in sy smart.
I wonder what troubles me!
Unrest in my heart again,

like a frightened butterfly
trembling softly in pain.

Anna sat down next to Dirk and joined in:

. . . of daar 'n bange vlinder
sag huiwer in sy smart.
. . . like a frightened butterfly
trembling softly in pain.

They swayed slowly as they sang. Dirk was gazing at the empty duck pond and Anna's eyes were half closed.

Jessie cocked her head and we got up and went inside. The kitchen was a mess: unwashed dishes, ants all over, cleaning up bits of food on the counters. Grace must have left already. I wondered how Lawrence's funeral went, and if she was in Cape Town yet.

Light was streaming in from the sash windows onto the metal sink and the wooden kitchen table. The fingerprinting dust had been cleaned up but the table was full of fresh crumbs and Karoo dust. It was strange seeing the place in the light of the day, messy but normal, without murderers or dead people. It looked a bit bigger: the open-plan kitchen and living room, with the couch where Martine died, the pantry with the door full of gunshot holes. I peeked inside the pantry—the jam and flour had been cleaned up, the cans and recipe books on the shelves were all wiped and tidy. I touched the spine of *Cook and Enjoy* and felt sad that Martine was never going to read that recipe book again. In the living room, the broken glass had been swept up. The wedding photograph of Martine and Dirk stood alone on a small table in its frame—without the glass.

We went into the study. Papers were all over the table and floor. There were books on the floor, their pages open.

"What happened here?" said Jessie. "This isn't how we left it."

"Did the murderer have time to make such a mess?" I said. "You'd think the police would've tidied it up. Or Dirk."

"Maybe Dirk was the one chucking things around. No harm in tidying up a bit," she said, "since the police are finished here."

Jessie sorted the papers back into Martine's filing cabinet, while I picked up the books and put them back on the shelf. I shook each one out, looking for papers hidden inside. Maybe it was silly of me, but I still wondered if she had kept our *Karoo Gazette* letters somewhere, hidden from her husband. The books were all empty. Then at last, inside a book on the Klein Karoo, a clipping from a newspaper fluttered out and down to the floor. But it was a recipe for an ostrich casserole. I read it in case my ostrich farmer might be interested. It was a lot like tomato bredie, but with more whole coriander. Coriander is very nice in ostrich biltong, so it made sense.

As we looked through the books and papers, they carried on singing outside:

> *'n Tortelduif se sange*
> *het in my siel gevaar.*
> A turtledove's song
> ventured into my soul.

Anna raised her voice, interrupting their song: "You are a fokken bastard, you know that, Dirk. I should've killed you dead."

"Ja," he said.

"Why did you donder Martine?"

"I'm fucked up," he said. "Sometimes I just go bossies . . . I don't know why."

"You should get help, y'know."

"Who would help me? Would you help me?"

"Not me—I'm not your fokken nanny. Haai, jou sissie se vissie, you're spilling again. I'll hold it for you. No, man, get counseling, join a group of other asshole men like you."

"Where?"

"Just look, man. Ask your doctor or go on the fokken vleisbroek Facebook . . . I can't believe you killed those ducks."

"I know you won't believe me, but I thought I was shooting the enemy. From my army days. I thought they were terrorists hiding there in the reeds."

"Christ. You'd better fix yourself up or I'll fokken kill you, for Martine's sake, y'know."

They were quiet a moment. I could hear a breeze swishing the leaves of the gum tree.

"I miss her," said Dirk.

"I miss her a moerse lot more than you."

He started to sing again:

'n Tortelduif se sange
het in my siel gevaar . . .

Jessie shook her head and said, "I wonder if bastards like him can ever get right." She pointed to the filing cabinet in front of her. "Well, there doesn't seem to be anything different here."

"Nothing missing?" I asked. "Since when you looked?"

"Not that I can tell," she said. "Her financial papers are in the biggest mess."

"Any sign of my *Gazette* letter?" I asked.

"No," she said. "There's a newspaper cutting about the frackers that I missed last time."

I heard a slow thumping sound, getting closer. Anna was bumping her wheelchair from one corridor wall to another on her way to the bathroom. She was humming the turtledove song. On her way back, she stuck her head in on us.

"We're just tidying up," said Jessie, closing the filing cabinet.

"Ag, there's no point in that," said Anna. "It just gets messed up again. He says it's her spook, but that's just nonsense twakpraatjies. I've cleaned the whole kitchen myself and seen him mess it up with my own two eyes."

Dirk's lonely frog voice called from the stoep:

'n Tortelduif se sange
het in my siel gevaar.

Anna's eyes went all misty and she rolled back toward him and the song:

'n liedjie van verlange
wat glad nie wil bedaar,
'n liedjie van verlange
wat glad nie wil bedaar.

A song of longing that just won't let go, a song of longing that just won't let go.

SEVENTY-ONE

I dropped Jessie back at the *Gazette,* picked up my ground meat from the fridge, and headed on home, the tin of padkos rusks on the seat beside me. The sky was gray with clouds, but it was still hot. The peak of the Towerkop was lit up by the evening sun, the rest of it in shadow. I started planning the spaghetti Bolognese I was going to make for supper.

Maybe because the Bolognese was on my mind, I didn't see the crows until I was nearly on them. Two of them, pecking at a flat red thing. I swerved and braked, and the car wiggled about but I managed to get a grip again. Then I pulled over by the side of the road to take a few breaths.

I looked back through my rear window. The crows were dancing around something on the road, ripping off pieces.

"I should go and make sure it's dead," I said to the tin of rusks. "Move it to the side of the road."

I turned around and drove back, pulled over, and walked up to the crows surrounding the roadkill.

"Shoo!" I said.

But the crows just glared at me with their shiny black eyes.

I stamped and said *Shoo!* again, and they went back to pecking at the red meat.

I picked up a stick and a stone from the side of the road.

"Voetsek!" I shouted, throwing the stone at them.

They hopped back a couple of feet, leaving the body on the tar. It really was a bloody mess. But I could see from its ears, its long furry ears, what it was.

I used the stick to push the dead rabbit to the side of the road, to the base of a groot-wolfdoring bush. There was some Karoo gold growing nearby and I picked some of the yellow flowers and dropped them on the body.

"It was a rabbit," I told the rusks, as I got back in the car. "It was very dead. I said good-bye."

When I got home I saw Kannemeyer's van. I left the tin of traveling rusks in the car and walked up my pathway to find him sitting on my stoep, sipping a cup of coffee. I guess it was later than I thought. I smiled at him as if my hair wasn't stuck to my forehead and my dress all sticky. And he said good evening as if he lived there.

"Koffie?" he offered.

No man had ever made me coffee in my own home, but I said yes please, as if it was something that happened every day.

I went inside and freshened up. I put on a clean dress, took off my veldskoene, and went barefoot back to the kitchen. I made the Bolognese while I drank my coffee.

Kannemeyer stayed on the stoep. I could see his legs, still and solid, through the door. He was watching the copper and flame colors of the sunset. Because of all those clouds, the sky was really showing off.

The Bolognese was marinating nicely in the hotbox. I popped the spaghetti in the boiling water and went out to the stoep.

Kannemeyer made a little grunting noise when I sat down, and together we watched the end of the sunset performance.

The red clouds did their last, slow dance. They reminded me of the bloody pattern I had seen that morning. It looked less like a phoenix now and more like a dead rabbit. The red faded away and the dark curtains closed. The show was over.

We ate supper out on the stoep.

"Mmm, lekker," said Kannemeyer.

The crickets were cricking and the Bolognese was delicious. I should have felt peaceful, but I knew something was wrong. Not just a small thing, like too little salt, or even a bigger problem like overcooked spaghetti. But something really bad.

So when the phone rang, I knew it wouldn't be good news.

It was Reghardt.

Jessie had disappeared.

SEVENTY-TWO

"She's not at her house," said Reghardt. "She's not anywhere."

I sat down slowly and held the phone tight in my hand.

"I dropped her at the *Gazette*," I said, "around six or six thirty."

"I've been there. I've been everywhere. I was going to fetch her at her house at seven thirty. She was coming to my house for supper."

"She might have forgotten?"

"No. She knew I was making her bobotie."

"You haven't had a fight with her or anything like that?"

"No. Nothing like that."

Kannemeyer came inside and stood in the kitchen.

"Henk, it's Reghardt. Jessie's gone missing."

"But she did phone me earlier, on my cell," said Reghardt. "I was on a field call. Mrs. Kromberg thought there was a burglar, but it turned out to be a mongoose. I said I'd phone back, and then when I did, the phone cut out."

"What did Jessie say, exactly?"

"She said, I need to talk to you. Are you at the station? And I said, no, I'm on a field call, I'll phone you back now-now. And she said, where are you? Shit. My phone. I heard a beep and the line went dead. I think her battery went dead. She's got one of those fancy phones that's always going dead. My phone I only need to charge every three days."

"Reghardt," I said, because he was losing the story.

"I called her two minutes later. But it just went to her voice mail."

"What time did she phone you?"

"Six fifty-three," he said. "It's on my cell. I was a bit worried but I knew I'd see her later. And we'd sort it out then."

"Did she sound upset? Cross with you?"

"No, not cross. Just like it was important. Jessie's like that, she gets excited about things."

"I wonder if she was on to something. A story. A lead in our case?"

"The murders. That's what worries me. After those threats . . ."

"She's only been gone two hours," I said to make him feel better.

But it didn't make me feel any better.

"Let me speak," said Kannemeyer, and I handed him the phone.

He listened for a minute before he rattled out orders to Reghardt in high-speed Afrikaans. Then he called the police station. In five minutes he'd organized a guard for Hattie, a policeman to visit Jessie's house, and someone to go with a photo of Jessie to all the restaurants and bars, and to drive the streets looking for her scooter. It was a small town. Not many places would be open.

He put down the phone and I called Hattie.

"Jessie's gone missing," I said. "They are sending someone to guard your house."

"God Almighty," she said. "I prayed this wouldn't happen."

"They're looking everywhere. She's only been missing two hours."

Kannemeyer was carrying in the dishes from outside.

Hattie and I sat in silence with the phone line between us. I could hear the crickets outside and a dull hum on the line. We were waiting for words of comfort to give to each other, but could not find any.

"God Almighty," she said again before we hung up.

"You'd better go," I said to Kannemeyer, taking an empty pot out of his hands.

"I'm not going anywhere," he said.

"You've got to find Jessie," I said. "It's your job."

"My job tonight is to make sure nothing happens to you," he said.

"Henk," I said. "You've got to look for her."

"I'm staying here."

I wanted to shout, but instead I did the dishes. In a way that was more noisy than usual.

"So you want us to do nothing?" I said over the clatter. "While she could be in the hands of that . . . that monster?"

Henk took the dishcloth and was drying what I washed. The noisier my washing, the quieter his drying.

"We have to do something, Henk," I said, banging down a pot on the sink counter.

"We are doing everything we can. They are searching all over. We could get word she's okay any minute now. It doesn't help to get all upset."

His phone rang. He put down the dishcloth and answered.

"Lieutenant Kannemeyer. Ja . . . Ja . . . And the hotel too? Okay. Keep looking for the scooter. When you've covered the dorp, move on to the farms outside town."

I turned to look at him.

"Nothing," he said. "Yet."

I put my hands into the warm soapy water, and closed my eyes and took a deep breath.

Henk was right. It didn't help to get upset. What would help was to find the murderer. I prepared a pot of coffee and took it onto the stoep with a tin of beskuit. I turned on the outside light. Then I went and fetched my notebook and pen.

"Come," I said. "Time to talk."

Henk poured the coffee.

"I don't suppose you will consider leaving town now?" he asked.

"The time is finished and over for you to tell us not to be involved. We need to work together."

Kannemeyer raised an eyebrow. The coffee was too hot, and he blew on it.

It was warm and muggy because of the clouds, and there were insects flying onto the stoep, attracted by the light.

"Henk, nothing you say will be reported in the *Gazette* until you give permission, I promise you. But there are two people dead, and now Jessie's disappeared. I know I am not a policewoman, but like it or not I am involved in the case. If we can work together, maybe we can save a life here. Jessie's life."

He twirled a tip of his mustache and said, "Okay, Maria. What do you want to know?"

"Everything," I said, opening the notebook. "We told you what we know. Now it's your turn."

We sat late into the night, talking about suspects and motives and investigations. The moonlight slipped through a gap in the clouds and lit up the big gwarrie tree in the veld as he told me what the police had been busy doing.

"Piet checked on John's tires at the farm. They don't match. He's also got an alibi from his girlfriend for both murders."

"But wouldn't she lie for him?" I asked.

"Maybe," Kannemeyer said. "Quin Crush delivered a pile of sand to the station. We're getting people with Firestone tires to drive across it. Once we've been through our suspects, we've also got a list of sales in this area from the dealers, HiWay Tires."

"Don't forget that Seventh-day Adventist," I said. "And Mr. Marius, of course."

"Marius was meant to come in for the tire test today, but he didn't, so I'm going to fetch him from his house first thing tomorrow."

"What have you learned about him?"

The insects were thick around the light now. Big moths, a green praying mantis, and some other little flying things.

"Shaft is his client, and they want to frack in this area. Marius has no alibi for the morning of Martine's murder. He has one for the night of Lawrence's murder. From his wife. But I visited there and it looks to me like they sleep in separate rooms."

The moths were all throwing themselves at the light. The mantis was sitting next to it. Hunting.

"Has he got a basement or anywhere he could hide someone?"

"Not that I could see. But if Jessie's still missing, I'll get a warrant to search tomorrow. I might bring his wife in for questioning. I have a feeling she knows something. She seems afraid of him."

I poured us both another cup of coffee.

"What else have you found?" I said.

"Martine's most recent accounts show a deposit of forty thousand rand."

I frowned, and said, "We didn't see . . . I suppose her most recent bank statements wouldn't have been posted to her yet."

"We got three years of statements from the bank."

"Do you think it could have been a deposit for the sale of her property?" I said.

"Could be. It was a cash deposit," he said. "Made at a Standard Bank in Riversdale. The name given on the deposit slip is V. Niemand."

"V. No one. A false name. Martine told me she was making a plan to leave. I wonder if this was part of it."

"Maybe. Up till now all there has been is her regular salary from the Spar."

A fat little gecko was heading down the wall toward the insects. My hand went to my arm, and I stroked the place where Jessie had her tattoo.

"And the pomegranate juice, with the sleeping pills in it?" I said.

"We think the murderer probably took it to her. The cashier

says Anna bought it. But we're not sure she's reliable. We believe Anna bought the six bottles today, but not necessarily the one on the day of Martine's murder."

"Thank goodness, I thought you'd take her word."

"We aren't fools. She's just trying to please her boss. And the other cashiers can't remember."

"What happened with those petty thefts at the Spar?" I asked.

"We didn't catch them, but it seems to have stopped." He looked at me. "What? What do you know about that, Tannie Maria?"

I opened my eyes wide and shook my head.

"Who else knew Martine liked pomegranate juice?" I said. "Anna, Dirk, David? Candice?"

"We can be sure that Dirk and Anna were in the hospital for Lawrence's murder. And Dirk's work gives him an alibi for Martine's. We are busy checking on the other alibis."

"And has forensics found anything?" I said. "What about my veldskoene that were cut up? And the letter sent to me?"

When the gecko was just behind the mantis, the mantis whirred up into the air and landed on the other side of the light. There were even more moths now, flying around, bashing their wings on the globe.

"Oudtshoorn LCRC tested for prints—there was nothing. For other investigations they have to send the shoes to the Cape Town forensics lab. No results there yet."

"Why not? Don't they know it's urgent?"

"The Cape Town forensics lab has to serve a hundred and fifty police stations. And there's a lot more crime in the city. Results will take a month, if we're lucky. The fluids are tested up here in Oudtshoorn. The red stuff on your letter was blood. Fresh blood. But it wasn't human. They have sent it off to the vet lab for tests. Everything takes time."

"We haven't got time," I said.

Kannemeyer looked at his watch and said, "We need to get some sleep."

"We haven't finished."

"Tomorrow."

I put out a sheet and pillow for him on the couch and I went to bed. I lay there in the dark, worrying about Jessie. I was still awake after the crickets went to sleep. My thoughts went around and around, like the moths at the light.

SEVENTY-THREE

I woke to the sound of thunder. I sat straight up. Where was Jessie?

It was light. I'd overslept. The last time I'd heard thunder was with Jessie, the night of Lawrence's murder. My spinning thoughts were now focused, hunting:

What was the murderer doing there that night? Why was he looking in Martine's study? Did he find what he wanted?

Anna told me that the study was messed up again. Dirk thought it was Martine's ghost. Anna thought it was Dirk. But what if it was the murderer? Still looking?

And if he didn't find what he wanted—where was it?

The thunder was rumbling but no rain was falling. I looked out of my window. The clouds were dark and heavy. It felt like they were about to burst.

Her office at work, I thought. She would have papers there.

I got dressed then went into the living room.

"Henk?" I called.

There was a crash of thunder and a flash of lightning and the heavens opened and fell onto my house. Rain battered down on my roof.

I looked out on to the stoep. Not Kannemeyer but Vorster. He spoke but I couldn't hear him above the rain.

I went closer and asked him, "Any news? About Jessie."

He shook his head. I stood on the stoep and watched it pouring down. It washed away the view of the hills and mountains. I could only just see the big gwarrie tree.

It was good to have rain, but I could feel no gladness. I was too worried about Jessie. I prayed she was okay. Can I call it prayer? I sent my feeling of longing, that was as strong as an arrow in my heart, up into the sky:

Rain down on Jessie. Keep her safe. Lead me to her.

I went and stood out in the rain. The water flattened my hair, ran down my face, wet my clothes. Vorster must have thought I was mad, but I didn't care.

Help me find Jessie, I asked the rain. *Alive.*

Since I was already wet, I walked around the back of my house to check on my chickens. They were all there, tucked under the shelter of their hok.

They gave me a couple of warm eggs and I cupped them in my wet hands. My veldskoene had handled the water, but I needed to change into dry clothes. I put on my pale blue dress with buttons down the front. I fried and ate the eggs for breakfast. Then I phoned Hattie at the office.

"Maria," she said. "Oh, heavens! I was about to call you. The police have just left."

My heart beat in my throat.

"Is Jessie . . . ?"

"Her boots, they were on the doorstep when I arrived. Destroyed. Burned."

"Burned?"

"Konstabel Piet thinks they were fried. They're all black and oily."

I could not find words. The rain was falling softly now.

"Piet reckons the boots were left here in the early hours of the morning," said Hattie. "They were sheltered by the eave, so they didn't get too wet and he could read some signs, don't ask me how."

"No sign of Jessie or her scooter?"

"No. They're still searching. I promised Kannemeyer I'd call you."

"We've got to find her."

"Poor Reghardt's a wreck. Before now there was a tiny chance of another explanation . . . I'd even hoped she was off investigating something. You know what a bloodhound she is when she gets on a trail. But now with the boots . . ."

"I'll come in to the office now, Hats. I'm just going to stop at the Spar on the way. I'll explain when I see you."

I called Kannemeyer but he wasn't answering his cell so I left a message. I told him I'd heard about the boots, and my thoughts about the messy papers in Martine's office. And that I was going to stop in at the Spar on my way to the *Gazette.*

"Wait," said Vorster, as I headed out. "Where are you going?"

"I'm going to work," I said. "You can go and look for Jessie."

Vorster nodded, but he stayed sitting. He wasn't taking orders from me. I walked carefully along the walkway, trying not to step in the streams and puddles.

The traveling tin of rusks rattled beside me as I drove. The veld and farms looked blurry in the soft rain.

"I'm going to find Jessie," I told the rusks.

By the time I got to the Spar, the rain had stopped. I knocked on the office door. But there was no answer. I peered through the mirror strips, and saw no one inside, but knocked again anyway. A young man came up to me.

"Can I help you, Mevrou?"

He had a pale white face with skin pulled tight over his bones, and a neat short-sleeved shirt with green stripes.

"Is the manager here?"

"He's coming in a bit later today, ma'am," said skull face politely. "I am the floor manager. Can I help you?"

"I need to look through Mrs. van Schalkwyk's papers in the office. It's important."

"I'm afraid Mr. van Wyk will need to let you in for that."

"Don't you have keys? It's really important. Life or death."

"You'll need his permission, ma'am."

"Can you call him?"

The young man frowned at me and walked away. He spoke on his cell phone then came back to me.

"He's on his way, ma'am. He won't be long."

I walked up and down the aisles of the shop, hoping it would calm me down. The sight of all that food usually does. But today it didn't help. I went back to that floor manager with the bony face.

"Did you see Jessie here yesterday after six o'clock?"

"Jessie?" he said.

"Pretty girl, reporter, works at the *Gazette*."

He shook his head, and said, "Sorry, don't know her."

"Her cousin works here. What's his name? Boetie. Can I speak to him?"

"Sorry, ma'am, Boetie called in sick today."

I walked past the cold meats and the butter and yogurts. Rooibos-flavored yogurt. That was a new one. I spotted Marietjie at a cash register.

"Marietjie, did you see Jessie last night?"

"Hello, Mr. van Wyk," said Marietjie, looking past me.

"Mr. van Wyk," I said. "I'm glad you are here."

Mr. van Wyk was blowing his nose. His eyes were red and puffy. His hair was smoothed across his head, but it had been done badly and a bald patch was showing.

"Excuse me," he said. "A cold. Nothing serious."

It looked pretty bad to me, but I wasn't going to let some germs slow me down.

"Did you see her, Marietjie?" I asked. "Yesterday after six?"

Marietjie shook her head and opened her cash register, then started sorting through the change. Mr. Van Wyk coughed.

"How can I help you?" he said.

"Can we go to your office?" I said.

As he led the way, he smoothed the hair on his head sideways, trying to get it in place. His shirt was creased, like he had no one to iron for him.

"I need to look through Martine van Schalkwyk's papers," I said.

He didn't invite me to sit. He wiped his chocolate-milk mustache, but it didn't go away.

"What are you looking for?" he asked.

"Um, I'm not sure," I said. "I'll know when I find it."

"The police have already been through her papers," he said.

I sat down at Martine's tidy desk.

"Would you mind if I looked through them again?" I said.

"I don't really see how it's any of your business . . . ," he said.

He was standing, his arms folded, looking down at me.

"It's part of the *Klein Karoo Gazette* investigation into Martine's murder," I said. "I'm Maria van Harten, a reporter and a friend of Martine's."

"Look," he said, "I don't think you should be sticking your nose into police business, but of course I want Martine's murderer to be caught. So I'll let you look through her papers. I'll even help you."

He pulled a chair up next to mine and we started going through Martine's desk drawer and her trays, labeled "In" and "Out." I didn't really want his help, but I was glad he wasn't stopping me. There was a big pile of books on her desk. They were full of columns with numbers.

"Don't you people do your math on computers these days?" I said.

"Sure," he said, "but the auditor needs hard copies as well. There's her computer." It was a little white laptop. "You want to look at it? The police took a copy of the hard drive."

"Another time," I said.

If the murderer had been searching through her papers, then

it was paper I needed to look for. I opened a book titled "Ladismith." It was full of columns and codes with numbers and ticks. I didn't really understand it, and I think Van Wyk could see that.

"She kept records of sales," he said. "She also noted all the stock coming in and out. These codes refer to items of stock."

He leaned forward to point them out. He smelled funny. Like spices gone wrong. Too much pepper. I wondered if his wife cooked for him. Marietjie had mentioned a wife.

"Does your wife like to cook?" I asked.

He sneezed.

"She's gone away," he said. "Staying with her sister in Durban. I'm looking out for myself."

He should use a recipe book, I thought.

I paged through the book, while he blew his nose. There was another book with "Regional" written on it.

"What's this about?" I asked.

"She kept a summary of the sales and expenses of all the Spars in this region. I'm the regional manager, you know. The bookkeepers in the other branches email through their information, and she puts it all together."

I nodded. I picked up a really fat book called "Salaries," which seemed to cover the salaries of all the workers in all the regions, their unemployment fund contributions, and pension and all. The workers didn't get paid very much.

There were too many books and too many pages. I was looking for a loose leaf of paper. Something that she might have been hiding. I didn't have time to look through each page, so I turned the books on their sides, shaking them. But nothing fell out.

"Have you looked through the papers at her house?" Van Wyk asked me.

He was also shaking the books now.

"Yes," I said.

"Nothing useful?"

I shook my head.

"What kind of paper do you want?" he said. "Any idea at all?"

"Well, it might be something to do with money," I said. "Maybe a sale."

I was thinking of that cash deposit.

I shook out the other books on a shelf above her desk. Two were about accounting and another was a novel. We skimmed through all the loose papers in her desk drawer and her trays. I scratched in the back of her drawer and I came across an electricity bill and a shopping list. On it was written "Lamb knuckles," and it made me think of that mutton curry recipe I'd sent her.

Then I had a thought. It hit me like a hand on my forehead and I had to clamp my mouth shut so I didn't cry out. How could I have been so stupid?

"Thanks for your help, Mr. van Wyk," I said. "May I use your phone?"

"What is it?" said Van Wyk.

"Oh, nothing," I said. "I just need to get going."

I looked up a number in the phone book and dialed and asked for Dirk van Schalkwyk.

"He's in a meeting right now, can I get him to call you back?" said the lady at the AgriMark.

"No, don't worry," I said.

I was sure Dirk wouldn't mind if I just popped in at his house.

SEVENTY-FOUR

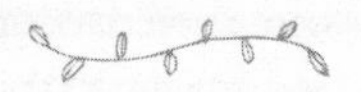

I parked under the big gum tree at Dirk's place. The house looked very quiet.

"Maybe I shouldn't have come here now," I said to the rusks. "But I've got to find Jessie." I opened the bakkie door. "I won't be long."

The sun had turned the clouds to steam and they were evaporating into the big blue sky. The ground was still cool and damp from the rain. I went around to the stoep and knocked on the front door. While I waited for no one to come, I wiped the mud off my feet on the doormat.

I tried the door; it was unlocked, and I went in.

"Dirk?" I called.

I knew he was at work, but it just seemed polite. The silence was like a heavy thing in that house, sitting quietly, waiting to jump. There was a pile of unwashed dishes at the kitchen sink.

I went straight for what I had come for. The recipe books. Martine's shopping list with ingredients for my recipe had made me think: I'd remembered the books I had seen on her pantry shelf. A recipe book is just the private place I would keep something important.

I put her four recipe books on the kitchen table, and opened them one at a time, carefully shaking them out. The first one, *Cook with Ina Paarman,* had a loose page with a handwritten recipe for butternut cheesecake in it. The second and third books, *Karoo Kitchen* and *A Celebration of South African Food,* were empty. The fourth and biggest book was *Cook and Enjoy.* I shook it and a page fluttered out: my reply to her in the *Gazette,* with the lamb curry recipe. It was there in her recipe book, just like I kept her letter to me in my Afrikaans version of the same book, *Kook en Geniet.* It was a spooky feeling. Like our recipe books could talk to each other after she was dead.

And then I found them, in the middle of *Cook and Enjoy.* Two pages: one full of figures, another with Martine's tidy handwriting. I sat down with the papers in front of me. A fly buzzed against a window. There was the sound of a car, and I thought for a moment Dirk might be coming home. I stood up to put the books away, but the car sound did not get any closer. It must have been going somewhere else.

I sat down again. I recognized the one page. It was like the bookkeeping pages I'd seen at the Spar. It had a heading—"Regional Pensions"—and lists of numbers and codes that were hard to make sense of. So I read the other page first.

Dear Mr. van Wyk, she'd written.

> *The pension records you have been passing on to me for the last three years are a lie.*

She'd crossed out "a lie" and had written "incorrect."

> *I found one correct report in your desk, which alerted me to what you have been doing.*

Then there were a few columns of numbers, then her writing again:

According to my calculations you have stolen at least 900,000 rand.

There were more corrections. This must have been her draft letter, and she would have given him her final version. She wrote:

I will not report you. But I would like 33 percent of the money you have stolen, 40,000 rand now and 260,000 rand by the end of the month.

You are to stop skimming from the funds within the next three months. The current level of loss would at present be covered by Old Mutual, who underwrite the pension plan. However, if you continue to do this, Spar will not be able to make the pension payouts that are due in the years to come, and the workers will suffer.

I will destroy my evidence of your crime only when you have paid me in full.

I read it through twice. Her "evidence" must be that bookkeeping page about regional pensions. It was strange that she was taking part in the stealing but at the same time trying to make sure that the workers would not suffer. Maybe even among thieves there are different types of wrongdoing.

But it wasn't the time to be chasing morals around in my head. These papers showed that Van Wyk had a big motive to kill Martine. He would probably also know about her love of pomegranate juice, and could have brought it to her, along with some other shopping from the Spar.

I thought I heard a sound. But I told myself I was just jumpy. I should not have come here on my own. I heard the sound again—something crunching? I got up to go and use the phone in the study. My heart was beating a bit too fast. I picked up the phone. It was dead.

I went back to the kitchen and put the books on the pantry

shelf. I picked up the two pieces of paper to take away with me. But before I could get to the front door, it opened.

Cornelius van Wyk stood there. His side-swept hair was in a mess, so his big bald patch gleamed like a china bowl. In his hand he was holding a gun. Aimed right at me.

SEVENTY-FIVE

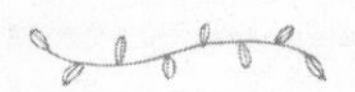

I stood still, my eyes wide, as he pointed his gun at me. My body and my mind were each going in their own directions. My knees were shaking, but my brain was pleased to have come to the end of the puzzle.

"So, it is you," my mouth said, speaking for my brain instead of my legs.

He stepped forward and pulled the papers from my hands.

"You found them," he said.

He pointed at me and then the door, with the gun.

"Let's go," he said.

My mind said, *Why go with him? If he's going to kill you, let him do it here.*

His eyes were a cold pale blue, but his face was flushed red, his chocolate-milk mustache twisted into a sneer. He was a man who took pleasure from another's pain.

Don't argue, do what he says, said my legs. *Walk.*

But my feet were frozen to the floor.

"You're looking for Jessie?" he said, his nostrils rising up.

My heart made my feet move. I would go with him.

We walked a way up the road to where he had parked his Golf. The ground was still damp, and I stepped carefully, pressing my veldskoen tracks into the ground, leaving a story for

Piet to read. Van Wyk kept his gun pointed at me as he drove. I could smell that strange spicy smell again.

"You do anything stupid," he said, "I shoot. Be a good girl and I'll take you to Jessie."

He wiped his nose with the back of his gun-free hand and sniffed. That smell, it wasn't food. It was pepper—the smell of Jessie, fighting back.

"She sprayed you, didn't she? With her pepper spray," my mouth said.

"The smell of skunks is much worse," he said. "I'm a hunter."

I held my hands flat on my lap so he couldn't see them shaking. *Am I meant to be impressed?* said my brain. *Look at that stupid little mustache. A schoolboy could do better.* I missed Kannemeyer.

I was glad my mouth stayed quiet about the mustache.

Van Wyk was driving us right out of town, toward Barrydale. He took a dirt road toward the Touwsberg. He slowed down as we drove through some muddy puddles. After a while there was a metal gate with a sign saying Kraaifontein Nature Reserve and he stopped.

"Open it," he said.

As I got out, my legs were still wobbly, but my brain noticed broken branches of klapperbos by the side of the road. The red flowers were trampled into the mud among the tracks of a big buck. *Probably eland,* said my brain, *they like to snap the branches with their horns.*

As Van Wyk drove through the gates, a little mouse ran into the bushes. *Run,* said my legs. But even if my feet had believed in running, my brain knew I could not run faster than a bullet. We drove slowly along the bumpy road until we got to a small shelter where a white 4x4 bakkie was parked.

As we climbed into the big 4x4, I saw it had Firestone tires, covered in mud. We drove toward the tall Touwsberg. There were fat gray clouds hanging in a bright blue sky. The kloofs were in purple shadow. Around us were low hills covered in stones and gwarrie trees and wild plum trees. We frightened a herd of zebra and they galloped up the hill. My heart galloped with them. *We are driving into the middle of nowhere. He's going to kill me.* But then my brain said: *You are still alive. And you are going to Jessie.*

"What happened with Jessie?" my mouth said.

"She found out about the pomegranate juice. That bloody packer, Boetie, told her I took a bottle from the storeroom. He's her cousin or something, Marietjie says."

The cousin who'd called in sick, I thought. Was he sick?

"Marietjie's in on this, these murders?" I said.

"Oh, no. She's just loyal, poor girl. Tells me things. I suspected the staff of petty thefts, so they accused me of stealing."

"Did Jessie come after you?"

There was a kudu in the road. The sun seemed to be shining through its big ears as it looked at us with wide black eyes.

Van Wyk didn't slow down. It leaped away, just in time, over a spiky bush. My mouth sucked in air. Van Wyk laughed.

"I've only once gotten one like that," he said. "Too messy. Damages the car. I prefer a bow and arrow."

"Jessie?" I said.

"I followed her," he said. "She was heading out, toward you. I got her on the dirt road to your house."

"Got her?" I said.

"I knocked her down."

"You knocked her down?"

I was sounding like an echo, but I couldn't help myself. I needed to hear about Jessie.

"Oh, she was okay, only out of it for a minute or two. Her leg was a bit damaged, though. A pity. I was hoping she'd be a runner."

"A runner?" I said.

My brain was irritated by my mouth's echo. Maybe Van Wyk was too. We didn't speak for a while. He pulled under a carport with a reed roof, next to a square house with a wide stoep. The walls were painted a dirty green.

He made me walk ahead of him, into a living room with

big leather couches and a cement floor covered in mats made from the skins of wild animals. On the walls were the stuffed heads of animals with long horns, staring at me with glassy eyes. Through a door I could see a kitchen with wide metal counters. He pushed aside a zebra skin with his foot. Underneath was a wooden trapdoor.

"Open it," he said.

My hands pulled on a brass handle and the square door lifted up. There were gray stairs leading down to a darkened door. He pulled a flashlight from his pocket and shone it down the stairs. The door was made of thick gray metal.

"Down you go," he said.

I shook my head. This time my body and brain agreed.

"You don't want to see Jessie?" he said, aiming his gun at my heart.

I stepped toward the stairs and he gave that ugly smile again.

"You people," he said to himself.

He followed me down the stairs and unlocked the door with a big key. The door was thick and heavy but made no sound as it swung open. A wave of icy air came out, like we were opening a giant fridge.

There was a low humming sound, and a faint blue light along one edge of the room. I could not see properly. Van Wyk pushed me in, and I bumped into something big and icy.

The door slammed behind me, and I heard him walking up the steps again, and the *thud* as he closed the trapdoor.

My eyes shut and opened, hoping to adjust to the dim lighting. They could just make out the outline of a big shape, which seemed to be hanging from the ceiling, not touching the floor. But it was my nose that confirmed it for me. The smell of meat. Cold flesh hung just in front of my face. My throat squealed as my feet stepped back.

"Jessie?" my small voice said.

Of course there was no reply. This was not a room for living things.

SEVENTY-SIX

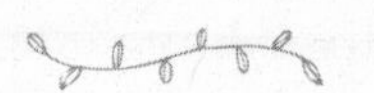

As my eyes got used to the darkness, I could see the shape of the hanging flesh. Small and stout. I went a little closer. It was a buck. I breathed out. I was sorry for the buck, but glad it was not Jessie.

I touched its shoulder. The body was very cold, but not frozen. It was a little klipspringer. What kind of man would kill a klipspringer?

I hugged my arms around my body, glad for every gram of fat I had. As I moved around the giant fridge, I rubbed my hands together and blew on my fingers. In the dim light I saw six more hanging bodies. My tummy was in a knot, but I made myself check each one.

A young kudu, his horns just starting to curve.

A female eland.

Two steenbuck, a male and a female. I wondered if they were mates.

A baby zebra.

And a mama zebra, who looked pregnant to me.

I am no expert on hunting, but I know there are some rules, and this man didn't care about them. He was also killing animals in summer when the hunting season was in winter.

Under the kudu was a dark pool of blood. It looked a bit smudged and I leaned down to have a closer look. There was a handprint in the kudu's blood on the cement. Next to it were small dark initials: J.M. Jessie Mostert had been here. But where was she now?

My heart called: *Jessie. Where are you, Jessie?*

I could picture her face, smiling at me, like she was glad to see me. It made a warm ache in my cold chest. It kept me going as I searched the room. There was a big freezer against a wall, with a strip of blue light under it. I was not ready to look in there yet, so I studied the floor and walls for more messages from Jessie. Nothing.

I went to the freezer. It had a big padlock on the lid, but was not locked. I lifted up the lid. Inside, there was a light, and I could see plastic bags of meat. Ground meat, sausage, steaks. There was no packaging on it, but it looked a lot like the game meat I had bought from the Spar. There was no sign of Jessie.

I heard a loud rattling sound. It was my teeth, chattering. I felt nauseous. I closed the lid and folded my arms on it and leaned my head down.

I saw Jessie's face again, this time frowning at me. *Don't give up, Tannie M*, she was saying.

It gave me that warm feeling in my chest again and my feet started stamping, and my hands rubbed my arms.

"I'm going to find Jessie," I told the frozen meat.

I heard feet on the steps outside. When the door opened and a flashlight shone in my eyes, I walked straight toward it.

"What have you done with her?" I said.

But I'm not sure if the words got right out of my mouth because I swallowed so hard when I saw the big knife in his hand.

SEVENTY-SEVEN

I need your help in the kitchen, Tannie Maria," he said.

He and his knife were silhouetted in the doorway.

I took a step backward and banged my head against a steenbuck.

He laughed, and said, "I am glad you are learning a little respect. But don't worry about this." He waved the knife in the air. "It's just for chopping meat." I could see a silver glint on the metal as well as dark stains of blood. "Come along, aren't you chilly down here?"

It wouldn't help Jessie if I died of cold, so I followed him up the stairs. The gun was strapped to his waist now. I knew from my days with Fanie that I was no fighter. I was just not quick or strong enough. I wished I had done some classes, or learned to use a weapon or something. I bet Jessie knew a thing or two. Maybe she had escaped. Maybe she was just fine.

He made me walk ahead into the kitchen. Along the big silver counters were all kinds of butcher's equipment, a meat grinder, a sausage maker.

It was warmer upstairs, but my shivering got worse. I was shaking like a rattle.

"What happened to Jessie?" I said, between the chattering of my teeth.

"Maybe a bit of cooking will warm you up," he said. "I haven't had a good meal since my wife left, and I know you are quite the little cook."

On the stove was a big cast-iron frying pan and next to it was a wooden board with three fillets of meat. There was also a jar of beets and a bean salad from the Spar.

"Now you go ahead and cook those steaks," he said. "That meat is really fresh."

I tried to turn on the gas stove but my hands weren't working properly. They were numb from the cold.

"Let me help you," he said, all Mr. Polite, and he put down his knife and lit the stove.

I hated this man, this murderer, but I let him light the stove. I held my hands on either side of the pan. My fingers were blue. The warmth made them ache. But after a while they started working and I poured a little oil into the pan.

I was about to put in the meat, but then my hands stopped working again. This time it wasn't the cold. It was my heart.

I cannot cook with hate, said my heart. *I just can't.*

You cooked for Fanie, my brain reminded me. *And you hated him.*

No, I didn't, my heart said. *I just didn't love him. And I did love to cook.*

I stepped back from the stove.

"I'm not going to cook for you," I said.

"You are going to cook for me," he said, pulling out his gun.

"Cooking is something you should do with love," I said.

My whole body believed this as my mouth spoke, but my brain said: *Are you mad? He'll kill you!*

I folded my arms and waited for the bullet.

But instead of shooting me, Van Wyk laughed. A cold, dry laugh.

"You people with your . . . love nonsense," he said with that sneering smile. "It makes you so weak."

I just stood there, my body still shivering from the cold, but my refusal hot in my belly.

"If you cook for me," he said, in an artificial-sweetener voice, "I'll tell you what happened to Jessie. I promise."

Of course, his promise meant nothing, but if there was even a small chance of finding out something . . . I would cook, for the love of Jessie.

I lowered the steaks into the pan. The oil spat up at me, but my hands jumped aside. Van Wyk laughed again.

"You see how strong your weakness makes me?" he said, putting his gun back on his belt. "You wouldn't even be in this mess if you didn't care. You cared about a stranger, one you hadn't even met. And look at the trouble it's gotten you into. It's unnatural, you know, quite unnatural."

"You are unnatural," I said. "A sick man."

I might be cooking for him, but I wasn't going to agree with him.

"Not at all," he said. "I'm the fittest of the fit. A predator. Looking out for myself."

He took out a comb from his pocket, and combed his few hairs across his head.

"Without care or love you are nothing, just a lonely man," I said, turning the steak.

"I like being alone. Though I do miss a good cook," he said, putting his comb away. "And when I need, what is it you people call it?" His gaze jumped around as he spoke, his pupils moving like water beetles on a pool. "Closeness, intimacy, then . . . I hunt."

He dished the bean and beet salads onto two plates. I added a fried steak to each serving. I left the third, thickest one in the pan, to keep warm.

"Have you killed lots of people?" I said, like I was asking if he wanted tomato sauce.

"Oh, it's a brand-new sport for me," he said. "I used to hunt only animals. Didn't realize that people could be so . . . satisfying."

He laid the plates on the counter with knives and forks, and started to eat, standing up.

Your body needs fuel, my brain told me, *to get warm.*

I pulled up a chair and made myself eat.

"But the chase," he said, "is so important. Killing—*bang bang,* you're dead—has its pleasure, but it's just not the same." He cut into the meat. "Of course, I try for a clean shot but when an animal is wounded, and I have to track it down, then the hunt is even better." He chewed. "I always find it, you know. Usually it's dead, but sometimes it's weak, and waiting for me to put it out of its misery. And I do."

He smiled. His eyes were empty as ice. As he ate his steak, a bit of blood leaked out of the corner of his mouth.

"Hmm. You are not a bad cook," he said. "Not bad at all."

I don't overcook a steak. The meat was tender and rich. I didn't recognize the flavor, but my taste buds were cold and confused. I hoped I wasn't eating a klipspringer or something. I left the steak and ate some of the salads. They tasted like shop food but I made myself swallow the beets and beans.

"What happened with Jessie?" I said.

"The bow and arrow. Great weapon, that. Very accurate if you're a good marksman. And silent. Don't know what's hit them. No adrenaline, so the meat tastes nicer. No noisy shots to give you away if you happen to hunt out of season."

"Jessie," I said. "You promised to tell me about her."

"But I am."

I pushed my plate aside. The knot in my tummy wouldn't let any more food in.

"You shot Jessie with an arrow?"

"She had that sore leg, which would make the chase boring. So I decided to let her take her scooter. I drained most of the gas out." He ate a mouthful of beans. "Didn't tell her that, of course, so when I caught up with her, she was frantically trying to get it started. Didn't see me coming."

"You hit her?"

"Oh, I never miss."

"Where is she?"

"Not far," he said, as he picked up his last forkful of steak. He waved it slowly in the air. "Very close, I'm sure, very close."

I looked at the meat on his fork and on my plate. I wanted to throw up.

"I'll have that last steak, Tannie Maria. Unless you want it, of course. I see you haven't finished yours?"

He popped his piece of steak into his mouth.

I went to the stove and picked up the handle of that heavy pan in two hands. As I got to the counter, I swung it at him. He swerved but I still hit him hard. I'm not sure if I got him on the head or neck. He fell onto the floor and I didn't wait to see if he got up. I moved, as fast as I could, out of the kitchen, across the dead animal skins in the living room, and out the front door. I headed down toward a line of trees. My breath was jumping in and out of my throat. I looked behind me and saw my footprints clearly in the damp sand.

SEVENTY-EIGHT

A woodpecker was hammering on a tree by the riverbed. It sounded like my heart. *Thud-thud-thud.* I was not made for running, but my legs were doing the best they could. They just kept moving, one in front of the other, taking me away from that man. Away from that last steak that had fallen on the floor when I panned him.

The clouds had grown thick and dark, and I heard a rumbling.

Rain, I prayed, *fall down. Fall down on me. Hide my tracks. Keep Jessie safe.*

My tummy groaned. I hoped it was not a piece of Jessie that was groaning at me. You should never exercise right after a meal. But my legs kept on going, taking me down to the cover of the trees.

When I was almost there, there was a crack and I jumped. My heart fluttered like a woodpecker's wings. But I had not been shot. It was lightning.

Then I felt it. The rain. It fell hard, streaming down my face.

Thank you. Thank you, thank you.

I walked into the cover of the trees that lined the riverbed. The wind roared through the leaves and shook the branches. I was hidden from the house, and I leaned against a camphor tree to catch my breath. My hands and teeth were shaking. I rubbed my arms with my hands.

Well done, Tannie Maria, my brain said. *You are still alive. Maybe Jessie is too.*

My tummy and the thunder rumbled together. My legs got me moving again. I walked down the narrow riverbed, and the rain washed my tracks behind me. I headed south, in the direction of the gate, I hoped.

A rabbit shot out from beneath a big wolf-thorn bush. It raced toward me and I stood still so I wouldn't frighten it. It swerved around me and headed up the riverbed.

Then I saw what had given that a rabbit such a fright.

About ten meters ahead of me, he stepped out from beneath a thorn tree that was covered with yellow devil's tresses. His hair was all mussed and his mustache was twisted in that sneer. The bow and arrow hung by his side.

Van Wyk shouted at me. It was hard to hear him over the storm, but he shouted again:

"Run, Tannie, run!"

My body shook with fear, but I did not believe in running. And I especially didn't believe in running as a favor for a murderer who wants a moving target.

He stepped over a slime bush and shooed me with his hand. But I stood facing him, the rain running down my hair, my clothes sopping wet. He shook his head, and lifted his bow and arrow, waving them at me.

When I didn't move, he walked backward, farther away. Ten meters was too easy for him. When he'd doubled the distance, he raised his bow again, put in the arrow, and pulled the string back.

In that tiny moment as his arm set the arrow free, my brain and body and heart all worked together and a strange thing happened. It is hard to describe but I can only try.

The cold and the fear had been shaking me like a leaf, but as he pulled his arm back, I was dead still.

There was no time, but there was all the time in the world. I could see a raindrop falling.

As he released the arrow, I did not run.

I flew.

I flew up and away, to the side.

I thought I was dead, but I was alive. I flew like a phoenix.

And the thing that made me fly was the fire of love that I felt in my heart. This is what made me stronger than Van Wyk. What made me powerful, and him nothing.

Love. I felt my love for my life. My love for Jessie, and Hats, and my chickens. And Kannemeyer.

It lifted me up. Gave me wings.

I flew up to the side and down again. My landing was not so gentle. I crashed down onto the ground. *Thud.* But I did not feel any pain. A part of me was still flying.

Then Van Wyk was standing above me, his lips pulled back, his teeth small and mean.

"You do make this interesting," he said. There were drops of rain on his feeble mustache. "Sorry to cut it short, but I have another hunt to get to."

The rain was less now. It fell down softly onto me. He put an arrow into his bow and pulled it back and pointed it at me. He aimed at my heart.

"I wonder if the arrow will go right through you at this range?" he said. "You are quite . . . dense."

I closed my eyes so I would not have to see his ugly smile. I imagined Jessie and Hattie drinking tea and eating rusks. And I saw Kannemeyer, with his thick mustache and that handsome smile of his.

I was not afraid.

SEVENTY-NINE

I heard a loud *crack*. Followed by a *thud*. Did the arrow make that noise as it cracked my heart?

But I still felt no pain. Maybe it was a crack of lightning? I opened my eyes. I saw no arrow sticking into me, but I did see the face I had been imagining. The one with the chestnut mustache. So I knew I was dead.

"Maria," he said, kneeling down beside me, "are you all right?"

He put his hand on my forehead. The rain had stopped now but my face was still wet. I pushed myself up so I was sitting. I wasn't dead. I was shivering like crazy.

"I'm cold," I said.

My teeth were chattering so hard, I don't know if he could hear me, but he got the idea. He unbuttoned his shirt and took it off and wrapped it around my shoulders.

"Get something warm," he said to Piet, who then ran off, up toward the house.

Van Wyk was lying on the ground in the riverbed. Dead still. With a red stain spreading across his shirt.

"You shot him," I said.

Kannemeyer helped me to stand up. His chest had that chestnut hair on it. He pulled me in, wrapped his arms around me. It reminded me of that time he had held Anna when she was fighting. I didn't fight. He was warm, like freshly baked bread. My skin drank up his body heat, but I couldn't stop shivering.

"We've got to get you warm," he said.

He put one arm around me and helped me up the riverbank. I turned to look back at Van Wyk.

"He put me in a big fridge," I said. I was still shivering, but if I kept my mouth a bit open, my teeth did not bang together. "Jessie. I think he shot Jessie. With a bow and arrow. When she was on her scooter. He said . . ."

We walked toward the house and Reghardt and Piet came running down to us. Piet had a big kudu skin that Kannemeyer wrapped around me.

"Is Jessie here? Have you seen her?" asked Reghardt.

His dark eyes were wet and his face was pale.

"No. But I . . ." My tummy growled and I felt nauseous.

"What?" said Reghardt.

"She was here. I saw her handprint in blood, and her initials on the floor. The fridge is full of dead animals. Hanging."

"Where? What are you talking about?" said Reghardt.

"Under the zebra skin. There's a trapdoor. Stairs down to a big fridge."

Reghardt started to head up to the house.

"It's locked," I said.

"Check Van Wyk for keys," said Kannemeyer to Reghardt, who then ran down to the riverbed.

"There was a fight," said Piet. "With a pan. You hit him?"

I nodded.

"He made me cook some steaks, then he said . . . He said . . . He made it sound like the meat was Jessie. That we were eating her. There's a steak on the kitchen floor. And on my plate."

Piet shot up to the house.

"We must get you in a hot bath," Kannemeyer said, as we got close to the stoep.

My belly twisted and groaned just looking at the house.

"I'm not going back in there," I said.

Reghardt brought me a bunch of keys and I pointed out the long one for the freezer door. Detective Kannemeyer barked a list of instructions at Piet and Reghardt. Reinforcements, searches, ambulance.

"I'll be back now-now," he called over his shoulder as he led me to the police van. "Warrant Officer Snyman, phone Harriet Christie and tell her to head over to Tannie Maria's house. Konstabel Witbooi, find those scooter tracks."

The van was parked at an odd angle next to the carport that made reed-striped shadows on Van Wyk's 4x4. Kannemeyer helped me into his van and tucked the skin around me. He didn't ask for his shirt back.

Just as we were driving off, Piet came running up to us.

"The steaks," he said. "I know that meat. It's aardvark."

My belly stopped groaning and went soft with relief.

EIGHTY

"Tell me what happened, Maria," said Kannemeyer.

We were bumping across the dirt road, the heater turned on full blast. The outside of my skin was warming up but the cold was deep in my bones.

I gave him my story, right from the beginning.

"I woke up this morning thinking about the study at Dirk's house," I said.

I told him my thoughts about the papers and my visit to the Spar, and my brainstorm about the recipe books. I did not care if Kannemeyer got cross with me for doing stupid things. What mattered was finding Jessie. Dead or alive.

He didn't get cross, he just listened, and asked me questions here or there. His chest was still bare and he smelled like earth and rain and nutmeg.

We stopped at the gate to the nature reserve and he said, "Look at that steenbokkie."

The little steenbuck was lying in the shade of a gwarrie tree, its big ears pricked up. When Kannemeyer got out of the car to open the gate, it darted away across the veld.

We drove through the puddles on the dirt road and back onto the tarmac. I told Kannemeyer about the smell of pepper and Van Wyk's feeble mustache and the dead animals and what I said to the murderer about love. And when it got to the end of my story, I even told him how I flew. But I didn't tell him that it was the fire of love in my heart that made me fly like a phoenix. Or that when I thought of him and his chestnut mustache I was not afraid.

Instead I asked him, "How did you find me?"

"I suppose we found you because of Boetie," he said. "And Harriet. She was looking at the notes on your whiteboard, and she remembered Jessie wanted to talk to her cousin at the Spar. You were also taking a bit long to come from the Spar, so she drove over there. But there was no sign of you, or Boetie."

He ran his hand across his chest. The sun was peeping through the clouds now, and the light showed off the red and silver in his chest hair.

"She was worried about you," he said, "and came to the police station. We had Marius there, driving his Firestones across the sand. Piet said his tracks were okay, but we were about to go and search his house anyway. Harriet convinced us that we must first find Boetie. She got me worried about you."

He glanced at me and I looked down at my hands. They were still shaking.

"It's funny they are still so cold," I said. "So did you find Boetie?"

"Ja. He had gone to Suurbraak to get gerook with his friends. He was still stoned but we sobered him up and the story came out. He didn't go in to work today because he was scared he'd pissed off his boss."

"I'm glad he was okay. Boetie. I thought maybe Van Wyk had gotten to him . . ."

"He'd told Jessie that Van Wyk had taken a bottle of pomegranate juice."

"Ja," I said, "Van Wyk told me. Marietjie overheard them and ran to her boss."

Kannemeyer went on, "Boetie doesn't know why Jessie got so excited about it, and rushed off like that. He realized Marietjie had overheard them and saw Marietjie going into Van Wyk's office right after Jessie left. He left work fast and hitched a ride to Suurbraak."

"Did you talk to Marietjie?"

"She said Van Wyk is allowed to take from his own shop. It's not stealing. Then she started crying and wouldn't say any more. We searched his house in town and then his game farm. Thank God we got there in time. Before he . . ." Kannemeyer was gripping the steering wheel tightly. His arms had that same soft chestnut hair on them. "If you . . ."

He looked at me, and I saw that sadness in his eyes. I wanted to reach out and put my hand on his. But I didn't.

His eyes were on the road now, as he turned the wheel, taking the turnoff toward my house.

Sergeant Vorster's gone to join the search," said Kannemeyer, as we parked in my driveway.

"That's where you should be," I said. "Where I should be."

"Ja, ja, I'm going back. Let's just get you warm and dry. Harriet will be here soon."

My hands were still shaking and I struggled to open the van door. He came around and helped me out, keeping that kudu skin wrapped around me.

He took me into my house and went straight to the bathroom and started the water running. Then he found the Klipdrift brandy, poured a small shot and stirred in a spoon of sugar. I enjoyed watching him moving around, without his shirt. I tried not to stare at the shape of his broad chest, and its layer of chestnut fur, and the soft hair that ran down past his belly button to the top of his pants. When he turned away I could look at the muscles moving under the brown skin on his back. He gave me the glass of sweet brandy. With the shivering and all, I spilled some, but a mouthful got down my throat and made a warm line to my belly.

He called me when the bath was ready, and I put my fingertips in the water.

"Eina," I said. "It's hot."

He leaned down and put his elbow in.

"No," he said, "it just feels hot because you're so cold. But I'll cool it down and you can add hot when you're in."

He added cold water then he took the kudu skin off me. He did not take his shirt back.

"I'll be just outside," he said. "If you need me."

He left and closed the bathroom door. I took his shirt from my shoulders and held it to my face and breathed in his smell. Then I put the shirt on the laundry basket and tried to undo the buttons on my pale blue dress, but my hands just couldn't get it right. I tried to lift the dress over my head but that was worse, so I pulled it down again.

"Maria," he said. He was still outside the door. "Are you doing okay?"

"My buttons," I said.

"Do you need help?" he said.

I nodded.

"Can I come in?"

I nodded again. It was hard for me to ask out loud for that kind of help.

"Maria?"

He knocked and came in.

"I can't undo my buttons," I said.

My dress was still damp and it clung to my breasts. He took a step toward me. I could smell his breath. It was like cinnamon bark and honey. My breasts were moving up and down with my breathing, though I was asking them to stay still.

"Maybe we should wait for Hattie," I said.

He took my cold hands between his warm palms. For a moment they stopped shivering. He looked into my eyes.

"I don't think we should wait," he said.

He let go of my hands and undid my top button.

EIGHTY-ONE

He went on looking into my eyes as he undid my buttons. His fingers were trembling a bit. I held my breath, to keep my breasts still, but then I started to run out of air, so I had to suck some in. His fingertips brushed against me, his hand looking for the next button.

I could feel the heat from his body, waves of it moving from him to me. When he had undone the buttons all the way down to my thighs he slipped the dress off my shoulders. I was glad I had my nice underwear on. White cotton.

He stood in front of me—his body so close that I was tickled by his chest hairs—and reached his arms around me to undo my bra. He took the straps off my shoulders, and the bra dropped to the floor. Then his body heat pulled me in, and I was pressing myself into his chest.

His hand held the back of my head, gently, like I might break. I heard the sound of a car arriving. He stepped back, and my arms moved to cover my breasts. But then I realized that I might've died today, without any man seeing me naked, so I let my hands drop.

He looked at me standing there in only my panties and my muddy veldskoene, and he smiled. That wide white smile that made my heart somersault.

"Lovely," he said.

He grabbed his shirt and left the room, closing the door. I finished getting undressed and climbed into the bath and lay back in the warm water. The ice inside me was slowly melting.

EIGHTY-TWO

"You all right in there, Maria darling?" said Hattie through the bathroom door.

"Hats! I'm fine, my skat."

"I'm just making us a spot of tea," she said. "The detective said I must tell you to add more hot water."

I heard the sound of a car driving off as I ran the hot tap. My shivering stopped, and the warmth filled my whole body.

I got dressed in trousers and a shirt, and put on fresh socks with my veldskoene and went out to the stoep. Hattie jumped up and gave me the biggest hug.

"Oh, Maria. Tannie Maria!" she said.

For a skinny lady, she was a good hugger. On the stoep table was a tray with cups and a pot of tea in a tea cozy, and an open tin of beskuit. I poured for us, as if this was an ordinary Friday-afternoon visit. The chickens came calling and I threw them a handful of mielies.

"I have been out of my mind with worry," Hattie said.

I told her my story, the bits she didn't know, and we drank tea and ate beskuit.

"Thank goodness that dreadful man is dead," she said.

"Thanks to you, Hats. Without your ideas about Boetie, they wouldn't have gotten to me in time . . ."

"Oh, pish-posh," she said, flapping her hand as if chasing a fly away. "We all did what we could. I can't tell you how happy I am that you are alive."

But she did not look happy. Her face was pale and pinched. There was a big emptiness in the chair where Jessie wasn't sitting. We sat looking at the afternoon sun melting away the last of the storm clouds, but the silence got too loud.

"We can't just sit here," I said. "Let's go and help find her."

"Are you sure, Tannie M? Don't you need to rest?"

"Can you rest?" I said, standing up.

She sighed, and stood up too. I grabbed the tin of rusks and a jacket and a flashlight, and we headed for her car. The Toyota Etios was squashed between a thorn bush and a eucalyptus tree.

"Why don't I drive?" I said.

"Don't be ridiculous, Maria, after all you've been through."

"We could go past Dirk's and fetch my bakkie."

"Let's get it later," she said. "When your nerves have settled."

"You're right. The sooner we get there . . ."

Apart from giving her directions, we did not talk on the road because I was holding my breath most of the time. Her driving was even more terrible than usual—maybe it just felt worse because of my shaken nerves or all those puddles and bumps on the dirt roads.

The tin of beskuit rattled on the backseat. I put them on my lap so that they did not all turn to crumbs. But I did not ask Hattie to slow down, because I wanted to get there as fast as we could. Luckily we did not kill ourselves or any wild animals on the way. I think the animals heard her coming and ran over the hill.

Goodness gracious," said Hattie as she bumped the Etios into a Combi parked outside Van Wyk's house. "What a circus."

"Looks like half the town has turned up," I said.

The circus was overflowing off the green stoep, into the driveway. We could see: a flock of Jessie's relatives; a line of nurses from the hospital, Jessie's mom standing very still among them in her white nurse's outfit, hugging her arms around herself; a troupe of Seventh-day Adventists; and the clowns—Dirk, Anna, and John—in their bandages and wheelchair.

Police in uniforms were herding the people into small groups. On the stoep, Kannemeyer pointed to a map that was stuck up on the wall. His shirt was back on; it was very wrinkled.

He said, "Only go to the areas that your policeman leads you to." He frowned and shook his head when he saw me, but went on talking. "We don't want to mess up the tracks in the areas that Konstabel Witbooi is still studying. No running off."

"But that guy's running all over like a mad thing," said Anna, pointing out across the veld at someone moving like a jackal, zigzagging across the slope of a hill.

"That's Warrant Officer Reghardt Snyman. He's working with Konstabel Witbooi. Listen, we don't have time for messing around. You do what we say, or you leave. Understood?"

There was a nodding of some heads. Anna took a silver hip flask from her side and had a sip then rested the flask on her plaster cast.

"Right. Now listen closely. Group one, you come with me. I'll give you directions when we get there."

As he was talking, a red sports car came racing up the road and skidded to a halt, spitting gravel.

"Group two, you are with Sergeant Vorster," said Kannemeyer. "You'll be following him, walking three meters apart. Group two, are you listening?"

But he realized he'd lost their attention; he shook his head and allowed a break as the people watched Candy's arrival.

Her legs seemed to have gotten even longer, and they came out of the car with a pair of midnight blue heels. Her short dress was sky blue and her gold hair loose and soft on her shoulders. Even on that bumpy ground, she moved like a catwalk model as she walked toward us.

She saw Kannemeyer but ignored him and looked at me.

"Tannie Maria," she said, as if I was the one running the show, "I came as soon as I heard. Is there anything I can do?"

"Come here," I said, because Hattie and I had been herded into group one. "And listen to what the detective is saying."

Candy pursed her pink lips and came and stood by me. She smelled of lemon blossom.

"Right," said Kannemeyer, pointing to a section on the map. "Group two will drive with Sergeant Vorster to the south side."

There were four groups, each to cover different areas. Three of them headed off, with their own police leaders. Group one stayed on the stoep, waiting for Kannemeyer.

"Pretorius. You're not going to get across the veld in that thing," Kannemeyer said to Anna, who was rolling along after group two.

"I've got binoculars," she said, pulling them out of a pocket of the wheelchair, and waving them at him.

"Best you stay here." He turned to the hobbling, bandaged Dirk and John. "All three of you."

"Ag, bloody hell," Dirk grumbled into his beard.

"Warrant Officer Smit needs backup here, at base camp."

Smit's eyebrows shot up.

"The ambulance will be here now-now," said Kannemeyer to the warrant officer. "To pick up Van Wyk."

"What?" said Anna.

"He's still here?" said John.

"I'll kill him," said Dirk.

"He's dead," said Kannemeyer.

"I don't care," said Dirk. "Where is he?

"I hear the ambulance now," said Kannemeyer.

There was a siren wailing across the hills.

He mouthed *Sorry* to Warrant Officer Smit. Then he led group one away.

"We are going to catch up with Konstabel Piet Witbooi," he told us.

There were ten in our group and those of us who didn't fit

into Kannemeyer's van climbed into Hattie's car. In the front sat a skinny young man with red eyes and a woolen cap pulled down over his ears. He smelled of some sweet herb. Basil?

Georgie, the Seventh-day Adventist, and Candy sat in the back with me. On my lap I held the tin of broken rusks.

"We are praying for her," said Georgie, patting my knee.

Hattie banged the Combi again as she reversed out.

"Ooh-woo," said Georgie in a high-pitched tone, and began praying in a singsong rhythm.

"How do you do?" said Hattie to the young man. "I am Harriet Christie."

"Uh-huh," said the man.

"And you are?"

"Boetie," he mumbled.

"Ah, the notorious Boetie Mostert," she said, shooting down the dirt road to catch up with Kannemeyer's van.

"You've got that glow, sugar," Candy said to me, gripping the seat in front of her. "What happened?"

I thought of Kannemeyer in the bathroom and my face went hot.

"Jessie might have gotten away," I said. "Sprayed him with pepper spray."

"You're blushing. I hope so. She's a wild one, Jessie." She looked down at my muddy veldskoene. "I've got just the shoes for you. I'll send you a pair."

Hattie was weaving all over the dirt road, avoiding puddles, and hitting rocks.

The more the bumps, the faster Georgie prayed, and the higher the notes on her Ooh-woos: "Lord, oh lord, ooh-woo, oh lordy, as we move through the valley of death, keep us all safe. Ooooh-woooooo."

"There's Piet," I said.

We pulled up behind Kannemeyer's van, only lightly hitting his back bumper. Maybe Georgie's prayers did work.

We all piled out and looked around at the wild veld and hills.

Some zebras were silhouetted on a faraway ridge. The rusks and I stood close enough to the men to hear them talking. Piet was crouched on his haunches by the side of the road, looking at the muddy ground.

"What are you doing?" said Kannemeyer.

"Watching ants," said Piet.

"Find anything?"

"The rain was heavy."

"Tracks?"

"Bike tires and the Firestones. They stop. The Firestones turn around, go back."

"And shoe prints?"

"Rain was too heavy."

Kannemeyer moved from one foot to the other.

Piet went on watching the ants.

Kannemeyer tugged at one end of his mustache.

"Here are the volunteers to help with the search."

Piet nodded and inched forward, following the line of ants.

"Will you tell them where to go?" said Kannemeyer.

"They are telling me," said Piet, keeping his gaze on the ground.

"Konstabel Witbooi," said Kannemeyer.

Piet pointed.

We looked at the ants. There was a long line of them heading one way, and another long line heading back.

Piet trotted forward. Kannemeyer and I followed.

We followed the line of ants between some vetplantjies, and then behind a porcupine milk bush. Piet prodded the earth with his foot. The ground was soft and disturbed.

"There is something under here that the ants are eating," he said.

Reghardt ran down the hill to us, his face streaked with scratches and dirt.

"What is it?" he said. "What have you found?"

"Get the spade from the back of the van," said Kannemeyer.

The other people from group one had wandered across and were standing behind us. They used their hands to shade their faces from the afternoon sun. They moved aside as Reghardt pushed through with the spade. Kannemeyer tried to take it from him, but Reghardt wasn't letting go.

Piet pointed out the area to dig. Reghardt's spade dipped in fast but shallow. Like he didn't want to hurt what was underneath.

Beneath the sand, there was just more sand. The sweat ran down the side of his face. Then Reghardt struck something solid. *Thunk.* The sound made me jump, and the rusks rattle.

Reghardt closed his eyes and stood still a second. His face went white. Then he crouched down and peered into the hole. Piet was squatting on the ground. He reached in and touched the thing that Reghardt had hit. He brought out his finger and smelled it. An ant was walking across his fingernail.

"Blood," Piet said.

EIGHTY-THREE

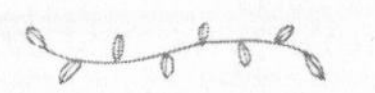

Reghardt let out a small sound like he had been hit in the belly, but then he swallowed and started digging with his hands, like an animal clawing the ground. Piet was working beside him. Reghardt's hand gripped something and he tugged at it.

"It's metal," he said. "It's metal."

Kannemeyer and Boetie joined them and they all dug together. They cleared the dirt away and pulled out a scooter. Jessie's red scooter.

I could see the ants and the dark sticky stuff on the seat of the bike. Piet ran his fingers across it. Touched his finger to the tip of his tongue.

"This is from today," he said.

Reghardt's face was now whiter than white.

"She'd dead, isn't she?" he said. "Just tell me."

Piet shook his head.

"Can't say."

Reghardt was breathing fast; I thought he was going to faint.

I clutched my tin of buttermilk beskuit. I wanted to give him something to help with the shock. But he needed something else even more than these broken rusks. Something we all needed: hope. We had to have hope.

"Jessie was on her scooter, and he shot her," I said, "with a bow and arrow. But when he caught up with her, she was ready for him. She sprayed him. With the pepper spray. I smelled it on him. He was blinded and she got away. She left her bike, but she got away, Reghardt. Then there was rain and it washed away her tracks, so he couldn't find her."

Piet was nodding, but Reghardt was shaking his head, holding back the tears. I kept on talking.

"She was like a wounded animal and he wanted to come back and look for her. He got a phone call that I was at his work and he came to get me. This morning he told me he had another hunt to do. He was talking about her. He hadn't found her. And he didn't find her."

I turned to the people standing behind me.

"Now he's dead and he didn't find her," I said. "But we can find her."

"Konstabel Witbooi," said Kannemeyer, "go back to where the scooter tracks stopped and see if you can find any foot spoor." He turned to speak to the rest of us. "If she was injured, I doubt she'd have gotten farther than two kilometers. She might have hypothermia too. Keep your eyes on the ground. Footprints are unlikely because of the rain, but you never know, maybe she walked after the rain. Also, look out for broken plants, blood, ants. You see anything unusual, raise your hand and call out for me or Konstabel Witbooi."

As he spoke, I offered the tin of rusks, and people helped themselves. A young nurse in a white uniform took the tin from me and offered it to those who stood out of my reach.

"Warrant Officer Snyman—you move in a wide circle around this point. Climb to the top of each of these hills around us. And use your binoculars to check out all the hiding places: bushes, trees, ditches."

Reghardt was just standing there, but there was some color in his face now.

"Go!" said Kannemeyer.

Reghardt blinked and shot off like a racing dog.

When he was gone, Kannemeyer turned to the rest of us and

said, "We are also looking for soft earth." He tapped the ground next to the scooter with his foot. "Like this. Where something is buried."

Georgie's hand went to her mouth. She caught an "Ooh-woo" in her fingers.

The nurse gave me the rusk tin back and I offered the last beskuit to Kannemeyer. He looked into my eyes as he ate it, and my chest filled with a strange warmth.

Then he pointed to a hill with a row of spekboom trees at its base.

"We're heading that way first. Walk two meters apart and follow me. I'll go ahead and sweep the area for anything obvious. You move slowly so you don't miss anything."

I ate the last few crumbs of hope—then I left the tin in the car.

We spread out and walked behind Kannemeyer, our eyes on the ground. I heard him talking to Warrant Officer Smit on the radio, telling him to have an ambulance on standby, and to get the other groups to come and join our search. Hattie and Candice were on either side of me. Candy was slower than me in those heels, and Hattie a bit faster. But I hardly noticed them.

My eyes were drinking in everything in front of me. Looking for clues. I found the tracks of a snake after the rain. A mouse scuttling into some Christmas aloes. The footprints of a rabbit, and the heart-shaped hoof prints of a hartebeest. Piles of big black shiny droppings. White stones, purple stones, stones the color of dried blood.

The sun was low and blasting onto the side of my face. I kept on walking and looking. The other groups joined the search. There were lines of them walking across the veld and up the hills. But I was keeping my attention on the two meters that were mine.

I scared a springbok out from the shade of a wild plum tree. I looked in dongas, the sandy ditches where the cancer bush grew, its flowers dripping red. The little faces of the lion-mouth flowers looked up at me. I studied a sterretjiebos, because the dried star pods looked like ants marching up and down its stalks. But they were not ants and they were not leading me anywhere.

I saw dung beetles, and spiders with golden bellies. I saw Karoo violets with velvet petals and little prickly plants whose names I did not know.

But none of them had signs of Jessie.

There were so many different kinds of life—insects, plants, creatures—that I had never really noticed before.

Life, I found myself praying to the life on the land, like I had prayed to the sky and the rain. *Life of the land. Keep Jessie alive. Show us where she is. I beg you, Life, keep her alive.*

We kept on looking and walking. The sun was setting now and the clouds were changing colors. Soon it would be dark. My heart was sinking with the sun. If we had not found her by nightfall . . . My eyes were sore from looking so hard, from seeing so many things, but none of them clues to Jessie. I put my fingers on my eyelids and closed them for a second. There was such a tiredness in me, I wanted to lie down on the ground and cry. I opened my eyes and saw Reghardt, reaching the top of a koppie. A herd of kudu were running away from him, down the slope of the hill. One kudu with big horns did not run. It stood staring at him, its horns gleaming in the light, while the others galloped away. Reghardt had his back to them, as he moved up to the peak of the hill. The running kudus came to a gwarrie tree that was growing between two big rocks and suddenly stopped. They turned and ran away from the tree, back up toward Reghardt. The big kudu barked, and the kudu herd ran down again, but on the slope away from the tree.

I raised my hand and shouted, "Henk! Piet!"

Kannemeyer was closest. I told him what I'd seen: The kudus were avoiding that tree.

"What did they see or smell there?" I said.

He radioed Reghardt: "The big gwarrie tree, southwest of you."

I watched Reghardt scramble back down the hill. Sliding on

the loose gravel as he ran. He disappeared behind the rocks at the gwarrie tree. Kannemeyer and Piet were running now, up the slope.

Then I saw Reghardt's head appearing, as he walked out from behind the rocks. He was carrying a body in his arms.

It was too far to see for sure, but I knew it was Jessie.

He was shouting something. The people who were searching closest to the base of the hill ran toward him, and soon they were shouting too, but I could not hear what they were saying. Then those a little closer to them heard the shout, and it got passed across the veld, between the thorn trees and the stones, until the words reached my ears:

"She's alive. She's alive!"

EIGHTY-FOUR

I bowed my head in thanks:

Thank you, Rain, for hiding her tracks.
Thank you, Life, for keeping her alive.
Thank you for showing us where to find her.

Tears were falling down my face when Hattie reached me and we hugged and cried together.

Then Candice joined us, stepping between the prickly plants in those heels of hers. Her legs were scratched and her face lined with dirt and tears, but when she smiled she was the most beautiful sight.

The ambulance got to Jessie before we could walk across the veld, and we saw Reghardt and Kannemeyer lifting her in. Reghardt got in too. A herd of mountain zebra galloped along the plain as the ambulance raced off, its *wee-waaah wee-waaah* tearing across the sunset sky.

We headed back to the cars, and Kannemeyer came to join us. We were smiling, but when we saw his face, we stopped.

"What is it?" I said.

"I'm no doctor," he said, "but she is unconscious and it looks bad."

A group of Seventh-day Adventists broke into prayer, and

Hattie joined them. If there was a god, the Adventists and Hattie had his phone number, so I left them to it. I walked away and watched the darkening sky. The clouds were streaked with a deep red. I looked at the veld, soft in the evening light.

The sky and the land. I had prayed to them and they'd delivered. Could I still ask for more?

Should I not be doing some work myself? Helping Jessie get better. I was no doctor, but I was her friend. I let my heart fill with all the love I felt for her. My love was big and red like the sunset. It pushed out the worry and the fear in my chest. When my heart felt so full I thought it would burst, I sent all that love to her. I had her phone number. She would get my love.

There was a warm hand on my shoulder. It was Kannemeyer. But he turned and walked to his van before I could see his face. The searchers were back in the cars, waiting to go.

"Oh, goodness," said Hattie. "Do you think she'll . . . ?"

"Turn on your lights," I said. "She's a strong girl, our Jessie."

We'd dropped the others off and it was just the two of us again, driving in her Toyota in the dark.

"She may have lost a lot of blood . . . ," said Hattie, hooting by mistake as she turned on her lights.

"Slow down," I said.

"She had injuries too. And maybe hypothermia—"

"Watch out!"

A kudu leaped across the road and Hattie swerved into a thorny bush.

"Oh, jolly hockey sticks!"

She got us out of the bush and went on driving at the same speed.

"So, darling, what's happening with you and the detective?"

"Pasop! The gate!"

"I see it, I'm not blind."

I got out to do the gate and she reversed to give me space to open it.

When I got back in, she said, "I've seen the way you look at each other."

"I don't know, Hats."

"He looks after you very nicely, I must say. I was wondering . . . did he run that bath for you?"

"He has been very nice. But he's just doing his job . . ."

"I don't suppose he'll be camping at your house anymore, now that . . ."

"No. No, he won't."

"He's a jolly good-looking chap."

And he could do much better than me, I thought.

"I'm too old for that kind of stuff," I said.

"Never too old. Has there been no one since . . . Fanie?"

I shook my head. We were back on the tar road now, so the ride was a bit smoother. And although we veered around the road, thankfully there were no cars or animals.

"Isn't it about time . . . ?" said Hattie.

"Fanie put me off men."

"He was a rotter. Not all men are like that, you know."

"I know, I know. But my heart is kind of . . . closed."

"Give him a chance, Maria."

"We'll see. Can you drop me at Dirk's farm? My bakkie is there. Your turn signal is on."

She flipped her turn signal off, but switched her hazard lights on. I didn't tell her. I think it was for the best.

Dirk's house was dark.

"I wonder where he is," said Hattie.

"He might not be back yet, we drove here quite fast."

"Fast? Perhaps he's with Anna. I wonder if they're still working together to drive one car."

"Dankie, skat," I said and kissed her cheek.

"I'm quite pooped, Maria. I'm sure you are too. Have something to eat and a rest. I'll see you in the morning."

She drove off, her hazard lights still flashing.

My blue bakkie was waiting patiently under the gum tree. On the passenger seat was my tin of rusks.

"The Spar manager was the murderer," I told the rusks as we drove. "He nearly killed me, but Henk shot him. Dead. We found Jessie. Alive. But injured and unconscious. It could be bad. We are going to the hospital now. This time you are coming in with me."

EIGHTY-FIVE

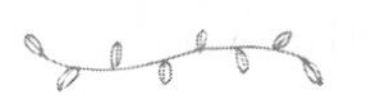

Jessie was in the intensive care unit. The ICU waiting room was full. Lots of the people who had been at the search were there. Reghardt was pacing up and down, wearing a path in the linoleum. There was no sign of Kannemeyer.

"How is she?" I asked.

Reghardt shook his head and bit his lip. His long eyelashes were wet.

"The doctor is coming to talk to us now-now," he said.

There was a big urn and Jessie's younger sister, Juanita, was making cups of tea. I helped her pass them around to everyone. Anna took out her silver hip flask and added a shot to her cup, and then to Dirk's. I gave Juanita my tin of beskuit and she handed that around too. It was empty in thirty seconds. I suppose most of us had not had supper. Dirk's head fell back and he started his warthog snoring. We heard footsteps coming down the hallway, and Anna elbowed Dirk in the ribs. He sat up, snorting. Jessie's mother jumped up. She was not in her uniform, but in a blue dress. Her clothes were fresh and clean, while mine were creased and muddy. But her face looked so crumpled.

The doctor arrived and we all turned to him like flowers to the sun. A very black sun in a white coat.

"Can I have a word with just the family?"

Most of us got up and moved toward him.

"Oh, okay. I'll address you all, if that's all right with you?"

He looked at Nurse Mostert and she nodded.

"Jessie's condition is critical. Her leg injury and the place where the arrow hit her shoulder are not too severe. There is some infection, but it's under control . . . for now. The problem is the blood loss. She lost a lot of blood. Her heart stopped for a while and we got it going again. She's still in a coma. If she comes through, our biggest concern is brain damage."

Jessie's mother clutched a fist to her heart. The doctor started talking in difficult medical language about the danger of "coning" and "neural probes" and things I did not understand and did not want to understand.

I closed my eyes and sent my love to Jessie. I could see it flowing into her, red like pomegranate juice. Like blood.

"Only one visitor at a time," the doctor was saying now in normal English. "And only those closest to her. Nurse Mostert and Officer Snyman will monitor who goes in. She is in a coma, but there's a small possibility that she can hear you. So, please, only say encouraging things to her."

People came and went from the waiting room, but I kept sitting. My eyes were closed a lot of the time but I wasn't sleeping; I was on the phone to Jessie:

Jessie, my girl, you're going to be just fine. That horrible man is dead. We got him. And you are in the hospital getting better. I'm going to make you the best chocolate cake you have ever eaten. And have you tasted my chicken soup? That will get you healthy in no time. And then you can eat all your favorite things: like bobotie and koeksisters.

I opened my eyes—the waiting room was almost empty. Anna and Dirk were still there. Anna passed out in her wheelchair, and Dirk snoring on the couch. Reghardt was sitting upright, his eyes red, his mouth a tight line.

I went on with my call to Jessie:

When you're ready I'll make a big feast for you with roast lamb and potatoes and vetkoek with curry. And salads: potato, and three bean and carrot with pineapple. And coffee and koeksisters and chocolate cake. And bread with appelkooskonfyt, of course. Ooh, you will eat so lekker, your tummy will be round like a potjiepot.

I heard footsteps and saw Jessie's mother coming toward us. It was just me and Reghardt in the waiting room. Now Nurse Mostert's dress was as creased as her face. Reghardt jumped to his feet.

"You can go in now," she said. "I'm going home to try and sleep."

I closed my eyes again. A while later I felt a hand on my shoulder, and I woke, saying, "Henk . . ."

It was Reghardt.

"Kannemeyer was here," he said. "He didn't want to disturb you."

"Is she okay?" I asked.

"The same," he said. "You can go in for a bit if you want. Then I can give you a ride home. He said I should give you a ride home."

"No, I'll be fine to drive. But I do want to see her, even just for a minute."

"All right, then I'll sit with her till morning. Her sister's coming early."

I went through the big swinging doors of the ICU and washed my hands with liquid soap. Then a nurse showed me to Jessie's bed. Attached to Jessie were drips and pipes, and beeping machines with numbers and moving green lines. Her left upper arm was bandaged, and her right knee and shin had dressings on them. Repairing the damage done by his car and arrow. There was a plastic mask over her face and a machine helping her breathe.

She was lying very still. The nurse left me alone and I sat on the chair beside the bed. Jessie looked so weak and pale; I wanted to rip out all the wires and tubes and hold her to me like a baby. I put my hand on hers. It was hot and still.

I watched her chest as it rose and fell with the breathing machine.

"Well, we caught him, Jessie," I said. "He's dead now. We make a good team. You and me. And Hats. The police helped too. Reghardt really loves you, you know. We all love you. Our girl with the gecko tattoo, hey?"

I looked at the ink gecko on her shoulder that wasn't bandaged. I had never seen it lying so still. I patted her hand. Her breath rose and fell.

"Now you just need to get better. I'll be making you your favorite chocolate cake." Her fingers twitched. "First thing in the morning."

Reghardt stood at the foot of the bed. Then he came and put his hand on her forehead and brushed her hair back. I saw the look on his face as he stroked her hair. It cracked my heart right open.

EIGHTY-SIX

My house was very quiet and empty. No police guard. No Kannemeyer.

I made a piece of bread and jam and took it to the couch.

There were dents in the cushions where Kannemeyer had slept. The couch smelled of him. I was so tired, I lay down, just for a second. I lay down in the shape he had made in the cushions. Was I stupid to think that he and I . . . ? I was the one who had taken the step forward in the bathroom, pressed myself against him. But he had said I was lovely. Maybe he was just being nice about the veldskoene and panty combination. Maybe he didn't mean anything by it . . . He was only doing his job. And now that job was over.

How could I even be thinking about him, with Jessie, lying there, almost dead? Almost dead, but with a man who loved her . . .

I lay in the cushion curves of Kannemeyer's shape. I fit just fine. I fell asleep in those curves.

When I woke, the sunlight was falling in through the open window in the living room. The phone was ringing. It was Hattie.

"She's come around. She's talking. She's going to be okay."

I could not say anything because I was crying. Why does good news make me cry?

"She's asking for you . . ."

I swallowed.

"I'm on my way."

I washed off my mud and sleep in a quick shower. My legs were sore from all that walking. I brushed my hair, but did not even put on lipstick or have coffee.

In the hospital, Jessie was propped up on some pillows. When she saw me, a big grin filled her face, but she was so weak she could not keep it for long.

"Jessie," I said, holding her hand.

"We did it, Tannie Maria," she said. "We got the bastard."

I squeezed her fingers. She squeezed back and closed her eyes.

"I dreamed of your chocolate cake," she said, a smile lifting her cheeks again for a second.

One arm lay across her chest, her fingers resting on the gecko tattoo on her other arm. She touched the head of the gecko as if she was about to stroke it, but then she fell asleep.

I went to the Spar to get the ingredients I needed. I was still planning what to buy as I pushed my cart down the aisle. I would need flour for the chocolate cake, of course. But also ingredients for chicken soup; a person cannot live on cake alone. And more flour for beskuit. I needed to make a lot more rusks. I stopped and looked at a 2.5-kilogram bag of Eureka Mills stoneground flour. I picked it up. And then I saw him. Henk Kannemeyer. He was at the other end of the aisle.

I thought he saw me too, but he couldn't have, because he disappeared instead of coming over.

I would make him a cake as well. A nice big chocolate cake for him and Piet and Reghardt. Still holding the bag of flour to my chest, I walked to the next aisle. There he was.

"Henk," I said.

I smiled at him. Now I was sorry I had not put on my lipstick. But he had seen me looking worse, and still said I was lovely.

He looked away and then looked back at me, as if he was not pleased to have been spotted. Perhaps he was there undercover. No, that's silly, everyone in Ladismith knows who he is.

I walked up to him and said, "She's fine. She's going to be okay."

"Yes," he said, looking down at me. "I heard. I am glad."

"I'm shopping for her cake. Chocolate cake. And I am going to make you one too."

"Oh, no, please don't bother."

He was looking up and down the aisle again. Was he avoiding someone? I hugged the flour to my breast.

"But you have been such a help. Looking after me and all. You saved my life, Henk."

"Mrs. van Harten, I was just doing my job."

He looked at me and he had that sadness in his eyes.

"Yes. You're right. You were just doing your job."

I took a step back, and bumped into the jars behind me. Two jars of strawberry jam rolled off the shelves and I dropped the 2.5-kilogram bag of flour. It burst all over the floor.

Detective Kannemeyer bent down to try and pick it up.

The floor manager with the skull face came running.

"Oh dear," he said.

"I'm sorry," said the detective.

"No, it was my fault," I said.

The detective and the manager were both trying to clean up. I just stood there, unable to move.

"Sorry," said Kannemeyer again.

"Don't worry," said the manager.

"It's my fault. I was stupid," I said.

"We'll clean it up," said the manager.

"It's such a mess," I said. "Such a mess. I'll pay for it."

Kannemeyer stood up. He had flour all over his pants and hands and even his mustache.

"I am so sorry," he said, and he walked away.

EIGHTY-SEVEN

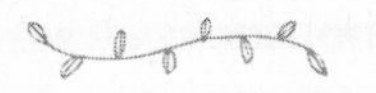

I had to make two trips from my car to the house with all my heavy groceries. But I walked slowly and I managed just fine.

The house was very quiet, and I had an empty feeling in my belly. I put the food on the table and stood on the stoep.

"*Kik kik kik*," I called.

The chickens came running and I threw out a handful of mielies for them.

"*Cluck cluck*," they said. "*Cluck*."

I helped myself to some of their eggs. It was about time I had a decent meal. I had a long day of cooking ahead of me and I needed to be strong.

I fried some eggs and bacon and sausage and tomatoes, and warmed up some cheese scones that I had in the freezer. Then I made toast and coffee and put them on a tray with butter and apricot jam, and took it all onto the stoep.

My garden and the veld were looking lovely after the rain, but I had eyes only for my breakfast. I ate and ate. I didn't even make conversation with the food, because I was too busy eating.

The empty feeling in my belly had just been hunger. After a good breakfast, I felt fine.

I thought I heard a car coming down my dirt road. Then I realized it was a truck on Route 62.

I was full now, no space for emptiness, but I had an extra cheese scone with jam, just to make sure.

I started with the chicken soup, because it is best to slow-cook it for a long time. I decided to make a big batch so I could freeze it and take some to Jessie every day. While I was chopping the celery, I kept looking up and seeing those bloody couch cushions. They had the curves of his shape in them and then the shape of my body on top of his. It was embarrassing.

I put down my knife and went and turned the cushions over.

"That's better," I said to the celery as I finished chopping. "I was stupid . . . A fool. I won't do it again. Honestly, at my age . . ."

I added the potatoes, celery, carrots, tomatoes, and parsley to the chicken that I had fried in olive oil with leeks, onion, ginger, and garlic. Then I added cold water. That's the important thing when making a good soup. The water must be cold so the flavor can seep into the broth, instead of sealing the taste into the vegetables.

Once the soup was simmering, I put it into the hotbox. Then I got out all the ingredients for the chocolate cake and the rusks. I decided to make my mother's muesli buttermilk rusks again. The ones with extra butter, as well as muesli, seeds, and raisins.

I started with the cake. Just one cake.

But as I was adding the ingredients to my big mixing bowl, I decided to double the quantity. I was going to bake Kannemeyer and his policemen a cake. Maybe he hadn't saved my heart, but he had saved my life. Surely that was worth something.

While the muesli rusks were still drying out in the oven, I left home with two chocolate cakes and a big glass jar of chicken soup.

I delivered the cake to the police station. Kannemeyer and Reghardt weren't there but Piet gave me a big smile of thanks.

Jessie was doing well, but sleeping. The doctor said she could have some of the broth from the soup when she woke. No solids and definitely no cake just yet. I left the cake with her mother, who looked tired but had a smile that lit up the whole hospital.

When I got home I sat down at my kitchen table. It had been a good day. Jessie was doing fine. I had cooked up a storm. I looked at the cushions on my couch. They were flat and empty.

"I do sometimes feel so . . . alone," I said.

Talking to myself, now there was a sign I was turning into a crazy old lady.

Then I remembered the rusks in the oven. They would be ready to come out. I took out the tray and laid it on the table.

"I'm not alone," I said. "And there's no need to talk to myself. I've got you."

I smiled. They were a golden buttery color, with brown crunchy toasted seeds and dark chewy raisins. There were at least fifty of them. And rusks are just the best company.

I made myself a cup of coffee, and took six of them outside, and sat chatting and dipping them into my coffee and looking out at the best view from my stoep.

I was just fine.

EIGHTY-EIGHT

Those next couple of weeks I fed Jessie something every day. I had a pile of *Gazette* letters to catch up on, but I always made time to get that medicine food into her body. Food made with love.

By day two she was eating cups of that chicken soup and on day three she even had a tiny piece of chocolate cake. She let her visitors polish off the cake. Soon she was able to eat some salads. When she ate her first vetkoek with curry, the doctor said she could go back home, so long as she rested a lot. We had a welcome-home party around her bed. Reghardt made us all his bobotie. It was delicious. It was obvious enough in his eyes, but if you ever had any doubts about his love, you just had to taste that bobotie. He gave me his recipe. He added appelkooskonfyt and sliced almonds to the spicy ground meat, and he used sour cream in his custard topping. But it was the feelings he held in his heart as he cooked that gave it that special Reghardt flavor.

Kannemeyer never thanked me for that cake. Not that I needed thanks—it was a thank-you gift to him and you can't just go on thanking each other back and forth forever. But it was an opportunity he could have taken if he wanted to call me. And he didn't.

I saw him now and again in town. Once he was in his van and

he drove past like he hadn't noticed me. But Piet, who was next to him, lifted his fingers to say hello.

When Jessie was back part-time at the *Gazette*, I said to her, "Jessie, my skat, you are still a bit thin. Those geckos have hardly got enough to climb on. I think it's time for that big feast I've been promising you. With roast lamb and all your favorite foods."

"Ooh, lekker, Tannie M. I can't wait. Check how this gecko is climbing towards a big star." She turned to show me the arrow scar just above her tattoo. "Cool, hey?"

A big pink box with long legs arrived at the door. Hattie's head popped around the side of the box.

"Good morning, darlings," she said. "Look what was at the post office for you, Tannie Maria."

She plonked the box on my desk, along with three letters. I looked at the postmark on the box: New York. And the return address: Candy's Boutique. I opened it with Harriet and Jessie peering over my shoulders.

"Goodness gracious," said Hattie.

"Ooh, sexy!" said Jessie.

Wrapped in tissue paper was a beautiful cream dress and a matching pair of shoes with a classy low heel. The sizes looked just right. Also in the box was some pearl nail polish and a thin pearl necklace.

Hattie picked the necklace up and rubbed a pearl on her teeth. "Fake, I'm afraid," she said. "But the dress is fabulous."

"Try it on," said Jessie.

"Ag, no," I said. "I'm not really in the mood."

"Later then, when you get home," said Hattie.

But I knew I wouldn't be in the mood then either.

I gave us all beskuit and rooibos tea; we were all drinking that now because the doctor said it was good for Jessie. Then I sat down with my three latest letters. The first was from my friend the mechanic. I recognized his envelope and writing, and I was happy to open it.

Dear Tannie Maria, it said.

Thank you so much, you have really helped me. The recipe trick worked! And I also made the best chocolate cake Lucia has ever tasted. It just gets better and better with me and her.

It hasn't been a long time together but we know we are just right for each other. We would be very glad if you would come to our wedding in Riversdale on December 21. Please sit in the front, next to my brother from Cape Town. You will see the announcement on page 3 of the Karoo Gazette. *My real name is Kobus (not Karel) Visagie, and Lucia's is Stella Vinknes. Feel free to bring a date.*

I am deaf, but I can lip-read quite well. My speaking isn't very good, so I don't do it much, which is why text messages and letters and food are a good way for me to talk. But I hope you'll come and talk to me at the wedding anyway.

Everything of the best,

Kobus

I smiled and finished my rusk. I didn't have a date, but I would go to Kobus's wedding.

The next letter was from Oudtshoorn.

Dear Tannie Maria, I read.

This is the sweet potato lady. You'll never guess what happened. On the Saturday morning after I saw your letter, I went down to the Farmers Co-op at 10 o'clock like you suggested, and there was a man hanging around the sacks of butternut squash, who looked like he was waiting for me. He was very friendly and kind. And then, not long after that, another three men and another four ladies all came, carrying things from their gardens or farms, and they stood around and spoke about ground ostrich meat and sweet potatoes. They had read the letters in the paper and wanted to meet and eat too! So we have formed an Ostrich Supper Club and we meet somewhere every Saturday night. It is lots of fun. If there are single (older) people who would like to join us, come to the butternut squash sacks at the co-op at 10 o'clock Saturday mornings, and we'll let you know the menu and venue for our next event. Maybe you would also like to come one day, Tannie Maria?

I thanked her and gave her that recipe for ostrich casserole that fell out of the book in Martine's study a while back.

The third letter was from someone who had not written to me before. As I read, my breathing shook and my heart beat faster. It was from a man with a lamb.

EIGHTY-NINE

Dear *Tannie Maria*, the letter said.

There's a special lady who I met not so long ago. She made me the best roast lamb I've ever eaten. And the best chocolate cake. I am very sorry to say I have not treated her well. When things got close between us, I kind of ran away.

I was married to a woman who I loved very much. She died of cancer over four years ago. It was very painful.

When I started caring about another woman, I felt like I was betraying my wife. My wife was also a good cook.

The other problem is that this special lady puts herself in dangerous situations. Again and again. I don't think I could bear it if she also died. I don't know if I could manage going through that kind of pain once more.

So I ran away from the special lady.

But I have been missing her. A lot. I keep imagining I am sitting with her on her stoep, eating her roast lamb.

I stopped reading. I wanted to crumple this letter up and throw it in the trash can. Who did this man think he was, marching off and on a woman's stoep when he felt like it? I had my last sip of rooibos tea, but it was cold and had bits of soggy crumbs in it. Then I made myself carry on reading:

How can I make it right with her?

What I was thinking was this. My uncle Koos has just given me some fresh meat from his sheep farm. In fact, the lamb is still alive. It is right now eating up the geraniums in my backyard.

Do you think it will be a good idea to give this lammetjie to the special lady?

My other problem is, I'm not really sure if this lady likes me as more than a friend. We got close because things threw us together. How do I know if she has that special kind of interest in me?

Yours sincerely,

A man and a lamb

I got up and walked outside.

"Tannie M?" said Jessie, but I just kept walking.

I leaned against a jacaranda tree and looked up at the sky. The sky was too bright, so I looked at the ground. I wanted to write to the man, saying, *You just leave that special lady alone to get on with her life instead of coming with your on-and-off nonsense and causing her more pain.*

"What's wrong, Maria?" said Hattie, coming out into the garden, a calculator in her hand.

"Nothing," I said.

"All right, you don't have to talk about it," she said.

We watched a car driving by. A Combi with writing on the side.

"Those Adventists are heading up the mountain soon," she said. "The world's ending this Friday. The twenty-first."

"The end of the world . . . ," I said. "I've been invited to a wedding on that day."

"Well, let's hope it ends after your wedding," she said.

"How many times can a woman make a fool of herself?" I asked.

"I beg your pardon?" said Hattie.

I went back inside and sat down at my desk with my pen and a fresh sheet of paper. I was already making a fool of myself by thinking that I might be that special lady. I needed to do my job as the love-advice tannie. I must answer this letter as if I was not involved. Maybe the special lady in this man's story would be very glad to hear from him. And his blerrie sheep.

Dear man and a lamb, I wrote.

These days a cook does not like to slaughter her own animals. It would be better if you just gave her a leg of lamb. The butcher can do the job for you if you are not the farmer type.

We can be sure that our lives will all end with death. There's not much we can do about that. But you can add love and good food to your life. That is your choice.

I know what you mean about the pain. But love should not live trapped inside your chest. Pain is not a reason to keep love in. You should let it out.

After I wrote this sentence I put down my pen and gave a big sigh. I wondered if I could follow my own advice. Then I read his letter again and carried on with my reply:

How do you know if you are more than a friend to her? That is something your heart will have to tell you. But if she gets a bit dressed up before she sees you, and has a glow on her face when she looks at you, then she probably likes you in that special way.

If she did care for you, then you have probably hurt her feelings by running away, and you may have to work quite hard to win her back.

I crossed out "quite" and wrote "very."

You may have to work very hard to win her back.
TM

I folded my arms on my desk and rested my head on top of them.

NINETY

Jislaaik, Tannie Maria. You can cook, hey?" said Jessie, as she helped herself to some more potato salad.

Reghardt nodded his agreement, his mouth full of carrot salad.

"This three-bean salad is the best, Maria," said Hattie.

It was Thursday the twentieth of December, and we were sitting on my stoep, the sun low on the hills, having that feast I'd promised Jessie. In case the world was ending the next day, I wanted to be sure I'd done what I'd said. It was also the thing I'd most like to do if I had only one evening left. Sit on my stoep with the best view, eating good food with my favorite people.

"That flippin' sexy dress," Jessie said. "Is it the one Candy sent?"

"And those shoes too?" said Hattie. "Maria, is that pearl nail polish on your toes?"

"Vetkoek?" I said, passing the bowl along the table.

Reghardt helped himself. "How'd you get the ground meat right inside the vetkoek?" he said. "I've never had that before."

"Some more roast lamb?" I asked Jessie as I sliced off a tasty crust of meat.

"Asseblief," said Jessie, holding out her plate. "What is in this gravy of yours?"

"Pomegranate juice and red wine," I said, giving her the sliced lamb.

"It's awesome," she said, pouring lots of gravy over her food.

"Goody gumdrops," said Hattie. "Super to have you top of the pops again, Jessie."

Jessie stroked the gecko tattoo on her arm before she started eating again. It was good to see her strong and happy.

I piled some more lamb onto Piet's plate. He was a small guy, but he could eat a lot of meat.

"Would you like some more?" I asked Kannemeyer.

"Please," he said, and gave me that big white grin.

I told my knees to stay strong, because you shouldn't wobble when you have a big knife in your hand. And anyway, a smile and a leg of lamb didn't mean he wouldn't go running off again.

"Ag, no, Kosie," said Kannemeyer, "I'm eating now."

A lamb was bumping its soft nose against his thigh.

He pulled a bottle from his pocket and the lamb sucked on it like a hungry baby.

Henk scratched Kosie on his head, between his little horns, and then the lamb wandered off toward the compost heap. My chickens hopped out of the way to let Kosie join their feast.

It was dark when I served the moerkoffie, koeksisters, and chocolate cake.

I turned out the stoep light and we all looked out at the stars in the big Karoo sky. We have more stars here than anywhere else in the world. If you look and look, you will see that there are more stars than there is darkness.

When you look at a sky like that, you can never be afraid of the dark.

While we were sitting there, Kannemeyer reached out his hand for mine. I let him take it, but I felt a tightness in my chest. I think it was the pain from all the times I'd felt a fool.

He squeezed, but I did not squeeze back. He kept holding my hand, gently, like it was a bird in the nest of his hand.

Everyone helped clean up, but Kannemeyer stayed after they'd left and did the dishes.

"Don't worry," I said, "I'll finish up. You go home."

"Nearly done," he said.

I put the last koeksisters in the fridge and didn't offer him more coffee.

"I'd better be going, then," he said, when the dishes were washed, dried, and stacked away.

He looked at me as if I was a tasty koeksister in that dress, and stepped toward me, but I stepped back.

"Can I see you again?" he said.

I looked down at my feet. My toenails did look pretty in those shoes.

"I'm going to a wedding tomorrow afternoon in Riversdale," I said. "If you want to come with, I'm leaving here at two o'clock."

"I'll be here," he said.

NINETY-ONE

The next day he was there at a quarter to two. The world had not ended yet, but maybe it was still coming. I wore my nice dress with the blue flowers, and the shoes Candy had given me. We set off in his car, with a tin of old-fashioned sweet cookies on my lap.

"You smell good," he said.

"It's the soetkoekies," I said. "But they're not padkos for us. I made them for Kobus and Stella."

I heard a bleating sound, and jumped. The lamb was on the backseat.

"You didn't bring the lamb!?"

"Kosie needs feeding every four hours," he said. "I can't just leave him."

I folded my arms to show I was not pleased, but turned my head to the window, so he couldn't see me smile.

I wished I *had* brought us some padkos—it was quite a long ride. We went through a beautiful pass between tall green mountains, full of fynbos plants. We did lots of looking out the window and only little bits of talking.

When we were coming down the steep pass, he said to me, "I've really missed you, Maria."

And I said, "Look at that sugarbird on the protea bush."

"Lovely," he said.

When he was all nice, it made my heart feel warm, but it also felt sore and too full.

Henk sat at the back with the lamb because it was too hot to leave Kosie in the car. I sat in the front of the church, next to Kobus's brother. It was a beautiful ceremony. She looked so pretty, and he so handsome. But what made it extra beautiful was the sign language that Kobus used. Somehow his moving hands gave even more feeling than the spoken words.

After the ceremony there was a nice spread of tea and food in a big tent outside.

Henk tied his lamb to a tree and we went together to congratulate the happy couple. Henk touched my arm as we walked but I didn't want to hold his hand.

Stella was surrounded by people, but we managed to get close to Kobus.

"Hello, Kobus," I said. "I'm Tannie Maria. Congratulations."

He grinned at me like I was a new bicycle on his birthday.

He held his hands at the center of his chest and then let his fingers flutter out, like birds flying away.

"Thank you," he whispered.

I remembered a line from his first letter to me: *When she smiled at me, I felt like a bunch of birds was trying to fly out of my chest.* It looked like those birds had escaped now.

I know he was signing "Thank you," but it felt like he was telling me: *Open your heart and let the love fly out.*

I reached for Henk Kannemeyer's hand.

And why not? I thought. *Why not?*

TANNIE MARIA'S RECIPES

Now the murder and love stories took up so much space there are not many pages left to write out the recipes. So I've chosen just a few of my favorite Karoo dishes. Some recipes that are not from the Karoo just pushed their way in because they are so lekker.

I am sorry for the vegan Seventh-day Adventists because most of the recipes have Karoo lamb or butter and eggs, but there are still a few they could try.

Make sure the meat and dairy you use comes from a proper farmer: a free-range or game farmer. Animals should live in the sunshine and eat from the veld.

USING A HOTBOX

A hotbox is a big cushion filled with Styrofoam balls with a soft hole in the middle for your pot and a cushion lid. Using a hotbox saves a lot of electricity, and it is the best way to slow-cook food. It cooks overnight or while you are at work.

These days you can buy hotboxes. I got one at a church fete long ago; it is covered with a lovely orange shweshwe cloth. My mother used to put her pot on a wooden board and wrap it up in a duvet and put a pillow on top, and it worked just as well.

It is important that the food is covered with fluid and that the pot is almost full. (A half-full pot will stay warm but won't cook.)

A hotbox is perfect for soups, stews, curries, rice, or other grains. Just bring the food to a boil and pop it in the hotbox. The pot will stay very hot for at least two hours. If you are cooking a grain, make sure you don't add too much water or it will overcook.

No moisture is lost in the hotbox so you may need to heat your dish in the oven or on the stove before serving if you want to cook off excess liquid.

MEASUREMENTS

T = tablespoon
t = teaspoon
cup = 8 ounces

All eggs used are size large.

MEAT

These meat dishes serve 4 to 6 people, depending on how hungry they are.

MARTINE'S TENDER MUTTON CURRY (WITH SAMBALS)

MUTTON CURRY

1 T ground turmeric
1½ T paprika
2 T ground coriander
1 t ground black pepper
1 t salt
4 T garlic, chopped (about 6 cloves)
3 T fresh ginger, chopped
2 to 4 chilis, chopped
2 pounds mutton or lamb neck or knuckles (i.e., cut-up lamb shank)
2 medium eggplants (about 1 pound), cut into ¾-inch chunks
5 T sunflower oil
1½ T cumin seeds
2 t fenugreek
1 T mustard seeds
6 cardamom pods, cracked open
½ cinnamon stick
2 large onions, peeled and thinly sliced
8 large ripe tomatoes (about two pounds), peeled and chopped
4 medium potatoes, peeled and chopped into ¾-inch chunks

1 T garam masala
1 cup fresh cilantro, chopped

Prepare 24 hours before serving—this is very important. The meat needs the long, slow-cooking to become tender, and the spices need time to give the best flavor.

Begin by mixing all the ground spices (except the garam masala) and the salt with the garlic, ginger, and chilis. Rub the spice mix into the meat very well and set it aside.

Salt the eggplant with about a teaspoon of salt and set aside. Heat the oil in a big, heavy ovenproof pot until very hot. Add the seeds and whole spices and stir until their smell fills the kitchen and the mustard seeds begin to pop. Add the onions and turn the heat down to medium-high.

When the onions are soft, rinse the eggplants, add them to the pot, and cook until they have a little color.

Now add the lamb with all its spices and keep stirring to stop the spices from sticking to the bottom of the pot. When the lamb is just brown, add 1 cup of water and cover the meat with the chopped tomatoes. Bring to a simmer and cook on the stove for about 15 minutes.

Prepare your oven or hotbox. (See instructions on page 379 on using a hotbox.)

In the oven: Cook, covered, at 300°F for 2 hours. Then switch off the oven and leave it to cool. Keep in the fridge overnight.

In the hotbox: Make sure your curry is hot and covered with liquid, and that the pot is almost full. (If there is a lot of empty space, the food will not cook properly.) A cast-iron pot of about 10 inches in width is best. Leave the pot in the hotbox for about 4 hours or overnight. Then reheat and put back in the hotbox. Repeat this about every 4 hours if you have time.

The next day, about an hour before you are ready to eat:

Boil the chopped potatoes in very salty water until they are well-cooked (about 15 to 20 minutes). Drain and add to the curry, together with the garam masala. Put the pot in the oven with the lid off, and cook at 375°F for about 50 minutes or until the liquid has thickened.

The hotbox method may have more liquid, so may need more time. It will be ready more quickly if you move the curry into a wider pot or dish when you put it in the oven.

Taste, and maybe add a pinch of salt or pepper. Garnish with fresh cilantro and serve with basmati rice, sambals (see below) and poppadoms.

SAMBALS

Cucumber Sambal

½ cup plain yogurt
½ t salt
1 T fresh mint, chopped
One 3-inch piece of cucumber, diced
1 small sweet red or yellow pepper, diced
½ red onion, finely chopped
3 T fresh cilantro, chopped
1 T vinegar

Mix all the ingredients together.

Tomato Sambal

2 to 3 tomatoes, chopped
2 T lemon or lime juice
½ t chili, finely chopped, or chili powder
½ t salt
1 t sugar
1 t toasted cumin seeds
1 scallion, chopped

Mix all the ingredients together.

REGHARDT'S BOBOTIE

⅓ cup raisins or sultanas
1 T ground coriander
4 t ground turmeric
1 t ground black pepper
1½ t ground cumin
½ t cinnamon powder
¼ t ground ginger
¼ t ground fennel seeds
¼ t ground fenugreek seeds
¼ t ground black mustard seeds
¼ t cayenne
1½ t salt
Pinch nutmeg
Pinch ground cloves
¼ cup butter
2 onions, peeled and finely chopped
1 clove garlic, crushed
1 t fresh chopped fresh ginger
1 pound ground meat (lamb, ostrich, or game)
1 cup grated carrot
1 slice bread, soaked in 3 T milk, lightly squeezed then mashed with a fork
¼ cup sliced almonds
¼ cup apricot jam—homemade is best (see recipe for homemade jam)
3 T lemon juice (or 2 T wine vinegar)
1 egg

Custard Topping

3 eggs
1 cup milk

1 cup cream or sour cream
½ t salt
½ t vinegar
Grated zest of half a lemon
6 lemon leaves (if you really can't get lemon leaves, use bay leaves)

Soak the raisins or sultanas in hot water and set aside.

Measure out the spices into a small bowl and mix together.

Heat the butter in a large pan and gently fry the onions until they just begin to change color. Now add the garlic, fresh ginger, and the mixed spices, and cook for a minute or two.

Add the ground meat and brown lightly, stirring to break up any lumps. Then add the grated carrots and remove from the heat.

Stir in the rest of the ingredients, including the drained raisins or sultanas, adding the egg last so that it doesn't cook. Taste to check the seasoning and then tip the meat mixture into a rectangular ovenproof dish (about 9 by 5 inches and at least 2 inches deep).

To make the topping, beat the eggs and add the milk, cream, salt, vinegar, and lemon zest, and mix well. Pour over the meat in the dish.

Stick the lemon leaves into the bobotie until just the tips are showing.

Bake at 375°F for 20 to 25 minutes until golden brown.

Bobotie is delicious with anything but is traditionally served with yellow rice (rice cooked with turmeric, raisins, and cinnamon, with honey and butter added after it's cooked), fruit chutney, sliced bananas, and a chopped tomato and onion salad.

Tips

* If you are not able to use homemade jam (made with apricot kernels), you can add two crushed apricot kernels to give the

bobotie that almondy flavor. You need to break the shell of the apricot pit with a hammer or half a brick to get to the kernel inside. You can also buy apricot kernels from health food stores.

* If you prepare this dish in advance, keep the topping separate until just before you bake.
* If you like it hot, add extra cayenne pepper, but then serve yogurt with your bananas to cool things down.

TAMATIEBREDIE

2 pounds tomatoes, peeled and chopped
5 T sunflower oil
2 pounds mutton neck or knuckles (if you can't get mutton, use lamb)
About ½ cup flour for coating the meat
2 medium onions, peeled and chopped
2 T butter
5 whole cloves
6 whole allspice
10 peppercorns
1 stick cinnamon
1 t whole coriander
4 t ground coriander
1 t ground cumin
½ t ground pepper
Pinch nutmeg
Pinch mace
2 to 3 cloves garlic, chopped
2 t fresh ginger, chopped
¼ cup tomato paste
2 t salt
2 t sugar
4 medium potatoes, peeled and cut into ½- to ¾-inch cubes
1 to 2 T vinegar

Cut a small cross in each end of the tomatoes. Scald them in boiling water for a couple of minutes and then put them into cold water. This makes the skins come off easily. Skin and chop them.

Heat the oil in a heavy ovenproof pot. Coat the meat in flour and then brown it in hot oil, frying only a few pieces at a time and being careful not to burn the flour. Once the meat has all been browned, take it out of the pot.

Fry the onions in the butter in the same pot for a few minutes. Add the whole spices and cook until the onions are soft. Add the ground spices, the garlic, and the ginger, and fry for another minute. Return the meat to the pot and add the tomatoes, tomato paste, salt, and sugar. Bring to a simmer.

Prepare your hotbox or oven. (See instructions on page 379 on using a hotbox.)

Either put the pot in the hotbox for the day, reheating every 4 hours if possible and returning to the hotbox, or cook, covered, in a preheated oven at 250°F for 4 hours. Remove from the oven and let it stand.

Boil the chopped potatoes in very salty water until cooked (about 15 to 20 minutes).

About an hour before serving, add the cooked potatoes, take the lid off the pot, and put it in the oven at 350°F or simmer it on the stove until the sauce is thick. If you are using the stove, be careful not to let the stew stick to the bottom of the pot. The meat should be very soft now (falling off the bone). Just before serving, stir in the vinegar according to taste. Taste again and see what it needs. It will probably enjoy a good sprinkle of salt and freshly ground black pepper.

Serve with rice and green beans.

Tip

- I usually use sunflower oil for frying and baking, but you can use any oil that doesn't have a strong flavor, and gets nice and hot.

GROUND MEAT FOR THE VETKOEK

This is the curried ground meat that you make to eat with vetkoek. The recipe for vetkoek is later on.

3 T butter
1 pound ground beef
1 medium onion, peeled and chopped
½ t ground turmeric
1 t ground coriander
1 t ground white pepper
4 whole cloves
1 bay leaf
2 large tomatoes, peeled and chopped
1½ t salt
2 cups water
¼ cup green tomato chutney (or any other tart fruit chutney)

Melt the butter in a heavy pan over medium-high heat. Add the ground meat and stir to separate any lumps. Cook the ground meat, stirring the whole time to keep it from sticking.

When the ground meat is a lovely deep-brown color, add the chopped onions and cook until soft.

Turn the heat down to medium and add the spices. Cook them with the meat and onions for a few minutes and then add the rest of the ingredients.

Simmer the mixture for about half an hour or until thick and delicious.

Taste it and see if it needs a little more salt or maybe a squeeze of lemon juice.

Tips

* Browning the ground meat properly at the beginning does take a while but it is worth it. It gives the dish a special flavor and richness.
* Cut halfway through the vetkoek (see recipe later on) and then use the tip of the knife to cut the rest of the way without cutting through the crust. This makes it easier to eat once you have filled it with the delicious ground meat. You can also add a little more chutney into the filled vetkoek.

SWEETS

APRICOT JAM

2 pounds firm, unripe apricots
2 pounds sugar
Juice of 1 lemon (optional, if fruit is ripe)
10 apricot kernels (removed from the pits)

Cut the apricots in half, and take the pits out before you weigh them. Measure exactly the same weight of fruit to sugar and mix together. Leave overnight.

Put the fruit in a large, heavy-based pot. Add the lemon juice (if your apricots are a bit ripe) and the apricot kernels to the fruit. Put the pot on the stove over low heat and stir until all the sugar has dissolved. Then bring to a boil.

Put the lid on for 3 minutes to dissolve any crystals on the side of the pot, then take the lid off and boil over medium heat until the jam starts getting clear and it reaches "setting point" (around 20 to 25 minutes). Stir the jam every now and then to keep it from sticking on the bottom, but not too often or it will crystalize.

To test if the jam has reached setting point, put a drop on an ice-cold plate. Make sure it is thick and sticky, not runny. If you hold the plate at an angle, the jam should make a little blob that does not run. When you have made jam a few times, you will see by the way it falls off the spoon when it is ready.

Pour the jam into sterilized jars, making sure each jar has a few apricot kernels in it. Once it has cooled a little, seal with hot melted candle wax and screw the lids on tight. You do not have to use the wax, but it will help the jam stay fresh for many years.

Tips

* The apricot kernels give the jam a nice almondy flavor. Use a hammer or half a brick to break open the apricot pits to get the kernels out. You can also buy apricot kernels from health food stores. The almond flavor takes a month or two to come out of the kernels into the jam, and just gets better and better.
* Use unripe fruit for the best jam. It has the most pectin and its flavor will last the longest. If your fruit it is a bit ripe, add lemon juice (which has extra pectin).
* To sterilize jars—wash them in hot soapy water, then put in the oven to warm and leave for 20 minutes to dry out. Put the jam in the jars while they are both hot.

TANNIE KURUMAN'S MELKTERT

Crust

1¼ cups flour

⅓ cup confectioners' sugar

¼ t salt

½ cup butter, cut in pieces and softened

2 egg yolks

Sift the flour, confectioners' sugar, and salt together.

Add the butter and egg yolks, and cut them into the flour with a knife. Using your fingers, knead very gently until the butter is mixed in. Wrap the dough in plastic wrap and leave to rest for 30 minutes in the fridge.

Roll out the dough onto a floured surface and fit into a well-greased 10-inch pie pan.

Prick the base with a fork.

Bake for 15 to 20 minutes at 400°F.

Filling

Ingredients A:

2 cups milk

1 T butter

Pinch salt

⅔ cup sugar

Ingredients B:

1 cup milk

2 T cake flour

¼ cup cornstarch

Ingredients C:

2 eggs
1 t vanilla extract

Topping:

Cinnamon sugar

Heat ingredients A (2 cups milk, butter, salt, and sugar) in a saucepan, stirring until the sugar has dissolved.

Mix ingredients B (1 cup milk, flour, and cornstarch) in a bowl, and pour A onto B. Mix well and return to the saucepan.

Cook the mixture, stirring all the time, for about five minutes, until it has thickened and the floury taste has gone.

Beat ingredients C (eggs and vanilla extract) in a bowl. Slowly whisk the hot mixture into the eggs and mix well. Return to the saucepan and cook gently until thick (2 to 3 minutes).

Pour the custard into the baked pastry shell and let it cool and set. Sprinkle on lots of cinnamon sugar before serving.

Tips

* To make cinnamon sugar, mix equal parts of ground cinnamon and brown sugar.
* You can dust the top of the milk tart with just cinnamon instead of cinnamon sugar.

MANGO SORBET

2 sweet, ripe mangoes, peeled and chopped
Yogurt or lime juice (optional)

Freeze the mango flesh for 3 hours, or until quite hard but not rock solid.

Blend well in an electric blender and put back in the freezer.

You can add a spoonful of yogurt or a squeeze of lime juice before serving.

Tips

* This recipe depends on the mangoes being very delicious. If they are only average, you may want to add cream or yogurt to your mixture before freezing, or drizzle a little honey on top.
* If the mango is frozen rock hard, you should wait a few minutes before you blend it.

THE PERFECT BUTTERMILK CHOCOLATE CAKE

Cake

¼ cup water
8 ounces butter
½ cup cocoa powder
1¾ cups brown sugar
2 eggs
1¾ cups buttermilk
1 t vanilla extract
2 cups cake flour
1 t baking soda
1 t baking powder
½ t salt

Preheat the oven to 350°F. Line the bottom of a 10-inch cake pan with parchment paper and grease the paper and the sides of the pan with butter.

First, put the water into a saucepan, then add the butter and cocoa. Heat until hot but not boiling.

Beat the sugar and eggs together, and mix in the buttermilk and vanilla extract. Then add the cocoa mixture and mix well.

Sift the flour, baking soda, baking powder, and salt together, and add to the mixture. Mix well again.

Pour the mixture into the cake pan and bake for 50 to 55 minutes. Let it cool in the pan.

Icing

1½ cups confectioners' sugar, sifted
½ cup butter
¼ cup cocoa powder, sifted
¼ cup buttermilk

¼ t salt
½ t vanilla extract
1 T rum

Heat all the icing ingredients, except the rum, in a saucepan over medium heat, stirring all the time and whisking out any lumps. Bring just to a boil and remove from heat. Add the rum.

Let both the cake and the icing cool completely before spreading or pouring on the icing.

Tips

* Make the icing while the cake is in the oven so it has time to cool completely.
* The warm icing also makes a delicious chocolate sauce that you can put on ice cream.
* If you don't have rum, you can use brandy, but rum and chocolate do make a special magic.

THE MECHANIC'S CHOCOLATE MOUSSE CAKE

8 ounces dark chocolate
½ cup butter
1 t vanilla extract
4 eggs
¼ cup superfine sugar
Pinch of salt
Zest (grated rind) of 1 orange

Melt the chocolate, butter, and vanilla extract over a double boiler. I put the ingredients in a small heatproof bowl and rest it over a pot of boiled water (off the heat).

Beat the eggs, sugar, and salt at a high speed until very thick and silky. This will take at least 5 minutes with an electric mixer on high speed. This is very important and must not be rushed. The mixture will get thick and foamy, about five times its original volume.

Add the orange zest and then fold in the melted chocolate butter.

Pour the batter into a greased, lined 10-inch springform pan and bake at 325° F for 35 to 45 minutes or until the top of the cake begins to crack.

Leave in the pan to cool, then take out and fill the hollow on top with whipped cream and berries or nuts.

Tips

* The "dark" chocolate here has about 35 to 40 percent cocoa solids. Do not use very dark chocolate or chocolate with more than 45 percent cocoa solids or your cake will be dry, bitter, and heavy.
* This cake may look a little flat but this is so you can fill the middle with delicious whipped cream and berries or nuts, or even poached kaalgatperskes (nectarines).

HONEY-TOFFEE SNAKE CAKE

Dough

½ cup milk
2 T sugar
1 T honey
1 t instant dry yeast
2 cardamom pods
2 cups cake flour
¾ t salt
Pinch nutmeg
1 egg, beaten
7 T butter, softened

Honey-Toffee Topping

3 T butter, softened
⅔ cup confectioners' sugar
1 egg white
2 T honey
1 ounce almonds, chopped

Put the milk, sugar, and honey in a saucepan and gently heat until warm. It must be slightly warm, not hot, or it will kill the yeast. Add the yeast and set aside.

Crack the cardamom pods in a mortar and pestle. Remove the pods and grind the seeds, with a little sugar, into a powder.

Sift together the flour and salt, and add the nutmeg and ground cardamom.

Add the yeasty milk and the beaten egg to the flour and work together for a few minutes. Add the soft butter and knead the dough until extremely smooth, about 10 minutes.

Put the dough into a clean buttered bowl, cover with a cloth and set aside in a warm place to rise for an hour and a half or until doubled in size.

In the meantime, make the topping by putting everything into a bowl and mixing well.

Line a roasting tray or wide, shallow cake pan with parchment paper. Turn the dough onto a lightly floured surface and knock out the air. Gently begin to roll and pull the dough into a long sausage. You can let it rest for a few minutes if it begins to fight back. Once your dough sausage is about 27 inches long, or ¾ to 1 inch thick, coil it into a loose spiral on your lined tray or pan. Do not let the coil touch itself—leave about ¾ inch between the coils of your dough snake, except for the tail, which you can tuck in underneath.

Pour the topping evenly over the cake and let it rise for another 20 to 25 minutes.

Bake the cake for 30 to 35 minutes at 375°F or until deep golden and cooked through.

Tips

* The cake is most delicious on the day it is baked, but it can be warmed in the oven or toasted to make it just as tasty again.

KOEKSISTERS

Syrup

2 pounds sugar
2½ cups water
½ t ground ginger
2 cinnamon sticks
3 T lemon juice
½ t cream of tartar

Dough

4½ cups cake flour
1 t salt
4 t baking powder
½ cup butter
2 eggs, beaten
About 1 cup milk
About 2 quarts sunflower oil, for deep-frying

First prepare the syrup by mixing the sugar, water, ginger, and cinnamon in a heavy pot. Place over medium heat and stir until the sugar has dissolved. Bring to a boil and let it boil for about 5 minutes to make a syrup. Remove from the heat and add the lemon juice and cream of tartar.

Once the syrup has cooled slightly, put it in the fridge or freezer.

To make the dough, sift together the flour, salt, and baking powder. Rub the butter into the flour with your fingers. Add the eggs and enough milk to form a stretchy dough that is easy to work. Knead very well—for at least 10 minutes—until smooth and elastic.

Put the dough into an oiled bowl, cover it with a cloth, and let it rest for 3 hours.

Turn the dough out onto an oiled work surface. Divide into 6 equal pieces (about 6 ounces each) and roll each into a sausage. Working gently but firmly, roll each sausage as much as it will let you without tearing the dough. Set it aside and move on to the next one. Once you have rolled them all, do this again until the 6 sausages are about 3 feet long, or no more than ½ inch thick. Leave the dough sausages to rest for 10 minutes.

Now make two braids with 3 strands each. The easiest way to do this is to start in the middle and work one way, and then work in the other direction. Make sure that the braid is nice and tight, and then let it rest for another 10 to 15 minutes.

Cut the braids into 2¾-inch lengths—you should get at least 12 koeksisters from each braid.

Fry about four at a time in hot oil, turning when they are golden brown (about 2 to 3 minutes a side). Once they have an even golden brown color, drain them for a moment (on old egg boxes or paper towels) before dropping them into the cold syrup. Turn them over and leave them in the syrup until the next ones are ready to go in. Keep going until they are all done.

Tips

* These are delicious and definitely worth the effort. They are best served chilled and will stay fresh in the fridge for a couple of days (although you will have eaten them before that). They can also be frozen.

MUESLI BUTTERMILK RUSKS

2 pounds cake flour
¼ cup baking powder
4 t salt
1½ cups toasted muesli
1 not-quite-full cup of sultanas or raisins
1 cup dried apples, chopped
1¼ cup sunflower seeds
½ cup desiccated coconut
¼ cup linseeds
¼ cup sesame seeds
¼ cup pumpkin seeds
2 cups brown sugar
3 large eggs
2 cups buttermilk
2 cups butter, melted

Preheat the oven to 350°F and grease four standard loaf pans or one 12½-by-17½-inch jelly roll pan.

Mix together all the dry ingredients.

Beat the eggs and mix in the buttermilk and melted butter. Add to the dry ingredients and mix well.

Spoon the mixture (about 1 inch thick) into the pan(s) and bake for about 45 minutes.

Leave to cool slightly before turning out onto a wire rack, and then cool completely.

Cut into rusks, about ¾-inch thick if they are in loaf pans or 1 inch by 1½ inch if they are in the larger pan, depending on how big you like them.

Dry overnight in the warming drawer, or set oven to warm and leave for about 4 to 6 hours, or until hard and dry. Store in an airtight container.

Dip the rusk into your coffee, like a cookie, until soft and delicious.

Tips

* Use a pair of scissors to cut the dried apple—it's much easier.
* You can also add dried cranberries, or your favorite nuts, seeds, or dried fruit, as long as the overall amount of dry ingredients stays the same.

BREAD

KAROO FARM BREAD

4½ cups whole wheat flour
3 t salt
2 t instant yeast
1 cup rolled oats
½ cup sunflower seeds
¼ cup molasses
1 T oil
2½ cups lukewarm water
1 cup All Bran flakes

Grease a 9-by-5-inch loaf pan.

Sift the flour (adding back the bran that is caught in the sieve) and mix in the salt, yeast, oats, and sunflower seeds.

Add the molasses, oil, and water, and stir together. Now add the All Bran flakes and mix well. Spoon the batter into the pan and put in a warm place to rise for about 30 minutes.

Sprinkle the top with a few more sunflower seeds and bake in a preheated oven at 425°F for 40 to 45 minutes.

Remove from the pan and cool on a wire rack before slicing.

Tips

* This bread stays fresh for up to a week. It's delicious with butter and apricot jam or thick slices of cheese.

VETKOEK

5¾ cups cake flour
3 t instant yeast
2 T sugar
3 t salt
2 T oil
2 cups warm water
2 cups milk

About 2 quarts of oil, for deep-frying

Sift the flour and mix in yeast, sugar, and salt.

Mix the oil, warm water, and milk, and slowly add to the flour mixture. It should form a workable dough. Knead the dough on a lightly floured surface until smooth and elastic (about 8 to 10 minutes). Oil a big bowl, put the dough into it, cover with a cloth and let it rise for about 2 hours or until twice its size.

Gently knead the dough to push the air out and divide into 10 portions (about 4 ounces each). Work into balls and then flatten them using the palms of your hands. Rub these with oil and let them rise for about 20 to 30 minutes.

In the meantime, heat the deep-frying oil in a large, heavy pot. Fry the vetkoek three at a time in the hot oil, turning them over when golden brown on one side (4 to 6 minutes) to brown the other side.

Drain them on paper towels or empty egg boxes.

Serve with vetkoek ground meat (see recipe) or with lots of butter, cheese, or homemade apricot jam.

TANNIE MARIA'S GLOSSARY

AFRIKAANS AND SOUTH AFRICAN TERMS

aardvark—a kind of anteater ("earth pig")
afdak—a verandah roof, usually made of corrugated iron
Afrikaans—comes mainly from the Dutch language, Nederlands, but has words taken from lots of languages (including Malay, Bushman, French, and English)
Afrikaanse Taal-en Kultuurvereniging (AKTV)—Afrikaans Language and Culture Association
ag—oh. But it has more feeling and meaning than "oh." It is pronounced "ach"—like in the German *achtung*.
appelkooskonfyt—apricot jam
asseblief—please
bakkie—what Americans call a "pickup truck." It has a "pickup" area with a canopy instead of backseats. The Klein Karoo is full of bakkies and 4x4s. And many of the big bakkies are 4x4s. The Nissan 1400 bakkie that I have is a very small car (and nothing like a truck), but it is tough and handles dirt roads.
berg(e)—mountain(s)
beskuit—rusk(s). I am told there are some poor people who don't know what rusks are. Is this really true? It is sweet bread, torn into chunks and oven dried. You dip the rusk into your coffee

and eat it. But don't leave the rusk in too long or it gets soggy. They are a bit like the Italian *biscotti* but quite different.
biltong—spiced dried meat
bitterbos—bitter bush, a toxic plant with little yellow flowers
blaasoppies—little puffer fishes
blerrie—bloody, damn
blikemmer!—a more polite way of saying bliksem! Blikemmer means "tin bucket."
bliksem!—means "lightning" but it is used like a swearword, meaning damn
bobotie—a South African spiced ground meat dish baked with an egg-based topping
boerewors—spicy fat "farmer's sausage"
bokkie—little buck
bokmakierie—yellow and green shrike with a very beautiful song and many different tunes
bossies—crazy
botterblomme—"butter flowers." Gazanias.
braai—barbecue
brandewyn—brandy ("burning wine")
bredie—stew
broekie-lace—"pantie lace." This describes the flowery patterns you get on the ironwork of the Victorian houses in Ladismith.
buchu—sweet-smelling medicinal plant (from a Bushman language)
Bushmen—or San, are the original hunter-gatherers in South Africa. Jessie says that both terms are okay (and used by Bushmen themselves), although neither was chosen by the Bushmen. They have no word in their own language to describe themselves as separate from others. People are just people. They were the first people in South Africa, and have lived here for more than twenty thousand years. They are famous for their tracking skills and their healthy relationship with each other, nature, and the spirit world. Bushmen were forced off their land and treated very badly by black and white South Africans. Many cattle and sheep

farmers saw them as "vermin" and killed them. Today most of the hunter-gatherer communities are destroyed and many of their languages are extinct. But you still find their strong spirit in some people and places.

Coloured—describes South Africans with light brown skin. Their ancestors are mixed and include Malay slaves and Bushmen, as well as white and black Africans. They speak Afrikaans and English.

daggakop—pothead. Dagga (marijuana) is from the Bushman word "daxa."

dankie—thank you

dassie—rock rabbit

deurmekaar—messed up

doek—a square cloth, folded into a triangle and tied over your hair. Americans call it a "kerchief."

donder—bastard. From the Afrikaans word "donder," meaning "thunder," but when used as a swearword it has lots of meanings.

dondering—beating

dongas—ditches

dorp—town

eina—ouch! Sore. This word is from a Bushman language.

eish—oh dear

Ek is op pad—I am on the way

Ek soek—I am looking for

English—English speaking. Both my parents were born in South Africa but I call them English and Afrikaans because of the languages they spoke. In South Africa the word "English" does not always mean "coming from England."

frikadelle—spicy meatballs

fok—fuck (but in Afrikaans it does not sound as rude)

gerook—stoned

goggas—insects. From the Bushman word "xo-xo," crawling thing. The "g" is pronounced like the "ch" in the German *achtung*.

Groot Karoo—Large Karoo. The Groot Karoo is a bigger area farther north from the Klein Karoo.

Groot Swartberge—Big Black Mountains (name of the mountain range)

groot-wolfdoring bush—big wolf-thorn bush

haai—hey!

hayi khona—no way (Xhosa)

hemel en aarde—"heaven and earth." Heavens above!

hok or hokkie—little hut (made with chicken mesh and a roof)

hotbox—a cushion or box where you wrap up your food in a cozy way so it can carry on cooking slowly

ja—yes

ja nee—yes no. It kind of means "all right then."

jakkalsbos—jackal bush

jammer—sorry

jinne—gosh. Stronger than "gosh," but not as strong as "jislaaik."

jirre—gosh. Stronger than jinne, almost as strong as "jislaaik."

jislaaik—gosh! Pronounced: "yiss like."

jou ouma se groottoon—your grandma's big toe, a swearword

jou sissie se vissie!—your sister's little fish! A swearword.

just now—soon or recently

kaalgatperskes—bare-bum peaches (stark-naked peaches), what we call nectarines

kaffir—a rude word for black people. It came from the Arabic word "kafir," meaning nonbeliever. It was used by Arabs to describe Christians, and then used as a rude word to describe Dutch colonists in Malaysia and Indonesia. The Dutch brought it to South Africa and they and the British whites used it as a rude word for blacks.

kak—crap

kareeboom—rhus tree

Karoo—the name of an area in South Africa, means "place of thirst" (from a Bushman language)

klap—hit

klapperbos—Chinese lantern bush

Klein Karoo—Small Karoo

Klein Swartberge—Small Black Mountains (name of the mountain range)
klipspringer—rock jumper (small buck)
kloof—ravine
knyp—pinch tight
koeksister—a South African braided, syrup-coated doughnut
kolskoot—bull's-eye
konstabel—constable
Kook en Geniet (Cook and Enjoy)—a famous South African cookbook
koppie—small, rocky hill
kossies—little foods
lammetjie—little lamb
lappiesgroep—"little-cloth group." They do patchwork and quilting and are associated with the Afrikaanse Taal-en Kultuurvereniging (AKTV).
lekker—nice, yum, delicious
loslappie—loose rag, describes a loose woman or casual relationship
ma—mom
maar—just
magtig!—heavens!
mama—mother (Xhosa). Like the Afrikaners, South African black people use family names for people even if they are not relations.
melktert—milk tart. Soft tart made with lots of milk, vanilla extract, and cinnamon.
Mejuffrou—Miss
Meneer—Mister
Mevrou—Mrs.
mielie—Indian corn
mieliepap—cornmeal porridge
moederliefie—mother's little beloved
moerkoffie—sediment coffee (not filtered)
moerse—very (quite a rude swearword)

'n liedjie van verlange—a song of longing
nee—no
netjies—neat
NGK—Nederduitse Gereformeerde Kerk—Dutch Reformed Church. This is the biggest and most powerful Afrikaans church.
niemand—no one
niks nie—nothing
nooit!—no way!
now-now—soon
oo, gats—oh dear
oom—uncle
op pad—on the road
oupa—grandpa
pa—dad
padkos—food you pack to eat on the road
pampoen—pumpkin
pap en wors—stiff cornmeal porridge and sausage
pasop!—watch out!
potjiekos—food cooked on the fire in a cast-iron pot
potjiepot—round cast-iron pot you cook with on the fire
reëngrassie—rain grass
Reghardt—an Afrikaans name that is pronounced "Rear-ghart." In Afrikaans the letter "g" is always pronounced like the "ch" in the German *achtung*. "Reg" means "right" and "hart" means "heart" and "reggeard" means "good natured" or "right minded."
Rooiberg—Red Mountain (the name of a mountain)
rooibos—red bush (tea)
rooikat—lynx ("red cat")
sambals—small Indian side dishes
shame—poor thing; something you say to show your sympathy
shweshwe—a printed patterned cotton that is very popular in South Africa (especially among Sotho and Xhosa people)
sisi—sister (Xhosa)
sjoe—phew

skat—treasure
skelling out—scolding
skrik—fright
slaan 'n bollemakiesie—do a somersault
slangbos—snake bush
slap chips—French fries that are limp (not crispy)
soentjie—little kiss
soetkoekies—sweet cookies
soetpampoen—sweet pumpkin (also known as pampoen)
Soetwater—Sweetwater (name of farm)
sommer—just
spanspek—sweet-melon
spekboom—"bacon tree," a small tree with succulent leaves
sterretjiebos—star bush
stoep—what the English call a verandah, but it's more comfortable and has a nicer view
sultanas—a type of sweet white grape common in South Africa
tamatiebredie—tomato-lamb stew
tamatiesmoor—chunky tomato sauce
Tannie—Auntie, the respectful Afrikaans way to greet a woman the same age or older than you. (You pronounce it "tunny.") The men we call "Oom," meaning Uncle. It may be a bit old-fashioned, but we still do it, especially in the small towns.
tata—father (Xhosa)
tjanking—howling, in a kind of sobbing way
totsiens—'bye
Towerkop—a dome of rock with a split down the middle, high on the Swartberge, next to Ladismith. "Tower" means "to put a spell on" and "kop" means "head."
trekking—traveling long distances
twakpraatjies—nonsense talk
veld—wild field, savannah
veldskoene—strong lace-up shoes (made from soft leather) that walk nicely in the veld
veldvygie—wildflower (a succulent)

vetkoek—"fat cake." This is a puffy deep-fried bread dumpling. Very tasty.
vetplantjies—little fat plants, small succulents
vlakvark—warthog ("pig of the plains")
vleisbroek—"meat pants." Anna's nonsense word that sounds like "Facebook."
voetsek—go away
vygies—small succulent plants that have bright flowers with lots of shiny petals
wildsvleis—game ("wild meat")

ACKNOWLEDGMENTS

Writing is such a solitary activity, but as I write my acknowledgments I am blown away by the army of supporters I have had. My heartfelt thanks to you all. I list some of you below:

Peter van Straten, Bosky Andrew, and Joan van Gogh gave feedback on early drafts. Miriam Wheeldon and Nicolene Botha were my music advisers. Anel Hamersma did the first Afrikaans language and culture edit. Christian Vlotman and J. P. Andrew answered questions about youth culture. Vilia Reynolds gave me information about Ladismith. Andrew Brown was extremely generous with advice on legal, literary, and police matters. Ladismith policewomen and policemen kindly educated me about certain police procedures.

Carole Buggé (of New York's Gotham Writers' Workshop) gave me hope and a fantastic first edit. Christopher Hope gave me insightful feedback.

Sisi Nono Silimela embodies Tannie Maria's do-the-right-thing spirit. Ditto Tannie Maria van der Berg, who also lent me her first name, is a brilliant cook, and along with her daughter, Crecilda, advised me on matters from swearwords to sheep. Danie Vorster of Merino SA taught me more on the latter subject. Ronel Gouws, Hanneke Verschoor, Chris Erasmus, Pieter Jolly, and Carl Wicht kindly answered questions on Afrikaans, literature, Bushmen, and broken limbs (respectively). I am grateful to

Vlok and Schutte-Vlok for their book *Plants of the Klein Karoo* (Umdaus Press, 2010).

If I were to sing all the praises of my agent, Isobel Dixon, I would sound like a mere sycophant, so let me just say in an understated way that she is a wonder woman and a goddess. Louise Brice is pure angel, Melis Dagoglu moves mountains, and I am extremely grateful to the full murmuration of darlings at the Blake Friedmann Literary Agency, including Hattie Grunewald (who even lent me her first name) and Tom Witcomb.

I am blessed to have received wild enthusiasm and careful editing from a collection of brilliant publishers, editors, and proofreaders, including Fourie Botha, Beth Lindop, Máire Fisher (Umuzi, South Africa); Louisa Joyner, Jamie Byng, Lorraine McCann (Canongate, UK); Dan Halpern, Megan Lynch, Bridget Read, Victoria Mathews (Ecco, HarperCollins US); Iris Tupholme (HarperCollins Canada); Mandy Brett and Michael Heyward (Text, Australia). It has been an amazing collaborative experience, in which many cooks perfected rather than spoiled the broth (with thanks to expert kitchen management by the lovely Louisa).

My gratitude goes to the full teams of all the publishers of this book across the globe. Thank you for the most beautiful letters that some of you wrote to me. I keep them in my box of love letters and use them as medicine whenever I have a bad day.

Thanks to my gorgeous man, Bowen Boshier, who supports me through everything and teaches me how to see and how to be.

The love and support I have received from you all is like the fresh stream from which I drink daily in the Karoo.

I am inspired by and grateful to the following literary icons: Queen of Crime, Agatha Christie, who sparked my love of cozy mysteries; master storyteller Herman Charles Bosman, who taught me that what you leave out of the story can be just as important as what you put in; and the charming Alexander McCall Smith, who showed the world that a slow-moving, soft-boiled woman detective from southern Africa can outrun many a fast-paced, hard-boiled PI from North America.

Titles of songs heard in Jessie's ring tones are with thanks to the following great musicians: "Girl on Fire" by Alicia Keys; "My Black President" by Brenda Fassie; "Light My Fire" by The Doors; "I'm Your Man" and "By the Rivers Dark" by Leonard Cohen.

The Afrikaans folk song "'n Liedjie van Verlange" sung by Dirk and Anna is derived from the German folk song "Ich Weiss Nicht Was Mir Fehlet." I made use of poetic license with my own English translation of this "Song of Longing." Much thanks to the Federasie van Afrikaanse Kultuurvereniginge and to Protea Boekhuis for kindly giving permission to use the Afrikaans version of this song, by Eitemal, in their *FAK Sangbundel* (Protea Boekhuis, 2011).

I am very grateful to the chefs, cooks, and bakers who helped me perfect the recipe-related parts of this book.

Nikki Langer (of Eat Love Feast caterers) kindly read the whole book in its early draft, helped me to plot the food, and provided me with numerous wonderful recipe ideas (many from Ina Paarman).

The magnificent baker and chef Martin Mössmer tested and adapted all the Tannie Maria recipes until each one of them was moan-out-loud-and-faint delicious. He provided the recipes for the tomato sambal, vetkoek, vetkoek ground meat, honey-toffee snake cake, koeksisters, chocolate mousse cake, and the buttermilk chocolate cake. The sublime melktert recipe is from his great-great-grandmother Ouma Alie Visser.

The legendary Ina Paarman allowed me to use her fabulous recipes for cucumber sambal and bobotie topping, and was so kind as to meet with me and share her ideas.

I am inspired by my sister, Gabrielle Andrew, who makes the most delicious meals. The tender mutton curry is an adaptation of her recipe (with ideas added by Martin and me).

My parents, Bosky and Paul Andrew, are the best hosts on the planet and cook every meal with love, and each one is divine. I am indebted to my mother's most-used cookbook, *Cook with Ina Paarman* (Struik, 1987), and my father's mother's cookbook, *Mrs. Slade's South African Cookery Book* (Central News Agency, 1951). I was also inspired by the classic *Kook en Geniet* by S.J.A. de Villiers (self-published by the author, 1955).

The bobotie recipe is my father's, inspired by Mrs. Slade (with additional ideas from Ina Paarman and Martin Mössmer). The tamatiebredie is my creation, with adjustments by Martin Mössmer.

My thanks to Barrie Pringle for her Karoo farm bread recipe, to bread baker Gavin Lawson, and to master baker Chris Johnston (of Main Street Café, Omaruru, Namibia) for great ideas (including the choc-banana), and to Laurian Roebert for her mother's magnificent rusk recipe.

Dan Halpern, Hattie Grunewald, Laurian Roebert, Teresa Loots, Jenny Wheeldon, Lindy Truswell, and Tova Luck are great cooks who tested out some of Tannie Maria's recipes and provided excellent feedback.

I was also influenced by ideas in *Karoo Kitchen: Heritage Recipes and True Stories from the Heart of South Africa* (Quivertree Publications, 2012) by Sydda Essop.

The recipes in my book are predominantly from the cooking tradition of Afrikaans-speaking people. However, they are enjoyed by a broad range of South Africans, and the sources of the recipes are very diverse. Despite apartheid's best efforts, cultures (and their foods) are intricately interwoven, and "traditional South African" recipes have many influences (including Malay, Indian, Dutch, French, and Italian) in addition to their African origins.

In my opinion, all the Tannie Maria recipes are beyond delicious, but please note: Any errors or flops are my responsibility and are not to be blamed on any of the above-credited cooks.

> There is no such thing as an original recipe. We learn from each other and we adjust. Something here, something there, a handful of this, a handful of that . . . from generation to generation.
>
> —Karen du Preez, cited in *Karoo Kitchen*

> When you prepare a meal, you must do it with your heart.
>
> —Carolyn Essop, cited in *Karoo Kitchen*

ABOUT THE AUTHOR

SALLY ANDREW lives in a mud-brick house on a nature reserve in the Klein Karoo, South Africa, with her partner, Bowen Boshier; a giant eland; and a secretive leopard. She also spends time in the wilderness of southern Africa and the seaside suburb of Muizenberg. She has a master's degree in Adult Education (University of Cape Town).

For some decades she was a social and environmental activist, then the manager of Bowen's art business, before she settled down to write full-time. This is her first novel. It will be published in at least twelve languages, across five continents.